A Poisoned Prayer

Michael Skeet

Five Rivers Publishing
www.fiveriverspublishing.com

Queen Street, P.O. Box 293, Neustadt, ON N0G 2M0, Canada.
www.fiveriverspublishing.com
A Poisoned Prayer, Copyright © 2016 by Michael Skeet.
Edited by Dr. Robert Runté.
Copy-edited by Sara Firmani.
Cover Copyright © 2016 by Jessica Allain.
Titles by Jeff Minkevics.
Interior design and layout by Éric Desmarais.
Titles set in Chopin Script Font designed by Dieter Steffmann as an airy homage to the formal writing of early nineteenth century France.
Text set in Tinos designed by Steve Matteson as an innovative, refreshing serif design that is metrically compatible with Times New Roman™. Tinos offers improved on-screen readability characteristics and the pan-European WGL character set and solves the needs of developers looking for width-compatible fonts to address document portability across platforms.
All rights reserved. Without limiting the rights under copyright reserved above, no part of this publication may be reproduced, stored in or introduced into a retrieval system, or transmitted in any form or by any means (electronic, mechanical, photocopying, recording or otherwise), without the prior written permission of both the copyright owner and the publisher of the book.
Publisher's note: This book is a work of fiction. Names, characters, places and incidents either are the products of the author's imagination or are used fictitiously, and any resemblance to actual persons living or dead, events, or locales is entirely coincidental.
Published in Canada
Library and Archives Canada Cataloguing in Publication
Skeet, Michael, 1955-, author
A poisoned prayer / Michael Skeet.
Issued in print and electronic formats.
ISBN 978-1-988274-11-9 (paperback).—ISBN 978-1-988274-12-6 (epub)
I. Title. PS8637.K43P64 2017 jC813'.6 C2016-903898-X C2016-903899-8

For Lorna, who knew first

Contents

December	5
One	6
Two	20
January	48
One	49
Two	76
Three	93
Four	119
February	156
One	157
Two	186
Three	197
Four	239
March	277
One	278
Two	292
Three	311
Four	334
Five	349
Six	366
About the Author	374
Books by Five Rivers	375

December

One

"**By God, Julien,**" Lise muttered, "if you've killed us I'll never forgive you."

Despite her orders to the footman, the carriage was slowing again. They were still, by her guess, a good two hours—call it four leagues at least—from Paris. It had been dark for ages, the moon was well up, and at this rate she would arrive too exhausted to take part in the New Year celebrations...if she arrived at all.

There were few reasons Lise could think of for the carriage to stop in the middle of the dark, dangerous, and very cold countryside, and all of them were bad. Father had specifically warned her against travel after dark, but there were so few hours of daylight at this time of year, and she had been so close to Paris when the sun began to set, that it had been easy for her to set the warning aside just this once. Normally she thought herself much more cautious than this; now she regretted the impulse that had put her here.

"What do you want?" the driver, like the carriage hired by Father, demanded of a person or persons unknown, confirming Lise in her fear that they'd met brigands, or worse.

"Who are you?" added Julien, one of Father's footmen.

"Please," a voice cried, as from a distance. "You've got to help me!"

The words were well-enough spoken, though the voice had something coarse, lower-born, about it. Lise felt her throat and stomach tighten as she heard the crunch of footsteps on snow; that meant that someone was approaching the carriage from the verge, because the road itself was a muddy slough. She lifted one of the heavy curtains to peek through the window in the door. The moon was full, which would mean good enough light were she able to withstand the biting cold. She was a daughter of the south, though, and the wind bit into her cheeks and fingers; in less time that it took her to breathe in she was forced to drop the curtain. At any rate, from the side of the coach she couldn't see anyone. The man who'd stopped them was obviously standing in front, or to the other side.

The tightness was spreading to her temples, and Lise shut her eyes for a moment. *Oh, no,* she thought. *Not now.* This was no time for one of her headaches. *I have to be able to think,* she thought, silently saying a prayer for calm. No calm came, but that wasn't really a surprise to her. She shouted through the partition at the front of the carriage, "Start up again! Get moving!"

"Please," the stranger said, and now his voice was much closer, "you've got to help me. They're after me! So close! Please don't forsake me!" Something odd was happening to his voice; it was thickening, becoming even more coarse.

The carriage jolted forward, then stopped. Lise fought to steady her breathing, wrestled with the lid of the small box on the floor beside her feet, and prayed for light. This time her prayer was answered: after a moment a wan, flickering glow appeared just above the open box. The light was pathetically weak, the sickly green of a winter dawn viewed through a cheap windowpane, but it was enough to let Lise find what she'd been looking for within the few moments the light remained. *I wish I had the grace God gave to Andrée,* Lise thought—not for the first time—as she worked.

"I told you to start!" she shouted to the driver, not looking up but unhappy with the desperation she heard in her voice.

"Mademoiselle, I'm sorry," the driver began. Whatever he'd been about to add by way of qualification, though, was obliterated by a shriek of pain or anger, followed immediately by the blast of a musket. The carriage shook, the horses screamed, and Lise was slammed back against the seat by the force of something hitting the carriage.

She heard a howl of animal rage, a prayer that was more of a scream, and a series of growls mixed with wet-sounding noises that her mind refused to comprehend. *Oh, God,* she prayed, *be with me in my hour of need. Sweet Mother Mary, do not abandon your child.* The prayers had come to her by instinct, not by any force of will. She knew, as she heard the tearing sounds coming from outside the coach, that she lacked the power to give those prayers any real force.

God can't help you, she thought. *In the end, it's only and always going to be you.*

And when the partition behind the driver's seat was torn away and the blood-soaked muzzle and glowing red eyes of the loup-garou thrust through the ragged opening, Lise was ready for death.

Not hers. She pointed her pistol as steadily as she could, and as the creature reared back to lunge for her, she pulled the trigger. The wheel rasped, sparks flew, and powder ignited. With a bright flash and a clap of chemical thunder, the pistol sent a silver ball at high speed directly into the *loup-garou's* brain.

Time seemed to have stopped. Lise could smell the bitterness of the powder, the higher, sharper scent of the pyrites of the wheel-lock—and the sweet-salt tang of blood. The smoke from her shot seemed to wrap itself around her, like a gauzy scarf that while beautiful to look at would give no protection against the weather.

She could hear her breathing, rushing in her ears like the sound of a stream in flood. Her cheeks stung with cold and fright—and wind that, she realized now, was coming through the shattered partition.

The carriage was moving.

Slow down, damn you. How was it that the horses hadn't spooked when the loup-garou had jumped onto the driver's seat, but the sound of a pistol-shot had frightened them into a panicked dash to disaster? Lise knelt on the front passenger seat and looked through the hole the loup-garou had smashed in the thin partition. Oh.

The loup-garou's body had fallen backward onto the traces, right between the rear pair of horses in the team. The smell of blood might not have been strong enough at first, in the bitter cold of this post-solstice night, but having a blood-soaked body right next to them would be impossible for the horses to ignore. So now they were, in their fear, trying to get away from the bad smell by running as fast as they could.

They were carrying the smell with them, but they wouldn't understand that.

Lise could see the reins, still wrapped loosely around the worn wooden rail that framed the driver's bench. *If I can get up there, I might be able to slow them down. Or get them to stop.*

Lise eased her head into the opening the loup-garou had torn in the front of the carriage. An instant and a bouncing jolt of the carriage later she pulled back inside the cabin, gasping in pain and clapping a gloved hand to her torn cheek. The opening was splintered, tiny daggers of wood skewed at crazy, dangerous angles. It was too narrow for her to get through. In his blood-lust the loup-garou would probably have been able to force it wider, but with the carriage jolting in this fashion, one bounce at the wrong time would slash her throat on one of those wicked points. Lise sat back down and began to look about the cabin for anything she could use to cushion the blow when the carriage crashed or rolled over—something it was going to do any moment now.

She became aware of the throbbing in her temples again after the horses had slowed from insane gallop to serene walk, and the carriage had stopped rattling like a badly made window in a thunderstorm. *So the only thing I need to eliminate my headaches,* she said to herself, *is to live in constant fear of my life.* Then it occurred to her to wonder why the horses had slowed. Looking through the hole in the front of the carriage, she saw the horses standing still, steam rising from them and their heads oddly motionless. She realized what had probably happened: something—or someone—had charmed the horses. Was this that sort of headache, then? *Even though I'm hundreds of leagues from my family?* She shook her head; this was no time to dwell on the mysteries of her headaches. What mattered was that someone had likely saved her life.

To what end? Were the keepers of that loup-garou now going to rob her? She fumbled on the floor for her pistol, prayed without success for more light, and in the end found the weapon only because a sliver of moonlight through the broken front of the carriage happened to fall on the time-polished metal of the barrel. Trying to remember everything Father had taught her about how to stay calm in a dangerous situation, she searched within her muff for the small bag of balls and flask of powder she'd stored there. Another silver ball? They were expensive; on the other hand, they were also charmed. Ordinary lead would not kill an enchanted or sorcerous creature.

Two such creatures would have fought each other before attacking me, she decided, and rammed a lead ball down the barrel to nest amongst the powder and wadding until such time as she called for it. She wound the wheel until she felt its spring tighten. Then she sat back, trying to guess from which direction the attack would come.

What came instead was the slow, steady crunch of hoofbeats on snow, the soft jingle of horse-gear, and a snorting sort of breathing that suggested a beast that was trying to recover its wind after having been galloped too far in air that was too cold. "Is everyone all right in there?" a voice demanded.

It was a well-formed voice, drawling somewhat lazily but with a suggestion of contained energy that reminded Lise of the wheel-lock that she had just wound. The voice, its tone, were just close enough to normal that, freed for a moment of fear, Lise could realize: *Julien is dead. The driver is dead.* "I think that I am in one piece, Monsieur," she said, feeling her heartbeat rising up from her breast. "If it is you who charmed my horses, I thank you."

"I heard the shots," the man said, "and only regret that I could not reach you sooner." There was a brief pause, and then, with a hint of amusement in his voice the man said, "Might I be allowed to introduce myself?"

This was not something Lise would consider under normal circumstances. After all, the man could be anyone, or anything. Politeness dictated that some third party of mutual acquaintance do the honours.

On the other hand, politeness had very little to do with an attack on a defenceless traveller, or with loup-garou. And the man undoubtedly had saved her life. "It is somewhat irregular," she said, making the caution she felt audible to him. "At the same time, I am grateful." She lifted the curtain, found no one there, and shifted across the seat to lift the other curtain.

Her rescuer seemed tall, and grey, and nondescript. Of course, the height was probably an illusion created by his horse, a magnificent creature that looked almost royal purple in the moonlight, but with a diamond-shaped white blaze down the centre of its nose. The gear, at least those bits of it not spattered with mud, glittered as if to emphasize that a horse such as this could only be ridden with the finest leather and metal.

The grey was just about all she could see. The rider's face was almost invisible, sheltered by a broad-brimmed grey hat—if it had ever had feathers, they had disappeared—and a heavy cloak, grey in the sickly light, that he had wrapped up over his chin. Even his big, leather gauntlets looked grey under the moon.

As for nondescript, if the man hadn't been mounted on such a magnificent beast, she'd have mistaken him for a cooper or a carpenter or a goldsmith. Still, he *had* helped her. Lise had been properly brought up; she knew how to show appreciation for a good deed performed. "Monsieur, I thank you very kindly for stopping my horses." She nodded, giving him permission to introduce himself.

He opened his mouth to speak, but at first no sound emerged. Eventually he said, "Mademoiselle, you are hurt."

"No, I assure you, I'm fine."

He carefully lifted his right hand from the reins and tucked it inside his cloak. "There is blood on your cheek," he said. "Rather a lot, it looks to me." Now his arm was shifting, giving the cloak a disquieting, crawling effect that suggested something evil burrowing into him. Lise remembered the shock of the splinter tearing at her cheek, but it no longer hurt, and she couldn't believe that her face was disfigured in the way he had suggested. *If there was blood on my face, wouldn't I feel it?*

If I can't feel the pain, perhaps I can't feel the blood either.

In a sudden flare, equivalent to the sparking to life of a candle, Lise understood the expression on her rescuer's face, and what his hand was reaching for under his cloak. Suppressing the gasp of breath her shock demanded of her, she brought out her own pistol and leveled it at the man.

"Please be at ease, monsieur," she said, hoping the trembling she felt wasn't audible in her voice. "The creature did not touch me. I scratched my cheek on some splintered wood, trying to gain control of the horses before you helped me." He relaxed in the saddle, a bit, but his hand was still invisible under the cloak. "I am not at risk of becoming a loup-garou, monsieur. Believe me, and show me your hand, or I will have to shoot you. In my own defence, you understand."

The dark eyes widened a bit, fixed on her in a fashion that made Lise feel unaccountably warm. Then, suddenly, a laugh burst from him, the cloak falling away from his mouth. For a moment his laughter echoed crazily, like a pistol shot, through the trees that lined the road.

"By God," he said, pausing to wipe his eyes, "my mother would like you." He carefully raised his right hand from beneath the cloak. He'd removed his gauntlet, presumably to make it easier to work the trigger of the pistol she had no doubt was hidden inside the cloak. "I am happy we have cleared up the state of your health," he said, "and happier still that you are not compelled to shoot me. In your own defence." He bowed as best he could in the saddle. "I am Rafael de Roublard, duc de Bellevasse. By your accent, you are from the south, I think."

"It is a pleasure to meet you, Monsieur. Yes, I have come from the south. I am Lise de Trouvaille." Then she realized what he had said, and she felt a chill numbness in her heart. Had he claimed to be a duc?

"Your devoted servant, Mademoiselle," he said. "De Trouvaille? I think I know that name, but not well."

"I am the eldest daughter of the Marquis Arnaud de Trouvaille. Not his heir," she added, feeling clumsy and stupid immediately after the words left her mouth. "Our estate is on the northern edge of the Pyrenees."

"Ah, yes," the duc said. "Your people were once in the service of the kings of Navarre, I believe."

"I'm afraid you have me at a bit of a disadvantage, monsieur. I know little of the great—of the families of the north."

"Look," he said, dismounting and walking over to look up at her. "Let's try to remember that this is not a social occasion. Who you are and who I am don't really matter that much right now. Honestly, I was more comfortable with you when you were threatening to shoot me." He nodded at her pistol. "Did you use that on the loup-garou?"

14

"I happened to have it loaded," Lise said, grateful for the change of subject. "It seemed a wise idea; this road has a foul reputation."

"Which makes me wonder why you were on it after dark. I also wonder how it could have seemed a wise idea that you keep your pistol loaded with a silver ball. I assume it was silver; our hairy friend back there is definitely dead."

"Yes, it was silver," she said, allowing herself a small sense of pride. "Carrying the pistol was Father's idea, but it was mine to use a silver ball. I decided that if I had to use it against a non-sorcerous creature the nature of the ball wouldn't make much difference. And if I was attacked by someone or something of the Devil, well…"

"Wise indeed," the duc said, "if a trifle expensive." He looked at her as if he were pricing a new cloak. "I would be honoured if you'd let me replace the ball for you."

She'd been hoping to be able to recover the ball from the loup-garou's head—though she hadn't progressed to the point of working out exactly how to do that. God knew, she couldn't afford to waste what was probably a good livre's worth of silver. She wasn't, however, going to accept charity from a stranger. Especially one who claimed to be exalted and who still looked at her that way. "That won't be necessary, monsieur," she said. She did not thank him for the offer, intending him to know that he'd over-reached himself. "I would be grateful, though, if you would help me with the bodies of my attendants."

"They are servants of yours?" The implication was that unless the dead men had long ties of service to the family, they could be left to rot by the side of the road for all the duc cared. "That looks to me like a hired carriage."

"One of the men was a footman for my father. He gave his

life trying to save mine, monsieur; the least that I can do is see that his body is returned to his family for burial."

"Your sentiments do you honour," the duc said. "This is not a safe place to tarry, though. We will have to throw the bodies onto the carriage without ceremony, and I warn you it's not likely to be something you want to look at."

"I've seen death," she said. The deaths of pigeons and stags, at any rate.

"Not like this, I'll wager. And I don't wish to be responsible for terrorizing your dreams. No disrespect, mademoiselle, but I think you're going to have trouble enough sleeping as it is, and for some time to come."

"Good," she said, with a determination she almost believed. "I will be able to stay awake until we reach Paris, then."

"Not tonight, you won't," the duc said. Before she could put words to her protest, he snapped out, "It's bad enough that you were on this highway after dark to begin with. Do you have any idea how many thieves—and worse—haunt this road between here and the city? Regiments of the emperor's guard don't travel this road after dark."

"I am expected in Paris," Lise said.

"You will arrive in Paris," the duc de Bellevasse said. "But tomorrow, not tonight." He dismounted, and tied his horse to a handle on the rear of the carriage. "There is an inn about a half-league from here," he said, mounting onto the driver's bench. He climbed a bit slowly; Lise wondered if he'd been riding a long time, to be so stiff. *And why are you out on this road after dark, monsieur?* "You can have your bodies attended to there, and get something to eat and perhaps some rest before a good fire. I'll arrange for a driver to take you and what's left of your carriage"—he ostentatiously wiped a gauntlet along the bloody bench—"into Paris in the morning."

Lise wanted to get to Paris tonight. Her aunt was expecting her, and the New Year celebrations were to begin tomorrow; Lise had planned to be cleaned up and rested in order to present herself most effectively to those members of society who would be in attendance. This shabby duc—if he really was a duc—was perhaps so far beneath notice that a good appearance didn't matter to him. To Lise, it was a matter of life, if not necessarily of life and death.

But she was completely at his mercy, and she knew it. Perhaps she could handle the horses, and even stay awake in this cold for the hours it would take to reach the Porte St-Jacques. But she would present an obvious target to any brigand who encountered her, and she knew she would not be able to withstand a second attack.

Knowing this, she resented it. Still, she'd been brought up well. "I thank you for your kind consideration, monsieur," she said, and pulled heavy woollen mittens from her trunk, the better to keep her hands warm while she assisted the duc in stowing the bodies of the unfortunate men.

After a glimpse of what the loup-garou had done to the driver, Lise could not bring herself to look at Julien's body. The young man had been eager to see Paris, even if he was under orders to turn back for Trouvaille the morning following his safe delivery of the seigneur's daughter to her famous relative in the capital. Now he would return to his family in a poorly made coffin—Lise could afford nothing better—and with only whatever letter she could coax from her numb fingers by way of explanation of his death. She left the bodies to the duc—ignoring his cheerful "I warned you, mademoiselle"—and busied herself, while he worked, picking up Julien's pouch and personal effects from the snow into which they'd been thrown.

Of the man who had stopped them, requesting assistance, there was little sign. There had obviously been a struggle beside the place where the carriage had stopped: the snow was flattened or in some places scraped entirely away from the matted mess of rotting leaves that covered the roadside. Where the snow still existed it was pitted in many places, holes of varying sizes sunk in the crust. It took her a while to realize that she was looking at the places where warm blood had struck the snow and melted through.

The disturbance went back into the woods; Lise followed the scars in the snow to a place where hoof-prints suggested that a man on horseback had stopped for a time. Had the loup-garou's master watched the attack from here? What had happened to the man who'd called for help? And why had he been out here looking for help in the first place?

"If you would really rather spend the night in these picturesque surroundings," the duc de Bellevasse said from the road, "shall I leave your late companions to keep you company?" His voice had a slight lilt to it that suggested amusement, but amusement of a sort that Lise guessed she'd probably find insulting. He was rude in the way that too many of his fellow nobles, confident in their God-given rights of dominion, were. It galled her to think that the best she could hope to accomplish in Paris was to end up married to one of these pompous lordlings.

He is being of service to you, a nagging, practical voice inside her head reminded her, interrupting her contemplation of the sorts of words she'd like to say to this not-so-impressive duc. *Go away*, she thought to the voice. She did not like being reminded, even by her own conscience, of her practicality. Her practicality, so often remarked on by Mother and Father, was what had brought her here.

"Thank you, monsieur," she said, as sweetly as she could manage through teeth that had begun to chatter with the cold, "but I believe that my work here is done. I'll accept your escort to that inn, now."

⁂

When the duc de Bellevasse left Lise at the inn, she caught a glimpse of his face in the ruddy light cast by the innkeeper's lantern. There was definitely something mocking about the eyes, but she also saw something warm in their depths, or at least something that began to warm her. His skin was smooth, his chin well-formed and perhaps projecting just a bit forward. His nose, when she looked past the redness it had acquired from the cold night air, was a bit long but possessed of that quality, said to have been handed down by the Romans, that people called *gravitas*. And while the face did not look young, neither did it look as though time had played rough games with it.

What a pity he's not just some ordinary baron, her practical voice reminded her. *He might have made a suitable husband.*

Two

LISE'S FIRST SIGHT of Paris suggested to her a silver-scaled dragon sleeping in the weak winter sunlight. Looking more closely, she saw that what had suggested the dragon's spikes and scales were, in fact, the spires of churches rising above low, snow-covered hills. There were dozens of spires, more than she had ever dreamed of seeing in one place. Seeing the city brought her breath up short, and for a moment she felt weak, child-like. If she was ever going to consider giving up and turning back, this was her last chance.

The dragon may have been imaginary, but it certainly breathed smoke. So many plumes rose above the hills, in so many shades of grey, that they were impossible to count, even at the slow pace at which the hastily repaired carriage moved.

In the end she had been unable to send Julien's body home to Trouvaille for burial. The duc had said the corpse was too mutilated to allow shipment in anything but a lead-lined box, and while he was generous in paying to have Julien's bag and two leather satchels sent back south, neither the duc nor Lise could justify the expense of purchasing such a box for a boy who had been, after all, only a servant. So Julien's mother would have only his possessions to remember him by, and Lise, with a new driver at the reins, was at last on her way to Paris.

Before she fully saw the city, Lise heard—and smelled it. A buzz reminiscent of a swarm of angry insects fought with, and surmounted, the rattle and jangle of the carriage. As for the smell, at first it was pleasant: the rich, warm animal scent she had grown up around. As the highway became the Rue St-Jacques, though, and the carriage began to move past buildings, first isolated houses and then entire blocks of them, other odours quickly overwhelmed anything pleasant. The eye-watering sting of urine and the rotting-meat stench of human feces assaulted Lise with a force that made her squirm. She tried to make the smell go away, but the city defeated her efforts—which, she had to admit, didn't amount to much. Even if she'd been better-Blessed, her education hadn't included any prayers that could deal with *this*. The stink of the city permeated the mud of the streets.

And even in the south, the mud of Paris was legendary. A peculiar, disgusting brown-green in colour, the stuff had the consistency and determination of week-old gruel. As Lise watched people on foot, and even on horseback, trying to move through the stuff, she began to wonder if she would be able to afford the new clothes she'd have to buy every week until the dry weather came. *One day of walking through this will ruin any dress I own*, she thought. They said that once you'd got Paris mud worked into your stockings or the hem of your dress, not even the strongest magic could get it out again.

Even so, when seeing meant also smelling the *faubourgs*—which was what the new driver called these neighbourhoods outside the city's boundaries—Lise could not resist a smile as the city stretched up around her. Surrendering to the olfactory inevitability, she tied back the curtains and leaned her head through the windows on first one side, then the other side of the coach, the better to see her new home.

It was the height of the buildings that impressed her the most, she decided. That there would be so many of them, and that they would be jammed together like so many teeth in God's smile, she had understood. But she had not expected every house to be as tall as a church. Nor had she expected to see everything built right up to the edge of the road. Now, though, she would have to stick her head out through the carriage window and crane her neck around in order to see anything of the sky.

At some point the carriage seemed to have entered the city itself without her noticing. There had been no moment at which she could have said: *I am outside the city; now I am inside it.* Somehow it had just happened, in much the same way as Mother and Father had somehow contrived to suddenly be as old as Grandfather, without going through any change that Lise could see.

Now all of the buildings were four or even five stories tall, and they loomed over the street. Sometimes she passed not houses but tall, featureless walls that hinted at hidden magnificence; a couple of times there were turrets in the walls or the houses, a feature that Lise associated with ancient times. Nowhere was there a comfortable, rambling old *château,* set in a broad, tree-lined park, that could speak to her of home.

"Porte St-Jacques," the driver shouted through the damaged front of the carriage. Lise peered out the window. *Where is the gate? Shouldn't a gate into one of the great cities of the world be a magnificent, intimidating thing?*

Evidently not. Porte St-Jacques, it appeared, was not a thing so much as a place named for a thing. There was no wall around Paris.

No, wait. There were the walls—or what was left of them, at any rate. However, while they might have impressed at one time, today they were afterthoughts, crumbling and sagging. Buildings loomed over them on either side, and whatever gate the Porte St-Jacques might have been no longer existed: the road just cut straight through the rubble.

The carriage stopped for a moment, and as the driver engaged in profane conversation with someone who was apparently blocking their progress, Lise took advantage of the pause to more closely study the cross-section of wall revealed by the street's uncaring passage. The outer facing, she saw, had largely gone: those were the best-cut, most regular stones, so of course they would be attractive to builders. Scattered, like so many currants in a cake, through the rubble that had once been the fill were blue- and red-glazed blocks, the colours now dulled by time and weather. She knew from her studies that these were ward-stones, repositories of prayers for the safety of the city. The power lodged in a ward-stone was potentially dangerous, which was why the stones were always hidden, in walls or foundations.

Nobody had maintained these stones for a long time, though. Looking at them now, Lise felt nothing. Normally, a ward advertised its presence through a definite lack of something people could ordinarily sense, in the same way you could tell, just by the things you could or couldn't hear, whether you were indoors or out. That absence was gone from these stones, and perhaps their strength and power were past reviving. She could not say for certain, but she was sure that the physical embodiment of the emperor's divine defences for the city now resided somewhere else. Paris no longer needed walls, it seemed.

Lise was still contemplating the faded ward-stones when the carriage lurched forward again. After a few minutes of stop-and-start, Lise took a deep, frustrated breath—and realized with a start that the city no longer stank. It wasn't that it smelled better suddenly, or that she'd got used to the stench. There was almost no smell at all. Had hearing been the sense she was using, it would be as if she'd stuffed her ears with woolen lint.

She understood what was happening when she saw a group of badly dressed young men fighting—or were they playing?—outside a cabaret. Bursts of violent colour appeared over and among them, ghostly emanations of odd (but silly) creatures faded in and out of sight, and once it appeared that the very fabric of creation had wrinkled like linen on a hot day. "Ah," she said to herself. "The university. Of course." Sure enough, there, out the left window of the coach, was the cluster of buildings where young men went to learn the rules and practice of natural philosophy, the arts, and religious magic. And sometimes, the rumours went, other sorts of magic as well. And somebody here was praying—with some strength—to blot out the city's stink. Watching the silly young men trying to trump one another, Lise hoped that she wasn't looking at a potential husband.

She was unaware that she had crossed the Seine until after she'd done it. Only the driver's throw-away reference made Lise realize that the street lined with exceptionally narrow buildings had been a bridge. She was still trying to figure out if she'd ever actually be able to see the river while crossing it when the coach stopped. Lise heard the driver curse, following the oath immediately with a prayer.

Looking out the window she saw a crowd gathered around an old-looking building. From inside the crowd pikes waved. Who, she wondered, used pikes in this day and age? Then the crowd parted, and Lise saw that the men with the pikes wore red surcoats.

The cardinal's guard. Lise had heard of the cardinal and

his grip on the city, but it startled her to see such obvious proof on her first day—her first hour—in the city. The cardinal's men were, on closer inspection, only acting as escorts. As Lise watched, a trio of men appeared in the door to the building's courtyard. These men didn't wear red. They wore black, and their leader wore a cloak so black it seemed to suck all colour from the world around him.

The other two men were dragging another man between them. This man might have been young, but didn't look it. He wasn't likely to get much older, though: he had a heavy iron collar around his neck, and iron bands on his wrists and ankles. Lise's religious education hadn't gone very far, but she recognized the signs of the cursed when she saw them. That man had been touched by the Devil, had become a vessel containing a magic so dark that society's protection demanded his removal. The heavy iron kept the dark magic in check. And the iron could only mean that the escort belonged to the—

"Inquisition," the driver said, making a surreptitious rude gesture in the direction of the black-caped man. Then he cursed and spat into the street before whipping the horses into motion again.

As the carriage jolted through the streets Lise tried to return her thoughts to the pleasures of a new city and the party to come. She could not, however, wipe from her mind the vision of the man in irons. The Inquisition was a frightening thing to the blessed, but to peasants and merchants—and to those, like Lise, with no blessing to speak of—it was terrifying. The Inquisition had little impact in the place where she'd grown up, despite its proximity to the Kingdom of Navarre; there were just too few people. In the capital, though, even the cardinal was reputed to fear the Inquisition.

The carriage stopped with a rattle that interrupted these thoughts, and Lise saw that beyond her window was a gate.

This gate did not compare favourably with those of the châteaux she had grown up around. But, looking at it now, Lise realized that few of the buildings she'd passed had been walled at all, and few of those behind walls had had gates as wide as this. A carriage could pass through this gate.

Which this carriage proceeded to do. Beyond the gate was a courtyard, and beyond that a garden, and beyond that the prettiest house Lise had ever seen. A mansion, more like—a four-story building of beautifully worn stone, white and yellow and gold. Every bit of the façade that wasn't pierced by a huge window was adorned with a statue or some other object carved from stone. Gods and goddesses of ancient Greece and Rome looked down on her as she climbed the steps to the doors.

This is my new home, she thought. *For a while, at least.*

"Rafael de Roublard?" Marie-Françoise, duchesse de Vimoutiers, laughed and shook her head. It was a carefully modulated laugh and sounded like a small crystal bell being rung by a little girl. Lise felt herself blushing, then realized there was no hint of amusement in that laugh. There might well have been anger, in fact.

It was the eve of the New Year, and the Duchesse de Vimoutiers was about to entertain. This was why Lise had been in such a hurry to reach Paris, and it seemed to her she ought to be much more excited about the coming party than she was. Partly it was the way she was dressed: her borrowed gown of copper-coloured silk with green and white trim left entirely too much of her breasts and shoulders exposed, and this was not, she decided, how she wanted to accustom herself to the Parisian mode of dress.

And then there was the question of the werewolf attack, and the name of her saviour.

Lise and her aunt were seated in a small salon, one floor above the ground and adjacent to the ballroom. A fire blazed in a small but ornate fireplace set against the outside wall—every room in this house had a fireplace, save those rooms warmed by a marvelous new invention called a "stove." Weak winter sunlight trickled through windows on the inside wall; below, on the other side of the glass, the garden slumbered under a dusting of new snow. Lise had tried to put off her aunt's questions about the delay in her arrival, but unpacking and cleaning up and dressing for this evening's party could only consume so many hours. Looking now at the expression on her aunt's face, Lise wondered what horrible error she'd just made.

"Oh, child," the duchesse said after a moment. "That one is most definitely not a man with whom I want you associating."

"I know that he's too exalted for me, Aunt," Lise said. Put that way, it hardly seemed fair.

"His social standing might be considered a barrier by some," the duchesse said. "But not by me. Any member of my family, no matter how...obscure...is good enough for a de Bellevasse. No, that is not why I forbid you to see him."

"It's because," a voice said from the doorway, "they say he's in league with the Devil, and I for one believe them."

Lise turned around. A somewhat foppish young man had walked into the room. He bowed, low, and said, "Mama, who is this lovely creature? Surely you can't mean to tell me she's family?.

The young man looked as if he'd taken it upon himself to

further increase the temperature in any room he entered. His coat and breeches were the orange of flames, while his waistcoat and the turned-back cuffs of his coat sleeves were scarlet. Everything he wore seemed to be heavily braided and embroidered in gold, silver, or white; even the hilt of his sword was richly enameled. Lise thought with regret of the old rapier Grandfather had given her: no jewels or enamel sweetened its appearance or gave it any air of gentility; it was a weapon, and nothing but.

"Don't be rude, monsieur," the duchesse said. "If you don't behave yourself, I won't introduce you."

"Very well, Mama," he said. "I apologize, mademoiselle, for my presumption." Lise smiled and nodded, not knowing what else to do. Until she'd been introduced, she certainly couldn't talk to the man. Not in front of her aunt, anyway. This wasn't a forest, and she hadn't just killed a werewolf in front of him.

After a brief pause, presumably to let her displeasure bury itself more deeply into her victim, the duchesse cleared her throat and said, "Monsieur le Chevalier de Vimoutiers, allow me to present your distant cousin, Mademoiselle de Trouvaille. Lise, this is your cousin and my younger son, Robert."

Lise rose from her chair and curtseyed while young Robert—and he was quite young, she could now see—bowed deeply. "Are you with us for long, cousin?" he asked as he straightened himself.

"I don't know," Lise said. "I have things to do in Paris, but I don't know how long they'll take."

"Well, they'll take a lot longer if you have anything to do with that man," Robert said. "He's not just working with the Devil—he *is* the Devil, I think."

"Few people care much about what you think," the

duchesse said, "unless you're paying for the meal at which you're expounding these theories. Please go away, Robert, and amuse yourself with the wine or the hot cider. Your cousin and I have things to discuss."

"Very well, Mama," Robert said, bowing again. "But you will do me the honour, cousin, of allowing me to speak with you at some point before the party's over. Or at least before you leave Paris."

"I promise, monsieur," Lise said, unable to resist laughing.

"Don't encourage him, my girl," the duchesse said after Robert had left the room. "He's silly enough as it is."

"He's a younger son," Lise said. "Isn't that what's expected of them?"

"He doesn't have to strive for exceptional achievement in that direction," the duchesse said. "The boy's mad, if you ask me. Not in the head, perhaps, but definitely in the heart. I see nothing of his father in him, sad to say."

"I'm curious about something he said just now," Lise said. She tried to keep the interest out of her voice. "Something you both said, I suppose. What is it about the duc that makes him so unworthy of your house? Aside from his being in league with the Devil, which, coming from your son, might not be the most accurate of accusations."

"On that score, I'm afraid, my son is quite accurate. The most horrible stories are being told of that man—he seems to be throwing away a rather considerable fortune in a search for texts on the blackest of arts. Death-magic is what I hear."

"But surely those stories are just stories. The church fathers destroyed the last of the old Greek and Roman texts centuries ago. Any black spells anyone can find these days are bound to be impotent forgeries. The Inquisition surely wouldn't stand for anything else."

A Poisoned Prayer
December

"The Inquisition chases after peasants who are cursed," her aunt said, "but it has little impact on those of our class. As for black spells, the paucity of outcome does not mitigate the crime of seeking out Devil's magic, my dear. Why are you so interested in this man? What did he do to you?"

"Nothing. He helped me, that's all. He seemed kind—I admit, in a fashion just short of being insulting. But I thought he might be a useful acquaintance, and that he might be able to help me in my search."

"Absolutely not." The duchesse turned and fixed her gaze on Lise. "The only people that man knows are people you would never be allowed near, for your sake as well as mine. It will only be a matter of time before the cardinal or archbishop obtain the evidence needed to burn him."

Lise couldn't match this picture to the man who had helped her last night. Duc Rafael certainly hadn't seemed Satanic. But the look in her aunt's eyes persuaded her that it would be prudent to respond in a different fashion. "Madame, this is why I wrote you, asking to come and see you. I have to find a husband, and I don't think I have a chance of succeeding without the assistance of an expert. Grandfather says that you know more about manners and society than anyone else in the capital."

The duchesse closed her eyes for a moment and seemed to be relishing some especially pleasing scent. A small smile played amidst the curves of her mouth, and she said, "And how is your grandfather? I have not seen him in many years."

Lise could not resist her own smile. "He is magnificent, Madame, as always. As he grows older he seems at times to be in the process of transforming into a saint, or at least the picture of one. But every time I find myself thinking that, he will say something, or even just smile at me in a way that makes me laugh at his wickedness and reminds me of the hero he was to me when I was a girl."

"He was a scoundrel, that one." The duchesse's smile broadened, but then vanished. "It has always distressed me that his mother married so badly. Your grandfather could have been a great man, Lise, had he been given the opportunities presented to many a better-born but inferior contemporary."

Lise turned her hands palm-upward and gazed at the ceiling, acknowledging God's will. "These things cannot be changed, Madame. I can only do what is within my power."

"Very well, then: so can I." The duchesse got to her feet. "We—that is, my friends and I—will take you in hand, dear Lise, and see what we can do to get you established. I can provide you with a room, but only for a short while."

"I will not presume on your hospitality for long, Madame," Lise said, anxious to convince the duchesse that she was not a leech.

"Thank you," the duchesse said. "You may think me abrupt, but I am old and set in my ways." *She must be all of forty,* Lise thought, looking at the smooth skin and red-gold hair. "Your gentle acquiescence does you credit—and will also be quite attractive to the men." Her aunt's expression suggested she had a relatively poor opinion of men, and that her advice might as likely be to dupe them as it would be to please them. "Now, let us see what we'll have to work with. Stand, please."

Lise got to her feet with considerably more grace than that with which she'd sat down a moment ago. Unsure of what posture her aunt wanted, she made a curtsy. "You do that well," the duchesse said. "You have a physical grace that can't be taught." *It can be learned, though,* Lise thought, *if you spend enough time playing with your brothers and their friends.*

The duchesse circled her, slowly—exactly, it occurred to Lise, as if she'd been examining a horse she was thinking of buying. "Your looks are not magnificent," the duchesse said, almost in a growl, "which is a pity. Still, your hair is good, and if brown is entirely too common a colour, I see some red in there that can be brought out. I will show you the appropriate potions and prayers. You will have to be taught the effective use of powder, young lady."

Lise had to fight to suppress a growl of her own. "Thank you, Madame."

"Wait." The duchesse stopped, returned to look Lise in the eye. "Oh, what a shame. It's gone."

"What is?"

"For a moment there your eyes were the most attractive shade of green. Now they're quite brown, and I'm afraid rather dull."

The clock on the mantel chimed four times, and the duchesse sighed. "The guests will be arriving," she said. "Come with me, Lise. I would appreciate your opinion on some matters of party management. And then your cousin can make himself useful by escorting you this evening."

Lise guessed that "I would appreciate your opinion" really meant "I am going to see how well you've been taught to run a household," just as she knew that the beginning of a party was a terrible time for a test. This was a different place, though, and she would be following different rules now.

Most of the people Lise met in the next hour were the duchesse's children, their spouses, and various parents of spouses. Her uncle had grunted a greeting and then disappeared somewhere; later, Lise learned that the duc de Vimoutiers spent most of the time in one or another of the family's country estates. He and his eldest son hunted, apparently, to the exclusion of all else, only appearing in Paris when required to attend at court.

The woman who passed this information to Lise also relieved Lise of any need to depend on the duchesse for accommodation. The comtesse d'Ombrevilles was yet another aunt—a cousin of Aunt de Vimoutiers. After demanding that Lise tell her in the fullest, most gruesome detail the story of the previous night's werewolf attack, this lady—a soft, rounded, pleasant-faced contrast to her cousin de Vimoutiers—informed Lise that having recently sold the family holdings for more affordable housing she was in a position to make Lise a very attractive offer: chambers in what she described as a lovely new building on the Ile St-Louis. Aunt d'Ombrevilles had the second floor above the street, and "the nice justice who owns the building" had given her the third floor as well, though she didn't need it. And so a deal was struck: for forty-six livres, Lise was able to take the entire third floor of the building—three good-sized rooms, each with a fireplace—for an entire year. It would require her to climb four flights of stairs, but at least she would have her own place. And she could almost afford it. The comtesse even promised to have Lise's things moved for her as soon as Lise was ready to leave the Hôtel de Vimoutiers.

As afternoon turned into evening, family members disappeared a few at a time, and other people began to arrive. Lise understood that the first part of the party had been a family obligation; what was happening now was the debt the duchesse paid to herself.

A Poisoned Prayer
December

Knowing no one and with no home to return to—yet— Lise contented herself with watching the way the women moved, and took note of their dresses, hoping to be able to emulate the former even if there wasn't much her purse would allow her to do anything about the latter. The singular thing about the most attractive women, she decided, was the fluid confidence of their movements. Mother had always criticized the way Lise and her sister had rampaged through the house—"you move like cattle-drovers" was a favourite expression—and now Lise understood a little of what Mother had meant. These women didn't walk, they flowed with the impervious arrogance of rivers, their dresses adding to the effect by shimmering and soughing with liquid insistence. *I can do that*, she thought, watching. Hadn't her aunt just complimented her on her physical grace?

Dressing like these women would be more of a challenge. The latest mode, apparently, favoured textured stripes or embroidered floral patterns for the multitude of petticoats, each of delicate silk or satin. The overskirts worn by these women were not just pulled sharply back at the sides, they were bound up on their edges with loops of silk or elaborate lace that seemed to her to shout, "I cost more than a year's income from your tenants". One woman's overskirt and petticoats bore matching patterns in reversed colours. To a one, the women had bare shoulders that showed off pale skin and the upper parts of smooth, plump arms, and seemed to be competing in how deeply their décolletage could plunge without inviting censure or arrest. The more modest, apparently, disguised the expanses of pale skin with froths of lace, or shawls so delicate they were practically transparent. All of the women had their hair curled much more elaborately than Lise had managed, and many of the younger ones were sporting tiny tufts of lace that, tied to their curls, appeared to mimic on a more delicate scale the feathers men wore in their hats. *I can't do that,* Lise thought. *Not without a fortune.*

"What in God's name is *he* doing here?" Lise, startled from her reverie by the vehemence in the voice, looked up. She didn't know the woman who had spoken, but she certainly recognized the dark-clad figure the woman was pointing at. At the entrance to the salon, his mouth curved in a mild, knowing smile as he spoke to the duchesse's man, stood Rafael de Bellevasse.

She had not had any opportunity the other night to get more than a fleeting glimpse of his face. Still, there was no mistaking him: the attitude with which he stood would have been sufficient to identify him to her. Looking at him now, she saw a face that was perhaps a bit too long and lean, as if something unfortunate had been drawing it out. His mouth, for all that it carried an infuriating smile, was firm. And the smile, she noted with dismay, extended to his dark eyes. He was not an exceptionally handsome man, even in her limited experience, but something in his appearance was having the most profound effect on her.

And then, as she found herself beginning to walk toward him, the duc vanished back through the doorway.

"What was that man doing here?" she asked the servant when she reached the doorway. "Was he invited? I beg your pardon, madame," she added to a tall, busty woman whose passage she had apparently blocked.

"Oh, most definitely not, mademoiselle." The servant smiled thinly at her. "That gentleman is never invited to this house. He was, he told me, merely inquiring as to your well-being. I assured him you had survived your journey and sent him on his way."

A Poisoned Prayer
December

I'm sure you did, she thought. She was on her way through the doors and down the staircase before her next thought had fully formed. *He has some other reason for being here. I'm just a convenient excuse.* Men like the duc de Bellevasse did not journey in person to a hostile household to inquire after the health of an unknown and unworthy young woman. She did not care for the idea she had been an excuse.

"Which way did the duc de Bellevasse go?" she asked the boy standing outside the hôtel entrance.

"Who?"

"Tall man. Dull, uninteresting suit and cloak."

"Oh, *him.*" The boy grinned. "That's not what ducs look like, mademoiselle. But if you want to find him, he went that way, toward the carriages."

Lise looked in the direction the boy had pointed. At the far end of the garden, just inside the gate, a half-dozen carriages were jammed together. Presumably these belonged to especially exalted guests. Most of the attendees of this party would have had to have sent their carriages away; these favoured few could leave at their leisure because their carriages were immediately at hand. Looking at the horses, obviously enchanted into an equine peace, Lise was once again reminded of the inadequacy of her Blessing. The aristocratic owners of these carriages clearly thought it more efficient to pray their horses quiet than to employ grooms to steady them, but Lise could not have calmed even a pony without exhausting herself to the point of being too tired. This convenience couldn't have come without cost: the horses seemed still only because they had been prayed into slumber. Lise couldn't imagine how such powerful prayers could be cast without making one too tired to enjoy a party.

The carriages weren't jammed too close together for men to hide amongst them. The duc's voice made it possible for her to find him even after she'd left the circle of light thrown by the torches at the door. "It was wise of you not to give your name, Poussier," she heard him say. "But why have you summoned me here at all? Didn't I tell you that when it was necessary for us to speak, I would send for you?"

"I'm sorry, monsieur," a rough-voiced man said. He sounded very unhappy. "Uh, most humbly. Your forgiveness. I'm thinking this be too important to wait." Lise crept forward until she could see the two men. The fellow Poussier was clearly a servant, though in the light thrown by the moon and stars he appeared to be the most common sort of workman or vagabond, wrapped against the cold in a very old cloak of indeterminate origin.

"At least you've had the foresight to put off your livery," the duc de Bellevasse said to him.

"Wouldn't have called you," the man said, "if I didn't think you should know about this."

"What is 'this,' exactly?"

"The prince, he's behaving strange, monsieur. Him and his eldest. This afternoon I heard them talking about the cardinal. I'm a decent man, monsieur, and I couldn't believe what they said."

"Did this have anything to do with what I'm paying you for?"

"No, monsieur. Like I said: they were talking about the cardinal. It sounded to me like they mean to kill him!"

The duc snorted. "They're welcome to try. I think they'll find that hook-nosed old vulture isn't easily disposed of." He sounded amused at the prospect. Then he darted forward, and was lost in dark shadow. Lise could only imagine what the duc was doing as he said, "I am not interested in what the Prince d'Aude or his brats think of the cardinal. I am only interested in the d'Audemar family for one thing, Poussier. Nothing else concerns me. Do you understand?"

"But monsieur! The safety of the cardinal concerns the emperor—the empire! Don't you owe a duty to—"

"I owe a duty to my family," the duc said. Lise was surprised at how level and low-pitched his voice sounded, despite the bitter anger that seemed to inform it. "Until that duty is fulfilled, nothing else matters to me. So if you have nothing of any use to tell me, Poussier, I will leave you now."

Lise, startled by the crunch of boots on gravel, did the only thing available to her, scrambling into the nearest carriage. She waited until the footsteps began to recede before shifting the curtain from the window to peer through. She was just in time to see the duc de Bellevasse join with another man—this one in servant's livery—and walk through the carriage gate to the street.

What does this mean? If the cardinal was being threatened, it was of no concern to Lise; like her parents, she was convinced the cardinal was himself a danger to the emperor. But if the servant Poussier was correct, and there was a threat to the emperor, shouldn't she say something about it?

To whom? she asked herself as she stepped down from the carriage and made her way back to her aunt's house.

⚜

"Where in the world have you been, cousin?" Robert, suddenly at her side, hooked her arm in his. "By the good Lord, you're freezing! What have you been up to?" He looked at her, a sly smile on his face. She looked at him and the smile faltered and melted away. "Never mind, then.

Best be on your most pleasing behaviour, though," he told her. "Important people Mama wants you to meet."

"It would have been better had you not mentioned that," Lise said, nerves beginning to assail her. "The last thing I want right now is time to think about the things I mustn't do or say."

"In that case, you probably don't want me to mention that one's a cardinal, one's a prince, and the other's an archbishop." He grinned.

"If I knew you better, cousin, I'd clout you for that."

"Oh, you don't have to know me well to want to hit me," Robert said. "Strangers do it all the time."

Lise interrupted him before he could speak further. "Who is *that*?" In an ocean of luxury, Lise's eye had found an island of simplicity and apparent strength: a young man, about her cousin's height but with none of Robert's softness in his features. His shoulder-length hair was more beautiful than any wig could be. He wore a heavy white coat and breeches of a military cut, and under the coat was a pale blue waistcoat embroidered in silver. The sword he wore was solid, business-like. An officer—but not an exalted one, or he'd be wearing more braid.

"Oh ho," Robert said, gripping her elbow. "You've a good eye, cousin. Mother's sort of adopted him, which means he's going places. And he holds his rank by virtue of his bravery, not simply because his parents bought it for him."

Too late, Lise realized what Robert was doing. "No, no," she said, trying to pull free. "I just wanted to know who he was."

"And so you shall." Robert laughed at her discomfort. And then she was face-to-chest with the young man, who looked simultaneously startled and embarrassed. "Cousin Lise, allow me to introduce you to Captain Philippe-

Emmanuel d'Oléron, of the imperial musketeers and the *garde du corps* of the princesse imperiale. Captain, my cousin Lise de Trouvaille."

Lise made her curtsy, cursing Robert silently and trying to keep her face composed and blush-free. "Monsieur," she said, aware that she sounded like a shy little girl.

"Mademoiselle." Captain d'Oléron sounded no more comfortable or happy than she did, which was both a relief to her and a credit to him: if he'd been more like the other guests here he'd have been more at ease—more glib.

For a lifetime of a moment they stood staring at one another. Finally, Robert grabbed her elbow again and pulled her away, saying, "You two are deafening me." As they passed back into the ballroom he added, "I have concluded that Mama has her work cut out for her, my poor cousin."

Lise was about to tell him what he could do with his conclusion when Robert thrust her forward, saying, "Mama, here is Lise, delivered as promised."

"Don't be impertinent, boy." The duchesse smiled a mother's indulgence. "Go and fetch me some spiced wine, there's a good son."

Lise, while her relatives had been exchanging banter, had been looking—although trying to keep from being obvious about it—at the three men standing beside her aunt. The first she knew by reputation; the others were strangers to her, though she could guess their identities from what her cousin had told her. Together the trio formed an artistic contrast in physical types—one, tall and lean and suggesting an elongated, scarlet bird of prey; a second short and rounded, in stained brown robes that made him resemble nothing so much as a ball kicked around by peasant boys; and the last a sort of compromise between the first two: of middling height, though bent somewhat with age, and dressed in rich blue with red and orange contrasts.

"Your Eminence, Your Grace, my Lord Prince" the duchesse said, taking Lise by the elbow and drawing her into the centre of the conversational triangle, "I have the pleasure to present my niece, Lise de Trouvaille, who has arrived just this day from the south. Lise, allow me to present His Eminence, the Cardinal du Plessis; His Grace, the Archbishop of Paris, and the prince d'Aude."

Lise was startled at hearing the name of the man so recently insulted by the duc de Bellevasse, but covered her surprise with an especially elaborate curtsy, dropping her head so that her chin rested on her breast-bone. The implied respect was justified, she knew. Men of God two of this trio may have been, but even a girl from the south knew enough to respect the strength such men possessed on the earthly plane. No one became a cardinal or an archbishop without understanding the ways of power. As for the prince, the title implied a power and fortune possessed by few outside the imperial family. She wondered what the duc's fight with the prince was about, decided it didn't involve a woman, and then had to stifle the giggles brought on by the vision of this simmering, unhappy old man cavorting with anything female.

"Please, young lady, stand up." The archbishop beamed at her, as though embarrassed. "You do us more honour than we deserve."

"Don't presume to understand the young lady's piety, Jean-Claude," the cardinal said; his voice was as severe as his countenance. "For all we know, she does us exactly the honour she thinks we deserve."

"I believe," the prince said, "that my presence here is unnecessary. If you will forgive me madame, messieurs,

I will go see what trouble my sons are getting into." He bowed, turned and left, and Lise, straightening from her curtsy, was impressed at the length of his stride. He may have looked old, but the prince d'Aude didn't act it.

Lise gave what she thought was a suitably demure smile to the two holy men and said, "I thank you both," in her most respectful voice, "for your attention and concern."

"Nicely spoken," the cardinal said. "Might I ask what brings you to Paris? You must find the climate at this time of year much colder than that to which you are accustomed. Do you perhaps wish to be presented to the emperor?"

"She is seeking a husband," the duchesse said, pre-empting any response Lise might make. *As is her right*, Lise reminded herself. "A good match will be of much benefit to her family. And, therefore, to mine."

"Though I would like, I think, to at least see the emperor while I'm here," Lise added.

The archbishop laughed, and clutched briefly at the cardinal's sleeve. "How's that, eh? Our lord and master, just one of the many sights to be seen in this great city!"

"I would hardly interpret the young lady's remark in that fashion," the cardinal said. *Why not?* Lise wondered. *What's so bad about a bit of fun from time to time, even for a holy man?* Her parents and their friends were convinced that Cardinal du Plessis, while ostensibly his servant and teacher, wanted to usurp the emperor's role. He would certainly wear the role of usurper perfectly. His very nose seemed aggressive, forward-thrusting like some hunting-raptor's beak. His robes were of a satin so rich and heavy that they shone in the candlelight, red with the Lord's life-blood. When the cardinal moved, his robes whispered like a congregation waiting for a sermon.

"However you want to interpret it, my dear Michel," the

archbishop said. "Surely a presentation can be arranged." If the cardinal was a hawk, the archbishop most closely suggested a partridge. "The young lady has the right, by virtue of her birth, to be presented to her sovereign. And Charles is certainly holding enough of your expanded levees in the coming weeks to be able to accommodate one more charming young woman."

"Of course that can be done," the cardinal said.

"Our Lise has had an interesting journey here, haven't you, dear?" Aunt d'Ombrevilles had suddenly appeared at her cousin's side. The duchesse scowled, but the other woman laughed. "Oh, come, Marie. Don't you think the cardinal and archbishop want to hear about Lise's loup-garou?"

"A loup-garou?" The cardinal's generous eyebrows lifted. "Not here, surely."

"It was on the way to Paris," the duchesse said, abruptly as though distracted—which surely she must have been, else she would not have treated Cardinal du Plessis that way.

"Is she all right?" the cardinal asked. "This sort of encounter is not part of most young ladies' introduction to the world."

Lise was trying to change the subject when Cousin Robert piped up, "Most young ladies don't have the ba—I mean the presence of mind—to put a silver bullet into a werewolf from point-blank range, either, Your Eminence. Hey!" he added when Lise smacked him on the back of the head.

"Werewolves in the forests, and under a day's ride from Paris," the archbishop said, as if Robert hadn't spoken at all. "Not good, Michel, is it?"

"Of course it isn't," the cardinal growled. "A single demon

anywhere in the empire is a demon too many. I don't need you to remind me of that."

"Except that it's not just one," the archbishop said.

"This is hardly the time or place for such a discussion," the cardinal said. "We are embarrassing our hostess, Jean-Claude. Come see me at my palace tomorrow if you are serious in your concerns." He turned to Lise. "In the meantime, if I might inquire of the young lady: why seek a husband so far from home? Are there no eligible suitors in the south?"

"Some," Lise replied after waiting for the go-ahead nod from her aunt. "But my circumstances are such, your eminence, that I decided that it would be more to my advantage to enlarge the circle, as it were."

The archbishop laughed. "Well put. But what are your circumstances that should require you to leave the warmth of the south and venture here in this cold?"

"Money and grace, your eminence—or, rather, the lack of them. My family's estates are not large, and I have decided that it will be better that they all go to my younger sister, Andrée."

"Your younger sister?"

Lise couldn't suppress her sigh. "Andrée has by far the stronger Blessing," she said. "Which is to say, I have no Blessing to speak of. I was the despair of our family priest, I'm afraid."

"Surely it can't be as bad as all that," the duchesse said, as the comtesse clucked sympathetically.

"Of course it can," said the cardinal. "God does not necessarily play favourites, but His Blessings are no more evenly distributed amongst us than are blue eyes, or wits. It does you credit, mademoiselle, that you accept this." Lise lowered her eyelids and bowed her head, acknowledging the compliment. *It's a credit I could easily live without*, she thought. "And you have certainly done the wise thing," the cardinal added. "A noble name is still worth something, and if anyone can help you obtain the best possible marriage, it is your aunt the duchesse."

"And we will begin first thing tomorrow," her Aunt de Vimoutiers said.

"Second thing, surely," the archbishop said. "After New Year Mass, my dear lady."

⚜

"You're not going to hit me again, are you?" Cousin Robert eyed Lise warily as she advanced on him, having tracked him to the small salon in which he was hiding from his mother. "I thought I was giving you a compliment back there."

"Of course you did," she said. "Every woman wants to be described as a cold-blooded killer to a pair of holy men."

"Well, the cardinal's not all that holy," Robert said. "And I'm pretty sure the two of them appreciate a cool head as much as they appreciate piety—at least in people of our sort."

"I wanted to ask you about that," she told him. "About the archbishop, that is. Is he as poor as he looks?"

"God, no." He squinted at her. "You really don't know anything about him?"

"Robert," she said through gritted teeth, "how long have I been in Paris now?"

"Ah. Should have thought of that. You're right. No doubt he's not as well-known in the South." He caught a glimpse of himself in a mirror, and carefully adjusted his wig.

"The archbishop is—or at least, he was—a Maillart. That's one of the great families of the old, Valois, nobility.

He gave up his name and his inheritance to join the church. Everyone says he was made a bishop only by virtue of his humility and good deeds."

"You sound doubtful," Lise said.

"Well, cynics like your friend de Bellevasse say it's all an act to impress the bourgeoisie. The way he dresses is supposedly part of that act. But I don't know, myself. The archbishop certainly does a lot for the poor."

"But the poor don't make bishops, much less archbishops."

"Oh, the archbishop part is easy enough explained," Robert said with a grin. "My mother and her friends more or less adopted him. They all made him their personal confessor, and their interest in him was more than enough to promote him to the top."

"I liked him more than I like the cardinal."

Robert laughed. "No surprise there, cousin. Nobody really likes the cardinal. He has more power than the archbishop, but if you wanted a friend you'd be better off looking in the archbishop's direction."

"Thank you, Robert," she said, favouring him with a smile. "You have answered the question that brought me here after you in the first place. I hope you enjoy the rest of the party."

January

One

THE CATHEDRAL OF Notre Dame de Paris was easily the biggest building Lise had ever seen, much less been inside. The real surprise, though, was how much of its interior was—empty. The congregation, numerous as it was, seemed shrunken into insignificance as Aunt de Vimoutiers lead Lise into the pew her family had owned here for generations.

Which was, Lise supposed, the point. Humans in general, and the French aristocracy very much in particular, probably needed constant reminders of their insignificance in the sight of God.

The impact of the reminder this morning seemed to Lise to be rather minimal. Seated between her aunt and her cousin, Lise felt less isolated and more like a participant in a continuation of last night's party. A number of her fellow congregants she recognized from last night. Over her head, the space that perhaps should have reminded people of their place in the order of things was instead filled with swirling twists of colour, animated icons of family saints and even representations of the Cross. Lise had never seen anything like it, and her attempts to follow the riotous celebration gave her another of her headaches.

The officiating priest was the archbishop, and he seemed not to mind the behaviour of his aristocratic congregants. Lise doubted the cardinal would have been so understanding, and with that thought she tried to relax and enjoy the show. This would have been difficult had she been attending Mass at her parents' home, because her Latin was almost non-existent. Here, though, she found French translations of the prayers somehow emerging through the pain of the headache; during the Collect someone even cast illustrations of the New Year-themed prayer overhead.

By the end of the service Lise had realized why the archbishop had corrected her aunt the night before: most of the people sitting around her, she saw, weren't using their Blessings to enhance the service, they were trying to stave off boredom. Without having to ask, she knew that neither her aunt nor her cousin attended Mass more than a handful of times during the year. Of her uncle and elder cousin there had been no sign. The rites of the Church seemed not to matter to these people, who from their chatter and ridiculous prayer-imaging seemed to be in church not for any reason of faith she could ascertain.

The sermon at least was in French, but it was brief and so mundane it might as well not have been delivered at all. It made no sense to Lise that the archbishop should waste the opportunity to speak to a congregation most of which wouldn't be in Notre Dame again before Easter.

After the Mass had ended, though, Lise realized what the archbishop had planned for this morning. As she and her aunt were leaving the cathedral, by the exit reserved for the high-born, they found the archbishop waiting, discussing with each family that passed the subject that was really on his mind this morning.

"I realize that I say this every time we meet in this place," he said to the duchesse, "and I likewise realize how little effect I have. Nonetheless I am compelled to remind you, my ladies, of the pope's encyclical of two years ago and the Church position on the matter of using one's Blessing to subvert God's plan for women."

Lise's lack of understanding must have been obvious, because her Aunt de Vimoutiers turned and said to her, in an unnecessarily loud whisper, "He's referring to those prayers that keep us from conceiving."

Lise felt the blush wash over her. "I don't—I haven't—"

"Don't worry, Lise," her Aunt d'Ombrevilles said, sidling up to her with a side-long glare at the blushing archbishop, "it's the sort of thing priests are required to say, for the sake of the bourgeoisie. The reality is that if we couldn't control conception our Blessings might become so diluted as to be unusable, and without our Blessings there *is* no aristocracy in France. And then where would the Church be?"

"Is it necessary that you be so blunt, Madame?" The archbishop had gone beyond blushing and was now tripping over his words like a first-year seminarian. "The pope's word on this subject is supposed to be final. You make my position extremely awkward by being so publicly obstreperous, you know. All of you."

"And you wonder why we so seldom attend Mass," Aunt de Vimoutiers said, her voice pure vinegar. "Lise, it's time to go. We have work to do, you and I."

Lise began following her aunt, but hesitated when she realized that Aunt d'Ombrevilles wasn't with her. Turning, she saw the woman standing very close to the archbishop, head tilted back so as to be able to look him in the eye, and berating him at some length. The poor man looked very much as if he'd heard this sort of thing many times.

When Lise looked around again, Aunt de Vimoutiers had disappeared. Running to catch up, Lise turned a corner and collided with another woman. The two fell to the frigid stone floor in a ruffling of silks.

"I am so sorry!" Lise said, struggling to help her victim to her feet. "Please forgive me, mademoiselle."

To her immense relief the other woman laughed, a sound of delight. She was, Lise saw, quite young—several years younger than Lise, and clearly unmarried. She looked at Lise in an unaffected way that Lise hadn't seen too much of in the city, where everyone seemed to be calculating all of the time. "I am Marguerite de Courçon. I hope you're not hurt."

"I am Lise de Trouvaille," Lise said, "and I thank you for your concern and your gentility. I am fine, believe me. And this was all my fault. I was in a hurry to catch up with my aunt."

"Not your fault at all," Mademoiselle de Courçon said. "It was I who wasn't looking where I was going. Mama is forever claiming that I'll be killed by something I've walked into without paying attention. Like the river." Her eyes crinkled as she smiled.

Lise laughed. "I should think that we would both notice the river long before we fell into it."

"Too true!" Mademoiselle de Courçon laughed. When they had both regained their feet and brushed their dresses into a semblance of propriety, she leaned over to Lise and asked, "So, did the archbishop give you the Lecture?" She finished with a giggle.

"He did. I confess it took me completely by surprise. I have never heard this particular homily before. Certainly my family's priest at Trouvaille never mentions it."

"I don't know that place. But if you've never been given the Lecture, you are a very lucky young woman. It's worse for me: my parents expect me to follow that rule."

"No!" Lise couldn't hide her shock. "That's barbaric! Not even the English expect their young women to be chaste."

"I know!" Mademoiselle de Courçon giggled again. "I once tried to tell my father that he was acting like a Spaniard. He was not amused."

"Why do your parents insist, then?"

"I don't really know. Though I think it's a way for them to keep me as I was when I was a little girl. Does that make sense?"

"It does." Lise remembered her father once saying something very much like that. "My mother always said that she wanted me to know my way around all aspects of married life, the way she had, so she took care to explain things to me very carefully around the time of my first Communion."

"That makes so much sense. Though I would have been horribly embarrassed to hear such talk at that age."

"Oh, so was I," said Lise. "And then my grandfather told me that I wouldn't buy a horse without first riding it, so why should I treat a man any differently?"

Mademoiselle de Courçon burst into laughter, then clapped her hands over her mouth. Her eyes continued to sparkle, though, even as she muffled her giggles.

"Lise, I just *knew* it was you responsible for that outburst." The duchesse de Vimoutiers rounded a corner and stood frowning, arms crossed under her breasts. Her eyes, though, were sparkling and Lise suspected she'd heard Grandfather's jest. "I was serious a moment ago, dear; we have to start work on your project today."

"Please forgive me, Madame," Mademoiselle de Courçon said, dropping into a quick curtsy. "I was the one making the noise." She turned to Lise. "You are staying with the duchesse?"

"Her aunt," the duchesse said. "If it would please you, mademoiselle, we would love to see you for wine in the next day or so, before Lise moves into her new place."

"Thank you very much. I would love that." To Lise she said, "It was lovely meeting you, mademoiselle. I will send you a note tomorrow."

"A pleasant young woman," the duchesse said after Mademoiselle de Courçon had left them. "Her parents aren't exactly in my circle, but they're certainly a good enough family. I am pleased that you have made her acquaintance, and so soon after arriving. It gives me hope that your southern origins and restricted upbringing won't handicap you too severely."

"She told me," Lise said as she followed her aunt out of the cathedral, "that her parents force her to follow the pope in the area of contraception."

"A number of well-born families do, Lise. It is purely a matter of controlling their women and has nothing whatever to do with God."

"I don't think the pope agrees with you, aunt."

"And is the pope a woman?" The duchesse smiled, but there was little amusement in it. "The truth, Lise, is that God would not provide us with any Blessing He did not expect us to use. I do not have much use for the Church— my communication with God the Father and Christ the Saviour, to say nothing of His Mother Mary, is personal and direct and does not require the mediation of some Latin-speaking tyrant—but I will point out that Cardinal du Plessis does not harangue the female members of his flock about which aspects of their Blessings they may use."

"I have so little Blessing," Lise said, "that I feel morally compelled to use every bit of it, no matter how horrid it makes me feel."

A Poisoned Prayer
January

"Horrid? Prayer isn't supposed to make you feel horrid, Lise."

"That is something, aunt, that I realize every day."

⚜

"What do you think of the cardinal's tale, Valentin?" Nicholas de La Reynie, lieutenant-general of police to the emperor, liked to enjoy the perks of his office whenever he could justify them; amongst those perks was having the Cardinal du Plessis himself officiate at Mass. The office also, unfortunately, carried the responsibility for the supervision of all law-and-order activities—down to enforcement of the food and drink and sumptuary laws—in the city of Paris. That, in turn, meant that he had the responsibility to pay attention when his instincts demanded it. They were demanding attention this morning.

Valentin was a trusted associate, the chief investigator for the lieutenant for criminal affairs and thus a man de La Reynie consulted on a steady basis. The story they had heard was not a sermon, but had been delivered to them in private following the New Year Mass. "I think the cardinal believes that the young lady he met last night may have been the last person to see the emperor's agent alive."

"It might, perhaps, be carrying things a bit too far to call Brother Marçal the emperor's agent," de La Reynie said, sucking on his pipe. Dragoons searching the site of the attack on mademoiselle de Trouvaille's carriage had discovered the torn robes and crucifix of the missing monk—a man who seemingly had carried proof of something dark and dangerous, dangerous if only because it was still so mysterious to de La Reynie. "Yes, we're reasonably sure that he was attempting to deliver information to the emperor at Fountainbleau. But the emperor himself claims to have had no knowledge of the man, and he has no reason to lie to me about this. Our interests in this regard are identical, after all."

"A fair point. Still, it would have been useful had the young woman seen just a bit more. We might not have learned from her for whom the monk was working, but at least we might have learned more about the loup-garou that killed him. From what the cardinal said back there, the transformation must have happened only a short while before the demon attacked." Valentin's right hand twisted around the hilt of his short sword.

Seeing this, de La Reynie couldn't suppress a smile. Valentine disliked being unable to see the entirety of a puzzle as much as de La Reynie did. He stopped for a moment to pray his pipe alight, and to hell with the cardinal's objections to smoking in the private quarters of his palace. "I have to confess, I'm more concerned about what the disappearance of this monk is all about than I am about the origins of a loup-garou. For all that I admit," he added, forestalling Valentin's protest, "that they may well be connected."

"And what a fortunate coincidence," Valentin said, "that the duc de Bellevasse just happened to be close enough to rescue the young lady."

"On this," de La Reynie said, "I believe you may be wrong, Valentin. My reports suggest that it truly was chance that put de Bellevasse's path and mademoiselle de Trouvaille's in conjunction that way. I realize that you don't like the man, Valentin, but remember what the late Friar John Punch used to say: given two possibilities, the one that is less convoluted is the most likely to be true. Friar Punch would argue that he simply cannot be responsible for every criminal act that takes place in or near this city."

"What do you want me to do next, then?" Valentin asked.

A Poisoned Prayer
January

De La Reynie puffed for a moment, thinking. "Because we still don't know what this is all about, I can't ask you to divert too much of your attention to our unfortunate missing monk. But I am convinced, in my bones, that something is happening that we will like less and less the more we learn about it. So please keep your eyes and ears alert, Valentin. And I think that perhaps I will pay a visit to the young mademoiselle de Trouvaille. It is possible she has remembered some details she did not share with the cardinal last night."

They stepped out of the palace and into the weak midday sunlight. "This has been Hell's own winter," Valentin said.

"I'm afraid it's going to get worse before it gets better," de La Reynie replied.

⚜

The small salon fell dark with a suddenness that startled Lise. Even at midday this room wasn't well-lit, at least not at this time of year. "Let's talk some more about your Blessing," the duchesse said. Gesturing at one of the candles, she said, "Light them again, please."

Shrugging in a way she hoped wouldn't be too obvious, Lise looked around the room to identify the candles. There were a lot of them, including an even dozen in a chandelier overhead—*girandoles* and *torchieres* seemed to be everywhere. Lighting them all at once would require more energy than she possessed.

Who had said anything about lighting them at once?

Lise felt herself smiling, and she began to pray.

Making light was a simple skill. Anyone with any God-given magical ability could do it, if taught—and many who'd never been taught could do it, though they were wise not to do so in the presence of a priest or noble. Even Lise, whose lack of power had so distressed her parents' priest that he'd actually threatened to give up holy orders, could make light and set a candle to burning. Most of the time, anyway.

This morning, she was pleased to note, was one of those times. One by one, the candles in the chandelier glowed yellow-green, then sputtered into flame.

By the time she'd relit all of the candles in the room, she had her usual headache, but for once she didn't mind. This perhaps hadn't been much of a test, but she had passed.

Her aunt the duchesse was looking at her, eyes narrowed. "That was... adequate," the duchesse said. Lise looked at her, trying without speaking to let the duchesse know that if she'd been any better at magic, any more gifted by God the Mother, she wouldn't have had to come to Paris to look for a husband.

"Now, extinguish them for me, please."

For a moment, Lise could only stare at her aunt. She was pretty much certain she wouldn't be able to extinguish a single candle, much less all of them. At the same time, she wasn't going to admit that without at least trying. So she smiled with as much confidence as she thought she could project—much more than she actually felt—and began praying again, this time the prayer to extinguish flame.

"You may stop now, Lise," the duchesse said after a moment. "Please stop," she said a heartbeat later, her voice now betraying a hint of concern.

Lise opened her eyes. A few of the candles had gone out, but most had flared up as if they'd been charged with gunpowder. The chandelier blazed like the sun; from one *girandole* gobbets of molten wax were spilling, spattering onto the carpet. "Oh!" she said, feeling the flush growing up her neck and into her cheeks. "Oh, aunt, I'm so sorry."

"Think nothing of it, dear," the duchesse said in a

somewhat distant tone. A flicker of concentration crossed her face, Lise's headache worsened, and the room dimmed, lit now only by the blaze in the fireplace. After a moment, the candles lit again, at a more natural level of light. "I think that we will downplay your potential role as a mother of gifted children," she added. "I am most sorry for you, Lise. Your first Communion must have been horrible for you."

Don't cry, Lise told herself. "It was," she said. "My parents tried to make me believe that this was nothing unusual, but I knew they were upset. So when my younger sister, Andrée, had her first communion and revealed a useful Blessing, they didn't try so hard to hide their relief. And all I have to show for my studies is headaches." *And they've been worse since I've been in Paris. They should have stopped.*

"Oh, there's that lovely green in your eyes again," the duchesse said. She smiled at Lise, the smile faltering when she stepped back and got the full impact of Lise's expression. "You would do well, mademoiselle," she said after a pause, "to consider ways of making your eyes sparkle in that fashion more often, but without the necessity of your showing the thundercloud expression you are currently wearing."

Lise flushed. She hadn't realized she was being so bold in her expressions, however angered her thoughts had been. "I'm sorry, Madame. I know I can't hope to understand the way God works, but it still angers me." She paused a moment, then decided to be honest. "And I'm not accustomed to being analyzed in this fashion."

"You would do well to get accustomed to it, Lise. If you are going to survive in society, much less make a good marriage, you are going to be inspected, analyzed, and perhaps even poked and prodded, by nearly everyone you meet. Society is a market, and your person is the currency."

"I had not thought of it in that way." *I should have, though.* "Aunt," she asked, "what about Captain d'Oléron? Could he make a good husband for me?"

The duchesse smiled, more warmly. "I'm glad you approve of him, Lise." *I'm interested in him,* Lise thought. *It's not quite the same thing.* "But I have to tell you, I don't think you made a very good first impression last night."

"I know." Lise shook her head. "Not my fault. Robert dragged me right up to him without any warning. I was so surprised all I could do was goggle at the man."

"I can have a chat with him. With both of them, I suppose, but with the captain, certainly. He would indeed make a decent match for you, Lise. But you'd be taking on a risk. Musketeers don't make that much money, even captains. You'd be gambling that he will rise as high as I think he will, and until he does your life is likely to be a poor one."

"It's relatively poor now," Lise said. Then she thought of something and her spirits fell. "He is assigned to the court, isn't he?"

"To the guard of the princesse imperiale, yes. Why does that matter?"

"It's my family's position. We are too close to the English in Aquitaine, and to the King of Navarre to the south. The emperor does not have much trust for his nobles in the south, Madame. I suspect that a marriage to a southerner might affect the captain's prospects. Oh, but if I married well, madame—or even well enough to maintain a modest household here—I could ensure that my family was properly represented and understood, in society if not necessarily at court."

"Don't worry so much," her aunt said. "Many girls with

less to offer than you have found acceptable husbands in my lifetime, and I doubt you'll fare any worse than they. As for the captain, your political situation makes things awkward, perhaps, but not impossible. Especially if you contrive to make yourself interesting to him." She rose from her chair.

"Now let's talk about dresses."

The duchesse circled her, calculating. "Fortunately, you have a good figure. Clearly you eat well, and yet you haven't let it go to fat. My woman can make much of you, I think. I'll send for her later today."

"What do you think I'll require?"

"You'll want at least one good gown for now, in addition to several dresses. Since you look to be the active type, you'll probably want riding gear as well; my husband won't miss a horse from time to time. Hunting clothes won't be necessary if you're going to make your mark in Paris. That's just as well; hunting gear is disgustingly mannish enough as it is."

"Madam, I have to warn you that my resources are limited." Lise thought of her grandfather counting out old coins from his precious cache, and of the loan—provided, reluctantly, by the local provost of the wine merchants— that she had told none of her family about.

"I understood that from your reasons for coming in the first place. Might I ask how much you have at your disposal?"

"I have six gold *louis* and thirty-four *livres*." Most of which she had already promised to pay as rent to her Aunt d'Ombrevilles.

"Good God. My shoes cost more than that, child. How do you propose to make that amount of money suffice?"

"I had thought it a reasonable amount, Madame. I guessed that rooms would not be cheap, but I still figured on being able to survive for a good four months on the contents of my purse."

"If you were prepared to live like a clerk or some other petty bourgeois," the duchesse said, not unkindly, "I've no doubt it could be done. But my dear, if you're to attract a suitable husband you're going to have to make yourself— well, *attractive.*"

If you are prepared to support my ignoring the pope where sex is concerned, Lise thought, *then my clothing shouldn't matter so much.* Aloud she said, "I do have an idea, Madame, for increasing the amount of money I have available to me. My intent all along was to treat those coins as a sort of beginning investment. A stake in my future, if you will."

The duchesse tilted her head back in an unspoken request for intercession by Christ or one of the saints. "A stake? You intend to go into business? *Child—*"

"Aunt, I am fully aware of the laws against nobles engaging in trade. Rest assured I have no interest in that. I intend to increase my funds in the most respectable of fashions, one that I understand the emperor and all of his retinue not only approve of, but practice on a regular basis."

"And what is that? What do you propose to do?"

"I propose to gamble. Except that it won't be a gamble, the way I play cards."

⚜

"Oh, I wish I had been there to see Mama's face when you said that," cousin Robert said. He paused, and looked at Lise more closely. "Do you really think that you could fund a proper household by playing at cards?"

"Of course." *That is the plan, at any rate.* Lise smiled

sweetly at him. "Who will anticipate a mere woman being a calculating card player?"

"In Paris," Robert said with a certain sadness in his voice and eyes, "just about everyone. Women may be kept in their place in the provinces, cousin, but here it's the women who run the show. We men are merely the audience."

Lise stifled a snarl. "Well, they won't be expecting much of me. Especially until I can afford to dress in what Aunt de Vimoutiers considers acceptable style."

"But—gambling? How can you make money at it? Isn't it—well, a *gamble?*"

"In most cases, yes," Lise told him. "But there are games of skill, cousin. And my grandfather is both very entertained by them and accomplished at them. He taught me a lot. I propose to dispense some of that wisdom amongst your friends." She gave him a small curtsy "Out of deference to your status as family, I shall avoid playing with you."

"Too kind, I'm sure," Robert said, his voice fading. "Just how, exactly, are we family, anyway?"

"I'm not entirely certain. I do know that your mother is not really my aunt; that's a courtesy title, I think. If Grandfather's memory is accurate, your mother is a niece of one of Grandfather's second cousins. What that makes you to me is even more confusing."

"Mostly, I think, I'm wary." Robert offered Lise his arm. "I do have an idea, though, that might help you catch yourself a husband without having to bankrupt yourself—or any of my friends—in the process."

"What is this idea?"

"It's not a 'what'," Robert said. "It's a 'who'." I know an old heretic who just happens to be an accomplished collector and seller of spells, prayers, and potions. He can give you prayers and things that will make the men overlook the fact that your dress is more than ten minutes old. Not that but I think it's really the women who notice these things anyway. Most of my friends are more concerned with the amount of fabric a woman's got on than with how it's patterned or cut."

⚜

The morning was cold. La Reynie could easily have justified staying in bed until it was warmer—say, February. But he had heard two archers discussing the case beneath his bedroom window, and what they had said demanded his attention and pulled him out of bed. Rest could wait.

Turning a corner onto the Place de Grève, he saw that he wasn't the only one who'd been drawn out of bed early. "Good morning, Valentin," he said. "I'm surprised to find you here. That, or I'm surprised that I didn't hear about this from you."

"My apologies, sir," Valentin said. "I didn't think it was important enough to justify waking you."

The two men had by now reached the edge of the quay. Beside them, the Hôtel de Ville was stirring into activity, as the city government slowly returned to action following the New Year holiday. In front of them, de La Reynie saw a cluster of men gathered around something on one of the docks. Out in the river, boatmen watched from their anchored vessels. A raucous, bird-like sound that could only be coming from the wash-boats on the Left Bank side of the Seine told him that the wash-women of the city had begun to pay attention as well.

"Not important enough?" he asked. "Two archers of the city watch are down there; I see a commissioner from the Châtelet with them. You're here, representing the lieutenant for criminal affairs. I'm surprised only that there's no representative from the Constabulary. Four police forces in

Paris, Valentin, all but one has a representative here—and you didn't think it important enough to summon me?"

De La Reynie looked more closely at the grouping on the wharf. "What exactly have they brought up, anyway?"

"It's just a servant, sir," Valentin said. He was trying to keep his voice diffident, but de La Reynie could tell the man was upset. *The question is, is it my presence that's upset him, or is it what they've pulled from the water?*

"I suggest you stop trying to deflect me, Valentin. It's not 'just' a servant if it justifies this much attention. And it does justify the attention, doesn't it?"

"I'm afraid so, sir. His name is—was—Poussier. He was a footman for the d'Audemar family. Worked for old Simon, we think, but we're not certain yet."

"Damn. I suppose there are no marks on the body."

"I was on my way down to look when you called me."

"But you suspect as much, or you'd have sent one of your men instead of coming yourself." De La Reynie drew in a long breath, letting it out in a sigh. "Too much to hope that this was another street-fight between lackeys."

"If it was him, you know, I wouldn't expect to see any marks. Not the way he kills."

"You mean the way he's rumoured to kill, don't you?" De La Reynie rubbed his hands together, part of him regretting the warm fire he probably wouldn't get back to until after dark. "We still have no proof that de Bellevasse uses dark magic. Nothing that would stand up to anything but an Inquisitorial court. And de Bellevasse's family is powerful enough that even the Inquisition won't go after him without more proof."

"Without meaning any disrespect, sir, why are you defending de Bellevasse?" They had reached the stone steps; Valentin stood aside to allow de La Reynie to precede him down to the quay.

"I rather thought that I was defending my own impartiality, Valentin." De La Reynie shuffled with care down the steps, reminding himself of an old man moving toward his pew in a church. He accepted the way he looked; it was preferable to pitching head-first from the frost-slicked stone. "Unless you know something you haven't told me, we don't have any reason to suspect that de Bellevasse is behind this. For all we know, the poor man got drunk and fell off the Pont Neuf."

"It is possible," Valentin said from behind him. "I merely remark that since September, whenever some misfortune befalls the d'Audemar family, the duc de Bellevasse seems to be standing nearby, watching with that infernal smirk on his face."

"No love lost between those two families, it's true. It's odd, that. If you accept that de Bellevasse is pursuing some sort of vendetta against the d'Audemars, the logical connection is with the aunt's death—except that there's no connection that I know of. She was married into old Simon's family, and her Bertrand was devastated by her murder. Both families lost out then." Reaching the bottom of the steps, de La Reynie turned to look at Valentin. "And anyway, why would anyone use magic against a lackey?"

"The duc de Bellevasse would, I believe, use magic against a flea if he thought it would further his aims, my lieutenant-general." Valentin produced a long pipe, in the Dutch fashion, and began filling its bowl.

"Hmm. You are probably right about that," de La Reynie said. "The question then becomes, how does using magic to kill a lackey further his aims, when a blow to the head would do the job as effectively and with less chance of discovery?

A Poisoned Prayer
January

Besides, given how he feels about the d'Audemars, I'd be more suspicious if he *didn't* take pleasure in their misfortune."

Valentin bowed his head. "You are right, sir. I apologize."

"Don't," de La Reynie said. "I understand that it's your frustration speaking. Since the emperor outlawed duelling, it seems we've had a lot more lackeys murdered in this city. I'm frustrated as well."

"So you keep pressing me. We never get answers if we don't ask questions."

De La Reynie was climbing the steps again after having given the body sufficient inspection to confirm that the servant had died by some mysterious means that would require investigation by priests when a flash nearly blinded him. Only Valentin's quick response kept him from falling backward and cracking his head. "Are you unwell, monsieur?" Valentin asked.

"I'm fine. Something on the bridge upriver flashed in the sun just as I was looking that way." Now back on dry ground, he turned and looked back at the bridge. "Oh ho," he said. "Speak of the Devil."

"It's de Bellevasse?"

"The same. Watching us, unless I'm mistaken." Closing his eyes, de La Reynie uttered a long and convoluted prayer. He didn't understand a word of it, medieval Latin not being a subject he had interested himself in, but he appreciated its value all the same.

He also well knew how queasy its effect could make him, and so he kept his eyes closed a second or two after finishing the prayer.

When he opened his eyes again, it was as if he was standing on the other side of the Pont Notre Dame, hovering over the river as he faced de Bellevasse. He was close enough—

in spirit, at least—to see the expression on the duc's face. Since the duc was either using a telescope or prayer to view the scene on the quay, de La Reynie was confident his expression was just as clear to the duc.

The duc did not look smug. He did not look pleased. "He looks rather upset," de La Reynie said to Valentin, "for a man whose enemy has just suffered another loss."

He walked away as the body was being brought up the slippery steps. "We should find out why this might be." He smiled at Valentin. "You have persuaded me that I should not let our powerful friend off so easily. I hereby formally request your assistance, Valentin, in the inserting of a—well, let us say 'an observer'—into de Bellevasse's household."

⁕

"So I have to admit," Lise said, "that I'm not at all sure you can help me—Rabbi, is it?" She had heard the word, once or twice, before Robert had given it to her as this man's title, but didn't know what it meant.

"Not an official title, but you're welcome to use it." The man smiled. "It's usually interpreted as 'teacher,' but in fact it means 'great one'. So you understand that this is not an honorific I have taken on myself."

Lise smiled. Rabbi Weiss was a sort of young-old man; his beard seemed to spread out, to flow, encompassing all of his skinny, sunken chest as he bowed his head, then contract once more as the rabbi raised his head again, and while the beard might have suggested age and wisdom, his eyes held something rather more young and wicked. While she doubted he would be of much use to her, she couldn't keep a small part of herself from hoping her instinct was wrong, and that the glint in his eyes meant he did in fact

A Poisoned Prayer
January

possess the sorts of prayers that would make the right sort of men more inclined to pay attention to her.

"You are obviously an astute young woman," Weiss said. "Which saddens me, because I would like for you to be wrong in this case. However, the sad fact is that so-called "practical" love prayers and potions are frauds, and anyone who tries to tell you otherwise is not someone to patronize—or to recommend to your friends." He smiled in a way that suggested disappointment with the universe. "I consider it a sign that God—however you perceive God to be—holds love in greater importance than many other aspects of creation."

"I'm not sure I understand. Why should prayer not work where love is concerned? Love is a part of the world, and prayer is part of our dominion over the world." Lise had no trouble at all believing that her cousin Robert had been taken in more than once by fraudsters, but the fact that Robert had recommended this rabbi had to have meant he was somehow satisfied with some service the man had rendered.

"An interesting point," Rabbi Weiss said, "So, let's talk about what you goyim call Blessing. Your priests train you to use this Blessing as part of the dominion God granted mankind over the earth. They call it prayer, but have you ever noticed, mademoiselle, how limited these prayers are?"

"Nearly all of my prayers are limited, rabbi. Believe me, I have noticed."

"And why should that be? God listens to everyone equally, does He not?" He smiled at her, stroking his beard with the lightest of touches. "What I think, my dear young lady, is that God grants precious few miracles Himself. What you think of as Blessing is, I believe, something delegated by

God. Wherever this power exists is beyond our ability to truly understand, but I am convinced it is not Heaven itself, but rather a place between Earth and Heaven."

"So you're saying that prayer is not holy?"

"Not at all, mademoiselle, not at all." He gestured at a candle, which obediently flared up. Lise's head hurt and she cringed at the memory of her disastrous attempt to extinguish her aunt's candles. "We pray and the world responds. Or at least it does if God has Blessed us, a Blessing your faith has decreed is bestowed only on those of noble birth. Clearly God meant some of us to have dominion over this physical world. And so the workings of the earth, the sky, the seas—all these are revealed to us through prayer, and we can bend them to our will, at least to the extent that God grants us the power to do so. But only the physical world, my dear mademoiselle, is revealed and given to us in this way. And even then God limits us: we cannot bend metal to our will, for example, and it frustrates our attempts to affect anything nearby." As if to demonstrate he waggled his fingers at the pewter base of the candle, which obligingly did nothing in response.

"As for the metaphysical—emotion, fate, success, failure—God treats us the same whether we are an emperor or a peasant. We have no influence over them, and God does what God wills."

"So my sister prays for rain and it comes, because that doesn't require God's direct intervention, but when I pray for a good marriage that does require God's intervention, and so it may or may not come to pass?"

"You have got it exactly, young lady," Weiss said, "or at least you have got it as I understand it, which is probably a small thing but seems to accord with the way I see the world working. And so you see, mademoiselle, the mysteries of the human heart are impervious to prayer, and known only to God."

"A good sign for humanity, perhaps, but not of much use to me." Lise extended her hand. "Thank you, though, for agreeing to see me without a proper appointment."

"What, leaving already?" Rabbi Weiss held her hand, his touch feather-light and paper-dry. "Just because the idea of a love prayer is a cheat and a lie doesn't mean I have nothing to offer you, my good young lady. There are plenty of things an intelligent young woman can do to win the eye and heart of an eligible man without having to call too much on God."

Lise carefully retracted her hand. What could the rabbi be talking of? And would it in fact draw the eye of a certain handsome captain in the bodyguard of the princesse imperiale?

She was about to ask him to elaborate when the door to the shop opened behind her. Turning, Lise found herself looking into the surprised eyes of the duc de Bellevasse.

"Mademoiselle." The duc bowed, and when he raised his head again the surprise had been covered over by the same narrow, knowing grin she had seen at her aunt's New Year party. "I am pleased to see you well," he said. "Though a bit surprised to see you patronizing this disreputable fellow."

"The one time I count on you to be late, my lord duc, you thwart me by being on time." Rabbi Weiss smiled with a resignation that looked centuries old.

I am intruding here, Lise thought. *I should leave.* Her feet refused to obey her head, though. The duc de Bellevasse was wearing dark green again, a colour so deep it could pass for black in all but direct sunlight. The cut of his suit was severe but skilled, owing little to fashion and nothing at all to convention. He held in his left hand a small leather case. The flap of the case was secured, she saw, by a small padlock of what looked to be very fine steel.

"Mademoiselle," he said, smiling when he eyes caught hers. "I am pleased to see that you arrived safely. Have you been enjoying Paris so far?"

"Thank you, monsieur, yes." The words sounded halting to her, stupid even. She struggled to make her voice even and smooth. "Thank you for asking after me. That was very kind."

"Oh, you saw me, did you?" Now his smile had something darker behind it, and Lise found herself convinced that somehow the man had known she was following him when he'd left her aunt's party. "It wouldn't have been polite for me not to inquire, mademoiselle. Though I'm certain your aunt would have preferred it had I kept to myself."

Though she knew he could not have been unaware of the stories told about him, Lise still felt her face flushing at the duc's words. Would it be rude to acknowledge the truth of what he'd said? Or would it be worse to pretend that Aunt de Vimoutiers had not in fact called him the Devil?

Lise pulled her cloak around her. "My apologies, Rabbi," she said. "I didn't realize I would be intruding on an appointment. Perhaps some other time." She accepted Weiss's salute as politely as her nerves would allow her, then edged past the duc to the battered old door. "I thank you again for your assistance the other night, my lord duc," she said as she passed, "and wish you more success with this gentleman than I have had. If you will excuse me."

She stopped, staring up at the sky and cursing herself when she realized she had slammed the door behind her. Then she cursed herself for being so upset. So she had wasted a part of her morning. What was that, in the end? *You always knew*, she told herself, *that in the end you were going to be responsible for your fate, and you alone.* When she looked down again she saw Juliette, the maid she had hired just this morning, staring at her, eyes wide with concern. "It's nothing," she said. "We should—"

Then she realized she could hear voices through the gaps in the door frame.

"What in the name of all that's holy was that?" Rabbi Weiss was asking. "I'm a poor man, my lord duc, and you seem determined to drive away any customer who isn't your exalted self."

"I would have thought I paid you well enough that you needed no other customer." The duc's voice was dry and sarcastic.

"Spoken like a man who has never had to question the source of his next meal," Weiss said in reply. He sighed, loudly and perhaps theatrically. "Very well: shall we to business?"

Now the duc's voice dropped in volume, and to her shame Lise strained to hear him. "I take it, then," he said, "that the translation is ready."

"I promised it for today, didn't I?" For a moment there was silence from behind the door. "Here you are," Weiss said.

"*Names of the Saints*," the duc said. "Interesting choice of title. Especially for you. I wouldn't think you'd know—or want to know—much of saints."

Lise did not hear the rabbi's reply, but the duc's next words chilled her: "The contents of my library," he said, "would start such a blaze as would be seen in London." His voice dropped off then, and she could not hear what followed. But she had heard enough. She stepped back so abruptly she nearly tripped into the gutter. "We go," she said to Juliette. "Now." She walked rapidly in the direction of the river, not caring how quickly or even if Juliette was following.

Is it all true, then? she wondered. *Is this why he's fighting with the d'Audemar family?* Another thought occurred to her. *Or is it* how *he's fighting them?*

Two

LISE AND JULIETTE were shifting a chest to its third location of the afternoon when a knock at the door gave Lise the excuse she needed to stop working for a moment. She was still reassembling her hair into something approaching order when Juliette appeared at the door to the parlour. The maid's face appeared waxy, as though she'd seen something horrible.

Which apparently she had, at least in her own limited perception. "A gentleman to see you, mademoiselle," she said in a thin voice. "He came with two archers, he did." Lise stiffened, automatically thinking back over the past few days and guiltily wondering what she had done to attract the attention of the archers. Had somebody seen her listening through Rabbi Weiss's door?

The man standing behind Juliette, though, was no archer. He was dressed not in their blue tabard, but in a dark, heavy coat of sober cut. He was also considerably older than she expected a policeman to be. He was a policeman for all that, though; Lise was sure of it. She was equally sure she didn't want those eyes to be on her with any more intensity than they were showing now.

"Mademoiselle, please forgive me for appearing at your door without prior notice." He bowed, almost, in response to her curtsy "I am required by my responsibilities to ask you about the story you told your aunt the other day."

The guilty pinpricks became something deeper, colder. "Who are you, sir?"

"I do not know whether to be relieved or concerned that you do not know me—yet." He brushed back his hair before making a second, more elaborate, bow. "I am Nicolas Gabriel de La Reynie, Lieutenant-General of Police for the City of Paris. And your description of the man who stopped your carriage—and was apparently killed by the loup-garou that then attacked you—is sufficiently, ah, interesting that I wanted to discuss the man further with you."

She had been so convinced that she was guilty of—well, of something—that for a moment Lise could only stare at him. Then it occurred to her that she was blocking the doorway. "Please, monsieur, come in," she said, backing into the parlour. "Though I have to confess I don't think I can much help you. I never actually saw the man before he—before it all happened."

"I understand, mademoiselle." De La Reynie pulled forward the one chair Lise had established in the parlour and gestured her into it. "But we will talk nevertheless. You might have seen something, or heard something, that you thought beneath your notice—but that could be vital to me."

Lise smelled something sulphurous drifting in from the apartment's small kitchen and nodded: Juliette had lit a brazier and was, Lise hoped, warming some spiced wine. "I will do my best to help you, monsieur, but I can't think I've much to offer." In as few words as possible she described the way the man had stopped her carriage, but had been attacked by the horrible creature and—according to the duc de Bellevasse, who had viewed the bodies—torn to pieces before he could speak with her. By the time she had finished her tale, Juliette had brought the wine.

"There was one thing," Lise said, sipping carefully to avoid burning her lip. "I don't know if it's significant, but you said you might be able to use anything." Monsieur de La Reynie nodded over his wine cup but said nothing. "Well," she said after a pause, "I was struck by the difference between his words and the way he said them. He sounded like one of my family's peasants, but his words were those of an educated man. I think he actually used the word 'forsake'. I wonder if he might have been a priest, perhaps."

"Or a monk." De La Reynie smiled at her, but his eyes looked unhappy. "I was right to come see you, mademoiselle. That is precisely the sort of detail a policeman likes to hear when conducting an investigation."

"Does that mean you know who he is—was?" Lise found herself leaning forward and on the edge of her chair.

"It does not, I'm sorry to say. It provides some reinforcement to a supposition, but that is all. To obtain proof I would have to examine the body, either myself or indirectly through the agency of someone observant—you, for instance. I don't suppose"—

"I did not see any of the bodies afterward, monsieur." Lise shifted, uncomfortable with the memory. "The man who assisted me would not let me see them. He said that the driver and the other man—the one you are asking about—were so badly torn that he could not—" She stopped for a moment, suddenly ill. She forced some wine down her throat, glad for the burning. "He said that what was left was pieces and shreds that were not recognizable as human. My father's servant may have been the last one killed, because he was torn but still recognizable, according to the man who assisted me."

"This would be the duc de Bellevasse," de La Reynie said. Now he smiled with his eyes, but the smile didn't last long. "I trust I don't have to emphasize too much that de Bellevasse's is not an acquaintance to cultivate."

Lise flushed. "I have had this pointed out to me, monsieur. Quite emphatically."

If de La Reynie was amused by her discomfort, it was a thin sort of amusement. "Don't worry, mademoiselle. You can't have heard anything about de Bellevasse in the past week that hasn't been said to me at some time in the last half-year."

What happened six months ago? Lise checked the question before giving voice to it: it wasn't her place to ask this, at least not of the lieutenant-general of police. What she could legitimately ask, she decided, was, "Are you investigating him?"

"Oddly enough, no. And I rather hope I'm not asked to. He amuses me, de Bellevasse does; my only regret is that he knows this."

De La Reynie turned to the door, then stopped and faced her again. "The fact that I am not investigating de Bellevasse does not mean that de Bellevasse is not being investigated, mademoiselle. The cardinal's office is quite interested in the subjects of the duc's many journeys. And there are at least two *lettres de cachet* drawn up against him—and possibly others that I don't yet know about—that await only the obtaining of more proof or more courage by his enemies."

The lieutenant-general bowed in farewell. "So you see, mademoiselle, your attitude concerning the duc de Bellevasse is wise. He may or may not be bad, but he could well be dangerous to know."

Lise scrambled to her feet and sketched a hasty curtsy

when she realized the de La Reynie's warning was also his valediction. He paused in the doorway to allow her to catch up to him. "I'm sorry I couldn't be more help to you, monsieur," she said as he stepped out of her apartment. "Could I ask why you—"

"It's nothing, mademoiselle. Nothing you need concern yourself about." Monsieur de La Reynie smiled, and Lise was sure she felt the temperature drop. "Just a search for a missing person, that's all." He thumped down the stairs, his boots hitting the steps like millstones. The archers, Lise noted, had preceded him to the next landing down.

After de La Reynie had left the building, Lise returned to her parlour and sat in the single chair. She ought to be upset, she thought, or frightened. Instead, she decided as she drained her wine cup, she was curious and perhaps a bit excited.

Why was a Paris police official so interested in an attack on a country road? What about the missing man—missing monk, if de La Reynie's hint wasn't meant to be misleading—was so important that it had to be kept secret?

Then there was the matter of the dangerous duc de Bellevasse. With a start she realized that the conversation she had overheard the other day would probably be considered sufficient evidence of blasphemy to draw him into the cardinal's web. Perhaps it would actually be safer for him if one of those *lettres de cachet* got its signature from the appropriate imperial official, and the duc find himself in the Bastille. All the more reason to take Monsieur de La Reynie's advice, then, and stay away from the wretched man.

And you could stop thinking about him at any moment now, she told herself when she realized how she'd allowed her mind to be overtaken. Shaking her head, disgusted with herself, she picked up de La Reynie's cup and drained it. Though the alcohol in it still burned her, the wine had gone cold.

※

The streets of the Faubourg St-Germain were for the most part not yet paved, so Lise was grateful for the winter wind that had frozen the mud on which she walked. A depressingly familiar pain stabbed inward from her temples as she crossed the rue Dauphine, but it disappeared as quickly as it had arrived. If her new friend Marguerite had told her true—and if she'd followed the directions properly—she should now be on the rue des Fossés-Saint-Germain, and the dressmaker's shop should be on the ground floor of one of the new buildings here. Juliette followed, rather less delicately. Juliette wasn't an especially big woman—when you lived on a third floor you wanted size and strength in a maid—but her shoulders were broad enough, and her deportment suggested that, like Lise, she'd grown up with several brothers.

In Lise's purse, a couple of gold *louis* and two dozen newly minted *livres* clanked. Over the past ten days she had attended three dinners and a pair of Thursday afternoon gatherings—a weekly event, she understood—in her aunt's hôtel. On every occasion someone had suggested playing a game of one sort or another, and sooner or later that game was always *reversis*. Lise had taken care not to win too much at first, but most of her aunt's guests were wealthy enough that they didn't pay much attention to stakes. It wasn't like playing in her parents' society. Very quickly she'd unleashed herself without regard to her opponents.

She now had enough money to pay for the new gown her aunt had ordered for her, and could probably have paid a full year's rent on the suite of rooms her Aunt d'Ombrevilles had provided and nearly finished moving her into. Madame d'Ombrevilles had been more than happy, though, to be paid a month at a time. From the way she'd laughed when Lise had explained where the money had come from, Lise was pretty sure she'd found an ally in her scheme to support herself at the card tables. Lise's only regret was in allowing her new landlord to organize the move: she still couldn't find some of her things, and most of the trunks she'd unpacked had been a shambles, as if things had just been tossed into them.

"Is this the place, mademoiselle?" Juliette nodded toward a door, facing onto the street, above which was a sign showing a needle and thread. Lise read the name.

"Yes. We're here." *Thank you, Mary Mother of God. This is not a city to be lost in, I think.* "You wait here, Juliette, in case Marguerite hasn't yet arrived."

As she opened the door, though, she heard Marguerite's voice. "Lise! How wonderful!"

"How are you this morning, Marguerite?" Lise offered her cheek to be kissed.

"Wonderful, and even better now. Listen," Marguerite said, "the seamstress tells me your gown is ready. Why don't you just have it shipped back to your apartment and let me buy you something to drink?"

"I think that's a wonderful idea," Lise said. "It's going to be lovely to talk to someone who isn't a relative"—or a potential reversis victim, or Nicolas de La Reynie with his unsettling eyes—"and I do think I'd like something to drink."

"Splendid! I'll wait for you."

"What shall we drink?" Lise asked as she emerged from the shop. "Is there a restaurant or cabaret you had in mind?" Lise had yet to enter any of Paris's infamous public eating and drinking establishments, and somehow she felt that her qualifications as a potential bride weren't going to be complete until she knew how to comport herself in a cabaret.

"I had in mind something a bit daring. I hope you don't object." Marguerite gave her a conspiratorial grin. "We won't tell our parents, of course."

"I certainly won't," Lise said, grinning back. "But now you've made me very curious."

"I won't torture your curiosity for long. In fact, we're already here." She gestured to a black-painted door that opened, like that of the dressmaker's shop, right onto the street.

Lise looked up. "Café Procope? Much as I hate to admit my ignorance, I must tell you that I haven't a clue as to what this place is."

"Monsieur Procope is"—Mademoiselle de Courçon's voice dropped to a whisper—"an Italian. But it's all right," she added, her voice resuming its previous happy lilt, "because he's been here forever. Certainly as long as I've been alive. He used to sell lemonade, and ices. Still does, I suppose."

"Then what is a 'café'? And what does the Italian gentleman sell in it?"

"It's both a Mohammedan drink, and the shop in which you drink it. My priest isn't at all sure it's a safe thing. He's heard it's the devil's brew, and much worse for us than wine. So of course I had to find out for myself. But I didn't want to go into such a scandalous place by myself."

Scandalous? How interesting. "I am glad to help, mademoiselle." Lise held open the door so that her companion could enter. "Do we send the servants on, or do they come in with us? I'm not too clear on the etiquette."

A Poisoned Prayer
January

"They come in, of course. Who would take our coats and cloaks, otherwise? There will be places for them to stand."

Coffee, delivered to them in tiny china cups by a man in an outlandish costume that Marguerite said was Armenian, turned out to be a hot beverage, which was a blessing on a day such as this. It was bitter at first, but the Armenian gentleman showed them how to stir in shavings from a block of sugar, and when sweetened the brew was almost tolerable. Lise still had to force herself to finish the cup, though. Even sweetened the stuff was harsh, bitter on the tongue.

Marguerite had a second cup, though, and Lise felt honour-bound to accompany her hostess. And at some point during this second cup, the world became a brighter place. Lise found herself anxious to explain the story of her life and plans to Marguerite, who was equally eager to tell Lise all about her own hopes and dreams. She noticed, seemingly for the first time, her surroundings: the finely dressed men, many elaborately bewigged, standing in front of the proprietor's long counter or in front of the steam- and frost-glazed windows, talking animatedly about subjects just beyond the reach of her hearing or comprehension; the sheets of paper being passed between some of the gentlemen; the brief flashes of light as some of the nobles in the warm, crowded room amused each other with competitions in small magics; the scarcity of women in this place.

"This is quite remarkable," Lise said, holding the twice-emptied cup so that it was bathed in light from the window, as if somehow daylight could illuminate the magic God was working through the rather grainy liquid. "I feel— refreshed, somehow. It's as if someone has put a cold compress to my forehead, while at the same time warming my heart."

Marguerite stared at her for a moment. "That is exactly right," she said. "It's just how I feel. This *is* a remarkable drink. And I should never have thought to describe it in that way." She shook her head slowly from side to side. "How did you come to such an ideal way of putting it?"

"How? I haven't a clue." Lise had never been made to think about how she thought, and now that she tried it she found herself stunned into silence. "I said what popped into my head. That's just how coffee feels to me."

"I envy you your facility with words. I never seem to come up with anything clever. I seldom think of anything to say at all, really, until long after the conversation has gone on to some other subject." Marguerite stared into her cup, as though trying to read some pattern in the brown-black residue on the bottom.

"You shouldn't be upset about something like that."

"I'm not upset," Marguerite said. The longing in her eyes was an eloquent contradiction, though. After an uncomfortable pause she continued: "It is awkward, though, to be so dull-witted in a city where everyone else is so clever."

"Do you sing?" Lise asked.

"Sing? What does that have to do with anything? I suppose I do."

"I'll wager you sing very well," Lise said. "I hear it in the tone of your voice. It reminds me of the sound of perfectly tempered steel on stone. Or a lark, when the sun's coming up."

"There you go again, being clever." Marguerite thought a moment. "My tutors thought my voice passable, I

A Poisoned Prayer
January

suppose." She reached across the table and touched Lise's hand. "You're very kind. But I still don't understand."

"I can't sing to save my soul," Lise said. "Quite literally, I'm afraid. My family priest only allows me into chapel on condition that I keep my mouth shut except to pray. I've always been deeply envious of anyone who could sing well, or who could *feel* music. I will never be able to experience what it is like to have music touch or speak to me.

"So you see," she said, "you shouldn't be upset if you don't do some things so well. There will always be someone better than you and worse than you, and envy doesn't make a bit of difference. I know that all too well."

"I had not thought of it in those terms," Marguerite said. "And it feels odd to think that others might envy me."

"Well, they do. *I* do. And I can say that even without hearing you sing a note, for you're sure to do it better than I no matter what you sound like."

Marguerite seemed to think about this for a moment. Then she laughed, lightly, and clapped her hands together. "You," she said, "must come with me this afternoon to tell my friends about our visit to this café. Your turn of phrase would be most welcome."

"Welcome? Where?"

"At my friend's get-together. Please say you'll come, Lise."

Lise thought about the gatherings her aunt held, and the men and women who frequented it. Marguerite should come some day; she'd see that not everyone in Paris was as witty as she supposed. "What sort of gathering is it? My aunt, Madame de Vimoutiers, holds one every Thursday, and so far it's all nobles talking about which minister is out of favor at Court, or which man's mistress is worthy of being received. Will there be musicians, or novelists in attendance?"

"Oh, yes! Especially writers: Madame de Taverner and Madame de Ressaisir come every day, and even Madame de Lafayette has come from time to time. La Champmeslé sometimes comes, representing the theatre—she's nearly forty and still incredibly beautiful. It's a brilliant gathering, really. Perhaps it's no wonder I so often feel inadequate there."

"You've excited my curiosity," Lise said. "If your friend will have me, I'd love to come."

⚜

Marguerite's friend was the marquise de Réalmont, the widow of, successively, a minor noble and a rich *financier*, and now owner of a magnificent new house in the Place Impériale, the beautiful square the emperor's father had built near the old east wall of the city, near the Bastille. Lise had heard the Place Impériale described at her aunt's home—both the emperor and empress had houses on the square, and in some noble circles competition was quite fierce to purchase property there—but she had never seen it until now.

The Place was beautiful, she thought, though in a way that wasn't necessarily in accord with the concepts of beauty she'd been taught. There was a regularity, a formality, to the buildings and the park in the centre of the Place that seemed unsuited to the rambling, improvised beauty of the rest of the city. The buildings were made of a pink sort of stone, faced with white, and their identical roseate forms suggested a gigantic confection. There was something fresh about these houses when compared with the ochre solidity of her aunt's mansion.

Standing in the antechamber waiting to be introduced,

Lise felt a sudden nervousness and a desire to retreat to the warmth of the fire in her rooms on the Ile St-Louis. The sound leaking from the second-floor room in which Madame de Réalmont held court had that peculiar, bubbling rhythm that suggested a close-knit group, happy in its insularity. It would, she thought, require more arrogance than she possessed to intrude on that self-sufficiency.

Her worries were compounded when the doors opened to admit her and Marguerite to the room. Her initial appraisal took in a dozen or so persons, in several small groups whose members seemed oblivious of everyone else. *How do I behave?* Lise wondered. *I will never be able to talk to these people.*

She felt no more confident after Marguerite had led her through a lightning round of introductions. Names slipped from her mind like glass beads through gloved fingers; only the clothes maintained any hold on her memory. A tiny woman who may have been an author wore a stunning outfit whose overskirt was patterned in a series of broad stripes formed by differing weaves of purple-blue satin. Another matched a bodice of apricot silk with a skirt and overskirt of two different shades of green, with no patterns discernible in the shimmering fabrics. A third set off a slender neck and an expanse of creamy skin on her bosom and shoulders with a single strand of pearls—but each pearl was the size of a field-pea.

The men had nothing memorable about them. They all seemed to be *bourgeois*, or nobles of the robe if they held any title at all. Their clothing was uniformly drab, in black or brown, and they inhabited it with a lack of panache that contrasted unkindly with the flair shown by Captain d'Oléron—or even the forbidden duc de Bellevasse.

Too unsure of herself to dare to even try intruding into one of the conversational groups, Lise attached herself firmly to her new friend, and spoke only when Marguerite forced her to. So she was close enough to Marguerite to see the sudden flush, the widening of eyes, and to hear the not-quite-stifled gasp when the very same Captain d'Oléron was announced into the room.

"Who is *that?*" Marguerite asked, grabbing Lise's arm with both hands. She gazed at the captain more ardently than was polite. "Is he not the most beautiful man?"

"He is a fine-looking man," Lise admitted. "His name is d'Oléron, and he is a captain of the musketeers. Would you like me to introduce you?" Lise couldn't suppress a wry smile, and at Marguerite's quizzical look she had to admit, "I have only just been introduced to him myself. He is an occasional attendee at my aunt's salon."

Marguerite giggled. "I should not want to do anything that would interfere with your interests, my friend. If you are determined to keep him to yourself, I will understand."

"I have no such feelings," Lise said. "My acquaintance with the captain is of such recent vintage that I cannot tell you with any honesty what my interests are."

"In which case I beg you to introduce me," Marguerite said. "I can tell you in full honesty that my interests are by no means permanent." She giggled again.

"I would think," Lise said with great care, "that Captain d'Oléron is not quite at your level."

"Oh, you're absolutely right, Lise. If he is merely a captain then his station is rather beneath mine, and doubtless he has no money to speak of. Mama certainly wouldn't approve of him on that score alone. That doesn't mean I can't flirt with him."

For a moment Lise found herself in sympathy with the pope: *This*, she thought, *is what comes of there being no risk associated with a young woman's dalliances.* Then she remembered that Marguerite was forbidden that sort of pleasure, and chided herself for selfishness. "Of course I will introduce you," she said, laughing. "And in return you can teach me about flirting, a subject on which I am woefully ill-informed."

⚜

Whatever awkwardness had possessed the captain on their first meeting had evidently dissipated, because when Lise introduced him to Marguerite he was all charm and good nature. She spent a very pleasant hour talking and laughing with him, and on taking her leave of the marquise felt that she was not deluding herself in thinking that the captain had found her the more interesting conversationalist. Not that he had ignored Marguerite; it seemed to Lise, though, that there was a qualitative difference between the attentions he paid to her friend and those he paid to Lise.

So when the marquise de Réalmont informed Lise that her quick wit had been noted with approval by several of the guests, and invited her to please attend the salon at any time, Lise was more than happy to accept.

The marquise had thoughtfully provided a footman to escort Lise and Marguerite on their journey home, but Captain d'Oléron insisted on accompanying them, at least as far as the Bastille. There he, with expressions of reluctance, left to attend an important meeting within the prison.

After watching the heavy door close behind the captain, Lise turned back to Marguerite to find her friend smiling at her broadly. "How can you not be in love with him?" she asked, squeezing Lise's arm.

"Love is not at issue here, Marguerite. Not for me, at any rate."

Marguerite's grip on Lise's arm tightened. "You cannot be serious. Love is always the issue between men and women."

"I would place respect above love," Lise said. "But in any case, sentiment is a luxury that someone in my position cannot afford. Not when seeking a husband."

"How can you say that, Lise? You will wind up betrothed to a—a *lawyer*, or maybe even something worse! If you do not listen to your heart you may well ruin the rest of your life!"

Lise looked behind them. Their maids were only a few paces back, but if they were listening to any of this they did not betray it. "I would that I had the luxury of being able to consider sentiment, Marguerite. But for people like me, that *is* a luxury. Your family is of excellent standing, my friend. The strength of marriage alliances is only one of the things you and your parents must consider when you look for a match. But my family is not wealthy, and our estates are in a disputed part of the empire. For me, marriage cannot just be about love, or even just about seeing to my own financial support. For me, marriage is more a matter of strategy than anything else." *I have to approach it in exactly the same way I play* reversis, *in fact.*

"Forgive me," Marguerite said, "but I find that a real shame. When I marry, I guarantee you that love will be my first priority."

"Allow me to envy you," Lise said. "So long as you forgive me if I must be somewhat more hard-hearted about it."

"Forgive you? There's nothing to forgive, dear friend." *Only to pity,* thought Lise. She said nothing more, though, and before a new subject of conversation could present itself they had arrived at her aunt's hôtel, where Marguerite hailed a chair to take her to her home. Waving farewell, Lise fought off her soul's attempts at making her depressed.

I have made a good start today, she thought, *and I did it myself, without having to have my aunt promoting me.* Still, there was room for improvement. *I ought to have paid more attention to those dull-looking lawyers and petty nobles,* she thought. *One cannot have too many potential suitors.*

Three

"HOLD STILL, LISE!" Aunt de Vimoutiers pulled at Lise's hair, Lise jerked away with a yelp, and the framework of the headdress disassembled and clattered to the floor—save for one piece that slid down Lise's back between her shoulder blades. "My God," the duchesse said. "Why in heaven's name did you try to do your hair in this way?"

"Madame, you know how weak is my Blessing. I have to have it dressed on a frame—I can neither build nor maintain a headdress in the fashionable style." Lise fought to keep her humiliation and anger under control. *This isn't my fault—why punish me?*

"I'm sorry, Lise," the duchesse said. "I know I'm making this harder for you than it should be." After a pause she added, "And it's not your hair—it looked fine, and I was only trying to make it a bit more elegant. No, the truth is, I think this is coming too soon, and I let it distract me."

"Too soon? Madame, I've been in Paris nearly two weeks, and not only have I no suitors, I haven't received a single proposal of any sort, even the indecent." Lise avoided looking at her aunt as she said this. While she was being truthful about the absence of proposals, her instincts told her it wasn't entirely true that she had no suitors. She had attended the salon at the Marquise de Réalmont's home several times since first meeting Marguerite, and she had noticed the same two men hovering around her and Marguerite on two successive afternoons. One was a lawyer, the other a very minor noble; Lise did not think that either of them was paying court to her friend.

It was a sin of pride, she knew, but Lise did not want to settle for a stuffy lawyer whose only interest was peasant riots in the north, or for an idiot younger son with no apparent interests whatsoever. "If I won't get invitations until I've been received by the emperor and empress," she said, "then this should have happened at New Year."

"You will refrain from talk of indecent proposals," the duchesse said, but she smiled as she spoke. "I understand your concern, child, but your presentation should still have waited until I could propose it to the emperor. As the senior member of the family in my husband's absence, that was both my responsibility and my right." She picked up the fallen sticks and lace; a brief gesture and the stick that had fallen into Lise's dress rose smoothly up her back and through the disarranged hair, coming to rest with its companions in the duchesse's hand.

"Instead of which, the cardinal has pre-empted me."

"Cardinal du Plessis?" *That horrible, hawk-nosed man?* "Why would he be interested in me? When we were introduced I found him cold and rude."

"His normal demeanour, I assure you. But your assumption is correct: he should have considered you beneath notice. That he has taken this step can only mean that he is making a move in a greater game against me, or my husband—or against the archbishop, who is a friend of mine."

Lise looked away from her aunt, not wanting to stare— or to betray her confusion and concern. It was not just that she could see nothing in her uncle's simple-minded determination to avoid the court and spend his time and energies hunting. "Why," she asked after a moment, "would the cardinal act against our family—or the archbishop?" And just how close was her aunt's friendship with that happy, outgoing—and supposedly celibate—holy man?

"You yourself spoke the answer to that question, Lise, after you were introduced to him. At best the cardinal has entirely too much influence over the emperor. At worst—"

"He may have designs on the throne. Oh." Certainly Mother, Father, and most of their friends back home were convinced the cardinal was a usurper who awaited only the right opportunity. "What should I do?"

"What you are doing? Finish getting yourself ready"—Lise's court gown and lace were on loan from the duchesse, Lise not yet having won enough money to buy anything appropriate—"and we will do our duty. Take comfort in the fact that his majesty is unlikely to talk to you for more than a minute; he will have many people to meet this afternoon. If the cardinal means to embarrass me, he will likely strike before or after the presentation and not during it. If we are careful, we will be able to get through this day without much difficulty."

Then, as Lise tried to absorb what she'd just heard, her aunt breathed a few words and Lise's hair stood up, twined itself around the sticks and lace, and settled into a design suggesting fairy architecture. Aunt de Vimoutiers smiled and gave Lise a kiss on the cheek. Lise bowed her head, but instead of thankfulness her mind was preoccupied with thoughts of headaches and Blessings and of a world that was much bigger than the one in which she'd been trained.

⚜

The Tuileries Palace had very nearly nothing in common with Lise's imaginings of it. The building, when her aunt's carriage approached, was tall and ornate, its solid magnificence suggestive of kings and emperors. But the interior displayed little of the colour, light, and sparkle of the castles in her dreams.

"Stay close, Lise," Aunt de Vimoutiers said, pulling Lise by the hand through the crowds in a large room on the ground floor, "and don't let yourself be distracted. If the cardinal plans anything, it will probably happen immediately before we go in to the audience chamber. I can't believe that even du Plessis would insult me in the emperor's presence."

What could possibly distract me? Lise wondered as she skipped across the dull, worn wooden floor, struggling a bit to match her aunt's aggressive pace. *The only difference between this place and one of your parties is that the people are slightly better dressed and the room is a lot less pretty.*

It was only when she saw the colour, light, and sparkle in the eyes of the people she was passing that Lise realized that the duc of Burgundy and emperor of France lived in a place that truly was enchanted: only the nobles, blessed by God, could see it the way it was meant to be seen. From time to time a prayer manifested itself to her, and for a second or two the room was a garden, or a diamond mountaintop. For the most part, though, it was clear to Lise that the degree of Blessing required to participate was higher than she possessed. Not for the first time she praised her aunt for the exquisite taste that manifested itself in a house that was beautifully decorated in the physical as well as the spiritual sense. *My home*, she told herself, *will not be like this place.*

The broad staircase leading to the emperor's suite on the second floor was jammed, uncountable numbers of men and women in brilliantly coloured silks—with the occasional black of the blatantly pious standing out like a raven in a cage of parrots—shifting minutely and only occasionally moving up or down. Lise was wondering what proscription kept the Blessed from simply flying up to the second floor over the heads of their inferiors, when the duchesse tugged her away from the base of the stairs. "I told you to keep up," she muttered. Lise began to wonder if she hadn't been mistaken in her enthusiasm for this project.

A man in blue and orange satin was pissing into the corner of the narrow stairwell into which the duchesse pulled Lise. The urine, the instant it hit the stone, vanished in a cloud of yellow-green fog that smelled of sandalwood; whatever sound was made was inaudible under her aunt's outraged intake of breath as she pulled Lise even more firmly up the stairs. The amount of prayer needed to maintain this palace's magics was stunning; Lise thought of the difficulties her sister and father had just ensuring sufficient rainfall on their estate, and felt even more depressed at her own absence of Blessing.

She had finally accepted the evidence of her headaches, and now she knew for certain that not only was she minimally Blessed, she was in a way cursed. The very presence of a Blessing at work, it seemed, was enough to spark the pain in her temples. When she had lived quietly at home she had been able to believe that it was just Andrée's prayers that brought on her headaches, and so ascribed the pain to God's punishment for her jealousy. But in Paris she had headaches all the time, to the extent that often she wasn't even fully aware of them. She didn't want to think about why God would be doing this to her.

The back stairs opened into a corridor on the second floor that turned out to be just a few paces from the anteroom of the audience chamber. Lise wondered if the nobles crowding the main staircase were simply more ignorant than her aunt—a distinct possibility, given her aunt's reputation—or whether they knew about the various secondary staircases and simply didn't care to go to the trouble of not being visible.

"Now we wait," the duchesse said. "We wait, and we watch to be sure the cardinal tries nothing to ruin your presentation."

The words had scarcely left her lips when a servant, in parti-coloured clothes combining the liveries of Burgundy and France, appeared in the anteroom and began calling names. His voice was soft, almost musical, and yet somehow he was audible over the hum of conversation—a hum that increased in volume as one by one, young women and their presenters began to move through the wide double doors and into the emperor's presence.

I think I would have rather waited a bit longer, Lise thought. *I'm not going to get a chance to study most of these gowns.* She was conscious of how her own gown fitted and felt, exactly as what it was: borrowed from her aunt and hurriedly adjusted to her own taller frame. This frustrated her, she knew, only because there was something she should have been able to do about it but had been prevented from doing—mostly by lack of funds. Some things like the colour and texture of her hair (brown, and mostly limp) she'd stopped worrying about long ago, because God had not seen fit to give her sufficient Blessing to overcome what nature had done to her.

That blue silk would do nothing for me, she thought as another young woman moved to the doorway. *But the amber and orange right behind her would work.*

Her aunt's sudden intake of breath interrupted Lise's study. "He is here," the duchesse whispered, in a voice suggesting an overwound spring. "Now we see what his game is."

But whatever the cardinal's game was, it apparently did not involve the duchesse de Vimoutiers. When he saw Lise, from his position across the room, he bowed briefly, his mouth bending upward in a tight, liturgical smile. Then he resumed his survey of the chamber and its feminine contents, at the conclusion of which he vanished through a previously invisible sidedoor.

"I don't feel as if I've been maltreated," Lise said, unable to suppress a smile.

"Don't be impertinent," the duchesse said, her own voice no less tightly wound than it had been before the cardinal left the ante-chamber. "The cardinal is a very dangerous man, and you dismiss his threat at your peril."

Lise knew better than to ask why she should share her aunt's apparently poor relations with the cardinal—*accept her help and support and you accept her reputation and burdens*—but she couldn't help thinking it unfair that she should be marked for her aunt's sins without having enjoyed them first, whatever they turned out to be. She had no time to dwell on this injustice, though, because in the next instant the parti-coloured servant was calling her name and her aunt was pushing her forward.

The Emperor Charles XIII was easily the most impressive man Lise had ever seen. His smile, when he acknowledged her curtsy, shone like the sun of her southern home. His very presence seemed to glow in a way that mocked the magics of his courtiers.

Then she was edged aside as another young woman was brought forward to be presented, and when Lise looked at the emperor again it was from a different perspective. Now she saw that while the smile was real enough, what had initially struck her as Olympian now seemed merely detached, and maybe even a little bit sad. The glowing presence owed far more to the gold, pearls, and gems that adorned his purple silks than to anything contained within

A Poisoned Prayer
January

those silks. Her grandfather, Lise decided, was a more imposing person, at least physically, than the emperor.

And yet there was still something about the emperor that impressed. After thinking fruitlessly on the subject for several minutes, Lise suddenly realized what it was: calm. She could not say whether the emperor was himself a calm man, but he projected calm, like a cooling breeze on a hot day or a warm fire in a Paris winter. Throughout her visit to the palace Lise had endured the throbbing headache that had always plagued her, but the moment she had entered the emperor's presence, she now realized, the headache had vanished. Watching now as this gloriously dressed man smiled benignly at yet another gawkily nervous young woman, Lise could not keep from smiling herself. He must have a truly amazing Blessing for him to have eased her headache as he had.

"I must say," her aunt said, shepherding Lise out of the audience chamber, "that went very well." After a pause she added, "Perhaps the cardinal was feeling unwell."

"Oh, madame," Lise said, not sure if the duchesse was joking or not.

"You're right, Lise; it really doesn't matter. Come with me. Since you're here, you really should meet the princesse imperiale."

"What?" Lise nearly tripped herself. "But I haven't been—I wasn't asked. I'm not—"

"You're my family, Lise. And the princesse is a very good friend of mine. Anyway, I'm sure she'll like you, if only because you're both having so much trouble getting husbands."

Lise had heard gossipy allusions to the emperor's supposed role in the princesse's unmarried state—the poor woman was nearly thirty—but knew little about the truth of it. She was sure, though, that the princesse's problems, cushioned as they were by wealth and power, were nothing like her own.

Still, she let herself be led. What would Mama think of her daughter being presented to two of the most exalted people in the empire—and on the same day?

The room the duchesse escorted her to reminded Lise a little of the emperor's audience room, but it was at once smaller and more lively. It was much more plainly decorated, too. Lise had begun to wonder what this signified when her aunt murmured, "This is actually the waiting room for the princesse's guards. She invites only her closest friends into her own chamber." Looking more closely at the crowded room, Lise was able to pick out a number of young men wearing the white and blue of the imperial musketeers—including, to her pleasure, Captain d'Oléron.

"Your Imperial Highness." Aunt de Vimoutiers intruded on Lise's thoughts. "Please allow me to introduce my niece, Lise de Trouvaille, who has just been presented to your exalted brother—long may he reign." She nudged Lise forward, a gesture Lise intuited more than felt. As Lise curtsied, the duchesse continued, "Lise, this is Her Imperial Highness, the Princesse Noël Elaine Marie de Bourgogne. Honour her as you do her brother the emperor."

"Your Royal Highness," Lise said, lifting her head. The princesse smiled, and Lise felt a shiver of relief.

"We are enchanted," the princesse said. "Please, help yourself to something to drink and stay with us a while. Our brother may even join us, when his audience is finished." A gesture from the princesse drew the duchesse near, and for the next few minutes Lise was alone in the crowd.

Pouring herself a glass of white wine from a jug that was cool to the touch, Lise overheard fragments of several conversations. One phrase caught her attention—"peasants are using witches and wizards"—but before she could locate the source of the intriguing words she heard her name being called by an unfamiliar voice.

Lise turned to find herself facing a magnificently dressed young woman whose golden hair, piled atop her head like a pyramid of bullion, sparked and glistered in a way implying either a munificent Blessing from God or a lot of work on the part of someone else thus Blessed. The woman was smiling, but her eyes suggested an amusement that wasn't meant to be shared —not with Lise, at any rate.

"Could we not hear Mademoiselle de Trouvaille sing for you, Madame?" the woman asked. "I am assured by all who have met her that the young lady possesses an enchanting voice."

"I am afraid you have been misled, madame," Lise said, offering the blonde a brief curtsy. *Who put you up to this?* she thought, struggling to keep from sounding as startled and off-balance as she suddenly felt. "I have, I am sorry to say, a dreadful voice." Inspiration struck. "One that has been known to frighten livestock. You will be doing Madame the Princesse no favours by asking me to sing for her." A few people laughed, in a way Lise hoped was friendly. But her attacker did not give up.

"I have also been warned of this maiden's modesty," the blonde said. *You could have put less emphasis on "maiden,"* Lise thought. "We will just have to try all the harder to get her to bless us with a song."

"Some music would be nice," the princesse said.

"Madame, I truly do not have a pleasant voice," Lise said. "What is worse, the songs I know are not nice. They are soldier songs my grandfather taught me"—*when I was a little girl, but I am certainly not going to share* that *information with your imperial highness*—"and are hardly suitable for a palace gathering." Lise looked to her aunt, and was rewarded with an expression that implied either impending heart failure or the frustrated desire to deliver a beating to Lise's blonde tormentor.

"Oh, how scandalous!" The blonde giggled and cast what Lise supposed was intended to be a simpering glance at the princess. "Your exalted brother wouldn't object, surely, to a bit of fun, would he, Mademoiselle?"

The princesse's face underwent a brief transformation, but her expression was composed again when she said, "By all means let us have fun. Mademoiselle, what sort of not-nice soldier song will you sing for us?" Lise surrendered. She had seen, many times, the expression that had flickered across the princesse's face. Her younger sister had worn it many times, when Lise had tried to exercise the eldest's prerogative to dictate acceptable behaviour. No doubt the princesse relished every opportunity to outrage her brother.

"I don't know what its real title is, Madame," Lise said. "Grandfather always called it 'The Soldier and the Maiden'." One of the musketeers made a spluttering sound, and Lise turned her head in time to see the man's companion wiping wine from his own face, the two men failing utterly to suppress their laughter.

"Some of us appear to be familiar with the thing," the princesse said. The laughter stopped. "We will not be upset by this, will we?"

"Of course not, Madame," said the blonde. "Anything the men can listen to and laugh about, women should be able to as well."

"Tell me that when you've enjoyed a week in the van of the army at a siege," Lise muttered. If anyone heard her, they did not acknowledge having done so.

"Perhaps one or two verses, to begin with," the princesse said.

"That might be better," Lise said. "The really dirty—uh, distressing things don't happen until six or seven verses in."

"Let us be grateful for small mercies," her aunt said.

"You will be singing without accompaniment," the princesse said. "We do not normally keep a harpsichord or an orchestra in the guard-room."

"It would not have made any difference, Madame." Lise closed her eyes, trying to draw forth the words of a song she had not sung in several years.

A stabbing pain shot through her temples, then was gone. She had just opened her eyes, alarmed, when the pain returned. It was not as strong this time, but it was still familiar.

Then she looked at her tormenter and it was as if she had just awakened from sleep. *Familiar.* The second incident of pain really had felt like an echo of the first, which she now knew had had something about it that was different from the headache she'd had before her presentation. *Prayer,* she suddenly knew, *can bear its own stamp.*

Without thinking further, she said, "Really, madame, it is not necessary for you to go to this trouble to make me sound bad. I can achieve that all by myself, and with the voice God gave me." The blonde's hair, she saw, no longer sparkled; now she knew why. *You can't maintain two prayers at once, can you?*

Startled, the blonde stammered. "I do not know what you mean, mademoiselle, but I think you are being rude."

"Who is being rude?" Lise rubbed the worst-afflicted temple with one hand. "Why are you trying to charm my voice, madame? I assure you, it is not necessary."

"Why, Denise," someone said. "What has happened to your hair? Is it true? Are you really trying to sabotage this poor girl?"

Now the blonde's face was blood-red; even the roots of her hair seemed to blush. "I have done no such thing!" The words came out in something dangerously close to a shout. Denise seemed to realize her error, for she paused for a breath and held it. No one else made a sound. "Madame, please forgive me," she said eventually, turning to the princess. "I am feeling unwell. May I have your permission to withdraw?"

Permission was granted, in a voice so carefully neutral that Lise half-expected to see musketeers following to arrest the woman once she was out of the room. Instead, the princesse motioned Lise to come forward. "I am very sorry about that," the princesse said. "It was never my intention to make you uncomfortable."

"I know that, Madame. You were put in an impossible position, just as I was. For either of us to say no would have seemed impolite." Lise wondered if it was safe to ask, eventually decided it was, and said, "Why do you suppose that woman did what she did? I have never met her, and have no idea even who she is."

"I cannot answer you," the princesse said. "This sort of thing does happen, but usually it is part of a longer war between women or between families. Why Madame de L'Este would want to make a new enemy is a mystery to me. She certainly doesn't lack for them."

"So her name is Denise de L'Este," Lise said. "That still means nothing to me."

"She is the mistress of the duc de Bellevasse," her aunt said, approaching the princesse's chair.

"Or was," the princesse said. She smiled at Lise. "It can be hard to tell. Those two fight a lot."

"I cannot imagine why," said Lise.

⚜

"But the most amazing thing happened *after* that," Lise said. For a moment the flow of her aunt's party had left her and Marguerite seated by themselves.

"What could be more amazing than being presented to both the emperor and his sister, and *then* out-duelling Denise de L'Este?" Marguerite turned to face her, eyes glittering. "I only wish I could have seen it. Such a story we'll have to tell at Madame de Réalmont's salon!"

"I don't know that I want to brag." Lise smiled. *Admit it. You're pleased with yourself.* "But it does get better."

"Well then, don't just grin. Tell me!"

"As the duchesse and I were leaving the princesse's guard chamber," Lise said, reliving the moment in her mind as she spoke, "a servant approached me. Not my aunt—me! He told me that the emperor had overheard my, uh, duel with Madame de L'Este. According to this man, the emperor is afflicted with an unmelodious singing voice just as I am. Apparently the emperor also has a sense of humour, because the servant gave me a note, signed by the emperor, applauding my wit and inviting me to a ball at the Tuileries in two weeks' time!"

"By the saints!" Marguerite grabbed Lise in a fierce hug that nearly toppled the two of them onto the floor. "That's amazing news, Lise! I always knew your wit would get you noticed. No doubt you'll be the shining star of the ball, too."

"Oh, I doubt that. And I'm not sure how much good it is, being noticed by the emperor. Do you suppose I could ask him to help my aunt find me a worthwhile husband? I seem to be having little luck on my own."

"You think you're joking," Marguerite said, hooking an arm into Lise's. "But perhaps this *is* the solution to your problem. Oh, you can't just walk up to the emperor and ask him if he knows of any good, moderately well-off courtier who's in need of a clever wife—"

"Damn. That's precisely what I was planning to do."

"Stop being silly, and let me finish. What you do, Lise, is have your aunt approach the emperor's *majordomo* and ask *him* to make the inquiries. It happens all the time, and now that you've officially been noticed it's sure to be an acceptable request. Perhaps an imperial nudge would persuade Captain d'Oléron to make an offer."

"The emperor's chief of the household includes match-making amongst his official duties?"

"Lise! Stop teasing—or do you not want to be married after all?"

"I'm sorry, Marguerite. Perhaps I just—you know, it was one thing to think about pressing myself forward in this fashion, but it's another entirely to have to do it."

"What are we doing?"

Lise looked up. Captain d'Oléron smiled down at her. "Good evening, captain," she said, returning his smile. "We were just discussing the upcoming ball at the Tuileries. Nothing more than women's talk, I'm afraid."

"Lise is hoping the emperor will—What?" Marguerite lifted her eyebrows at Lise's warning glare, then burst into giggles. "Oh, never mind then," she said. "You'll no doubt learn it all soon enough."

"But will this knowledge make me happy?" Captain d'Oléron didn't wait for a reply, adding, "Mademoiselle, your aunt requests your presence and that of your friend. There are introductions to be made, I gather."

"Both of us?" Marguerite got to her feet, pulling Lise behind her. "Lead on, captain. I'm definitely interested."

The first person Lise saw when the captain escorted them into the side salon was the prince d'Aude, the disdainful man she had been introduced to at the New Year and against whom the duc de Bellevasse maintained an as-yet unexplained animus. Beside him, her aunt de Vimoutiers stood radiating polite displeasure. *If I can tell how unhappy she is,* Lise thought, *the prince can't be in any doubt.* Presumably he was powerful enough that he could afford not to care.

At her aunt's other hand stood a tall, well-built man whose sharply etched face could have been any age from thirty to fifty. In his eyes and the straight line of his nose Lise could see the prince or at least a hint of him. *Cousin,* Lise thought. As she drew closer to him she could see that the man's clothes, though well-cut and tailored, were a bit past their prime. *Poor cousin,* she amended.

"Mademoiselle de Trouvaille, Mademoiselle de Courçon," the prince said, "please allow me to introduce my nephew once removed, Bertrand de Montauban, chevalier de Bonpré and marquis de Valérien. Monsieur, Mesdemoiselles Lise de Trouvaille and Marguerite de Courçon."

Lise curtsied alongside Marguerite; as they rose again Lise looked at her friend to see her already surreptitiously examining the still-bowing Monsieur de Montauban with a critical eye. That made sense, she realized; if the prince had brought his great-nephew here to seek a bride—and why else introduce him to a pair of unmarried young women?— Lise would be beneath consideration but Marguerite would be an ideal object of interest. And Marguerite, much more experienced in the Paris marriage market than Lise, couldn't fail to know this.

"It is a great pleasure to meet the both of you," Monsieur de Montauban began. He got no further; whatever he tried to say next was drowned out by a howl of laughter that caused Aunt de Vimoutiers's face to flush an alarming shade—an action matched, Lise noted, by the prince.

A moment later four young men burst into the salon. The one laughing, Lise was embarrassed to see, was cousin Robert. He stopped short when he saw the look on the duchesse's face, and stammered an apology—at which one of the other young men, behind Robert's back, rolled his eyes in a loathing that affected Lise almost as if he'd hit her.

"Mesdemoiselles," the prince d'Aude said with a weariness that to Lise sounded calculated, "please allow me to introduce my ill-behaved sons: Guillaume, comte d'Audemar and my heir; and Étienne, comte de Culle and chevalier d'Audemar. Guillaume, Étienne, you have insulted the ladies Lise de Trouvaille—niece of our hostess—and Marguerite de Courçon. Your apologies?"

The young men bowed exaggeratedly low; the younger smirked as he rose and Lise decided she despised him as a spoilt and self-absorbed brat. "Mesdemoiselles," the elder said, "we truly are sorry. Had we known we were interrupting our cousin we would not have suffered de Vimoutiers here to laugh so loudly at our feeble jests."

"Mademoiselle de Trouvaille, might I be permitted to escort you to the table for something to eat?" Captain d'Oléron's request was rushed and no doubt inspired by the anger Lise felt building in her, but she was grateful for it all the same.

"What horrid men those are!" she said once she was sure

they were out of earshot. "Why in the world does my aunt allow them into her home?" The fourth young man, she realized, remained anonymous. No doubt Robert would identify him, when she approached him after the party to learn what in hell he had been thinking of, barging into his mother's path like that.

"I'm sure that just now she is wondering the same thing," the captain said with a dry laugh. "The truth is, she and the prince d'Aude have similar political interests. I have no idea why his sons are here tonight; as a rule, they avoid any affair that doesn't involve gambling, whoring, hunting, or horse-racing—and in about that order."

Lise laughed at this, and for a moment wondered if this was a sign of another step being taken in what seemed a very slow courtship. "Do you know Monsieur de Montauban, captain?"

"Not really. But I do know that it would have taken all of the prince d'Aude's skill and influence to persuade her to invite him this evening. Bertrand de Montauban is the widower of Génie de Bellevasse, and I believe you know how the duchesse feels about that family."

"What an unfortunate man," Lise said. "Born into one odious family and married into another." *If he offers for Marguerite*, she wondered, *what will I do?*

⚜

"This is a long way to go," Lise said, "to a place that isn't even open yet. Why the St Germain fair, Marguerite? And why today?"

"Why today? Because you need a gown for the ball," Marguerite said, "and we don't have much time. As for the fair, it's true that it doesn't start for another few weeks. But that doesn't mean there won't be people there. And there will be coffee vendors, Lise. We can discuss the merits of different dressmakers as we drink coffee."

"Why can't I just wear the same thing I was presented in?"

Marguerite made a fizzing sound that Lise recognized as indicating polite frustration. "Absolutely not! Not if you want to make any sort of impression, you can't. Besides, didn't you say that gown was your aunt's? For your first imperial ball, Lise, you absolutely must have a new gown, one that's made to fit only you."

"Why are we in such a hurry?" Lise turned to Marguerite. "You haven't said a word about what happened after Captain d'Oléron dragged me away from you—and Monsieur de Montauban."

"Oh, la!" Marguerite laughed. "Lise, he is so *old* for such a young man! I hope he doesn't offer for me; if he does I am going to have fifty lovers before I've been a year a bride!" She grabbed Lise by the arm. "Come. No more excuses. You need a quality ballgown and we are going to get you one."

"Marguerite," Lise began, "I'm not sure I can afford a new ballgown—" The words were choked off by a sudden blast of pain lancing through her temples. "Oh," she said, and then she was on the paving stones, slush cold against her cheek. Desperately she grabbed at more snow, packing it against her temples, willing the icy crystals to deaden the pain.

"Lise? Lise, what is it? What's wrong?" The voice seemed to be Marguerite's, but Marguerite had been right beside her and this voice was far, far away.

The snow wasn't working. Lise's throat burned; a second later her stomach heaved, and this morning's breakfast spattered the cobbles. She retched again, and the pain appeared to diminish a little.

Now hands were on her and she was moving, up it seemed and forward. Her feet dragged behind her as she was carried; one smacked against a protruding paving stone, but the sensation registered only as impact. There was no pain that could compete with the fire burning her brain.

And then, as suddenly as it had assaulted her, the pain was gone. She felt outside herself, almost euphoric, the sort of bliss that usually happened only in church. Sound rushed in on her again.

"Lise, what happened?" Marguerite, tears like diamonds on her eyelashes, dabbed a scented handkerchief at Lise's temples, while Juliette, the maid, fumbled with coarser cloth at the stains on Lise's bodice.

"I don't know," Lise said. "I often have headaches, but nothing like this has ever happened to me before. I thought I was becoming accustomed to it." *I know the headaches are caused by prayer, but what prayer could do this?*

"Headaches? Lise, I thought you were dying! You must see a physician."

"I have. They find nothing wrong with me. I just get headaches, Marguerite. This one was worse than usual. And truly, I feel fine now." She braced herself, trying to get up. Stone crumbled under her hands.

"Mademoiselle, are you certain you shouldn't stay down? I will fetch you a chair." An older man—a puritan devot, to judge by his plain black suit—leaned in beside Marguerite. "You were indeed taken very ill. Surely it's by God's grace alone that you did not break your head open when you hit the pavement."

"I am grateful, monsieur," Lise said. "But truly, I feel fine now. I do not know what happened to me, but it appears to have stopped."

"Lise! Oh, my darling Lise, what has happened to you?"

Lise shifted to see her Aunt d'Ombrevilles rushing toward her, a tiny round bundle of agitated brown and lavender silks. "Aunt? What are you—?"

"I wanted to shop with you, my dear," her aunt said, looking dangerously flushed and worn, "but you young women have been walking much too quickly for an old thing like me to keep up with you. And when I finally do catch up it is to see you stricken down! We must send for a physician at once!"

"I have just been telling this gentleman," Lise said—her aunt favoured the man with a nod—"that I am feeling much better, and no physician can help me."

"Oh!" Marguerite clapped her hands together. "I see help for you, Lise! Stay where you are!"

When Lise tried to get up, her aunt gently pressed her back down. "Please, mademoiselle," the devot said. "This lady is correct."

"All right, monsieur." Looking around her, Lise understood why she had felt crumbling stone when she tried to propel herself to her feet. She had been settled down amidst the collapsing ruins of a part of the ancient wall. Beyond the wall was St-Germain, and the dressmakers she was not likely to be visiting now. In the other direction were the bridges and home. Looking across the street, she saw more crumbled wall, including fragments of a ward-stone.

A ward stone? An uneasy feeling sparked into existence.

And then Marguerite was back—and she had brought the duc de Bellevasse with her. "Monsieur the duc," Marguerite said, pausing to catch her breath between just about every other word, "says he would be honoured to escort you to the duchesse your aunt's hôtel, Lise."

Lise looked into the duc's eyes and saw, if not disgust, then at least a detachment that was almost as bad. "Thank you, Marguerite," she mumbled. "But this is not necessary." A glance at Aunt d'Ombrevilles showed a twisted smile on the older woman's face, as if she were struggling between the desire to laugh and the desire to be as condemnatory as the duchesse de Vimoutiers would have required.

"I assure you, mademoiselle," the duc said, "that I consider it a duty of honour to escort you and this lady to the duchesse." He turned to the *devot*. "The chair you have offered, monsieur, we gratefully accept. You," he said to Juliette, "help your mistress to her feet."

He's behaving as if this were a chore, not a favour, Lise thought as she stood up. *How could I ever have thought this man might be interested in me?* "Thank you for your assistance," she said to the duc. "But I would rather go to my own home than to my aunt the duchesse's. For one thing, my Aunt d'Ombrevilles is in the same building—she is my landlady, in fact. For another, it is much closer. And I assure you, I feel fine now."

"As you wish," the duc said, and for a brief moment his smile was civil, even warm. "I do seem to be making a habit of encountering you at difficult moments."

"Believe me, monsieur, this was not my idea." She hoped she sounded witty, but what she really wanted, she decided, was to be home in bed.

Being on her feet was easier than she had expected it to be, though, and for a moment Lise thought the worst of the day might be over. Then, looking down the street to see the devot returning with a chair and bearers, she saw a man glaring at her with a loathing so bitter its impact was nearly physical. She had to prop herself on the wall to keep from falling again. *What have I done to you, monsieur?* A moment later she recognized the man; she had met him at her aunt's home recently. *The comte d'Audemar,* she thought. *Guillaume; that was his name.* Her next thought was that she should warn the duchesse of this; everything she had heard about the d'Audemar family since her first meeting with the prince had ended with warnings of their power and the danger they posed to those they considered enemies. *And what makes you think your aunt doesn't already know this?* Lise tried to smile at the comte in a disarming fashion, but he turned on his heel and stalked away, disappearing around a corner just as the chair arrived.

"I'm still not convinced I need this," she said as Aunt d'Ombrevilles helped her inside the enclosure, but shortly after they started moving Lise found herself grateful for the sedan chair when she was assaulted by the mysterious pain again. It was not as fierce this time, but it lasted for longer. God, it appeared, wanted to punish her for something. It had to be that; it couldn't be prayer. *The ward-stones are dead,* she told herself. *There's no more magic in them.*

And suddenly, in a flash, she understood. *It's coming back.*

⚜

Lise was wrapped in blankets, sipping hot mulled wine, when her Aunt d'Ombrevilles poked her round, white-capped head through the bed curtains. " Are you certain you're feeling better, child?" she said. "You don't look better."

"My head is fine now, aunt. Thank you for asking."

"Then why do you look so miserable, Lise?"

"Men."

"All men? I can see why that might sour your expression."

"Well," Lise said, chuckling into her wine, "perhaps not all men. I would like to believe that Captain d'Oléron, for example, would have behaved with a bit more sensitivity than his self-possessed almightiness the duc de Bellevasse."

"Captain d'Oléron? The musketeer? The protégé of your Aunt de Vimoutiers? That captain?"

"Yes." Lise stared into her cup a moment, then sighed, rippling the surface of the wine. "I don't know what's the matter with me, madame. Until a moment ago I thought the captain would make a most suitable husband. Now, after having been ill-treated by a man everyone insists is a horrid wretch and the Devil incarnate, I suddenly find myself thinking the captain a rather poor excuse for a man." There was, she knew, absolutely no justification for her conclusion. The duc had spoken to Aunt d'Ombrevilles in a steady, reserved but polite fashion throughout the journey but had more or less ignored Lise. He had delivered her to her apartment as if she'd been a package placed in his charge. And he hadn't even tried to come in once Juliette had gone ahead to stoke the fires. The duc de Bellevasse had probably been down the stairs and out the door before Lise had removed her cloak.

"Oh, poor Lise." Her aunt pulled back the curtains and sat down on the edge of the bed. "I did not know. Not that there's much an old lady could have done to help, I suppose."

"You were magnificent," Lise said. "You did more than he did to get me safely home." She tried to think about her situation, and failed. *Don't pout,* she told herself. *Forge ahead instead.* "I don't know what's the matter with me right now. I'm sure I'll be fine by tomorrow, and married by the weekend. It's not the end of the world."

"Well, you're right about that. Even if you don't actually

believe it at the moment." Her aunt smiled at Lise's expression. "Don't think you're fooling me, young lady. You're trying to be hard and strong, but don't try too much. You may disdain that nasty duc—and you're right to do so—but it's not a sign of weakness to admit that his indifference hurt you. It would hurt anyone. But Lise, you have to let these hurts heal a bit before you go back into the fray." She patted Lise on the shoulder, then held out her hand for the winecup. "For a start, why don't we replace this sour old wine with something that will do more to cheer you up? You settle back into bed, young lady, while I have us some chocolate warmed up."

After her aunt had returned to her own apartment, having first plied herself and Lise with both chocolate and pastries, Lise had Juliette reheat the mulled wine. *I want to forget about this,* she thought, *and since I can't achieve that through prayer, I'll let Bacchus do the work for me.* And it wasn't just the disappointing behaviour of the men in her life that she wanted to forget. *I told Marguerite I was going to be practical about marriage, and I'm just going to do what I said. This is a business I'm in, and there's no more room for self-indulgence.*

She swallowed half the wine from her cup. The room felt deliciously warm, and though it was still light outside she pulled the curtains and doused the candles. No, the real trouble she wanted to forget was the realization that had crashed down on her when the second headache had attacked.

If anyone else learned that her headaches were signaling her about prayer, she would surely be receiving a visit from the Inquisition.

Against her will, she found herself thinking through the logic of her recent conclusions. With Madame de L'Este at the palace she had been certain of a distinct character to the prayer she had felt; she was confident she would recognize a prayer from Denise de L'Este again. But this afternoon had confused more than enlightened her. She didn't know what magic had been done near her in the streets of St-Germain, but she knew it had been powerful—more powerful than distinct. *A test*, she thought. *I need to test this theory. Which means I have to go back.*

Four

"I'M GOING TO have to beg off the emperor's ball at this rate," Lise said, counting coins. Aunt de Vimoutiers was out of the room, saying good evening to a marquise from one of the more exalted families of Burgundy, and Captain d'Oléron had been called back to duty at the palace; his reluctance to leave had been small consolation for the disappointment she felt. "Nobody wants to play for anything approaching decent stakes here, and if I can't get a new dress for the ball I can't go." Now that she'd been several weeks in Paris, Lise had realized that her early optimism about her success at the gaming tables had been premature. Yes, she'd already earned enough to pay for her chambers for a full year, and if she continued to win at her current rate she would eat reasonably well, too. But the price of even a single ball gown was far beyond the amounts she'd won thus far, to say nothing of building the sort of wardrobe she would need to continue her matrimonial campaign.

Cousin Robert made a sound that fell somewhere between a sigh and a grunt of disgust. "You win every afternoon," he said. "What could be wrong with that?"

"It's not the winning. It's the amounts. Robert, I don't have your resources." *If I did, I'd show more respect for them than you do.* "I can hardly afford to live in this city, much less make an impression. I need money, Robert, and playing at *reversis* is the only way I can think of to get it. Unless you have any suggestions. Do you?" She didn't give him time to reply. "I didn't think so. Why do such wealthy people have to be so close-pursed, anyway?"

"Mother's rich friends didn't get rich by being frivolous with their money, cousin," Robert said. "And the rich are not all close-pursed, either. You're seeing a rather specialized subset of society here, you know. Mama's friends tend to think as she does. Else she wouldn't be friends with them."

He picked at the remains of a pastry. "I happen to know plenty of people who play for higher stakes. They just don't come here to do it, is all. That's a nice dress, by the way. Your dressmaker is good at picking colours that do well by you. Pity she wasn't a man. The fellow who makes my clothes is a dreadful chooser of fabrics."

"Don't you choose the fabrics yourself? I do." Lise was waiting for Robert to realize that his compliment about her dress should have been directed to her and not to the dressmaker when she realized what it was he'd said. "Go back a minute," she said. "You know of games played for higher stakes?"

"What? Oh, that. Well, of course I do. Surely you didn't think for a moment that my gaming activities were going to be confined to the maiden aunts-type games at Mama's salon. Good God, Lise, where's the sport in that?"

"Where indeed?"

"Exactly."

"No, idiot, I mean *where*. As in, where do you and your friends gamble? Are the stakes sufficiently high that a few good days—oh, I suppose they'd be evenings, wouldn't they? At any rate, could I win decently at one of your tables?"

"I imagine you could, at that. You're a strong enough—

now, wait a minute. You've got me talking ahead of my thoughts. It wouldn't work, you know. Couldn't be done. Not a question of it."

"Why not?"

"Didn't I say 'not a question'? You've just asked a question, haven't you?"

"Don't be supercilious, Robert. It doesn't become you in the least. Why couldn't I game at one of your places?"

"Mama calls them 'haunts,' and that's as good a reason as any. Lise, ladies don't go to gaming houses."

"What, there are no women there at all?"

"I never said there were no women. I said *ladies* don't go there."

"Couldn't I go in disguise?"

Robert gave her a sad-eyed, disappointed look that he had apparently inherited from his mother. *She does it better than you*, Lise thought. "Not satisfied with driving Mama to an early grave, cousin? Do you want to shame *me* into God's hands as well? Think about what you're asking. You want to go to one of my clubs in the guise of a *courtesan?*"

"I was thinking 'actress,' actually."

"In those places, there's no difference. Nor anywhere else, come to that," he said. "I grant you that you're forward enough— annoyingly so, most of the time—but you could never successfully impersonate an *horizontale*—I mean, one of those women." Lise was about to demand that he provide particulars to support this assertion when Robert evidently realized the danger he'd left himself open to, for he quickly added, "And even if you could, you'd never keep it a secret from Mama, who would clap us both in the Bastille for our sins."

"She could do that?"

A Poisoned Prayer
January

"By the good God, Lise, have you never heard of a *lettre de cachet*? It's a warrant to have you locked up, and most of them are sworn by family. At any given time, they say, about every third prisoner in the Bastille is a fellow—it's almost always a fellow, but not *absolutely* always, so you'd best take care, cousin—who's been locked up by mama or papa or wife or husband."

She was reminded of the two *lettres de cachet* de La Reynie had said were waiting for the duc de Bellevasse. *Does every family Paris do this?* "Have you ever—?" This was as interesting as it was horrifying. *It could mean something, I suppose, to know that if I accidentally find myself married to a complete pig, I could at least commit him to prison if he went too far.* She had assumed from the way the policeman had spoken about de Bellevasse that these letters were political weapons.

"Absolutely not," Robert spluttered. "I've never had a *lettre de cachet* sworn at me in my life. And I'm not about to pay my first visit to those towers on your account, my girl."

"*'Not on your account, my girl'!*" She pitched her voice low, as close to his timbre as she could, and was amused at his blush. "Do you have any idea how *old* you sound, Robert? I swear, just now I'd think your mother was younger than—" She stopped, staring at him as an idea took shape.

A shape that was a lot like Robert's.

⚜

"Please promise me you'll send word the moment you arrive at Respire's," Marguerite said to Lise, rubbing some sort of chalk-stick into Lise's eyebrows. "I may not be able to be there when you do this, but I want my spirit to be with you."

"I wish, Marguerite, that you could find a way to come, if only because you were so much help to me in obtaining Madame Champmeslé's aid." Marie Champmeslé was arguably the most famous tragedian in Paris today—and an habitué of Madame de Réalmont's salon. It was her tutoring—to say nothing of the paints and guises she had provided—that had allowed Lise, with Marguerite's assistance, to transform herself in a way that would get her into a gaming-house. Lise took the hand mirror Marie offered and looked, carefully, at the startling face that gazed back at her with her own critical eye.

It was really difficult not to stare at her new moustache, pathetically scraggly thing though it was.

A knock on the door announced Juliette's return; Lise told the servant to come in. "Have those clothes been delivered?" she asked, getting out of the chair as the door clicked open. Then she stopped abruptly, as she came face-to-face with her cousin Robert. "I've brought them myself," he said. "I only hope this tailor's as good as you—what in the name of all that's sacred is going on?" For a moment he simply stared at Lise. Then his eyebrows launched upward, as though clambering for safety beyond his hairline. "Oh, no. Lise, no. I forbid you."

Feeling sick, Lise forced a smile onto her mutated face. "You're very quick to catch on, Robert. I was hoping to keep this a secret from you."

"How decent of you. What if I'd accidentally conspired to be at the club tonight? Or worse: what if I'd gone to a different club, and stories started about there being two of me? Your wanting to go to a gambling haunt wasn't funny before, Lise. Wanting to go as me is too much."

"I think it's a brilliant idea," Marguerite said from behind them. "And I'm sure she'll do splendidly."

A Poisoned Prayer
January

"If I don't disguise myself as you," Lise said, "I'll have to invent a whole new identity, and that can only increase my risk of discovery. Which will, of course, bring shame and ignominy on the entire family, driving you and your mother into an early grave, etcetera, etcetera."

"You'll never get away with it under any circumstances," he said. "For example, a gentleman always wears a sword, the cardinal's laws notwithstanding. How are you going to manage that?"

"Look beside the fireplace," Lise said.

"What, that? It's a rapier, for God's sake. Hideously old-fashioned. I've never carried one, wouldn't in a million—wait a minute. You own a sword?"

Lise smiled. "Have since I was eight. Since I insisted on playing with the boys, Grandfather thought I should learn how to handle myself. My sister Andrée studied, too, until her gift became clear and we knew who'd inherit the estate."

Robert's flush had paled considerably by now. "Can you use it?"

"Do you want to learn how well I can use it?"

"Thanks, no. I'm happy to take your word for it. By God, Lise," he said after a long pause, "this is too fantastic to work."

"Which is precisely why it *will* work," Lise said. "Who would suspect?"

"Besides me? Only nearly everyone."

"Bah," Lise said. "You don't know that. And anyway, you won't be there. Or, rather, you will be, but through me. I will be you. And since I'm much better at *reversis* than you, think of the gain to your reputation when I win."

"You mean 'if' you win."

"That implies doubt," Lise said. "Of which I have none. Not where *reversis* is concerned."

"You mean to do this regardless of what I say."

"But of course, Robert." Lise smiled sweetly.

"I do have one thing you need, though, in order for this to work."

"Oh, I rather doubt that." To herself Lise wasn't quite so confident. Then she knew what he'd been talking about, and the knowledge must have appeared on her face. His triumphant grin threatened to crack his cheeks. "All right, then," she said. "What will your silence cost, cousin?"

"Nothing so serious," he said. Lise heard the slightest catch in his voice. *You're not so sure of yourself, either.* "A small percentage of whatever you take at the tables—it's in my name, after all," he added when he saw her expression. "Did anyone tell you that your eyes turn green when—"

"Yes, they did. Idiot. How much of a percentage?"

"Oh, ten, I should think. No, no. Five. Five would be fine." He wiped his forehead, dislodging his wig. "Five and the promise that you'll never give me that look ever again." He swallowed.

"Agreed, then. And now," Lise said, "I think that you should leave. Your presence here is no longer useful."

"It might be, Lise."

"Whatever could he do that was useful, Marguerite?"

"Since he's here anyway," Marguerite said—Lise was pleased to see that Robert was now squirming—"he might tell you things that might help you."

"By the Mother, you're right! Robert, while we work on getting my face to look like yours, you can tell me all about the sorts of people I'm likely to meet at Monsieur Respire's."

A Poisoned Prayer
January

⚜

The Rue des Francs Bourgeois was only fitfully lit, and Lise shivered with more than the cold. This was the first time she had been out alone after dark, since the loup-garou had attacked, and she did not think that her trembling was doing cousin Robert's reputation any favours. Not that Parisians—or Parisians of quality, at any rate—normally ventured out at night. Dinner parties took place in the afternoon, the meal being served no later than four, precisely so that guests could be safely back home before darkness came. It was a good thing that the new lieutenant-general of police had undertaken to force the neighbourhoods to provide street lights, but Paris still wasn't a safe place to be after dark. *I hope the rewards justify this risk,* Lise thought.

"It's just nerves," she added aloud. "I'll be fine. If I'm not sick. All over Robert's hideous clothes." Lise was grateful for the opportunity to claw cousin Robert, even in absentia, because it took her mind away from the sudden, awful, realization that she had been fooling herself in believing that she could succeed with this masquerade. The closer they'd come to the gaming house, the worse she'd felt. Now, as she so often did when under pressure, she was developing a headache.

Just remember what you're there to do, she told herself. *Play cards. Nothing more.*

She and Marguerite had decided that Lise should stay away from the supper table, stay away from the drinks. Let everyone think that she—or, rather, Cousin Robert—was mad on *reversis* and nothing but.

"I'll never get away with this, you know," Lise had said when trying at the last second to abandon the project.

"Don't be silly," Marguerite had said. "You're forgetting the most important thing about tonight. Everyone there is expecting your cousin Robert. When they see someone about his height, in his clothes, appear at the *reversis* table they will fill in the rest of the details of his appearance themselves. They'll *make* you look like Robert, to their eyes. That's why it doesn't matter that your moustache doesn't exactly match his: I guarantee you that none of Robert's gaming acquaintances has ever really *looked* at his moustache. It's enough that he has one, and therefore so do you."

"I'm still not sure I believe that," Lise said.

"Well, you must *act* as if you do. The only key to your getting away with this is to be confident. If you think you're going to be found out, you'll somehow contrive to make it happen. If you're confident—even a little arrogant—I guarantee no one will think twice about you."

Then she had hooked her arm inside Lise's. The contact sent a mild shock through Lise, something she had not expected.

"Go on, enjoy yourself. Make us both proud, and get rich."

Monsieur Respire rented an imposing, older mansion just west of the Hôtel de Ville. Lise didn't know who'd owned it originally, but clearly the place had been built by someone with money. The house wasn't big, and it retained a couple of the corner towers that had been the fashion a hundred years ago, but the gate was wide enough to accommodate a carriage and the courtyard was cobbled so carefully that she never once felt in danger of slipping as she made her way, escorted by a torch-bearing lackey, to the double doors at the far end of the yard.

The house had been brought up-to-date in a style considerably more ostentatious than her aunt's. The windows were large and modern and their glass, she saw as she drew closer, was almost as thin as vellum. The narrow space between each window was occupied by an allegorical statue, some of whose meanings Lise was pretty sure she didn't want to understand. From those windows the light of hundreds of candles spilled, the colour of polished bronze, onto the cobbles. A lot of prayer had to have gone into making candles give light of that purity. That, or a lot of money spent on the very best beeswax.

There was a heavy wooden door hidden in the gloom of the alcove just inside the gates, but Lise was escorted past that. Beyond the courtyard there was far pavilion and a flimsy set of doors, set amidst glazed windows on the ground floor. A tall man, whose bearing shouted retired soldier and whose dark cloak and pike remade the point for anyone who'd missed the posture, leaned across one of the doors in an obviously much-practiced movement and swung the door outward. "Good evening, monsieur le chevalier," he said, and Lise felt a gratifying surge of confidence that, for a moment at least, overpowered her headache. Perhaps she *could* do this. Nodding to the man, she went in.

The ground floor was relatively quiet, and the rooms through which she was escorted looked like comfortable refuges—much more comfortable than her own suite of small rooms, still inadequately furnished with hand-me-downs from her aunts. The nearer she got to the grand staircase, though, the louder the noise became. *The gaming rooms must be upstairs, and they must be madness.* She fumbled trying to remove the hat without dislodging her wig—how did men manage this, and whatever possessed them to think that wigs were *at all* attractive?—and tried to memorize the face of the servant who took the hat and her cloak.

"Now! Go! Jean-Luc! No, down with Jean-Luc! Up with Thomas!" Lise heard the shouting well before she understood its meaning. On reaching the staircase, she saw two young men, dressed in what she had to assume was the absolute last word in fashion, hovering in mid-air, at least twice a man's height above the steps. They appeared to be racing up the stairs using only the drafts—both natural and those provided by friends who stood at the bottom, blowing and waving arms and fans—to propel them. Both men were straining with the effort of maintaining the state of grace required to float above the stairs, and their faces had purpled in a way that did not match either of their costumes—one mostly green, the other gold and yellow.

This, she decided as her temples throbbed, was easily the stupidest thing she'd seen young men do, in a city where there seemed to be a competition amongst the nobles and wealthy bourgeois to do ever more spectacularly stupid things. Then she realized that she was supposed to be one of these idiots herself, and so she joined in with the shouting and hooting of encouragement, meanwhile trying to determine—and yes, she could!—whether she could pick apart the sources of the pain the prayers caused her.

When one of the men finally reached the top—or at least close enough to it to be pulled across the threshold of the first-floor landing by his friends—Lise was stunned to see bags of coins immediately begin to change hands. *That was a bet? They* bet *on things like that? Ridiculous.* Then she stopped herself. *Don't jump to hasty conclusions*, she thought. *See if you can use this.*

She thought about the consistently negative way most of the younger nobles—and not a few of their elders—had impressed themselves on her. They all seemed to think with something other than their brains. Someone who *looked* like a man but *thought* like a woman might be able to take advantage of the male approach to life. And money.

A Poisoned Prayer
January

Entering one of the gaming rooms, she felt her confidence increasing, and her headache dissipating. *That's more like it.*

A small notice proclaimed that the gaming rooms were warded. It shouldn't have been necessary; young men were stupid but they had rules about cheating at cards. Still, someone had obviously thought that rules by themselves weren't enough. Perhaps Monsieur Respire had learned that the hard way. Lise knew nothing about Respire, but the mere fact of his running a gaming house meant he was not well-born himself and hence had no power to speak of. So presumably he'd paid some impoverished noble—or perhaps he had a noble silent partner to lay and maintain the wards. From what little studying Lise had done she could guess that these weren't very sophisticated. They were strongly emplaced, though. That was reassuring; the last thing Lise wanted to worry about was having some inquisitive sort go prying under her costume without her knowledge. Sure enough, the candles and lamps that lit the rooms were of the highest worldly quality—but they were worldly, and not of the spirit.

She quickly found a room dotted with tables at which *reversis* was being played. Taking care to remain unobtrusive, she spent a few minutes observing play at each table before deciding on which one to join; or rather, one to be asked to join There were distinct advantages to cousin Robert's reputation, not least of which was that he was very popular as a gamesman, mostly because he played so poorly and lost so cheerfully.

"Vimoutiers! Good to see you! Come join us." Lise thought for a moment, trying to place the man's face. It was a narrow face, one that suggested cruelty. That would be Du Rochefort; Robert had said that he was much nicer than he looked.

This was not the case for his companion. The round-faced, straw-haired young man sitting beside the Comte Du Rochefort was the chevalier d'Audemar. Nothing she had heard of him since their unfortunate meeting at her aunt's salon had changed her opinion of him. Étienne was a very reckless player, according to Robert, but an arrogant and angry one as well. *Happy enough when he's winning,* Robert had said, *but I don't much like him when he's losing and in his cups.*

Perhaps he's in a good mood tonight, Lise told herself, *and at least he's not looking at me the way his older brother did last week near the Temple.* She went to join them and their third, the young man who had accompanied Étienne and his brother to her aunt's party, and to whom the prince d'Aude had so carefully not introduced her. She had learned from Robert that this was the comte de Ferreulle, a familiar of the younger d'Audemar.

As she crossed the room she caught a glimpse of Rafael, duc de Bellevasse. He was simply dressed, as always, in black and dark green and with no obvious jewelry, and yet somehow he conspired to outshine most of the men here. *Damn him.* For someone who was both too exalted and too dangerous for her to know, he seemed to spend a remarkable amount of time crossing her path. Tonight he was a distraction she really couldn't afford. She glared at him as she passed, silently wishing he would disappear.

⚜

She played a double game and, she thought, played it quite well. At *reversis* she played carefully, showing what she thought of as cautious recklessness: losing far more frequently than she won at first, and even letting herself be forced to play the occasional ace; but ensuring that her losing hands were for small stakes and those she won for rather larger amounts. At the same time, she played the game of impersonating her cousin, acting the genial fool and congratulating the others—and especially d'Audemar—on what she declared to be the cleverness of their play.

The stakes were astonishingly high. When d'Audemar had informed her how much the other three men at the table were paying per *fiche*, she had had to swallow an oath. Buying the fifty markers she needed just to get into the game very nearly exhausted her entire savings. Only by appearing to accidentally break up du Rochefort's attempt at a *reversis* during the penultimate trick was she able to build enough of a cushion to let her continue the game without the constant worry that threatened to cloud her judgment and cripple her skills.

When the serving girl appeared with wine, Lise declined, and instead created something of a sensation by asking for coffee. Apparently this had never been done before in Monsieur Respire's establishment, and he was not immediately able to accommodate the request. Within an hour, though, coffee had been obtained from a street vendor, and by the time d'Audemar suggested they all take some time to refresh themselves, Lise was gratified to see that about half of the men in the room had at least tried a cup. Some were drinking it heavily, to the great pleasure of the beaming, red-faced vendor who had been given a place near the wine-table for his grinder, pot, and portable alcohol stove.

"Good evening, monsieur."

Lise, by herself in a small alcove just outside the *reversis*-parlour, started when she realized that the carefully painted young woman who had sidled into the alcove was addressing her. This was something Robert hadn't discussed, and she was horrified to realize that it had never occurred to her that he might actually know some of the women whose presence at Respire's he had so disdained.

"Evening," she said, trying to make her voice sound husky. To her it sounded tight, strained.

"You haven't called in a week." The woman pouted, thrusting out her lower lip and dropping her eyelids in a fashion that Lise found slightly nauseating. *Please tell me we don't all look like that*, she prayed. The dress wasn't quite new, but it still showed signs of the quality with which it had been made. The silk was pale blue, shot through with bright green and gold threads, and the petticoats were of a rich yellow that perfectly matched the woman's hair. She wore no cap, though, nor lace, and her shoulders and breasts were alarmingly bare, even by contemporary Parisian standards.

"You've found a nice place here, though." She edged closer, her dress rustling as she pressed against Lise. "It's very comfortable. And no one can see us." She leaned across, fluidly and deliberately, and pressed her teeth into the lobe of Lise's left ear.

"Ai!" Lise jumped, unable to restrain herself. "Please!" she hissed. "Not here!"

"But if not here, then where?" The woman's voice had dropped a bit; she sounded throaty, the vocal equivalent of good honey. "It's too crowded everywhere else. Unless you like the idea of performing for the others." She giggled. "Do you? If so, why not tell me? Why treat your little Minou with such disdain?" One cool hand flowed up, stroked Lise's cheek, then drew her face down.

She wants me to kiss her. God. Lise could feel her pulse beating in her hands, her throat. She also, she realized, felt a bit of interest in this opportunity beginning to warm her. Minou smelled just a little of some rather pretty flower. Well, it was too late to do anything else now. *What the hell; she'll never notice. It's not as if any of the men* I've *met knew anything about kissing.*

It was only when she felt her mouth touch Minou's, and felt Minou's lips part—and felt the bristles of her false moustache dig into her lips—that Lise realized with a start the risk she was taking. And by then Minou was whimpering slightly, and pressing herself against Lise in a way that was making her uncomfortably warm. Lise hoped that the binding that had flattened her breasts would be enough to convince Minou that it was a man she was beginning to rub herself against.

Do something else, she told what remained of her mind. *What did the men do? What do they always do?* She snaked a hand up between herself and Minou, and captured one breast. At the same time, she carefully disengaged her mouth from Minou's. When the latter tried to protest, Lise used her thumb to pull down the fabric of Minou's dress, then caught the nipple between thumb and forefinger. Minou's protest emerged as a startled squeak, which evolved into a giggling purr of pleasure. "Monsieur," she breathed. "You are taking liberties."

"I can see how much it bothers you," Lise said in what she hoped sounded like a growl. Minou's reaction wasn't exactly what Lise had hoped for. *How do I get out of this?*

Inspiration struck: stepping back a bit, she gripped Minou by the shoulders and turned the woman around. Then she reached around over Minou's arms, pinning them to her sides, and grabbed a breast in each hand. Remembering how she'd been handled by her cousins and their friends, she massaged Minou's breasts as though she were working bread dough. Dipping downward a bit, she planted a sloppy open-mouthed kiss on the side of Minou's neck, licking around to the base of her throat. In Lise's own experience, this treatment was about as exciting as being caught in a late-autumn rainstorm; with luck Minou would take the first opportunity to flee.

Instead, the yellow-haired little idiot threw back her head and moaned, loudly enough that the archbishop himself must have heard her, clear across the city. *You bitch,* Lise thought. She looked from side to side, hoping nobody was watching—it was too much to hope nobody had heard—as the moaning continued, now enhanced with a wriggling of Minou's hips backward, from which Lise was only by luck able to disengage. *Robert, you are an idiot if you fall for this.* Minou was obviously trying to persuade "Robert" that he was magnificently virile, no doubt with the aim of wheedling some gift or other from him. She was no doubt about as transported by lust as Lise herself was.

No; that was no longer true. To her surprise, Lise was beginning to find this contact disconcertingly interesting. Warmth had started to build below her navel, and suddenly the idea of playing with this woman's breasts didn't seem quite so ludicrous. She found herself touching a bit more gently, stroking instead of grappling. And Minou, to Lise's sudden interest, stopped the theatrical moaning and murmured something that Lise couldn't quite comprehend. *You'd better stop this,* she told herself.

In a minute.

⚜

The sounds the voices made attracted Lise's attention even before she understood what it was they were saying. They were tense, urgent sounds, the sort people made when their need to conspire warred with the need to stay hidden. One speaker was a stranger; the other voice was one Lise had heard recently. As recently as tonight? She thought a moment: it might have been d'Audemar's friend, de Ferreulle, to whom the stranger was talking.

"Quiet," she whispered to Minou, who by now seemed to have forgotten that she was only supposed to be pretending arousal. "Here—get along, will you? I want to listen to this."

"And I want to keep playing."

"If you don't behave yourself and leave me, I'll never touch you again!" Lise tried to keep her voice low, and to a whisper, but found it difficult. For a heart-gripping moment the voices beyond the far wall of the alcove stopped, and Lise was convinced they'd heard her.

Then the murmur of conversation started up again, and Lise exhaled the breath she'd been holding. Not caring how rude she seemed, she pushed Minou away. There was a small screen, set into the wall just above her knees; no doubt it was intended to provide some air to the small space. It was through the screen that the voices were coming, and once Minou was safely on her way Lise dropped to one knee and closed up on the screen. Now she was able to hear the conversation clearly.

"It's certainly a powerful enough prayer," the other voice said. "Thank you for providing it."

"Is d'Iberie going to be strong enough, do you think?" *That definitely sounds like de Ferreulle. But what was he talking about?*

"Oh, I think so, my lord. He promises to test it for us, but he claims to have done this sort of thing before, to speed the way for, ah, family inheritances. Which is really what we're talking about, isn't it?"

A family squabble, then? Lise wondered. It wouldn't be

the first time that someone had resorted to prayer or poison to hasten the death of an inconvenient relative. If the stories her maid had told her were true, at any rate.

"I'll thank you to keep your voice down. The cardinal has ears everywhere, and I for one would rather not come to his attention any more than I already have."

"I saw none of his creatures tonight. Unless you're telling me that de Bellevasse is working for the cardinal."

"Do you really believe that those stories about death-magic are true? If they were, the cardinal would have de Bellevasse over a fire before the night was out." A snort from de Ferreulle, then: "No, it's a sham to make us think that the cardinal hates and fears the man. But I'm convinced that de Bellevasse is, in fact, the cardinal's man. So keep your damned voice down."

Lise was trying to digest this when things got worse.

"Come the day," de Ferreulle said, "will the others be ready to act? Much depends on everyone being prepared to act together, my friend."

"We are all aware of the significance of our actions. We are all prepared." The statement came through the screen sounding half-growl, half-hiss. "And now it's you, my lord, who is being too free. Talk like that could cost us our heads."

"Yes, yes. You're right." A sigh, perhaps of resignation. Then the sound a door opening, and Lise held her breath.

"What are you doing, Ferreulle?" That was d'Audemar, Lise decided, letting the breath escape silently through her open mouth. Judging by the eroded edges of his consonants, he'd been drinking heavily during the break.

"Attending to some small business on your family's behalf," de Ferreulle said. He sounded smug, much more so than he had at any time during the game.

"Well, stop it. My family is less important now than skinning that pig de Vimoutiers. He bores me with his pretensions to skill and I want to clean him out quickly, so I can choke down some of the slop that Respire calls supper and move on to a more interesting place."

"As you wish, my lord. I believe that de Vimoutiers is finished with his little dalliance now."

Three voices laughed, a sound that suggested to Lise vultures arguing over carrion. "If the pig believed that tart for even a minute then he's an even bigger fool than I thought," d'Audemar said. "Much as they deserve each other." The hidden door opened again and a chair scraped against a floor; Lise scrambled to her feet and out of the alcove. "I want another drink," d'Audemar said, his voice fading.

Lise felt sick. So her suspicions from the night of the party were true. *Robert believes these men are his* friends? *They despise him, and don't try very hard to hide it.* Coming back into the gaming room she thought back to what she had been doing with Minou. She flushed, both with shame and with anger at what d'Audemar had said. Then she remembered the happy grin the blonde had sported as she'd been pushed out of the alcove. Minou might have been acting at the beginning, but that grin had been genuine. *That'll give Robert something to live up to,* Lise thought. *No matter what d'Audemar might say.*

⚜

She was back at the table with a fresh cup of coffee when d'Audemar and the others returned. As she had entered the room she'd caught a glimpse of Rafael de Bellevasse sitting at a table near the doorway. For a moment he stared at her and she was sure he'd penetrated her disguise, but then a confused expression came over him and he hurriedly turned away. *Good,* she thought. *Let* him *be the uncomfortable one for a change.* It hurt, for some reason, to think that de Ferreulle might be right—that Rafael was the cardinal's man and would help the cardinal to usurp power.

The more she thought about it, the more it seemed to her that the conversation she'd overheard had nothing to do with the cardinal. It didn't seem to have anything to do with any family conspiracy, either, however it had been couched. But she could not determine to her satisfaction what it really had been about. Anyway, there were more important things to think about now. "Did you enjoy your break, my chevalier?" d'Audemar asked, and the others laughed. He looked flushed, self-satisfied, and stupid—*male,* she thought—and Lise decided that she hated him as much for what he was as for Robert's sake.

"Damn," she said, trying to modulate her anger so it seemed more pretense than truth. "I couldn't get the cat to leave me alone!"

"Well, we'll soon take your mind off her," d'Audemar said. "Who's the dealer this round?"

Before the game had made one circuit of the table, Lise realized that unless she gained control of her anger it would destroy her by ruining her chances of winning more than a few *pistoles*—in other words, by ruining everything she'd come here for.

She didn't try to quash the anger, though. Instead, she channeled it, focused it until it became a weapon in the game. She abandoned pretense, and began to play as she'd been taught by Grandfather. And she found that between the anger and the spirits in the coffee she was amazingly clear-headed, even as du Rochefort, de Ferreulle, and d'Audemar became progressively fuddled with drink. Though she took money from each of them, she took particular pleasure in

A Poisoned Prayer
January

taking *fiches* from the Chevalier d'Audemar. By observing and counting cards she was quite easily able to force him to play the Quinola—and not once, either, but twice in three games. The second time she did this she won the game, drawing in addition to d'Audemar's penalty payment a further five *fiches* from each of the others.

Throughout the remainder of the evening she kept her countenance pleasant, her manners coolly polite, and her voice never less than friendly. She claimed to be perplexed at the run of luck that led her to a *reversis* and won her no less than one hundred twenty-eight *fiches*. Her only regret—and she left this unvoiced—was that d'Audemar was on her right rather than across the table from her. Had he been her opposite, he'd have had to pay double of everything she won. As it was, du Rochefort had that unfortunate honour.

It was also du Rochefort who ended the game. "By the good Lord," he said, looking down as the points were tallied and the *parti* divided up, "I appear to be completely done. And is that Monsieur Respire's supper I hear calling me?"

"I do believe it is," said de Ferreulle. "And not a moment too soon. You've had a damned good run tonight, Vimoutiers. You going to stand us to a bottle?"

"Not tonight, gentlemen." Lise got to her feet, her winnings clinking heavily in Robert's leather purse. "One of the disadvantages of coffee, I've just learned, is that it leaves you with a full bladder and a sour stomach. I think I'm for bed."

"I am sorry to hear that," d'Audemar said. "I thought the evening was just beginning to be interesting." *Lying bastard*, Lise thought.

"Easy for you to say, d'Audemar. Your purse is deep enough." Du Rochefort clapped him on the shoulder.

"Come, dine with us. We'll keep you company after, if you want to keep losing."

"Safe journey home, Vimoutiers," d'Audemar said. "Tomorrow night you'll have to give me the chance to win some of that back."

"It will be my pleasure—d'Audemar," she said. *Be familiar,* she reminded herself. *They believe Robert thinks them friends.* "Good night, all."

After a visit to the privy to empty her bladder—and count as best she could her winnings, which appeared to number over a hundred gold *louis*—Lise wrapped Robert's cloak around her, pulled his hat down over her ears, and set out for the Ile St-Louis. She thanked God that Respire's was close to the river; in ten minutes she could be on the island and in fifteen she could be home and out of these clothes.

She had to admit they were not all that uncomfortable. They were a bit more restrictive than the breeches and tunic she'd worn on her wild rides as a girl, but they were considerably more pleasant to wear than the sorts of dresses and gowns that Paris expected to see on a woman.

"In such a hurry to spend my money, chevalier?"

She stopped. That was d'Audemar's voice, she was almost certain. Any doubts she'd had disappeared when the man himself emerged from the dark shadow cast onto the street by the wall of an hôtel. He had de Ferreulle with him, she noticed. *Oh, and a couple of lackeys, too.* She tried to think: how far had she gotten from Respire's? Was there a hope of assistance if she called out? She couldn't be sure how far she'd travelled, and she realized that she knew nothing that might help her cope with this situation in a fashion that didn't involve swords. Her head began to hurt.

"I'd say it was my money, monsieur," she said, trying to keep her voice level. It occurred to her that a noble who would stoop to robbery couldn't afford to leave his victim alive to tell the tale.

"To the Devil with you!" D'Audemar spat and made a sign. "I don't know how you did it, Vimoutiers, but I know you cheated me of my—*us* of our money. You would never in a thousand years beat me in a fair game."

"Unless I had practiced, my lord." If she could just keep him talking, she might persuade him to leave her alone. Or perhaps he would simply fall down. He seemed to her quite drunk. "*Reversis* is a game of skill, not of chance. It is permitted to improve one's skill, I had thought." From somewhere she thought she heard a snort of suppressed laughter. At least one of the lackeys had a sense of humour, then.

"It is not permitted to do so at my expense. Didn't your mother teach you anything?" The sound of d'Audemar's short sword leaving its scabbard was a slow, steady susurration—a mother shushing a cranky child. For a moment Lise did nothing: did that sound mean deliberation on her opponent's part, or uncertainty?

Her headache increased, and now that she knew the reason why, her anger flared up as strongly as the pain. She let her anger run free into her voice, as a field might catch fire on a hot summer afternoon at home. "Surely that's beneath contempt, my lord chevalier d'Audemar," she said, and for once it took no effort to force her voice down low. "If you intend to attack me, should you not be using a sword? Is this how gentlemen fight?" Then, as suddenly as it had flared up her headache vanished, and she felt a cool comfort that reminded her of the emperor in his throne room.

"You've been practicing more than your card play," de Ferreulle said. His voice was dry and hoarse with effort—

perhaps his own Blessing was no better than hers. "His defence is too strong, d'Audemar."

What defence? The question fled her mind when d'Audemar drew his sword. She felt sick, and it was worse than the headache. *I am going to have to fight. I will probably die.* Her mouth felt sticky, her tongue thick. The world around her seemed dull, suddenly, and somehow far away. *But,* she thought, *I am my parents' daughter.* And when she drew her rapier, it was with a swiftness that made the blade ring, briefly but with the purity of a bell calling the congregation.

The chevalier d'Audemar, with deliberate care and an ugly sneer marring his face, unhooked his cloak with his left hand. A lackey caught it before it hit the street. As there was no one to catch her cloak as she dropped it behind her, Lise kicked it and the heavy purse to the edge of the street. She tried not to think about the money she'd kicked away.

"I had regretted the need for your death, Vimoutiers," d'Audemar said. "I don't any longer. That insult means that I will take a great deal of pleasure in this." The words were slightly slurred, but not enough to give any encouragement to Lise.

"Ah," said de Ferreulle, "is that to be the end game, now? Your father the prince will not be happy, monsieur. And his mother – "

"Don't you dare talk to me about my father and what he might or might not like," d'Audemar said, nearly spitting his words. For a moment Lise wondered if the man was so drunk as to be capable of murdering his own friend.

"As you will," de Ferreulle said, and d'Audemar's attention was back on Lise. He held out his left arm, and the lackey wrapped his cloak around it. *Épée and cloak,* Lise thought, and drew the long dagger from its sheath on her right hip. Automatically, her left thumb found its place in the spoon-shaped cavity in the *forte* of the blade. She lifted the dagger to *quarte*, raised the tip of her rapier, and—spreading her feet a bit further apart—awaited d'Audemar.

"Good God," de Ferreulle said; "is that a rapier?"

At the same instant d'Audemar shouted a blasphemous curse and leaped at her, thrusting *imbroccata* from *prime*. Her body reacted to the thrust before her brain, and she parried easily; then, commanding his blade with her dagger, she feinted high and thrust *punta riversa* to his breast. It was with considerable lack of dexterity and dignity that he got his cloaked forearm in the way of her thrust in the instant before the blade would have pierced him.

As they sprang apart, d'Audemar's eyes were wide, and Lise—thinking again—realized that his attack had been every bit as aggressive and clumsy as anything her cousin Justinian had done during all of her practice sessions with him, supervised by Grandfather. *Perhaps I'll survive this yet*, she thought.

Provided my arms don't fail, she added after another bout of thrust, parry, and counter-thrust. Her skill was greater than his, and she knew it: he was as subtle as an Englishman, prone to the flamboyant guards, *prime* and *seconde*. She could even guess, by the way he bent his foreleg and dragged his back foot—in contravention of the strictures of nearly all of the current schools—that he was waiting for the opportunity to lunge into a full pass. Very well; let him try. She was sure she had his measure as a swordsman.

What she didn't have was his strength. It had been months since she'd practiced regularly, and while she'd been getting a bit of exercise helping with household chores (when no one was around to see her thus betraying her class), she could already feel the dull ache beginning in the muscles of her upper right arm. The left would be hurting too, and soon; she could parry d'Audemar effectively with her long dagger, but it was tiring work.

Here it came: d'Audemar, with a grunt that might have been intended to be a curse, lunged, then threw his whole body forward and down, swinging his left foot forward in a full pass. His épée dipped, then flashed upward to her breast.

Or, rather, to where her breast had been a moment ago. Lise stepped back, shifted into a *volte* as though she were a Spaniard dodging a bull, and extended her rapier. With its long blade extending her reach, she didn't even have to thrust. The point of the blade went into d'Audemar's upper arm, just below the shoulder.

He yelped, then swore, nearly falling over because he'd rolled his trailing foot by extending so far forward. Lise cursed as well, but silently. Had she got her blade up just a bit more, she'd have ended the fight instead of just blooding him.

"You have been practicing, Vimoutiers," d'Audemar said, standing back and taking deep breaths while he raised a delicate finger to the wound in his sword arm. "Not that it will make the slightest difference, in the end. You can't beat all of us."

"Perhaps not," Lise said. "But if you're dead, what impulse will the others have to carry on your quarrel?" She didn't give him a chance to reply, but moved to the attack. *Let's see how he parries.*

He was better at defence than attack. She tried every trick she knew, including a *mandritto* and even the tricky *coup de Jarnac*, a very old attack Grandfather had taught her from the sword-and-buckler days. She was able to get the edge of her blade onto the back of one of d'Audemar's thighs, but she didn't have enough strength left in her arm to make it a crippling cut.

She did succeed in making him even angrier, so the blade must have drawn blood. Now he returned to the attack, and he was, if anything, even more predictable in his anger. He was still stronger, though, and what his thrusts lacked in accuracy they made up in ferocity. Her left arm stung and buzzed and tingled as his épée hammered the dagger, the blade making an ugly clanging sound as it crashed into the knife. After only a few such blows she was forced to use her rapier to parry, and now the sound that echoed up and down the deserted streets was something from a blacksmith's shop, each blow a brief gust of wind ending in a metallic ringing. He was wearing her down, and if he seemed in his drunken anger to be unaware of that, Lise knew it too well.

She was gasping for breath, and she no longer felt the cobblestones of the street through the soles of her sore, tired feet. *Any moment now, I'll fall.* Her guard by now was a sad cross between *tierce* and *quarte,* and the tip of her blade was barely at the level of d'Audemar's breast-bone. Had she been using Robert's épée, she'd be dead by now; only the rapier's longer blade kept her safe by extending her reach.

She stepped back when he gave her the chance, and without intending to found her shoulders slumping, the blade dipping toward the street. *Only one thing to do now.*

When d'Audemar, with a shout of triumph, leaped toward her, blade high and point thrusting down, Lise, instead of attempting to parry, leaped forward as well. She let the rapier take the full force of the blow, letting go of her sword as d'Audemar struck. The rapier, as it spun away, deflected the point of d'Audemar's sword from her neck to over her shoulder. More importantly, by rushing in to meet his thrust she'd brought herself inside the space he was thrusting to. The edge of the blade sliced through cloth, and then skin, and for a moment Lise felt the cold touch of winter on her left shoulder. But the point passed her by.

Then her right hand, no longer holding the rapier, grabbed d'Audemar's cloak and pulled his left arm down. Into the gap thus revealed, Lise, channeling all of her remaining strength into her bleeding left shoulder and arm, drove her dagger into what she hoped was his heart.

⚜

It seemed to take forever for her to regain her senses, but common sense told her it must have taken no longer than the space of a single breath. They were both on the stones, and Lise's hand was wet and sticky, and d'Audemar was screaming his pain. *So he's not dead*, Lise thought. She felt neither good nor bad about this. *How odd*, some distant part of her thought.

"What are you waiting for?" d'Audemar shouted as Lise scrambled to her feet, looking in the dark for any hint of a reflection that would show her where her rapier had come to ground. "Kill her, damn you!"

Lise's shoulder was on fire, and she could feel warm stickiness dribbling down her left arm. *No more dagger work tonight*, she thought. The voice in her head seemed very distant, not the *her* she was used to having speak her thoughts. Somewhere out of sight she heard the slow drag of metal being reluctantly drawn from a scabbard. *Why don't you just go home*, she thought, bending over to pick up her rapier. *I'll even let you take that cheating bastard with you.*

When she straightened up, something like enchanted stars sparkled behind eyes that couldn't quite see properly

A Poisoned Prayer
January

anymore. It was only when one foot automatically shifted that she realized that she'd lost her balance and was about to fall over. And her headache had returned, much worse this time. She turned; at least they hadn't stabbed her in the back.

The reason why wasn't immediately evident, but that there *was* a reason was clear on de Ferreulle's face. He was staring, drop-jawed, at something Lise herself could not see. The two lackeys were gone; now that she saw this, she thought she could hear rapid footsteps clattering in the distance. A sound rather like crying drifted back toward her along with the sounds of the running.

"Who *are* you?" de Ferreulle asked, now staring at Lise. "What have you—"

He didn't finish. Dropping his épée, he turned and ran, a sobbing shriek escaping his mouth as he went. And now Lise saw what he'd been staring at. Something that looked a bit like a greyhound went bounding after him, massive glittering claws striking sparks on the cobbles.

As she watched, its wings unfurled and the creature easily took to the air. A cold but unmistakably feminine laugh echoed from the upper walls of the mansions.

That, Lise thought in a daze, *might explain why that creature showed me a woman's face as it went past me.*

A noise from behind her caused her to turn to her left. The Chevalier d'Audemar was back on his feet, and if he was a bit unsteady the glazed look of animal hate in his eyes told her that he would keep fighting until the last of his blood had left through the hole she'd put in his chest.

"Please stop," she said. "I don't want to kill you." She meant it, too, she realized with some surprise.

"Yes, stop," a familiar voice said from behind her. "I don't want her to kill you, either, d'Audemar. That's my task—in the proper time and place."

As d'Audemar collapsed to the cobbles like a stone wall hit by a cannonball, Lise turned, head throbbing, to see the duc de Bellevasse walking towards her. His right hand, crossing his waist, rested casually on the strange-looking hilt of what she guessed was a sword. His face bore a smile that was equally odd-looking.

"The first time I met you," he said, in a voice like a night time breeze in late spring, "I said that my mother would like you." He stopped just short of her; she had to look up to see his face. "After tonight's demonstration, all I can say is that I wish with all my heart my father was still alive. After seeing you handle a rapier, Mademoiselle de Trouvaille, he would have loved you."

Lise dropped her sword. "You know?" She tried to recall all that she'd done tonight, thinking she was secure in her disguise. At least one thing she'd done took no effort at all to remember. "When did you know?"

"Almost from the moment you walked into the *reversis* parlour," he said. His voice seemed a little husky to her, and for some reason she shivered. *It's not that cold,* she thought. *I should get my cloak anyway. And my money.* He cleared his throat, so perhaps he also thought he sounded odd. "You did a very good job of your disguise, mademoiselle. I must congratulate you."

"Obviously I didn't do that good a job," she said. Her own voice seemed to be acting up as well.

"It wasn't the costume," he said. "You could not, I don't think, disguise your eyes. Not without holy grace, something I recall you telling me you'd don't possess in any great quantity."

"My eyes?" She felt very stupid.

"When you're angry," he said, "they turn the most fascinating shade of green. I've never seen your cousin's eyes do that."

He wrapped his cloak around her; she was shivering, though she still didn't feel cold. "In a way, I'm glad I recognized you as early as I did," he said. To her wordless query he replied, "If I hadn't known it was you, seeing you with that cocotte in the alcove might have made me very jealous of your cousin, a position I assure you I have no desire to be in. As it is, knowing it was you I'm merely extremely confused."

She wanted to say something clever in response, but felt herself losing her balance again. And when she reached out in the hope of breaking her fall, a saw-blade edge of pain ripped through her shoulder, she saw the stars spin, and the night turned dark red for a moment. She seemed to be falling, but there was no contact with the paving stones. Still falling. Still turning.

Then she felt nothing. Coming to her senses again, with the world seeming as if no time at all had passed, and all the time in God's universe had, she felt a moment's peace, a sense of warmth and well-being.

She breathed in something sharp and acidic, and the night and the world came back to her. "What?—"

"You fainted." Rafael laughed, sounding bitter. "My usual effect on women, I'm afraid. No wonder Mother despairs of me. Why didn't you tell me you were wounded, mademoiselle?"

"I think I forgot."

"Ah. Now *that* is an effect I seldom have. You do me great honour, mademoiselle."

"What have you done to me?" Now her head was pounding. "Some sort of charm?"

"If I had left you to the care of the surgeons, mademoiselle de Trouvaille, there would have been too many questions. And you would not have escaped a scar. It would have entirely ruined your appearance in a court gown, I'm afraid, for all that the wound looked clean. This way, by tomorrow there will be no sign that you were ever injured. You should feel no pain, either."

"That will be an immense relief, my lord, because at the moment I feel very little that isn't pain." She looked at him, saw what she hoped to be good humour in his eyes, and decided to take the risk. "And that which I feel and which isn't pain I am, I regret to say, unable to act on. At the present moment, that is."

"Tell me," the duc—Rafael—said, smiling. "Is it dressing as a man makes you this bold? Is it my effect on you—I seem to recall you earnestly threatening to shoot me when we first met—or have you always been this way?"

She was unable to keep from laughing, in spite of the pain and the ache she was now aware of, an ache that had taken up residence in all of the muscles of her arms and hands and legs. "I am afraid, my lord, that you see me as God made me. Well, save for the costume. My friend Marguerite and my cousin Robert can take credit for that."

The smile vanished from his eyes. "What game have you been playing, mademoiselle?"

"The same as everyone else at Respire's tonight," she said. Seeing his eyebrows lift, she added: "A money game. I have little of my own, and had planned to support myself in Paris with my winnings at the games I play at the salons I attend. But that wasn't enough, so I decided to try my luck for higher stakes. Oh! My money—"

"Rest easily," he said. "I hid it, in the event that one of d'Audemar's lackeys decided to take it while you were occupied." He muttered some prayer under his breath. "It's just behind us, I think," he said. "We'll pick it up when we go to take you home. And I trust you won sufficiently tonight, my clever young woman, because this is a game you mustn't attempt to repeat. It's not worth the risk you run."

"I thought I did well." She wondered if she might be able to stand, now. She tried to get up, and was grateful when Rafael raised her the rest of the way.

"That is, indeed, the trouble. You did too well. Your cousin, if he is noted for anything, is known for the affability with which he loses. Were he to suddenly embark on a winning streak, questions would be asked. As it is, I'm going to have to cast some pretty prayers over our friend d'Audemar there, in order that he not remember exactly what transpired here tonight."

"But I want him to remember!"

"Trust me, you don't." Rafael offered her his arm. Taking it, she was relieved to discover that her shoulder did feel a bit better.

"The d'Audemar family aren't fond of being bested," he said as they walked. "They *are* fond of carrying a grudge. If d'Audemar here had any clear memory of what you did to him tonight, his pride would demand that you die. Well, your cousin, at any rate."

"He could try!"

"No, it wouldn't be like that. If he remembers, then he remembers that he can't beat you in a fair fight. Recall that he didn't even have the honour to attack you magically himself, but had his friend do so while he thought you were distracted."

"So what I felt was you, defending me?"

"What you felt? Yes, I cast a sort of ward over you; it's the type of defence that Robert would have instinctively thrown up. Not that hard to do, because prayer works poorly in the presence of metal and you all had swords out."

"And yet the ward spells are prayers which I cannot do, even though I know them well. Thank you, sir. I've no doubt you saved my life."

"Yes. Well, I had my reasons. And all of them selfish." He stooped to pick up the purse. "Here. Now pick up your cloak and sword while I see to our friend here. If you'll come with me, I'll take him to a priest who will deal better with his wounds than I could—or than I would wish to, at any rate. Hello," he said a moment later, "you've broken his collar-bone. Excellent. I'll make him think that he challenged you, but that his horse threw him."

"Rabbi Weiss told me the sort of prayer that fixes men's minds doesn't really work."

"This isn't a prayer so much as a technique of persuasion I have learned in my travels. In his current state, all I have to do is put the idea into his head by repeating it sufficiently often as I carry him to the priest. The priest will repeat the story, and when he sobers he will choose to believe it."

"What about the others? The lackeys—and that friend of his? Won't they tell him the truth?"

"Not when my Shahrbàz has dealt with them. She'll see to it that they remember what I wish them to."

"Your who?" Was this Shar-something his mistress? *No. That is Denise de L'Este. Or was.*

"I believe you saw her chasing after de Ferreulle a moment ago. I would imagine she's taken him up to some rooftop by now; I suppose I should speak to her."

"That—creature is your—"

"Is a *djinniyah*. And, I suppose I misspoke a moment ago.

Shahrbàz is not 'mine' in any real sense. If she belongs to anyone, she belongs to that rabbi friend of mine of whom you just spoke. He claims she became attached to him while he lived in the city of Cordoba. Are you familiar with the *Thousand Nights and a Night?*"

She shook her head.

"A most interesting book, I'm told. Rabbi Weiss has described some of its chapters to me, and I'm told someone is translating it into French. Think of it as a sort of history of certain aspects of life and faith in the Mohammedan lands. At any rate, there is much in it about the *djinn*, the spirits from those lands that can take on corporeal form. There may have been such creatures in France, once, but they were destroyed." He sounded unhappy about that.

"If this Shahrbàz does not 'belong' to you, why was she with you?"

"Ah. Something of a complicated tale, that. Shahrbàz is a bit—I suppose 'jealous' is the word you'd use, though if so it's the jealousy of a small child. At any rate, she didn't take kindly when my friend Weiss married. So she left him and settled herself on me. She claims to find me amusing. I sometimes find her helpful."

"A jealous demon. You have the most interesting friends, my lord duc." She approached him as he hauled the inert d'Audemar up from the street. Rafael's face was slicked with sweat, which steamed from his face in the cold night air. A look at d'Audemar showed her to what end he'd been exerting himself: the blood that had soaked the front of d'Audemar's coat was no longer there.

"You should not propose to set yourself above them, mademoiselle," he said. He was grinning for all that his face looked drawn. "This is yours, I believe." He handed Lise her dagger. It, too, was clean.

"You have the advantage of me, sir," she said, replacing the dagger into its sheath and wrapping her cloak around her.

"Not nearly so much as I hope to have," he said, and as they walked to the nearest church it occurred to Lise to wonder how it was that she'd been able so completely to forget that she was supposed to fear him.

February

One

"Keep talking, Robert." Lise tried to tuck an errant tendril of hair back in place. "If I don't have something to distract me I think I may go mad." Snarling, she jammed the offending hair behind her ear.

"I don't know what's the matter," Robert said. "You look fine."

"What am I wearing, then?"

"Um."

"As I thought. You're not the most inspiring escort, Robert, but one thing you are good at is mindless chatter. So please take my mind off the fact that I am about to throw myself into a ball at the emperor's palace in a dress that feels like twenty pounds of plate armour."

"Y'know, cousin, you could probably guarantee a much better reception for yourself in the great houses of Paris if you managed, for at least tonight, to avoid insulting me. Oh, and talking of plate armour is probably not the most ladylike conversational gambit either."

"Robert..."

"Very well, very well. Babble you want, babble you shall get. Why haven't you won me any more money at the high-stakes tables? It was very, very nice to receive that alarming

A Poisoned Prayer
February

pile of coins from you after that night. I dined quite well there for a few days."

Lise closed her eyes. This was not a subject she wanted to visit, not tonight, not ever. "I thought you were horrified at the prospect of my risking your reputation."

"I suppose I owe you an apology for that. I think I was worried that you'd—well, embarrass me. Instead, I keep getting the most outlandish invitations from—well, from all sorts of people." He paused for a moment, as Aunt de Vimoutiers's carriage came to a halt inside the palace's carriage port. "And when I do show up, they seem horribly disappointed somehow." Robert looked around the interior of the carriage, as if trying to locate his train of thought.

"I've been persuaded that it's too dangerous for me to continue impersonating you," Lise said as a footman opened the door. "So consider your reputation saved."

"At the cost of my purse," Robert said. "And you really do look very nice, cousin." He followed her out onto the cobbles. "That mix of green and violet helps bring out the green in your eyes that otherwise people only see when you're angry. Which means, I suppose, that I see it more than most. Should consider myself lucky, I suppose."

"Idiot," Lise said, but she smiled at him. *I wish I could be as mindlessly happy as he always seems to be,* she thought as she inserted herself into the crowd snaking its way into the palace. The past two weeks should have been the best of her life. Instead, they had seen frustration piled on frustration. She had had to spend entirely too much time with dressmakers and hairdressers as her Aunt de Vimoutiers searched for a dress and hair-style that would make her appear at least potentially fashionable. And she had had to wrestle with two sides of her heart: one that thought she had spent too much of the money for which she had risked her life; the other that she would never find a suitable husband maintaining such a parsimonious attitude.

"I may be an idiot," Robert said with a sly smile, "but I know when my cousin's been given a signal honour. You shouldn't forget what the emperor's done for you, cousin."

"Oh," Lise said. It was all she could say, because Robert was right.

The anteroom to the Long Salon of the Tuileries Palace was decorated in the rich colours of autumn: oranges, ochres, rich red-inflected browns, with here and there a touch of green that hinted of spring to come. For Lise it was perfect: the colours were a comforting warmth against the early February chill. Better still, these colours were the result of human handiwork; one didn't have to be Blessed in order to enjoy them.

As Lise and Robert, having been announced to people who seemed all to have ignored them, passed from the antechamber to the ballroom itself, the unity of the décor began to collapse, in the way that light tore itself into colours when it passed through a prism. The dancers wore an astonishing variety of colours, and they glittered so brightly it sometimes hurt Lise to look at them. Many of the masks they wore reflected light, whether by means of jewels, polished glass, or magic she couldn't say. She wondered if her own poor mask would dazzle anyone tonight. The emperor, when she had been announced, had acknowledged her with a distracted nod of his head, destroying with that gesture her fantasy that she and Charles of Burgundy shared anything more than an inability to carry a tune.

Something—besides the emperor's indifference—wasn't right. "Isn't there supposed to be dancing?" she asked her cousin. "It is a ball, after all."

"They'll get around to it," Robert said. "Eventually. Dancing's not exactly what a palace ball is about, Lise."

She looked more carefully at the revelers. What had at first appeared to be a solid mass of beautiful people now revealed itself as a collection of small conversational islands, surrounded by a sea of people trying, with desperation more or less visible, to make landfall on them. Under this scrutiny, even the beautiful costumes didn't seem to sparkle quite so much. "Well," she asked, "what am I supposed to do, then? I can't talk to these people—I don't even *know* any of them."

"You were here more recently than I," Robert said. "So don't look to me for introductions. This isn't my crowd either." He turned to wave dismissively, but the wave turned into something more direct. "Oh, there you go," he said, pointing. "There's someone you know."

Lise had only to look in the general direction of Robert's gesture: even masked and wearing green and silver silk instead of his usual dull grey-green, there was no mistaking the duc de Bellevasse. *You should say something cutting,* she told herself. *People still think you fear and hate him.* All she could think of, though, was how she'd felt when he'd healed her wounds.

Then she realized who it was Rafael was talking to.

"I wish de Bellevasse would make up his mind about Denise de L'Este," Robert said. "If she's still his mistress, fine. But if she's not, others of us might be interested. I gather she's quite... talented."

"I never knew you were a connoisseur of that sort of talent," Lise said, swallowing an oath. The duc de Bellevasse seemed to be making a career out of confusing her. First he had rescued her from the werewolf; then he had treated her like a package when escorting her home after the incident near St. Germain. He had made her heart sing when rescuing her from the comte d'Audemar. And now he was frustrating her again, rubbing her nose into the fact of his having a mistress.

Then she had a wicked thought, and felt her mouth curling up into a grin. "Tell you what: let's go ask them. I'm sure that either or both of them would be happy to set your mind at ease." *Though I doubt it's your* mind *at work here,* she added silently.

She had nearly reached Rafael and Madame de L'Este before Robert could catch up with her. "Lise, for God's sake stop. You can't—"

"Good evening, Vimoutiers," Rafael said. He nodded, almost imperceptibly, at Lise. She was certain, though, that his eyes were smiling. At her. Her confusion redoubled. "What, if I may ask, are you trying to prevent your cousin from doing this time?"

Lise curtsied to Rafael, then to Madame de L'Este—who looked as if she'd swallowed something unpleasant. "Good evening, monsieur, madame." Turning back to Rafael she said, "My cousin is, alas, too shy or too smitten to ask you himself, so I must be his go-between. Tell me, please: Is Madame de L'Este still your mistress, or may my cousin consider himself free to make his interest known to her?"

The result was disappointing. Lise had hoped for some sort of sputtering explosion, but only Robert obliged—and really, it was too easy to do that to Robert. Rafael only looked down his nose at her, his mouth curled up in the smallest of smiles, as if she'd done exactly what he'd expected of her. And Denise de L'Este was the most disappointing. She said nothing, and her face betrayed no emotion at all. Then Lise felt the familiar headache—and *yes,* she had been right and she did recognize it—and knew that not all angry emotions were visible.

"What, again, madame?" Lise opened her eyes wide, hoping to persuade madame de L'Este that Lise knew more than she did. A spell was coming; beyond that it was all guesswork. "How much of a triumph will it be if I know that you've done it—and how you've done it?" She glanced around. The waiter with the tray was a likely mechanism, she decided. Perhaps Rafael or Robert knew a prayer for removing wine stains.

"Idiot slut." Now madame de L'Este's face betrayed emotion, ugly and red. "The triumph is exactly that you *will* know who did this, and how. Enjoy your evening, you Devil-cursed witch." Her eyes closed tight.

The water seemed to come from nowhere. Possibly it had. *Not fair,* Lise thought as she felt the rain of droplets spatter, then splash, on her face, shoulders, breasts. Then a sharp pain was followed by a strangled shriek—

—And it was Denise de L'Este who stood, soaked and open-mouthed.

She appeared to be screaming, but made no sound beyond the frenzied gasp of her breathing. Then her eyes glazed and seemed to stare, unseeing, at something above her, and she crumpled to the floor.

It had happened so quickly that Rafael had led her nearly to a narrow doorway before Lise identified both that the second prayer had—well, *tasted* different in comparison with the first, and what it was she'd smelled as the sodden Denise de L'Este had collapsed. "Cat's piss?" She couldn't suppress the giggle. "You turned her deluge into cat's piss when you turned it on her?"

Rafael flushed, and for a moment he stammered. "How did you—?" He shook his head. "You're dangerously clever, mademoiselle. But you are also unarmed in the sort of combat Denise started in there. I did not want you to think that I approved of what she was doing." After a pause he added, with what seemed like surprise in his voice, "Or of her."

"Oh. So you are—"

"Of course not. Your cousin is welcome to her. Though he'll run, if he's wise."

"He isn't." Looking back as he closed the door behind them, Lise saw—and felt—a shimmer. "What did you just do?"

"Your cousin was about to follow us. I'd rather he didn't. So I—well, I hid the door."

She brought up her hand to her face, hiding her smile. *I'm just as happy he won't be following*, she thought. "Where are we going, that you'd rather he didn't follow?"

"You're wet," he said. "I know where to find towels. Follow me please."

You could erase these few droplets with the simplest of prayers, she thought. She followed him anyway. "Why did you change madame de L'Este's prayer?" *You are unarmed* was how he'd put it. But... "If what you wanted was to defend me, all you had to do was make the water vanish. Oh, my God," she said, following him through the door he'd opened. "What is this?"

"The Hapsburg ambassador's suite," Rafael said. "The situation in Flanders being what it is, he's not using the place at the moment. Give me a minute, please." He opened a door at the opposite end of the room and disappeared through it. Through the doorway she could see one corner of what looked like a rather large bed. *Is he going to seduce me?*

The thought hung in her mind, blunt and matter-of-fact.

A Poisoned Prayer
February

Isn't there supposed to be a sweeping of me off my feet? Lise was sure she had a lot to learn about the arts of love, but she was still pretty certain that an accomplished seducer would never have left her standing here—however beautifully appointed the room—to second-guess him.

Rafael re-emerged from the bed chamber, carrying something impossibly white and thick. "Allow me," he said, dabbing the soft cloth against her forehead and cheeks.

She couldn't resist her laugh. "This is remarkably convenient," she said.

"Not so much, no. The ambassador and I are cousins—distant enough to allay any suspicions at court, near enough to occasionally be useful. I have often attended on Karl—on the duc—so I know my way around here." He lowered the towel to her shoulders, and now she could feel the warmth of his hand through the thick cloth. *I didn't even notice him remove his gloves.*

Then the towel was on her breast, and somehow his hand was cupping her breast even as he pressed the cloth down. *That's nice,* she thought, and then he bent to kiss her and "nice" was no longer an adequate word.

He was hot and cool, firm and yielding, and Lise reveled in him and in the realization of what he was doing to her. *I'll bet prayer feels like this, to the Blessed,* she thought. Something teased her nipple—not grappling with it, the way boys always had, but a touch that was light without being an annoying tickle: just enough to get her attention, make her interested in feeling more of that.

The touch vanished, and she heard a muffled complaint that was, she realized, coming from her mouth and going straight into his. Then the touch was on the back of her neck, just below the hairline, and a jolt went straight from her head down to the pit of her stomach, and below. She had to break the kiss in order to catch her breath.

"If you want to stop," Rafael said, "now is the time to say so." His voice had become thick, and there was a hint of urgency to it that Lise, to her surprise, found flattering.

"Why would I want to stop?" She stood up on her toes to kiss him, a quick darting kiss. "Shouldn't I be saying this to you? I'm not exactly prime mistress material."

"Who told you that?" He bent down and kissed her again, and this time a fingernail lightly scratched its way from her neck down to below the top of her bodice. "Whoever it was, he lied." She felt cold, then hot, as the nail teased her skin.

Then his hand was back on her breast, and it was the flat of his thumb teasing her, working its way into her gown until she felt the soft pressure of the flat of the thumb pressing against her nipple. This time the jolt that went through her seemed to lift her from the earth, so that she felt dizzy and somehow outside of time.

"If you stop that," she said gasping, when she broke the kiss again to breathe, "I will kill you."

He laughed, said, "I believe you," and then his mouth was on hers again and he was pressing her nipple and somehow it was directly connected to her very core and Lise felt a rushing like a powerful wind seeming to encompass her. *Is this what it's like under prayer?* she wondered, and then she knew that Rafael hadn't invoked any magic beyond what he—they—could do with body and spirit. *How wonderful,* she thought. Then she clutched at his shoulders and pressed herself to him. There ought to be something she could do for him, she told herself, to make his body sing the way he was making hers. But for now she was more than content to let herself be carried off by the sensations he was bringing out of her.

She stumbled; he was moving her. *The bed*, she thought. *What a good idea.* She broke the kiss—not enthusiastic about it, but it made movement easier—and looked into his eyes as he directed her toward the Hapsburg ambassador's bed. Rafael was, she realized, watching her as intently as she was looking at him. *What do you see?* She couldn't generate the courage to ask the question aloud.

"Am I interrupting?"

Lise stumbled, horrified, and fell into the bed. She flushed, felt a wash of shame that was utterly unbidden and unjustified.

Then she realized who it was in the doorway. "Damn you, Robert!" she shouted. "Didn't your mother teach you to knock?"

"I won't ask what sorts of lessons your mother neglected," her cousin said. He was smiling, but only his mouth was involved. "I was worried about you, cousin."

"As you can see," she said through clenched teeth, "I am fine." She wanted to throw something at him. Looking around the room for something suitable, she saw instead the expression on Rafael's face. He was smiling, but unlike Robert's, this smile reached his eyes. There was still something about his smile that maddened her, though. She was struggling against the urge to kill her cousin, and he seemed no more than amused by it all. Without willing herself, she stepped away from Rafael.

"I am quite capable of looking after myself," she told Robert. "You, on the other hand, should be better at taking a hint."

"I think that perhaps I should leave you two while you discuss this," Rafael said. "I suspect that my presence here will only impede the free exchange of...ideas. Please pull the door shut behind you when you leave." He was shaking his head as he left the room, but Lise was sure she heard him laughing. She found it impossible to share in his amusement.

"Was this really necessary?" She turned on Robert, wanting to be furious with somebody. She suppressed the idea that this should be herself. "I am perfectly capable of looking after myself."

"Oh, is that what you were doing? Not what it looked like to me, you know."

Lise stepped toward him, expecting him to scurry out of her way, but Robert didn't move. "He's not a good person to get yourself involved with," he said. "How can you not have seen the black all around him, Lise?"

She stopped, and looked more closely at him. What she had first seen as petulant anger was, she realized, anguish and fear. He was afraid for her. Which was nice, and said very good things about his character, but he was wrong about Rafael.

Wasn't he?

"I know you say he deals in death-magic, but I don't see that, Robert." *Or perhaps I'm just choosing to ignore it.* "I just see—" She had to stop, there. What exactly did she see in him? Excitement, certainly. Was that enough? It wasn't something she was going to tell Robert, though, not if he was this upset about something as simple as her sneaking off with Rafael.

Oh, stop that, she told herself. *Of course it's enough that he excites you. Why else would you let him lead you here?*

"Yes?" Robert turned to the door. "Lise, you're here to find a husband. Rafael is not going to be a husband. Not for you, not for anyone. If he doesn't destroy himself, he's

A Poisoned Prayer
February

going to take his magic—whatever it is, why ever he's doing it—so far that if the emperor doesn't condemn him, the cardinal most certainly will. I don't know what he's thinking or what's behind this death-magic that everyone's talking about, but I do know that it can't be good for you. So please, listen to me when I tell you that you're better off ignoring Rafael de Bellevasse."

He stopped in the doorway and looked into her eyes, clearly wanting her to agree with him. There was no chance that this was going to happen. But Lise couldn't make herself say this; she found it endearing that he should care so much. So instead she said, "I think I've had enough of this ball, Robert. I'd like to go home now, if it's not a problem."

⚜

Lise looked across the room at her aunt. "I'm sorry, aunt; I didn't quite hear that. Could you please say it again?"

"I shouldn't, but I will. I don't know what's got into you, girl, but you're behaving very rudely." Some of the guests giggled and Lise flushed at the rebuke. It may have been rude of her, not paying attention to her aunt; but wasn't it ruder, then, for her aunt to point it out?

"As a matter of fact, I was asking you what happened to you last night, after the ball." Lise flushed; had Robert told his mother about what he had seen in the ambassador's suite? Then the duchesse smiled, saying, "I had expected you to come see me after, to tell me all about it, and instead I was left to imagine it." Lise was relieved to detect some warmth there, after all. "The only excuse for such behaviour is that you were having too good a time to worry about me. I trust you enjoyed the event."

"I did, aunt, and I'm sorry I didn't seek you out before going home. I think I was just—overwhelmed by it all.

I asked Robert to take me home and didn't think about anything beyond sleep." Lise looked around. "Isn't he here tonight?" Robert was almost always present at these soirées, despite his frequently stated desire to be anywhere but; tonight, though, she hadn't seen him.

As for last night, it was her memories of it that were the cause of her ignoring her aunt just now. She had been thinking for most of the day about Rafael's touch and his kiss. The fact that he was even interested in her, much less that he could do what he had done, was a wonder. What her aunt's question had interrupted was Lise trying to decide whether it really mattered all that much if she married right away.

"Robert is a guest tonight at a dinner given by the princesse imperiale," her aunt said. "I don't know why he's suddenly the recipient of so many invitations; he has never struck me as a necessary fixture in the social scene, but evidently I have been wrong." She looked genuinely happy for her son, if perplexed about what had happened to suddenly make him a social asset. Lise, who suspected this increase in popularity was the result of her impersonation of him at Respire's, felt a flush. But then the vision of Rafael kissing her at the ball slashed into her imagination, banishing embarrassment and leaving desire in its wake.

"Well, I for one am pleased that his worth is being recognized." Aunt d'Ombrevilles strode into the room, beaming her ruddy-faced smile, impervious as always to the duchesse's disapproving glare. "He's a good boy, much more appropriate to a social gathering than some men, the sorts who are so full of themselves they are blind to everyone around them. Oh, that reminds me," she said, her voice a little girl's, "your Captain d'Oléron is on his way up, Marie-Françoise."

A Poisoned Prayer
February

"Thank you very much," the duchesse said; Lise was sure the temperature in the room dropped, and she prayed to God that the duchessee wouldn't cut back at her cousin. Aunt d'Ombrevilles was a nice woman and Lise enjoyed her sense of humour, one more wicked and cheerful than Lise expected in an older person, but she was really out of her depth against the sophisticated experience of the duchessee.

To Lise's embarrassment, the captain came straight to her seat the moment he had kissed the duchessee's hand. "Good evening, mademoiselle," he said, feathering a light kiss on the back of the hand she extended to him. "Might I beg the privilege of a few moments with you? I would very much like to hear your thoughts on the ball. I was unable to attend myself—on duty, you know."

Lise looked at him, at the nervous smile and the hollow self-confidence, and suddenly saw her cousin Robert. Was it that Captain d'Oléron had always been so—so *young*—and she just unaware of it? Or was it that Rafael had spoiled the captain for her? She smiled at him, not really feeling the smile, and let herself be led to the far corner of the salon where Captain d'Oléron pressed her—without much enthusiasm, she thought—to describe the ball. She knew that her tale was flat and without any spark, but she didn't care. And his attitude suggested to Lise that the captain wasn't really paying attention anyway. *So this is what it's like*, she thought, *when a man will do anything to be with you*. It was what she had wanted, she had thought. And the captain was a man her parents would have liked; perhaps even Grandfather would have approved.

And she couldn't wait to be shut of him.

After a painful five minutes that felt more like an hour, Lise was able to attract the attention of her Aunt d'Ombrevilles.

That worthy lady came immediately to her rescue. "Young man," she said, "I believe your good friend the duchessee would like a word with you." The captain dutifully bowed and vanished, and the marquise flowed over to Lise and sat herself down. "Now, then, Lise: tell me all about meeting the emperor. And what's this I hear about you getting into another fight with de Bellevasse's mistress?"

Lise couldn't help smiling as she started telling her aunt the full story of her encounters at the palace. It was perfect, really: she could continue to let Rafael occupy her mind, and justify it by virtue of her aunt having ordered her to do so. And her aunt was clearly interested in the story for its own sake. That story grew a little, and glistened a bit more brightly in the telling. But Lise told herself that was only because, because Aunt d'Ombrevilles was such an appreciative listener.

By the time Captain d'Oléron had made his way around the room back to her, Lise's mood was so good that she was able to smile at the captain—in a suitably appreciative fashion—as she spoke with him. It didn't bother her any more that she couldn't make sense of the change in her response to the captain. She might, she supposed, let him continue to woo her. But he would never have the hold on her he had once had. Most young men grew up; in the time since her encounter with the duc de Bellevasse at the ball, poor Captain d'Oléron seemed to have become younger.

⚜

"Is it a curse, or is it a Blessing?" Lise looked at her friend from the corner of her eye. "I don't feel cursed, Marguerite, unless you count headache as a curse."

"Sometimes I do." Marguerite giggled. "I'm sorry, Lise, but it's really hard for me to see you this way and not laugh."

A Poisoned Prayer
February

"I have the same problem, and I can't even see myself!" Lise looked down at the breeches, gold-threaded stockings, and red high-heeled shoes. "Well, I can't see my face, at any rate." She was dressed in Robert's clothes again, her breasts bound and the false moustache glued to her lip; in this guise she had collected Marguerite and her maid to go for a walk, the better to further test the theory she had developed about what had been happening to her since coming to Paris. "You'll note, Marguerite, that as silly as we think I look, nobody else is paying me the slightest attention."

"And is that fair?" Marguerite giggled again, vainly trying to stifle the sound by putting her hand in front of her mouth.

"I happen to think it is. Though I suppose you're right, too, and it's not fair that men have so much freedom of movement in this city, and we women are little more than prisoners most of the time. I wonder if I could persuade Robert to slip away to the family estates, so that I could be him all the time, and see all of Paris that I want to see, without fear of my aunts committing me to the Bastille or a convent."

"What do you want to see of Paris that you can't already?" Poor Marguerite really did seem to be perplexed at Lise's desire for more freedom, and she wondered how she could explain herself without appearing to be mad. *Would I be happier if my own desires were as narrow as hers?*

"Well," she began, "look at what we're going to be doing in a few minutes. Dressed as my cousin, I'll be able to climb around the old walls to my heart's content. All you'll be able to do is stand on the street and watch me—and then only because you've got your maid here as a chaperon."

"But why would I want to climb around the walls?"

"All right, perhaps you wouldn't. But I want to, and in a

dress I'd probably be arrested or something if I tried. You have to try it, Marguerite, before you can properly judge it. I feel so wonderfully free in this costume. Without it, I would probably never be able to come to any useful conclusion about my...condition."

"Your curse," Marguerite said. "Or not."

"I'd love to be able to call it a Blessing," Lise said, taking Marguerite's hand to assist her across a muddy street. "But it doesn't seem to *do* anything."

"Except give you headache."

"And when prayers are uttered, I wonder who it is who is doing the uttering. It might even be that I can tell when those prayers are heard and responded to by God." As Lise spoke these words she looked at her friend; Marguerite's eyes opened in a fashion Lise thought encouraging. *At least she's not going to report me to the Inquisition.* "So I have two questions. First: is my guess about this correct? And second: does it qualify as a Blessing if it doesn't actually have any effect on the physical world, the way Rabbi Weiss told me Blessings are supposed to?"

"You'll have to ask that rabbi person about your second question. Or you could ask a priest about it, I suppose. Though I'm not sure how safe that might be."

"I agree with you about that. Marguerite, you're the only person I've breathed a word to about this. Please promise me to keep it a secret—from everyone—until I say otherwise."

"Of course, dear!" Marguerite reached out to hug her, remembered how Lise was dressed, and let her hand drop limply to her side, a perplexed expression on her face.

"Thank you." Lise pointed up the street. "The Temple," she said. "There's a gate there, and where there's a gate there are ward-stones."

"Yes?"

A Poisoned Prayer
February

"Do you recall my ... accident near St-Germain, when we were shopping for a dress for me?" The traffic through the gate wasn't unusually heavy, and Lise hoped this would mean nobody would pay much attention to a young man should he suddenly start climbing the ruins of the old wall.

"How could I forget? You were so ill, Lise! And then that wicked duc de Bellevasse came to our aid and brought you home."

Lise kept her expression carefully neutral. Her feelings for the duc—Rafael—had changed considerably since that day; it felt as if some other person entirely had been hurt by the duc's indifference. Now, of course, there was a whole other level of concern to occupy her mind where the man was concerned, but she suppressed all those thoughts and instead smiled at Marguerite. "Well, I think that what happened to me was that I was near an especially strong source of magic. The headache it caused was so strong it made me faint."

"But Lise, that doesn't make sense. Those ward-stones are *old*. They haven't held any magic since my great-grandparents were children. If you do have this... condition, the ward-stones couldn't be responsible for what happened to you."

"They could," Lise said, "if someone were pouring magic back into them."

⚜

The weather had soured while Lise and Marguerite visited the Marquise de Réalmont's salon. Lise hadn't objected at first; the day had been a good one and a bit of inclement weather wouldn't detract from it. Before visiting the marquise, Lise had completed a very successful investigation at the Temple gate—she was in no doubt that the Paris ward-stones were being tampered with in some way—and the visit to the salon had seen her the object of an unexpected amount of attention from a lawyer who seemed impressively well-off, even if he hadn't yet been able to buy himself a title.

A few minutes in the raw late afternoon weather took some of the shine off her day, though, and she found herself walking at a faster and faster pace as the afternoon lapis lazuli sky gave way to something pewter and sullen, threatening snow. *I may have to break into my savings and hire a chair,* she thought.

She did not notice the man until he was right in front of her and his hands were on her shoulders, pushing her across the sidewalk and against the façade of a building. "What in heaven's name are you doing?" she shouted when breath and sense returned to her. Ahead of her she could see Juliette struggling as a pair of lackeys pushed her further away from her mistress. Juliette had a strong, carrying voice, and one of the lackeys clapped his hand over her mouth.

"Shut up, idiot girl, and listen to me." The man whose face thrust itself so close to hers was, she realized, the elder d'Audemar son, Guillaume. His breath stank of wine and burnt tobacco. "You are putting yourself at risk when you associate yourself with that bastard de Bellevasse. If you know what's good for you, you'll avoid him in future."

"What are you talking about? I hardly know the man!"

"Shut up! I'm not stupid! I saw you with him just the other day in St-Germain! And do you think that your ludicrous spectacle at the Tuilleries Palace went completely unnoticed?" D'Audemar tightened his grip on her shoulders. "I was told you were reasonably clever, for a woman. Show me some of those brains, and do yourself and your aunt a favour."

A Poisoned Prayer
February

"What does my aunt have to do with this? She hates de Bellevasse." Lise struggled under his grip, but his hands were unpleasantly strong. *If I were a man I'd have a sword on my hip,* she thought, *and he wouldn't dare put his hands on me.*

"What you do reflects on her," d'Audemar said. "Nothing in this city stays hidden for long. Sooner or later our sins are visited upon us and on our families. Think about that the next time you feel compelled to prostitute yourself to that demon-spawn bastard."

"What did you just call me?"

"Was I not speaking clearly enough, Mademoiselle Putain?" He grinned evilly. "This is the only warning you'll get, you stupid slut. Stay away from de Bellevasse or your family will suffer the consequences." He released his grip on her, stepped back two paces and ran north into the late afternoon gloom. His lackeys followed, with Juliette howling abuse after them.

Lise could not move. Shaking, she pressed back against the building, sure she was going to be sick. A single thought circled through her mind, turning on itself until it filled her awareness: *He could have killed me, had he wanted to, and there was nothing I could have done to stop him.*

The feeling of cold on her forehead brought her back to the world. "I came as fast as I could, mademoiselle," Juliette said. She dabbed the wet cloth onto Lise's forehead again. "Why doesn't the emperor do something about people like that? Nobody should attack young ladies in the street. It's a sin!"

You're right about that, Lise said to herself. Aloud she said, "Thank you, Juliette. Please find a chair for me. I'm not sure I can walk home from here."

At the entrance to her building, the concierge called her

as she exited the hired chair. "This package has just come for you, mademoiselle." He handed her something soft, wrapped in heavy paper; a page, folded and sealed, was tied to the package. The seal wasn't embossed, but Lise was pretty sure she knew who had placed it. She snapped the wax and unfolded the page.

The handwriting was tall, narrow, with a pronounced slant. It suggested a man in a hurry.

My dear Mademoiselle de Trouvaille, he'd written, *please accept this small token of my appreciation for the skill you have recently shown me. I would be honoured if you would present yourself, in the guise of my cousin from Picardy, at my hôtel tomorrow morning. While you show admirable courage, your technique is rusty. Bellevasse.*

The package contained a suit of men's clothes. "Thank you, Mother Mary," she whispered, "for answering my prayer so promptly."

※

She didn't think she'd got the moustache on completely straight, but looking at herself in the mirror, Lise was at least confident that in this latest disguise nobody would mistake her for cousin Robert. *My days of impersonating family are done with,* she decided.

She waited until the concierge was busy shifting a bucket of water for another tenant before slipping out the gateway, then made her way quickly off the island, onto the right bank and west past the Hôtel de Ville. *At least if I'm to be a country cousin,* she told herself, *I can gawk at will, and not worry about looking a fool.*

Rafael lived in an older part of the city, uncomfortably close to the Palais Cardinal but tantalizingly near the Tuileries palace, the emperor's primary residence when he was in Paris. The Hôtel Bellevasse wasn't quite as large as

A Poisoned Prayer
February

her aunt's Hôtel Vimoutiers, but somehow it managed to look more imposing. The stone walls, blackened in their upper reaches by centuries' worth of smoke, were at street level worn to an almost glazed smoothness, as though polished anxiously by generations of clients waiting for admittance.

Lise wasn't made to wait. "If you're not careful," Rafael said, looking up from his book as she was escorted into his library, "you're going to find yourself permanently employed in the theatre, making actors look like what they aren't. You are even more convincing this morning, mademoiselle, than you were yesterday." Lise was at first startled—he had seen her at the gate, had seen through her disguise again?—but couldn't suppress a happy grin; *Could it be that I'm no judge of what a man should look like?*

"Of course," he added, deflating her mood instantly, "it could just be that you're not trying to look like your ridiculous cousin that impresses me."

He set down his book—it was a slender volume, she noted, and at least part of the page she'd seen had been filled with some strange and angular script—and stood. "It's time, I think. I have a busy day ahead of me, so we should get to your lesson right away."

Lise felt what she knew to be an unjustified pang of disappointment. *I wanted to talk first*, she thought. *What's that book you're reading? How did you see through the disguise yesterday—and at Respire's, for that matter? How often do nobles attack each other magically, and how dangerous is it when they do?*

The room he took her to was a large salon. Whether it was used for entertaining she couldn't tell: this morning what furniture there was in the room was covered and pushed back against the walls. On a sideboard along the far wall, metal glinted in the pale light that snuck in through a window. Swords, Lise saw, of varying lengths.

Rafael led her to the sideboard. "Your rapier gives you an advantage in terms of reach," he said. "But it's heavy, and you don't seem to have the strength in your upper body that a man your height would have. So you tire quickly."

"I thought I had enough endurance," she said. "I've never tired when practicing at home. That fight the other night just went on too long, that's all. I was trying not to kill d'Audemar."

He grinned. "Fine words." He picked up two swords and handed them to her. "But the fight only seemed long to you. It always does, when you're in it. Really, it was a matter of a few minutes. And anyway, you're not good enough yet to be able to toy with an opponent. If you find yourself forced into a fight, end it as quickly as you can. If he dies, serves him right for giving you no choice. God will take care of him, if he's led a good life." He paused; when she looked up she saw him staring at her hands as she picked up one sword after the other. "Which of those is most comfortable? Try each one in both hands."

"I like this one," she said without hesitation, lifting the point of an épée. "It has good balance."

"They're both well-balanced," he said. "That one is a bit less heavy. I told you that was your problem."

"But now I have another problem. This blade is so short! I know my arms aren't long."

"They're long enough, if you know what you're doing. Who taught you the sword?"

"My grandfather." She was prepared to defend Grandfather's reputation against any slur Rafael might propose, and the words emerged in a sullen tone she hadn't heard from herself in years.

A Poisoned Prayer
February

Rafael backed away, his hands raised in mock horror. "Don't be that way," he said. "I meant no disrespect. I should have guessed that your instructor was an older man. I didn't recognize the school, but some of your thrusts and parries probably haven't been seen in Paris since before the last war."

"They seemed to work well enough."

"Very true. In fact, now that I think of it, an older style will aid in your disguise. It's just the sort of thing a country cousin would do, fighting in an ancient style." He paused, eyes glazing as he stared at the sword in her hand. "Though I'm damned if I can think how I can teach you much, if we're to keep your style from looking too modern."

"Wouldn't you teach a cousin what you could, and not worry about whether you were corrupting his 'ancient' style?" She couldn't suppress a grin.

"The results will look hideous, and will probably bring shame on my family. But I don't suppose you'd mind that too much."

"You suppose correctly, monsieur."

"Very well. Let's begin, then. You guard fairly well, but there are some thrusts coming into vogue in this city that your current skills might not be able to save you from. You'll have to recognize and learn to anticipate them." He stepped to her side, put his left arm around her, gripping her waist, and seized her right wrist with his other hand.

A shock went through her, and she flushed. It was impossible to believe that he hadn't noticed her shake. *I thought I knew what* want *felt like,* she thought. *Obviously I didn't know anything.* This was a feeling far more intense than she'd ever experienced in her tumblings with boys back home, and for a moment she was terrified that it would overpower her, rendering her completely incapable of responding in any way that would bring her credit.

Soon, though, and to her immense relief, she began to feel a distance from the intensity of the sensation, as though she were somehow floating above herself. She became conscious—on a level that was more than physical, lustful—of a smooth strength guiding her through the motions of guard, parry, thrust. Rafael seemed simultaneously new and ancient, his presence a marvelous discovery and something she had somehow always known. The tingle and churn of desire conflated with the stretch and strain of physical exertion, and seemed to melt into a single soul-releasing pleasure that intensified even as her exhaustion grew and her arms and legs began to ache. Fragments of prayers crept into her thoughts and tumbled together, flashes of light bursting behind her eyes whenever the power of the words managed to draw something from Lise's meagre store of magical Blessing.

Rafael became a more tangible presence again when the arm around her suddenly tightened, pulling her back against him. "Enough," he said, and she was surprised to hear exhaustion, or something like it, in his voice. "You nearly fell there, and that's dangerous when you're carrying a blade."

Something stung her eye, and she reached up to wipe the sweat away. "Hold," he said, and she realized she still held the épée. "Allow me." He gently pressed her arm back down, then lifted his own hand to her face. He was, she realized, using the mirror they faced to guide him. A finger brushed against the corner of her eye, and Lise held her breath. She did not recognize herself in the mirror, and for a moment it seemed as if she was stealing a forbidden glimpse of two other people.

A Poisoned Prayer
February

At that thought the molten rush hit her again and she had to close her eyes. She sank back against Rafael, and was rewarded with the sound of his sudden intake of breath. His hand came back, and now the tips of several fingers were stroking her cheek. Bells rang, and his other hand was on her hip, steadying her against him. It took a moment for her to realize that the ringing sound had come from her sword, which had fallen from her hand.

The hand on her hip shifted her, and the hand on her cheek tilted her head back and to the side, and he kissed her. The room seemed close, the humidity indistinguishable from the sweat. She could feel now she was no longer moving. Something seemed to be buzzing in her ear.

It was Rafael. He was laughing.

"God," he said, sputtering. "If that's what kissing a man with a moustache feels like to a woman, I'm going to shave mine off first thing tomorrow."

Drawing back a bit, Lise traced the false moustache with a finger. She'd forgotten she wore it. "Not on my account, monsieur," she said. It wasn't necessarily a pleasant sensation, feeling that curious combination of stiffness and softness on her upper lip, but she was pretty sure she could get used to it.

"As you wish," he said, and while there was laughter in his voice there was a huskiness as well. "For me, my wish is for that thing to be gone. It distracts me." He raised a hand, thumb and forefinger pursed together, toward her face.

"I think," she said, hurriedly interposing her own hand, "that I had best do it myself. The glue hurts sometimes," she added by way of explanation.

A tentative pull proved that she had been a touch too generous with the glue this morning. She had to disengage herself from Rafael's embrace and turn her back to him, closing her eyes, before she could work up the courage to pull the false moustache away. She did it in one swift tug—there didn't seem to be a better way to do it—and couldn't suppress a small cry at the pain as the glue finally gave way.

He put his hands on her shoulders and turned her around again to face him while she was still wincing and blinking back the tears that had sprung to her eyes. "Poor little fox," he murmured. "Can I make you forget the discomfort?" He planted the most chaste of kisses on the tender skin beneath her nose, and this time the feel of his moustache was soft, reassuring.

She realized that this was not what she wanted. Wrapping her arms around him, she pulled him down into a deep, open-mouthed kiss that had nothing chaste about it. *This is how to stop thinking about pain*, she thought.

She seemed to have sprung some sort of lock. Rafael's grip on her shoulders tightened for a moment, then his arms went around her back, one dropping down to force her hips against him. His mouth was still soft against hers, but now there was a pressure that threatened to overwhelm her. She tried to make herself think about what he was doing—*How is he doing that with his mouth? Where exactly is his right hand, and how much pressure is he putting on the small of my back? I may have to do this myself if I wind up having to defend my imposture against one of Robert's type of woman*—but it was impossible to concentrate. So she let herself be overwhelmed by sensation, and left thought to fend for itself.

He tasted of spices, something rich and a little sweet. His tongue sliding, thrusting against hers was startling in the intensity of the sensations it invoked. Every contact seemed to generate a corresponding spark between her legs, sparks that made the pressure of his body on hers delicious and simultaneously not enough. She felt an absurd desire to force herself into him, to merge not just their physical forms but their souls.

The pressure slackened; she realized his hand was tugging at the cloth of her sweat-soaked shirt. She loosened her grip on his upper back to give him space, and he broke the kiss.

For a moment they just stared at each other. He seemed to be having as much trouble with his breathing as Lise did. Then he smiled crookedly. "Forgive my clumsiness. If you were wearing skirts I would know exactly what to do."

Lise laughed, and was impressed at how deep and throaty she sounded in her own ears. "I think you have the knack of it pretty well, monsieur." She felt a kiss of moving air as a part of the shirt came out of the waistband of her breeches, and then the heat of his hand against the skin of her belly; she could not suppress her gasp of surprised pleasure.

"I asked you once before if I should stop," he said. "I will ask you once more—"

"No."

He smiled. "I will not ask again." He leaned back a little, looking into her eyes. "You perplex me, mademoiselle. In fact, your mode of dress is probably entirely appropriate: it, and you, are completely outside the bounds of what I understand to be normal. You are shaking me up."

"How is it," she asked, "that you can talk such nonsense and still move your hand about that way?"

"I had a very broad and extensive education," he said. "The priests said I would either travel very far indeed, or make the shortest of journeys up to the scaffold."

"No priest taught you that," she said as his fingernail scratched lightly across her ribs, and then he was kissing her again, hard this time, and his hand was hot in the small of her back.

For a few moments Lise let herself be swallowed up by sensation that blocked out the world. Rafael's hands alternately stroked and pressed her back, sides, belly as they moved to and fro against each other; from time to time she could feel his fingernails scratching his frustration with the cloth that bound her breasts. At some level she was aware that they were moving, a slow dance that seemed almost drunken in its haphazard progress—but to where?

Then she was being lowered onto her back and his lips were on her throat and shoulders and chest; his hands fumbled, then tore at the binding cloth until it came away. She was, she realized, on a chaise—*did we leave the ballroom?*—and now Rafael's mouth was on her breast and he was saying "Let me make this even better"—

And then something wild and powerful and horrific sawed into her brain. The heat and glorious sensation were gone and she felt the need to scream but couldn't. Her last thought, when oblivion overtook her, was that death would be preferable to what Rafael was doing to her.

Two

LISE PULLED THE quilt up to her chin. *Why is it so cold? Why hasn't Juliette made the fire?* Then she remembered where she was. A moment later, her head began to ache.

The room was gloomy. A glance at the window told her that while it was while it was technically still day, dark clouds that promised snow to come had choked off most of the daylight. A glance in the opposite direction revealed an elderly woman in servant's dress watching her with the perplexed apprehension of a father at a birthing. When the woman realized that Lise was looking at her, her eyebrows lifted and she started up out of her chair.

"What happened to me?"

The woman bowed her head nervously, jerkily. "You was sick, mademoiselle. The master, he didn't know what to do. So he and his man—that would be Alain—put you here. Then they called me to undress you and clean you up and watch over you."

"Clean me up?"

"Like I said, mademoiselle. You was sick."

"Oh." *Just the way I was in St-Germain.* And she knew what had happened to her. "Where is—is the duc?"

"Don't know, mademoiselle. In his library, most like. I don't go there myself. Off limits to us in the kitchen. To everyone but the master, Alain, François, and Master's uncle, really."

"How do I get there from here?"

The woman looked so unhappy at this that Lise wondered if it wouldn't be easier to let the headache guide her. But she didn't know enough about how her curse worked to know if she could trust herself to be led that way. "I will find it myself if I have to," she said.

"Down one floor and opposite end of the house," the woman said. "But wouldn't you rather I sent word you was up?"

"It's not necessary." Lise got out of bed, briefly amused to find herself wearing an old night-shirt. *His? More likely it belongs to that "man" of his. What was his name? Alain.* "I thank you for watching me, madame." A gesture with her head dismissed the old woman.

"Just doing what I was told," the woman muttered as she went through the door. "Nothing good going to come of this," she added as she was closing the door behind herself.

"You're probably right about that," Lise said to herself.

Her mannish clothes had been crudely folded and sat on top of a very ancient-looking chest of drawers. Well, none of the women in this house—and it was doubtful there were many of those, if Rafael lived alone—would know anything of a maid's duties. It was bitterly cold in this room, but she did not allow herself the luxury of dressing beneath the bed-clothes. The way she felt, to return to bed would be to surrender to the Curse and its headache.

As she shrugged into shirt and breeches she thought, *If I were better Blessed, I could warm myself and this room and not need a fire.* Perhaps that was why Rafael hadn't bothered to have a fire set here. *Why did he go? And what did he do to me?*

A Poisoned Prayer
February

There was only one way to find out; she walked to the door and pulled it open, taking care to make as little noise as possible. The short walk convinced her that this house was too cold to make going barefoot a workable proposition; something, though, made her leave the solid shoes where they sat by the unlit fire, and she satisfied herself with pulling on the thick woollen stockings Rafael had given her.

A single *torchiere* at the near end of the hall provided the only respite from a near-darkness that seemed to generate its own cold. Walking toward the light, though, Lise felt her headache lessening. *Interesting,* she thought. *Perhaps I can follow my pain.* Nevertheless, she continued forward to the nearest stair. And when she had reached the next floor down and started along the hall. It seemed the pain increased a little with each step.

The pain, when she found Rafael after what felt like a quarter-hour of wandering through the chilly hôtel, was so intense she could scarcely keep her eyes open and focused on the door to the room in which he hid. It took all her will to grip the knob and turn it.

The room in whose threshold she stood was a library, and some small safe part of her mind told Lise that it was a nice one, easily the most lived-in looking of the rooms she'd seen here. Rafael sat at the far end of the room, his back to her. She guessed that he was sitting, at any rate: he seemed to be floating in the midst of some sort of magical sea, and the rippling and flickering of the blue-green fluid that surrounded him—if fluid was what it was—obscured most of his lower torso. He was chanting, and though she could hear him little more clearly here than she had in the bedroom, she was sure it wasn't French he was speaking.

Movement from behind her caught her eye, and she

turned to find herself being glared at by a cat. She flushed, as though she'd been caught trespassing. Then she saw the cat's eyes more clearly, and knew where she'd seen them before.

The tail flicked once, twice.

Rafael's voice assaulted her ears; whatever had been muffling it disappeared or lost its power. Turning back, Lise was horrified to see the Devil's sea expanding, reaching out to her. She heard her gasp in her ears, but there was no sense that the sound had actually left her mouth; turning, she reached for the door, but the door was not there. It had vanished, apparently, with the cat. And the room. The house.

The distorting waters disappeared as well, before she had been given any sense of their true nature. The green-blue light was gone too, and what was left was no lavender dusk; she could see only a sickly orange in the velvet-black distance, suggesting the poor light of a torch.

She was seated. Or, rather, the spirit to which she had apparently been fused was seated. *A chair,* she realized. *This is a sedan chair.* She had gone elsewhere, apparently—and else-when, as well, because the night (if night it was) was mild, more late summer than midwinter.

The body she was in shook, and Lise was aware of a hand reaching out to grab for support. She heard gasping and choking sounds from outside; the hand pulled back the curtain.

The dark shape that filled the window, darker than the starry night, would have frightened Lise had she not seen the building just yesterday. *This is the Temple,* she thought. *But what is happening?*

Then the sedan door flew apart, and Lise felt a horrified, chilling numbness, followed instantly by searing heat.

A Poisoned Prayer
February

Something assaulted Lise's senses, something wild and awful. If prayer as Rafael practiced it was as old cognac, powerful but subtle in its way, then this assault was by the equivalent of the rawest, fiercest of marcs. As this perverse prayer battered her mind and that of the woman she occupied, and swords came from out of the dark and pierced the body, Lise screamed.

She shifted in pain. She was on the carpeted floor; looking up, she saw Rafael standing over her, staring down with an expression she could not understand—and hoped never to see again.

"It's true, isn't it?" she said, getting to her feet with as much speed as she could muster—and that was not much. "You really do practice death-magic."

His face softened, and he reached to help her up. "What in God's name are you doing here?" he asked.

She felt the pain beginning again. "No!" she said, clutching her hands to her temples. Then, realizing how loudly she had shouted, she added, "I am sorry. But please—no more prayer. I can't stand anymore."

"I was trying to help," he said.

"Believe me," she said, "it's not helping."

Then, before he could say anything more, she ran out of the room and back down the hall.

If he tried to follow her, he did not succeed. Lise retrieved her shoes and escaped from the house without seeing Rafael again. The servant, the man she had decided was Alain, was the only one to see her leave.

⚜

Lise was able to keep herself from crying. But it was harder to avoid despising herself. Why had she persuaded herself that there was no truth to the rumours about Rafael?

Everything she had heard and seen had argued that it was all true. Why had she let him kiss her today—much less touch her the way he had—when he had been so maddeningly inconsistent in his treatment of her?

She found herself shaking her head. It would be easy to believe that he didn't actually care that much for her, that the experience had merely constituted a physical release for him. But her experience of men, while perhaps not deep by Parisian standards, was still deep enough to argue that the way he had looked at her, and laughed with her, meant more than just lustful indulgence. And while it was true that he had made her ill to the point of unconsciousness—twice—she could hardly blame him for that. He didn't know the nature of her Curse.

She was, she realized, no surer about Rafael now than she had been the night she'd met him. That there was something between them she did not doubt. That her family would be horrified by her interest in him was equally certain. *At least I have a better idea now why he's never married,* she thought.

She refused to allow herself to wallow in the sort of self-pity that other women indulged themselves in, though; as she walked along the Rue St-Honoré she found herself becoming increasingly irritated with Rafael's attitude. As much as he'd be appalled by the comparison, he was very much like Cousin Robert—who would likewise doubtless be appalled at the comparison. Why did men all have to be so selfish?

Passing by a ground-level shop window, she caught her reflection in it and paused. That was an unpleasant expression, she decided, and it signified an unproductive state of mind. *Don't waste time grumbling or being frustrated,* she told herself. *Do something about it.*

A Poisoned Prayer
February

⚜

Lise pulled the coverlet up to her chin. It was cold in the bedroom, but Juliette had been in bed for a long time and it didn't seem fair to punish her back into wakefulness just because her mistress couldn't sleep.

It was too bad that Lieutenant-General de La Reynie had been out of his office when she had called. She should not have wasted time coming home to change back into her dress before going to see him. Now it would be tomorrow at the earliest before she could ask him about the wardstones.

But that was not the thing keeping her awake. *Stop trying to fool yourself,* she thought. *It's Rafael, and it has been since you left his hôtel. And you know what the problem is, too.*

"I can't see you again," she whispered. She looked at the dying fire, and thought it looked appropriate to the sentiment.

I'm not being dramatic, she told herself. *I'm being practical.* The problem, which she should have admitted the night he'd first kissed her, was that while he was exciting and clever and certainly knew his way with a woman, he could never be more than a distraction for her. And distraction was precisely what she didn't need right now.

A husband, she told herself. *You're here to find a husband. If you want distraction, look for it once you've ensured you have a future.*

Worse than a distraction, in fact. It now occurred to her that if she became Rafael's mistress, and anyone learned it—and how could they not?—then he would at best get in the way of any potential suitors, and at worst he would serve as an active impediment. *I can just imagine what Aunt de Vimoutiers would say about that.*

She should be working more closely with her aunt. She should follow her aunt's advice; what of the men her aunt had been proposing as possible matches? There was also the lawyer at the Marquise de Réalmont's salon.

What of Captain d'Oléron?

She sighed into the coverlet. She had dismissed him too easily, it seemed. The captain's behaviour had never been anything less than friendly, at least in their meetings since that awkward introduction. And lately, it seemed that he had been increasingly solicitous of her. Should she perhaps take him more seriously, despite the fact she found him more amusing than arousing?

And that's exactly the kind of attitude that always gets you into trouble.

Sighing, she folded back the coverlet. There was a jug of wine in the sitting room; it would still have a cup or two left in it, and it was obvious she wasn't going to get to sleep tonight without some sort of assistance. She got out of bed, suppressing a shriek when her feet touched the cold floor.

⚜

Lise wasn't entirely sure of what sort of reaction she had hoped for from Marguerite, but she was certain that it hadn't been the reaction with which she was presented. She had gone to the Marquise de Réalmont's salon, the afternoon following her late-night decision about Rafael, hoping for at least a comforting hug. Instead, all Marguerite could say was: "I envy you your freedom, Lise," in a voice that was as thin and dull as cheap pewter. "You can do anything, it seems. And I—" She paused for a series of shuddering breaths, finally seeming to regain control of her emotions—but not her powers of speech, for she did not finish the sentence.

"What is it, Marguerite?" Lise asked after waiting politely for clarification that did not come.

"My father tells me I am likely to be married soon," she said, and the effort of saying the words evidently required the strength she'd been using to hold in the tears. "It's funny, in a way," she said, her soft voice denying that humour could ever exist again. "You have been learning fencing from the duc de Bellevasse. And even if you are determined not to see him again, I am, it seems, going to become his aunt."

"What?"

Lise was surprised to find that Marguerite's speechlessness was communicable. She tried to elaborate, to make the demand less abrupt, but words would not come.

"My father is negotiating with Bertrand de Montauban. That man we met at your aunt's place, de Bellevasse's uncle by marriage. He's a widower—his wife was murdered, you know. Because he's also a cousin of the Prince d'Aude, I would be marrying into the d'Audemar family. They're suitably powerful for my father."

Lise's first wild thought was that perhaps this marriage might throw her back into Rafael's company without her being responsible for that. The selfishness of this indulgence was soon clear to her, though, and she smiled, putting an arm around Marguerite's shoulder. "Isn't that good news? You've said you wanted a good marriage, and this sounds like all you wanted."

"I suppose," Marguerite said, wiping tears from her cheeks. "And it's not as if he's horribly old or anything. He's just a few years older than his nephew." She smiled. "I suppose I've just been enjoying my flirtations, and yours, and I don't want to give them up. I am not sure I'm ready to be married. And—and it was a shock to me, that's all."

A hearty laugh from the entry hall announced the arrival of Captain d'Oléron, and Lise realized what flirtations her friend was going to miss. Turning to face Marguerite, she quietly said, "I shouldn't worry about flirtations, you know. A good marriage doesn't have to be the end of love, Marguerite."

"But Lise—Mama tells me that d'Oléron is likely to offer for you!" The tears started afresh, and Lise thought, *And this is what's really upsetting you, isn't it?* Then Marguerite added, "I don't see how you could—I don't think that I could bring myself to just toss my own husband to whatever amour he happened to want to keep seeing. I would be miserable, I think. Wouldn't I?" And Lise felt horrible for what she'd thought.

Then Captain d'Oléron joined them, and the opportunity to comfort Marguerite disappeared. The captain, as seemed to be the way with men, looked confused and uncomfortable from time to time, as though he had determined that something was wrong with Marguerite or Lise, but couldn't work out what it was, much less whether it was something he'd done. Still, his presence seemed to cheer Marguerite and that was enough to persuade Lise to not only endure the awkwardness but even to offer the captain the occasional word of encouragement.

When he had finally gone—whether it was for good or merely to relieve himself, Lise didn't care—Lise turned back to Marguerite. "He hasn't offered for me, Marguerite, and even if he did I have to be honest with you: I don't think I love him, as good-looking and nice as he is. Anyway, I think you're putting the carriage ahead of the horses. Who knows how our marriages will go, Marguerite—or even who I'll marry."

Marguerite, evidently still warmed by the glow of the captain's presence, smiled. "You're right, of course. So sensible—you're a good friend, Lise." Her smile broadened. "Besides, it might not anyway come to pass. Father tells me that de Montauban hasn't promised anything yet. And the marquise told me that he is actually offering himself to *two* women—do you believe it?"

"Really?" Now, this is interesting. I might be able to learn something from these negotiations. "Who is it?"

"Nobody you want to know, Lise. Trust me. If what Madame de Réalmont tells me is true, if de Montauban doesn't take me it will be some *bourgeoise*! The family's called Serre, and they're in the wine trade." She widened her eyes. "Can you imagine? Me or a wine-seller's daughter? I think I should be offended, were I not hoping with all my heart that her money is worth more than my dowry and name."

"Well, that's something you can pray for, Marguerite, if you really want to. Let this daughter of the grape have all the luck, then."

Three

"Perhaps I should become a fisherman," Nicolas de La Reynie said. "I seem to be developing an expertise at drawing things from the water. As I understand it, fishermen also do their best work when the day is still young."

He pulled his cloak tighter around his throat, flexing his fingers as he did so in the hope that they would warm a little. Was he simply getting old, or was this winter really lasting longer than it had any right to?

"Will I get into trouble if I point out that you did not actually draw this unfortunate girl from the water? Nor that servant the other day, if your comment was in reference to him." Valentin looked tired, and de La Reynie felt a second's guilt for his own self-pity. Valentin had been out here a lot longer.

"She's connected with the servant, in a way. Isn't she?" He smiled at Valentin, a smile he didn't feel. "Your note said you'd already identified her, and since you don't normally call me to these scenes unless you think it's especially significant, I suppose I should get right to the point and ask you why you think this young woman's death should be laid in the doorway of the duc de Bellevasse."

"She was about to marry his uncle."

"Who, de Montauban?" De La Reynie took a second look at the dead girl. She had been pretty, more or less. If you could ignore the vicious marks, now purple and blue, around her throat. "It hasn't been a year since his wife was killed, has it? Oh, but I recall your reports on de Bellevasse as saying the uncle was in desperate financial straits. A marriage would have brought in welcome coin, I suppose."

"But de Bellevasse couldn't stand the thought of his beloved aunt being abandoned by her husband," Valentin said. "Or he wanted to maintain his control over his uncle."

"I wonder if you aren't trying to force a round peg into a square hole," de La Reynie said. "It seems to me that de Bellevasse would have stood to gain if his uncle married into some money. The alternative is that de Montauban becomes a bigger and bigger drain on de Bellevasse's purse."

"But the loss of control," Valentin said. "That's a valid motive."

"And one that can be applied to others as well. I think you should get some sleep, my friend, before you try to think too much further on this case." De La Reynie extended a hand to Valentin and pulled him into a hug. "There is another family connection here you haven't explored," he added. "The servant you pulled from the river worked for the d'Audemars. Bertrand de Montauban is a distant cousin of old Simon. Perhaps we should be looking more deeply into that family's affairs, and leave young de Bellevasse's indiscretions to be dealt with by the cardinal's guard. My agent in de Bellevasse's household has reported nothing unusual from our hot-headed friend, and in fact I am told they emptied several bottles of Burgundy the other night in celebrating de Montauban's coming nuptials. Go to bed, Valentin. This will make more sense after some rest."

"I am tired," Valentin said. "And this has been worse than any of the other cases I've worked on lately. Dead servants, idiots knifed in tavern brawls—those I can deal with. A young girl is strangled for no good reason, that makes me angry. And I suppose it affects my mind; that and the tiredness."

"Don't worry. It happens to us all. Get some sleep and I guarantee you the world will look at least a little bit better." He looked back at the girl for what he hoped would be the last time. "You were able to identify her because of something she was wearing? Or did her family report her missing?"

"Both. There's a locket on a chain—a nice one, too, so this wasn't a robbery. And her father reported her missing late last night. They don't know how or why she left the house."

"The family?"

"Is *bourgeois*. Serre's the name."

"The *prevot des vins*." De La Reynie blew out a long, low whistle. "We'll be hearing from the *parlement*, I'm afraid."

"No doubt. The judges and merchant provosts are kindred spirits," Valentin said. "And there's more than just Serre's money at stake. Monsieur Serre has just lost his best chance at entrance into the nobility."

"To say nothing of a daughter."

⚜

As February shook off its covering of snow and shuffled towards March, word from both north and south was that the peasant uprising—the *Fronde*—was not only spreading, it was growing in audacity. The peasants had gone beyond attacking the emperor's tax collectors and were now—so the stories had it—abusing and even murdering those nobles who opposed them.

The idea of magic-deprived peasants attacking the

A Poisoned Prayer
February

Blessed was hard for Lise to believe. On the other hand, logic suggested that there were plenty of nobles in the empire whose Blessing was as meager as hers, who could be vulnerable to even the crudest of assaults. And even the most powerful magic could be defeated by enough metal, wielded with sufficient strength. That was the argument behind the creation of the emperor's musketeers, after all. And the chevalier d'Audemar had been warded as well, and yet she had still stabbed him.

The *Fronde* was not something that concerned her aunt, though. "Nor should you be worried, my girl," the duchesse said. They were drinking wine—the duchesse refused to serve coffee in her house, or to drink it anywhere—in a salon overlooking the garden in the hôtel de Vimoutiers's inner yard. "Not that I disapprove of women being interested in politics. I'm not one of *those* old women." Lise smiled, and the duchesse laughed. "But in the case of young, unmarried women, I fear that a little politics goes entirely too far." She sipped her wine. "You should be concerned with securing your position first. And while I agree that many men enjoy discussing politics with intelligent women, it is my sad duty to tell you, Lise, that unmarried men are seldom among this group." She bestowed a conspiratorial grin. "They're too unsure of themselves, you see, because their *own* positions aren't secure."

"What about widowed men, like Bertrand de Montauban?" Would he discuss politics with Marguerite? Had he even met Marguerite?

"Lise, I really do wish you would follow my advice and stay far away from that family. They are neither safe nor likable."

"I wasn't proposing to marry him, madame. I was merely curious whether widowed men are also so unsure of themselves that they're afraid to talk to young women about anything more substantial than the height of the emperor's heels this year."

The duchesse couldn't suppress a small giggle, but she also sighed heavily. "Lise, your vinegar tongue is going to prevent you from ever *meeting* eligible men, much less marrying them."

She smiled, with what looked like sympathy, or possibly regret. "I know you think most of the men you meet are weak, even disappointing. As it happens, I agree with you. But you must try harder to meet them part-way."

Weak? Lise thought about that word. *An interesting choice, Aunt. I would have said "dull," myself.* "It's not that," she said, setting her wine cup on a side table. "I'm just finding this a bit harder than I thought it would be."

"You dislike having to think of yourself as a commodity that men bid for. Well, none of us likes that, Lise." She paused, closing her eyes in concentration. Lise's cup filled, the dark surface of the wine shimmering. "So don't think of yourself in those terms. Think instead of how you're simply accelerating a process that God would eventually conclude the same way. I hear from that handsome Captain d'Oléron that you will scarcely give him the time of day."

Lise was startled by her aunt's directness, but recovered after only a moment's discomfort. Her aunt was, she reminded herself, as clever and determined as any military strategist, and whatever shock she had initially felt at the sudden flowering of the captain's interest in Lise, she seemed to have recovered well and now appeared to support the idea of his peculiar suit. Captain d'Oléron may have been part of the duchesse's promise to help Lise, but that didn't make him more attractive. In a curious way it made him less so.

A Poisoned Prayer
February

"I did not think I was being so cold," she said. "When he is polite to me I am very polite in response—I am not unaware of his suitability, Aunt. But I can hardly be blamed, madame, for failing to talk with the man at the Réalmont salon, when he so clearly can only focus on another woman."

"You refer, I presume, to your friend Marguerite." The duchesse sniffed, then took a sip of wine. She drank from a crystal glass rather than a cup, and Lise couldn't suppress a bit of envy when she saw pale winter sunlight sparkling through the glass, lightening the colour of the wine until it resembled cherry juice. "The captain has mentioned her to me. He tells me that he only speaks to her in the hope that by doing so he will be able to get closer to you. He also admitted that she flattered him, and no man is immune to the attentions of a pretty young woman. You should try that yourself sometime, Lise. Even if you're only pretending to be interested."

The only man I'm truly interested in has no need for pretend flattery, she thought. *Or for me,* her practical side insisted on adding.

⚜

That afternoon Lise went for a walk. It was only after she'd reached the Ile de la Cité that she realized how angry she was—and why. The last time she'd walked this far in the city she hadn't had to drag her maid along behind her, because she'd been wearing the young man's clothes that Rafael had given her. *And I'm supposed to be grateful,* she thought, *that I'm even allowed out at all.*

Lieutenant-General de La Reynie was on his feet, smiling in what presumably he thought was a friendly fashion, when Lise was escorted into his office. "My dear Mademoiselle de Trouvaille," he said. "I am pleased to see you again. Is it possible that you have remembered something about my missing man?"

Lise blushed; she had hardly thought of the man in weeks. "I'm sorry, but no. I wanted to see you because of something I noticed a few days ago."

"Was that you who so mysteriously visited me earlier? I was told a young lady had called on me, but you didn't leave your name. Next time, mademoiselle, please be more considerate."

"My apologies, monsieur; I had rather a lot on my mind at the time." *And you still do,* the vinegar voice in the back of her mind proclaimed, mocking her. *Why did you decide never to see him again?*

"I'm afraid I am rather busy these days. But I will certainly listen to you. Would you like some wine?"

"No, thank you." She swallowed a gulp of air; this was proving to be just as difficult as drawing a sword against d'Audemar. Possibly more difficult; against d'Audemar she hadn't had a choice. "Monsieur, I think that someone is recharging the ward-stones in the old city walls. Is this supposed to be happening?"

"What, the Augustinian walls? Those rock piles?"

"Yes." From the look on the policeman's face, Lise guessed that no, this wasn't supposed to be happening. "The walls might not stop a cannon shot, or even a determined herd of cattle. But if the ward-stones were activated, would the physical nature of the walls matter at all?"

"No." He stared at her—into her. "And how did you come by this information?"

"That's not easy to explain." She had, in fact, never come up with a suitable way of explaining it that didn't sound completely blasphemous. Only her despair at getting anyone to listen to her about this had brought her here.

"I know that it's asking a lot, but can I please have your word that you won't tell the cardinal or the Inquisition—especially the Inquisition—anything of what I'm about to tell you?"

"Are you asking me to pervert the course of justice, mademoiselle?"

"No, no! Nothing like that. It's a—it's a religious matter."

"If it doesn't involve the civil law, mademoiselle, you can count on my discretion."

"Thank you, monsieur." She took a deep breath. "What has happened is that I have somehow learned to feel magic. Or perhaps I always knew, but I have only recognized what it is I can do. And I can feel the magic in those stones, when I know they're supposed to be dead."

De La Reynie's eyes snapped shut for a second, and Lise could see his jaw working. *Should have kept my mouth shut,* she thought. Then her head began to ache, and she realized that she'd been watching him say a prayer without opening his mouth. A moment later the door to the office opened—there was no knock—and a younger man with a pinched face stood there, holding a sword. "What's the matter?" he asked.

"How did you call him?" Lise turned back to de La Reynie. "I've never heard of anyone being able to speak through prayer—to anyone but God, at any rate."

"I moved a small object in his office," de La Reynie said. "It's a signal we have. I'm sorry, Valentin, to have abused it," de La Reynie said to the pinch-faced man, who sheathed the sword with a look of tired relief, "but under the circumstances I couldn't think of anything else to do to test her."

"Test her? For what?"

"Come here and I'll explain it." De La Reynie beckoned

to the man he'd called Valentin, and then whispered something to him.

Immediately Lise felt the headache again, as God-light began to glow—but she was getting better at identifying what she'd begun to think of as the different voices praying, and this time she felt two different sorts of pressure in her head. "You both cast prayers that time, didn't you?"

The God-light abruptly went out. "How did you do that?" Valentin asked. His voice was sharp, accusatory. Inquisitional.

"Easy, friend," said de La Reynie, looking at Lise. "I don't think the young lady wants anybody passing judgment on her Blessing." He emphasized the latter word, and Lise was grateful. If de La Reynie called what she was enduring a Blessing, then perhaps she wasn't Cursed after all.

"Nevertheless," de La Reynie continued, "my associate's question is a valid one. You must explain yourself to us, mademoiselle. Please."

"I'm still learning about this myself," Lise said, hoping she sounded more confident than she felt. "I've always suffered from headache; the priest back home used to say it was from trying too hard to exceed the paltry Blessing I'd been given. For myself I always thought I was sensitive to my sister's Blessing and reacted badly to it." She felt her face flush. "I thought God was punishing me for my jealousy of my sister. But since coming to Paris I've been exposed to a lot more magic—and I've realized that not only am I sensitive to anyone's blessing, I seem to be able to tell one Blessing from another. Just now, I felt—well, I can't really say what it was I felt. I just knew there were two voices praying."

"You say you knew there were voices praying," de La

A Poisoned Prayer
February

Reynie said. "Were you able to tell what prayers were being spoken?"

"No." She felt herself blushing. "I can't tell. I can only tell that there's prayer. And how strong the Blessing is, I suppose, because my headaches are sometimes strong, sometimes not so strong." *And sometimes the opposite of ache entirely,* she thought, remembering the bliss she'd felt in the presence of the thoroughly warded emperor. *Will the walls make me feel that way, when the ward-stones are fully charged?*

"If you can't tell what prayers are being spoken, how do you know that the ward-stones are being re-charged?" Valentin clearly enjoyed his work, she decided.

"I guessed, monsieur. Just as I'm guessing that your prayer a moment ago was for light."

De La Reynie laughed. "Spoken like a policeman, mademoiselle. Still, while it wasn't all that hard to guess the prayer we were attempting—what impresses me is that you realized we were both praying—I have to think that it is a bit less obvious that the presence of magic at the old gates means that the ward-stones are being recharged."

"Only the fact that my headaches happen every time I pass the stones makes me think this," Lise said. Sometimes men were so slow to figure things out, and while her aunt's advice might be applicable where potential husbands were concerned, she wasn't attempting to persuade either of these men to marry her. There was something wrong in Paris; she was sure of it. Her job was to make these men equally sure.

"There's an easy way to test your theory," de La Reynie said. "Valentin, could you summon a priest?" Lise stiffened.

"No need for that, monsieur," Valentin said. "I know

the location of the appropriate books. I'll get the prayer myself."

"You're sure you can do it? It's not an especially easy prayer, I'm told."

"Sometimes brute strength can overcome a lack of dexterity," Valentin said. "And the strength of my Blessing is why you promoted me."

"One of the reasons, Valentin. One of them."

⁂

"Mother of God," Valentin said. "Who do you suppose is doing this, and why?"

Lieutenant-General de La Reynie waited until the man had safely climbed back down from the sloping rubble of the wall at the old Temple gate before asking, quietly, "So she was right, then?" Lise couldn't resist a smile of triumph, but it faded rapidly when she got a better look at the expression on Monsieur de La Reynie's face.

"It's true. It hasn't gone dangerously far, yet, and the stones wouldn't stop a child's wish at this point. But someone is definitely putting the spirit back into them." Valentin turned to Lise, and she saw now that the pinch-faced look he wore was a symptom of fatigue, not of disdain. *Is it really so hard,* she wondered, *to maintain order in this city?* "Restoring the stones isn't something that can be done quickly, or others would notice. Whoever is doing this is doing the equivalent of filling a wine barrel using a soup spoon." He turned back to his superior. "But if I've spoken the prayer properly, these two stones are just over half-charged. I can't say yet how rapidly they're being recharged, but I think we should probably take them out now, before they're put to use."

"Not yet," de La Reynie said. "Taking them out now tells whoever is doing this that we know what they're up to. I

A Poisoned Prayer
February

want a chance to find out what priest—or noble—is trying to restore the wards around Paris, and why." He bowed, low, to Lise. "Mademoiselle, we owe you a debt. I hope someday soon to be able to repay you. Thank you for bringing this to our attention." Turning back to Valentin, he said, "You are to keep a watch on this gate and the Porte St-Jacques. Let me know when they're three-quarters restored. If I haven't identified the culprit by then—"

"Culprits," Lise said. When the two men stared at her, she flushed and said, "I still can't explain how I know it, but I do know there are at least two different voices reading the prayers that are charging these stones."

"Without a proper explanation, it's hard for me to simply accept what you say," de La Reynie said. "But you did identify it when both Valentin and I cast our prayers in my office." His face had taken on a grey cast the made Lise feel unsure and perhaps even queasy. "As I was saying, Valentin, if I haven't identified whoever is behind this behaviour by that point, I will take steps to have the stones taken out." He flagged down a chair and helped Lise into it, ordering the bearers to take her wherever she wished, and submit the bill to him. The way he said this made Lise think that the chair-men, if they were wise, would undercharge. "Thank you again, mademoiselle. I thank you both for myself and on behalf of the emperor whose servant I am."

"I am just grateful that someone listened to me at last," she said.

"Oh?" His eyes locked on hers. "Have you mentioned this to others, then?"

"Well, yes. My cousin, Robert de Vimoutiers. And my friend Mademoiselle de Courçon. Nobody has taken me seriously. I don't know whether it's because I'm a woman or because they don't believe anyone would do such a thing.

And I don't know which of those reasons should make me angrier."

"I wouldn't worry about it, mademoiselle." De La Reynie looked dreadfully serious. "In fact, if I were you I would cease discussing this with anyone. Until I know more, I would appreciate it if you would treat this as an affair of state, and consider yourself sworn to secrecy."

"Oh!" Lise felt a flush, and sinking feeling, going through her. "Did I do something wrong by talking with the others?"

"No, mademoiselle, you couldn't have known. Now, however, you do."

⚜

"Lise, what in the world were you doing at the Porte du Temple this afternoon with that dreadful man de La Reynie?"

Lise looked up from the veal she'd been busying herself with, and understood why her aunt had been so insistent that she come for dinner today. "Who told you I was with Monsieur de La Reynie?" she asked.

"In my house, young woman, I ask the questions." The duchesse smiled, but it wasn't a happy smile. "Since you were so impertinent, though, I will tell you that no fewer than three of my friends have sent notes to me asking about this. God only knows how they learned of it."

Lise looked around the table. It was all family tonight; her aunt d'Ombrevilles gazed at her distractedly, while Robert seemed to be finding her discomfort amusing. *He's probably just grateful someone else is under attack*, Lise reminded herself. "I'm afraid I can't exactly tell you what I was doing, madame. Please forgive me."

"Can't tell me? Lise, what am I supposed to say to my friends? These are people who are important to your social success! They are also extremely sensitive to any hint of scandal. Do you really want to destroy your decreasing chances of making even a half-way decent match?"

"I'll bet you I know what it was about." Robert's grin had become unbearably smug, and Lise felt time beginning to slow, as awareness grew of what Robert was about to do to her. She tried to warn him off with a glare, but evidently he was too proud of his deduction to notice. "Honestly, Lise, did you really try to persuade de La Reynie to believe that ridiculous story of yours about the stones?"

"Stones? What stones? What story?" The duchesse turned on her son. "Robert, I swear with each day you become more and more obtuse!"

"It's nothing, madame," Lise said, looking down at her veal.

"She thinks someone's trying to restore the ward-stones in the old walls," Robert said. "I tried to tell her how silly that is, but evidently she didn't listen to me."

"I can't imagine why," Lise muttered.

"The walls?" The marquise d'Ombrevilles looked up from the plate she'd evidently been focused on. "Someone's rebuilding the old walls?" Her face, as she looked at Lise, seemed to sag, weighed down by some sadness.

"Not the walls, cousin," the duchesse said, with more acid than the older woman deserved. "Lise thinks someone is playing with the ward-stones. Ridiculous." She sniffed her derision, and Lise was glad for it: if people continued to refuse to believe her, and wanted to discuss only that refusal, they'd forget all about de La Reynie.

"Oh, that would be even worse," the marquise said. In a voice that held a hint of the sing-song cadence of childhood, she said, "When I was a very young girl, my grandmother told me stories of what it had been like to live in Paris during the civil war. In those days the faithful were fighting the Huguenots and the nobility fought amongst themselves. There were cannons in the streets. Those stories terrified me, so that I couldn't sleep. Eventually Mama told Grandmama to stop telling them to me."

She set down her fork, misjudging so that it clattered against the plate. "I would not like my Paris to go through that again," she said, in her grown-up voice now, but with surprising steel in it. "So I hope that you are wrong, Lise."

"Of course she's wrong," the duchesse said. She gestured to a servant, who spun on his heel and sped in the direction of the kitchen. "We will talk no more about it."

After dinner, though, Lise insisted on talking about it. "You have put me into an awkward situation, Robert," she said to her cousin, pitching her voice low enough that none of the others could hear.

"Oh, come now, Cousin Lise. It's not like you to be so overly dramatic." Robert grinned his pleasant, idiotic grin and Lise wanted to brain him with a candlestick.

"Robert," she said, trying to keep all inflection from her voice, "I have been talking about this with Lieutenant-General de La Reynie. He has confirmed the truth of what I suggested to you."

Robert goggled at her for a second, then he frowned. Or sneered; Lise often had trouble telling the expressions apart. "Lise," he said, "didn't Mama tell you that nothing good ever comes of involvement with the police? Why would you take such a tale to de La Reynie?"

"Because it's true, you idiot! It's happening: someone is pouring magic back into the old city ward-stones! And de La Reynie is taking this seriously enough that he warned me not to speak of it with anyone. And now you've gone and involved your mother and our Aunt d'Ombrevilles, because you couldn't resist making fun of me over dinner."

As soon as she'd finished Lise realized that she'd gone too far, but before she could apologize to Robert he was on his feet, a hand on each of her shoulders. "I'm so sorry, cousin," he said, head bowed. He took her arm in his, saying, "Let's take a walk." If anyone noticed them leaving the salon, nobody spoke.

The hall was much chillier than the salon had been—*or,* wondered Lise, *am I just a bit more frightened now?*

"I know I do that too much—talk before thinking, I mean—and I want you to know how sorry I am," Robert said. "It just seemed so ridiculous to me, Lise. Who would be doing such a thing, and why?"

"Well, you weren't the only one who thought it silly," Lise told him, squeezing his arm. "I told Marguerite, and even she wouldn't take me seriously. And de La Reynie and his man Valentin wouldn't believe me until I could demonstrate to them how I'd figured it out."

"Valentin? Oh, Lord. If the criminal investigation people are involved, then this really is serious. Wait," he said, stopping and turning to face her. "How *did* you figure it out?"

"I can't tell you that," she said, feeling helpless and even a bit stupid. "It's too dangerous for you to know."

Robert grinned at her, weakly. "I'm beginning to think that you're a better match for the duc de Bellevasse than Mama would care to admit."

"Please, Robert," Lise said. "No jokes about that."

⚜

If one were safe indoors it would be easy to think that a day as bright and sunny as this was warm and pleasant.

Being out in the streets, though, the bold sunlight mattered much less than the cold and the bitter wind. Lise moved as quickly as etiquette allowed, and trusted that Juliette would keep pace. She should have waited until the next time one of her aunts wanted to go to Mass. But de La Reynie's words had frightened her more than she had realized at the time, and she did not want to wait.

It was nearly as cold in the empty cathedral as it was on the streets, but when Lise sank to her knees in the confessional she found herself suddenly, blissfully, warm. Someone— either the previous occupant or the confessor himself—had prayed for warmth, and some of the heat lingered after the force of the prayer itself had dissipated. She knew the prayer was long gone because her head told her so by not aching.

As the confessor began to chant, and Lise felt the brief jolt of pain overtaken by the soft, comforting bliss of the warded invitation to confession—so like the sense of being protected by the emperor's wards—her courage failed her. "Forgive me, Father, for I have sinned," she began, and then stopped. Why had she thought of her condition as sinful? Aside from original sin, wasn't sin a matter of volition? She certainly hadn't wished this upon herself. And de La Reynie, whatever he had said to her, had not suggested that she had sinned.

"Yes?" The priest's voice was soft, bland, perhaps even indifferent.

"I, uh—" Lise stumbled over her words, no longer certain of the wisdom of being here. "It has been—" how long?— "four days since my last confession. And—" She knew now that she could not tell this priest about her condition, whether she thought it Blessing or Curse. Not and hope to avoid a visit from the Inquisition, at any rate. What was said in confession was supposed to stay between you, your confessor, and God, but confessors answered to bishops and bishops to the cardinal or the Inquisition or both, and were she a priest, Lise thought, a story such as the one she had been on the verge of telling would certainly be repeated. *I couldn't stay silent about what sounds like the Devil's work either.*

"Is something wrong, my child?"

Suddenly the words poured from her. "I have lost my heart, Father, to a man of exalted standing but scandalous reputation. In doing so I have disobeyed my—my guardian"—it wouldn't be wise to be too specific—"and possibly ruined my chances of making a good marriage."

"Have you... given yourself to this man?" He definitely sounded more interested now.

"No." *But only for lack of opportunity.* "And I will not." *But I want to.* "I have promised myself that I will not see him again, but I want to, Father; I desperately want to."

"This man is a sinner?"

"Of the worst sort, I fear." She remembered the strange, awful spell she had been pulled into at Rafael's hôtel, and could not suppress her fear and disgust. "And I love him anyway."

That came as a surprise to her. Lise had assumed that what she felt for Rafael was mostly driven by lust, but in this uncomfortable wooden cell what she found herself thinking about was the gentle way he had touched her when healing her wounds after the fight with d'Audemar, and the way he had laughed—as much with his eyes as with his voice—at seeing her dressed as his "cousin." *It's no wonder I hurt.*

"I do not see that you have committed such a great sin," the priest said in a voice soft with reassurance. "A sin, yes, if by loving this man you dishonour your guardian, but not a sin that puts your soul in any great peril. Continue to avoid him, child, and steel your heart against thoughts of him. I will not assign you a specific penance; instead, I will instruct you to say a Hail Mary every time you find yourself thinking of this man."

"Every time?"

"Yes, my child. Go with God, and sin no more."

I am, Lise thought as she left the cathedral, *going to become very familiar with that prayer.*

⚜

"I have had archers of the police watching the gates," Valentin told de La Reynie. "I also rotated off-duty members of the musketeers of the princesse's guard through watches over each gate. Nobody has touched any of the stones."

He sat down heavily in the chair facing de La Reynie's desk. Valentin had actually taken a full day off, and claimed to have slept deeply two nights in a row. He still looked tired, though, and de La Reynie was sure that neither of them would be restored to vitality until at least some of the immediate threats to the peace were dealt with.

He picked up Valentin's report. "The stones are still taking on power, I see."

"Yes, but the priests say that the rate of increase has slowed considerably in the past two days. It's still happening, but they're not willing to predict it continuing."

"Shit." He noted but ignored Valentin's raised eyebrows. He should be forgiven the occasional obscenity. "That means somebody knows that their work has been discovered. The question is, what will they do about it?"

"To say nothing of, 'Who are *they?*'"

"Yes. About the only thing I think I can be sure of is that

the emperor and the cardinal are innocent. Pretty much everyone else of noble birth is a suspect."

"Could it be peasants? The *fronde?* We know there are peasants whose curse compels them to usurp aristocratic powers and privileges. That might explain the inconsistent behaviour, the slow rate of increase in the stones' power."

"I don't think so." The words came from him while he was still thinking it through, but in his experience this sort of instinctive reaction was usually the right one. "I sometimes wonder just how much of a threat this *fronde* is—or if it even exists. Oh, I know," he said, waving away Valentin's attempted interruption, "there are plenty of reports of riots and even some attacks on tax collectors. But organized? I think not. Certainly not to the extent that this little mystery suggests."

He picked up a quill and opened his inkwell. "No, I'm sure that when we eventually find our culprits we'll find that their blood runs blue." Scratching instructions into the space at the bottom of the page, he said, "I'm ordering you to get a group of men—best to use a different set, I think; try the cardinal's guard—and have them tear out all of the ward-stones. Probably should have been done a century ago."

He handed the report back to Valentin. "Let's see if this scares anyone into emerging from hiding."

⚜

A ringing clatter interrupted Lise's gloom. She knew she had been wasting her time sitting in the gloomy parlour and staring at the fire, but she hadn't been able to make her mind concentrate on anything else. What she wanted, she realized, was the chance to discuss de La Reynie's injunction with Rafael. But she couldn't risk seeing him—not given what he had been doing when he had come so agonizingly close to seducing her—and it was the knowledge of this unfortunate fact that had made her so miserable.

Looking across the room at the source of the noise, Lise saw that Juliette, cleaning, had knocked over her swords: the rapier Grandfather had sent north with her, and the épée Rafael had given her. As Juliette picked up the swords, softly cursing herself, an idea flickered into life in Lise's head like so much God-light.

She might not be able to study fencing with Rafael any longer—even had he not been in league with the Devil, given her feelings it still would have been too dangerous—but that didn't have to mean that Rafael's "country cousin" had to retire from Paris so soon after his arrival. Walking into her bedroom she opened the trunk and pulled out the dull brown and ochre clothing, laying it on the bed. Then she went back to the sitting room and picked up the épée.

Marguerite, it occurred to her, hadn't seen her dressed in her country-cousin guise, though she'd expressed her desire to. It wasn't yet midday; perhaps it was time her friend got her wish.

⚜

"Do you know what is most delightful about all this?" Marguerite asked as they walked in front of the Louvre Palace. "It's that Anne-Marie"—she nodded back at her maid—"still hasn't worked out that you're not a man." She giggled. "Thank you so much, Lise, for thinking of this! They are going to fall over themselves at the salon."

Lise smiled back at her friend, grateful for her appreciation and eagerness. After the initial burst of enthusiasm that had got her dressed up in the dull brown costume she had felt self-conscious, and more than once on her way to meet Marguerite had considered sending a note of apology and turning back. Seeing the pleasure Marguerite was drawing from her masquerade, Lise was happy—and a bit proud—that she had resisted her timidity. "Let's not tell her," she said. "Perhaps the scandalous rumours will get back to your parents and they'll think twice about Rafael's uncle!"

Marguerite laughed out loud at this, then clapped her hand over her mouth to stifle the sound, her eyes continuing to flash. Then, abruptly, she dropped her hand. "Speaking of Rafael," she said.

Lise turned to follow Marguerite's gaze. And there he was. Rafael looked up, as if hoping to guess the time by the angle of the sun. It was overcast, though, typical for late February, so it wasn't really possible to tell by the sun what time it was. So perhaps he was just preoccupied with something; at the moment he seemed to be sauntering more than walking, and his aimlessness reminded Lise very much of Cousin Robert.

"What's that?" Marguerite asked, and Lise stiffened. A man had collided with Rafael—deliberately, Lise guessed—and stumbled with exaggerated alarm into the gutter.

"Shit!" the man shouted, and Rafael was on his guard instantly. The man who had collided with him, Lise knew, had taken advantage of the fact of Rafael's being distracted; otherwise he'd have seen the man coming out of the archway. Then the assailant turned to confront Rafael, and Lise caught a brief glimpse of his face and immediately understood the collision, if not the immediate reason for it.

"That man deliberately walked into your Rafael," Marguerite said.

"I know him," she said. "His name is de Ferreulle, and he's a friend"—*or something*, she thought—"of the younger d'Audemar son. What is he up to?" A memory of d'Audemar's attack on her crept in but she banished it before it could take hold.

"I think I know," Marguerite said. "He's trying to goad the duc into a challenge."

"*Him?*" Lise couldn't suppress the disdainful laugh. "I've seen him hold a sword; he wouldn't last a minute." *In a fair fight*, she suddenly realized.

Rafael stepped back, giving him ample room to draw his rapier if necessary. "I always guessed you'd end up in the gutter, de Ferreulle, but I rather hoped you'd take your master d'Audemar with you," he said. An indescribable sound from the recess of the arch told Lise that Rafael's thrust had hit home, and he smiled at de Ferreulle as he moved his hand to the hilt of his curious rapier.

"Pig." De Ferreulle looked angry, but Lise was certain she recognized fear under the pretense. "You will apologize for all of this. Now."

"What?" Rafael couldn't resist his laugh. "To you?"

Lise smiled at the unconscious synchronicity of his comment with her own.

"You knocked me into the street. I've killed men for less."

"In your fantasies, perhaps. I've seen you with a sword, de Ferreulle." Despite the seriousness of the situation, Lise giggled. Marguerite stared at her, eyes grown huge with surprise and outrage.

"What's the matter with you, de Bellevasse? Are you afraid to fight?" De Ferreulle stepped up to him. "Did your encounter with that idiot slut niece of the duchesse de Vimoutiers completely unman you the way Denise de L'Este is telling everyone it did?"

Lise felt as if she had been slapped, but it was de Ferreulle who ended up on his backside in the gutter. When he stood up again, though, de Ferreulle was smiling.

Lise couldn't hear what was said, but it was clear to

A Poisoned Prayer
February

her—and Marguerite confirmed it, breathlessly—that the two men were making arrangements. For a moment after de Ferreulle left Rafael simply stood, staring after the departing man without really seeing anything. Then he hitched up his sword belt and marched off to the east. *Not a fair fight*, Lise said to herself over and over.

Then she grabbed Marguerite's hand. "Come on," she said. "Follow me."

⚜

A crowd blocked their passage through the centre of the Place Imperiale. A very noisy crowd. "Damn," said Lise, not liking what the crow's-call sound implied. "We're going to have to walk all the way around."

"Oh, no," said Marguerite. "Let's keep going. The crowd will be just as bad on the other side of the statue."

"What, just push my way through?"

"You're dressed as a man, silly. Why can't you behave like one? No man would let a crowd like this keep him from getting close enough to see a duel here!"

Push, Lise thought, and then found she was doing it. "Out of my way, damn you!" she shouted at anyone and everyone. It felt rather good, the shock of contact and the way people melted away or—once in a while—pushed back. Until they saw the sword.

"What are you going to do?" Marguerite asked again. She had asked the question every other minute since they had set out after Rafael, and Lise was no more aware of the answer now than she'd been then.

"I don't know," she said. Then: "Oh."

They had reached the centre of the crowd. Rafael circled around de Ferreulle on the muddy, piebald snow in front of the equestrian statue of the Emperor Charles. The emperor's town house was directly behind Rafael, on the northern side of the Place Imperiale. Duelling here was the grossest of insults, because it was at the emperor's request that the cardinal had outlawed the duello. Not that the emperor was likely to be watching this fight: he was almost never in residence here. It was the gesture that made the insult, even if there was no one to receive it.

Some of the less-seemly members of the growing audience shouted at the men to get on with it, but for now both seemed content to circle one another like dogs, snuffling the cold air and insulting one another. The Comte de Ferreulle looked straight at her for a moment, and though her disguise today was different, for a moment she was convinced that he had recognized her and would betray her to the crowd.

Just as quickly, though, it was apparent that de Ferreulle's glance was searching for someone else. Someone he'd been waiting for, because for a moment he smiled a mad dog's smile and then he turned to face Rafael and drew his sword. Lise could hear the satisfaction in his voice when he said, "Now perhaps we can bring this sad affair to a conclusion, monsieur, and I can resume my journey before my luncheon gets cold."

"Your meal isn't all that will be getting cold," Rafael said. As de Ferreulle pulled a dagger with his left hand, Rafael drew in a fluid motion that somehow involved both hands. Now Lise understood why his scabbard and its contents had looked so odd when he'd come to her rescue that night: it held *two* swords, both of them rapiers. Grandfather had called this style the case of rapiers; it was an older style when he'd been a boy. He had admired it, though, mostly because it took strength and skill to fight with two swords. No one today would likely be familiar with the style.

Rafael had shed both cloak and coat, which were now

wrapped around one of the hooves of the large bronze horse on which the emperor's statue rode. Now he circled de Ferreulle wearing just the whitest of shirts, as though daring the other man to try to mar that blinding blankness; far more white than the snow he was trampling into mud. The onset of that headache, with which she was so achingly familiar now, announced to her that Rafael was fully warding himself against magical attack. He seemed to be doing more than that, in fact: where de Ferreulle's breath was emerging in dagger-like jets of steam, Rafael's breath was as invisible as if today had been the first of May. Would he use magic to attack de Ferreulle? It was something no gentleman would do, and it wasn't supposed even to be possible. But Rafael supposedly consorted with the Devil and collected spells from the Horned One, so who knew?

Movement on her left caught her eye, and she understood why de Ferreulle had been waiting and watching so anxiously: two young men advanced toward Rafael's back, drawing épées as they did. She did not recognize them, but their dress clearly marked them as nobles of the sword. If they were with de Ferreulle, they were probably clients of the d'Audemar family.

Almost before she was aware of it, she had moved forward, drawing her épée. Marguerite's choked-off cry of alarm did not dissuade her, nor did she think about the possible outcome, should she actually have to fight. In the moment before her mind cleared of all thought, her only concern was that Rafael not have to face three attackers at once. *Have they no honour?*

The two men turned to look at her, and she flushed at the realization that she'd spoken that last thought aloud. "Who is this... this *turnip*?" one drawled. "And why is he so anxious to be cut up?" The two men split up, one continuing to advance on Rafael and the other taking up a guard position just beyond Lise's reach.

"Should I ask your name, turnip, before I stain those"— he giggled—"rustic clothes?" The giggle became a laugh, a sound to which even a mule would object. "Now that I think on it, bloodstains could only improve the appearance of that ghastly ensemble. Where *do* you come from, turnip? At least tell me who your people are, so that I can know where to send the remains."

"He comes from southern Picardy." Rafael's voice was clear and steady, and from the sound of it he was vastly amused. "He is my cousin—a number of times removed. I have been teaching him to use an épée instead of the heavy cleaver he's accustomed to wielding." Someone in the crowd laughed. "I believe my cousin is anxious to demonstrate what he has learned," Rafael continued. "You are right, though, Baillard: he is something of a turnip. He doesn't know, for example, how important you are. Or at least think you are." More laughter; Rafael shifted slightly—Lise's notice was drawn to the way he arched his right foot and somehow pivoted left, cutting off a tentative advance by de Ferreulle. "Which of course means that you probably shouldn't be too surprised if he treats you more like a pig in the slaughter yard than like some sort of exalted demigod." The man he'd called Baillard took a step back, and Lise smiled when she saw his épée quiver a little. "After all," Rafael said, his voice the very embodiment of reason, "back in Picardy they've never heard of you, either."

A burst of reflected light flared from the hilt of his rapier as Rafael suddenly darted forward, and the first of de Ferreulle's companions was on the ground, screaming curses and trying to force closed the long red gash on his

A Poisoned Prayer
February

forearm. Lise's eyes widened at the wonderful audacity of the attack, and then she bellowed her grandfather's old war cry and charged at Baillard, not even bothering to set up a guard. Startled, Baillard only just managed to hold onto his épée as Lise hacked at the blade with what she hoped was suitably turnip-like enthusiasm. Satisfied that her opponent was sufficiently rattled, she settled into the stance that Rafael had taught her, drew her dagger, and set up her guard in *terce*. Feinting at Baillard's chest, she aimed a slashing blow at his left hamstring. She felt the shock in her wrist before she heard his yelp of shock and pain.

He kept his balance, though, and while he was apparently too surprised to take advantage of the opening she had clumsily given him, he was not yet *hors de combat*. Lise settled back into a guard position and made a couple of tentative attacks while waiting to see how he'd respond. With each clang of blade on blade she felt her confidence grow—*I can do this!*—and when Baillard seemed reluctant to respond she yelled again and returned to the attack, this time using a series of thrusts Rafael had taught her.

Baillard evidently recognized the style, because his eyes widened as he hurried to parry, and his face lost all of its colour. He was a heartbeat too late responding to one thrust, and Lise felt another tremor shiver up her arm as the point of her blade made contact with Baillard's shoulder.

Shouting a curse, he scrambled backward. "Damn you, de Ferreulle!" he shouted. "I did not agree to be your second in order to fight *peasants!*" When Lise held her ground, Baillard sheathed his sword and dagger—with a notable lack of grace—and said, "Go back to your fields, turnip. I won't sully my blade with the shit in your veins." He spat at her feet.

"Pig!" Lise screamed, lunging at him. Baillard's mouth

dropped open, and with a baby-like cry he turned and fled into the safe anonymity of the crowd. "Oh, dear," said Lise quietly. "Another day in Paris, another enemy."

Stabbing pain cut through her satisfaction, and she whirled around to where Rafael and de Ferreulle continued to circle one another. A huge man in the uniform of an archer of the Paris Watch charged across the snow and mud of the Place Imperiale, a massive broadsword held over his head. At first he seemed to be charging at Rafael, but his eyes suddenly locked on Lise. "I know you!" he shouted, and behind her Marguerite gasped, a shuddering sound that told Lise fearful tears would begin soon if her friend wasn't already crying.

And yet.... The pain behind her eyes argued that there was magic at work here, rather than the work of Nicolas de La Reynie. Looking the giant up and down, Lise discovered that there was no mud, no melting snow, on his legs and feet. He wasn't even leaving footprints behind him. Turning her back on the roaring phantom, she lowered her sword and told Marguerite, "Don't worry. It's an illusion. And not a very good one, either."

"Illusions can still kill," Marguerite said. She stood alone, now: the rest of the crowd had backed away, apparently less sure of the giant archer's intangibility than Lise. *That's a good friend*, she thought.

"Thanks for standing by me," she said. Her voice came out small and thin, a little girl's voice, and Lise felt a prickle of shame, as though she had somehow displayed weakness in front of Marguerite. She'd never thought much about friends, and now it occurred to her to wonder how she'd managed to grow up without really having any.

Marguerite's eyes widened; she tried to scream, but it came out as a squeak. Lise's headache grew worse; turning

A Poisoned Prayer
February

back to the fight, she was just in time to see the last traces of the giant archer's eyes—now the red of burning coals—as he faded away. At the same time, a wall of flame thrust up around Rafael like a Devil's hedge. When a similar thicket of hellfire sprang up around her, Lise was so shocked she dropped her sword. This illusion had *heat*.

"Why, Ferreulle," Rafael said with a slow, lazy laugh, "your master has bought you a priest!" The fire around Lise shimmered for a moment, turned to snowflakes that hung suspended for the space of a breath, then vanished. "I assume it's a priest," Rafael said after a moment, "because I know that you aren't this well-Blessed, and none of your so-called friends are either."

"That's just a taste of the fire you'll be feeling in a few minutes, bastard," de Ferreulle said, "when I send you to meet your father in Hell." He didn't press forward, though; in fact, he stepped back. Lise felt a sudden, sharp pulse of pain.

A heartbeat later Lise heard a dull ringing and Rafael darted to one side, a single choppy blasphemy emerging from his mouth as he clapped his right hand to his left shoulder. Lise couldn't help but be impressed: he'd managed to maintain his grip on the right-hand rapier.

For a long moment she couldn't figure out what had happened. De Ferreulle had been nowhere near Rafael when he had been wounded, so the attack had to have come from a distance. But there had been no gunshot—and surely no honourable man would have an accomplice ruin a duel by shooting.

Then she saw the dart at the base of the emperor's statue. No, it was a quarrel—a bolt fired from a crossbow. Grandfather had one that he sometimes used for hunting; as a military weapon it had been obsolete for a century or more, and outlawed by papal decree for even longer. Was someone was shooting a crossbow at Rafael from a great distance? She looked more closely; the entire quarrel was metal, even the fletching. No prayer would have been proof against that. It was a good thing the assassin's aim had been poor.

The pain stabbed at her again and she shouted, "Move!" before she was aware she'd done so. A second quarrel smashed into the base of the statue with another clang; Rafael had escaped completely this time, and his hand was no longer clutching the wounded shoulder. Someone in the crowd booed loudly, a sound followed quickly by a shouted "Unfair!"

"I don't know why," Rafael said, in a flat, angry voice, "but I expected better of you, de Ferreulle. If you weren't going to be a gentleman—and of course there was no reason to expect *that*—you could at least have bought someone with a semblance of fair play." He said nothing more, made no gesture, but suddenly huge green crystals began sprouting from the earth around de Ferreulle. In a matter of moments, a fence of gems surrounded the man.

"God damn you," de Ferreulle began. He was cut short by a scream that echoed weirdly from the walls of the buildings surrounding the Place.

"That's your priest taken care of, then," Rafael said. "Really, de Ferreulle—was that a crossbow he was using? Not just bad form, you've actually broken papal law. Or had you forgotten it was a mortal sin to use crossbows against Christian nobles?"

Now the crystal fence surrounding de Ferreulle began to evaporate. There was something unsettling about the way the gems disappeared, the crystals not so much crumbling or evaporating as they seemed to dissolve, like sugar in wine—as if the air were liquid. Lise had to look away, and apparently the sight disturbed de Ferreulle as well, for he shouted out something vulgar whose anatomical preciseness was so uniquely vile its very possibility had never occurred to Lise.

Rafael seemed to take it in stride, just in the way she imagined he must dodge the content of chamber pots as he walked, rather than rode, through the city. "What's the matter?" he asked de Ferreulle. His voice was caustic. Mocking, in fact. "Are things not working out as you'd planned, Ferreulle? Are you upset at the thought of having to attack me on your own, without any sort of unfair advantage? Do you find yourself doubting your abilities?" he snarled. "I *weep* for you, de Ferreulle. Really, I do."

"Who are you to accuse me of anything unfair?" There was an hysterical edge to de Ferreulle's voice. "You're working with the Devil himself, for God's sake! Who *wouldn't* want to recruit priests, saints, even the Holy Mother Herself to his side against you?"

"Why does everyone assume that my soul is for sale to the Devil?" Rafael paused, then his voice rose to a shout. "Why assume that my soul is for sale to *anyone?* I am de Bellevasse! I am beholden to *no one!*" After a pause for breath he continued in what at least suggested a more reasonable tone. "I might be able to understand—though not forgive—your refusal to understand that, de Ferreulle. But your patron should have known better."

"I am not acting on anyone's behalf but my own," de Ferreulle said. Straightening himself, he managed to project a small sense of wounded dignity. It suggested to Lise the rectitude of a boy who had been accused of something not quite exactly matching what he had actually done.

"I give you credit for that much honour, at least," Rafael

said. He raised his rapier *en garde.* "I hope that this is some consolation."

Whatever de Ferreulle might have thought of this gesture was not displayed on his face. Lise saw nothing in his face at all, just a waxy immobility as the man stared at Rafael, raising his own sword and dagger. There was a tightness across her chest that she had not felt when she was herself fighting, and that had nothing to do with the bindings flattening her breasts.

Then Rafael moved forward, and it seemed to Lise as if Rafael, freed of the need to deal with de Ferreulle's efforts at spiritual distraction, could now reveal his true self. That self was supremely fit, highly trained, and ruthlessly focused. *He was toying with me,* she realized, thinking of the lesson that had exhilarated and exhausted her—and apparently hadn't scratched the surface of Rafael's true skill.

Rafael and de Ferreulle came together with the abrupt, explosive fury of dogs that have abandoned posturing and given themselves over to fighting in earnest. She saw a flurry of white as shirt-clad limbs bearing steel blades flailed, heard the ring and scrape as the blades met. Only when the two men separated was Lise able to breathe. As for the combatants, both were now breathing heavily—though Lise guessed from his wild smile that it was excitement rather than fatigue that quickened Rafael's breath.

De Ferreulle seemed to be regretting a great deal now. As Lise watched, a thin red stripe on his left sleeve expanded, the crisp edges blurring as the blood spread through and under the linen of his shirt. His forehead was wet and his hair, despite being shorn to allow for the wig he'd doffed for the fight, was slick and matted. He appeared to be mouthing obscenities as he checked his stance, then—to Lise's surprise—moved to the attack.

She recognized his mistake well before he did. The young men of Paris were deeply enamored of a lunging thrust that showed a good leg to maximum advantage and—if it connected—put a man's full weight into the point of his sword. The lunge dramatically extended a swordsman's reach. Unfortunately, it also hobbled him, crippling his balance and exposing his entire body to a counter-thrust. While teaching her, Grandfather had often expressed his contempt for a method of attack that emphasized style over substance—or even security. Now Rafael expressed that same contempt in a brutally efficient fashion: as de Ferreulle lunged toward him, Rafael stepped forward into the thrust, his parrying rapier flashing outward and deflecting de Ferreulle's épée. Then, as de Ferreulle's lunge reached full extension, back leg almost on the ground and his body leaning forward and down, Rafael smashed down with the hilt of his attacking rapier on the top of de Ferreulle's head. De Ferreulle flopped face-down onto the muddy turf. A ragged gasp from the crowd followed him down. Perhaps the audience had hoped for some more flamboyant *coup de main.*

For a long moment de Ferreulle lay there, motionless, while voices from amongst the watchers called for an end to him. Rafael watched, one blade at the ready, but made no other gesture; he did not acknowledge the crowd in any way. Lise could see that Rafael's breathing was now heavy, but it remained measured, and he appeared to be thinking—weighing his options, perhaps. As de Ferreulle finally shifted, then began to lift himself out of the muck, Rafael's blade flicked to the side of de Ferreulle's neck. For a sickening moment Lise was sure Rafael would end the duel by butchering his opponent.

"No," she said. Rafael turned to look at her; she hadn't realized she'd spoken loudly enough for him to hear. "You can't kill him," she said. A howl from the watchers disagreed with her, but she ignored it as Rafael had. She was certain de Ferreulle and his friends would have killed Rafael in any way open to them, but as she watched de Ferreulle lock into immobility on feeling the point of Rafael's rapier, she understood why she'd spoken out.

"You've broken the law here, but so far it's just duelling," she said. "Kill him and it's murder and the emperor will have to take your head—if the cardinal doesn't burn you first."

Rafael glared at her a moment, and Lise felt cold. Then he smiled at her and she exhaled. Nodding to her in salute, he turned his attention to the man on the ground. "You really should think more about your fencing style, de Ferreulle," Rafael said. If he felt any sense of triumph—if he felt anything at all, for that matter—he kept it out of his voice. "Now, then, should I pay attention to my cousin, over there? What do I do with you?"

"You bastard," de Ferreulle spat. "You know what to do. Get it over with."

"Do you know," Rafael said, and now his voice drawled, lazy with contempt, "I am inclined to agree both with my cousin and with what your cowardly friend Baillard said a moment ago. I refuse to dirty my blade with the shit that runs in your veins." Whatever de Ferreulle had intended to shout in response was silenced when Rafael kicked him, savagely, in the side of the head. The man dropped as though he'd been a sack of coals. The crowd screamed its disappointment, thwarted in its desire for life's blood.

"Now," he said, "we have one more item to finish with." He closed his eyes, and Lise felt a stinging in her head—a sting she recognized from the last time she had been with Rafael, in his hôtel. She blushed with shame at the memory; she had just saved the life of a man who practiced death-magic! What could she say to her confessor now?

The crowd, which had settled into sullen grumbling when Rafael had kicked de Ferreulle into unconsciousness, seem as a single voice to utter a low, frightened moan before falling into abrupt silence. A shadow passed over Lise's eyes.

Looking up, she saw a man apparently flying overhead. No, he wasn't flying: he was being flown, brought to Rafael by some invisible force. *Is this death-magic?* The man wore a priest's robes, but they were torn and filthy — as, Lise noticed, was the man himself. He seemed to be bleeding from a number of places.

At a gesture from Rafael, the man suddenly fell to the ground. "What possessed you to use a crossbow against me, Father? And more to the point, perhaps, how did you do it?"

"Please don't let that thing have me!" *What thing?* Lise wondered, noting that the man's naked legs were stained with his own urine. Then she realized the identity of the demon responsible for his apparent flight.

"You have to answer my questions," Rafael said gently.

"The bolts are Damascus steel, so they could penetrate your wards," the man said, the words tumbling over themselves. "The crossbow itself is mostly wood and so susceptible to prayer. I used prayer to aim and to enhance the strength of the bow, to give the distance required." *He's not just dressed as a priest,* Lise realized; *he* is *a priest. Or was,* she appended, based on the state of his robes. The thought of a priest acting as a hired assassin was sickening.

"And why were you trying to do this?"

"It was what I was told to do! By—by my employer!"

"Not de Ferreulle, I'm guessing. Was it the chevalier d'Audemar, Father, or was it the prince d'Aude?"

"They'll kill me!" the man screamed. "Please, I beg you!"

"I suspect that somebody will, yes." Rafael looked up, smiling, and Lise's imagination painted the currently invisible form of the Mohammedan demon Shahrbàz, hovering overhead, proud as a hunting-cat. "I am going to let you go, Father," he said to the priest, "because I don't believe your heart was truly in what you were doing. Or trying to do, at any rate. I must warn you, though, that my—ah, my Blessing—now has your scent. And I don't just refer to that ghastly mix of onions and sour wine. So I bid you aware that, even should you escape the Inquisition or the cardinal's court, if you ever again try to call God down on me, you will be found. And next time I will not be lenient."

As the man scrambled to his feet and, filthier now than before, scurried away, a woman in the crowd screeched, "Devil!" As if that had been a signal, the viewers exploded into a cacophony of shouts, laughter, and insults. For a moment Lise wondered if the crowd would turn on the fleeing priest, but though one or two threw clumps of mud at his back the people seemed for the most part to have decided that he was of less interest than Rafael and his death-magic.

Their intensified interest seemed to have no more impact on Rafael than a summer breeze on a mountain. Checking his wound—he seemed not to have prayed it closed, yet— he sheathed his rapiers, bowed briefly to Lise and, with a quiet, "Thank you, cousin," walked over to the statue. There he picked up his jacket, cloak, and hat and, without another word, began to walk away. As he approached the crowd

A Poisoned Prayer
February

that blocked his way there was a ripple and a clear path opened in front of him, as the sea had parted for Moses.

"No," said Marguerite as Lise began to follow him. "You can't. You mustn't."

"But he might have been killed," Lise said. He hadn't looked back at her. Not once.

"Did you see what he did? That man hasn't moved. He may be dead." Marguerite tugged at her sleeve. "And if he *is* dead—or if he dies because of this—then what you told him will certainly come to pass: the cardinal's guard and the archers will be after your Rafael. You don't want them after you, Lise. You don't even want them to *notice* you. Come with me; we've got to get you to the marquise's house and out of that costume."

"You're absolutely right, my darling Marguerite," Lise said. "That's why I have to catch him, before he does anything stupid. More stupid," she corrected herself.

Like Rafael, she didn't look back.

She ran, not caring how ungainly she looked, past people who suddenly seemed to be paying too much attention to her. She felt sick. Throughout her training she had believed that a real fight, once she entered into it, would be exciting, would make her feel more alive. That was how the novelists described it. Certainly every young man who'd ever spoken to her about duelling had claimed this: to them, fighting was as ecstatic as communion with God.

Lise didn't feel ecstasy. She felt weak, nauseated. She couldn't banish the thought of de Ferreulle, abandoned by his friends, laying face-down in the mud and snow of the Place Imperiale.

It took her longer to catch up with him than she had expected. Even walking, his stride was long, and he'd had a good head start. When she did reach him, she could think of nothing to say, and so she simply fell into step beside him, waiting to speak until he acknowledged her.

When he did speak, it was with a smile. "You fought very well," he said. "I can see, though, that I have more to teach you."

"I want to learn," she said, and was surprised at the passion in her voice. "Rafael, where are you going?"

"I suspect it's time I paid my mother a visit," he said, his smile souring a little. "Forgive me if I seem a bit distant, Lise. "I'm trying to—"

"Heal yourself, yes." She tried to rub the pain from her temples. *Why can't his Blessing affect me the same way the emperor's wards do?* "Isn't your estate in Picardy? You're walking west, not north."

"Have to stop at home first," he said. "There. That's the first of them done, at any rate." His shoulder closed up as she watched, skin knitting together like the skin on a pot of warm milk after you'd stirred it. He turned to look at her. "Why were your rubbing your temples like that?"

"Why in heaven are you going to your home?" she asked in return, feeling the worry emerging from her mouth in a shrill, angry tone. "The cardinal's guard will be looking for you!"

"It takes time for word to get to them," he said, "and I doubt they'll be in any hurry to pay me a visit. The cardinal knows what I'm going to do, Lise, and he'll be happier if he lets me alone to do it."

"You assume the cardinal is going to be the first to hear of it," she said, "and that somebody hasn't spread the word already. Or spread the word before the fight even started."

He stopped. After a moment's pause he threw back his head and gave vent to a long, angry sigh. "I feel rather stupid just now," he said. "I'm sorry you have to see this; I don't like looking stupid around attractive women."

Ignoring this, she said, "What do you think is happening here?"

"What do I think? I think I've been duped, Lise. In fact, I'm sure of it; what I don't know is why."

"Duped? By whom?"

Rafael paused to do the next of the healing prayers. To Lise he looked fine, but as she watched him pray, he winced as if the same sort of stinging pain that afflicted her was lancing through him, as though the Devil was tormenting them both with needles. "The d'Audemar family, Lise. They're the only logical villains. Nobody who knows the both of us would think that de Ferreulle would have even a hope of beating me in a fair fight. So why was he so anxious to goad me into a duel?" He waved away Lise's interruption. "No, dear cousin. If the sole purpose was to assassinate me, they could have used that crossbow trick without the theatrics. Which reminds me, I must have a word with the cardinal about that. He may want to get his priests working on enhanced warding spells that target this sort of attack at its source.

"No," he went on, "there has to have been a reason this attack took the form it did. And unfortunately I won't be able to properly investigate it, not for a good while."

"Should I be leaving the city as well?" The thought hadn't occurred to her until now.

"For you, dear Lise, disappearing is as easy as putting those clothes into a chest for a few weeks." Rafael paused in the act of testing his left arm, lifting his head to look at her. "Is that it? Could the prince d'Aude or his brats have engineered this duel simply to get me banished from

Paris?" He started walking again. "That could explain a lot, you know."

Lise grabbed his good arm. "Not that way. Weren't you listening? You can't go home right now."

"So where do I go?" His smile was infuriatingly complacent.

She was pleased at the way it faltered when she said, "Come home with me."

Now it was her turn to shush his protests. "I've thought about this; I know what I'm doing. Nobody knows that I am, well, me. So if we move quickly and don't draw a lot of attention to ourselves, you'll be much safer at my apartment than you will at your hôtel. We can send word to your man Alain to get your things and meet you outside the city. From the Ile St-Louis you can get a boatman to take you beyond the walls, which will put you beyond the cardinal's interest. And anyone else looking for you won't think of looking east."

He laughed softly. "My mother would love you—will love you." He turned to look at her, and his grin was that of a scheming child. "You should come with me. We can be two vagabonds, on the run from the law."

Lise was startled when tears stung her eyes. "Please don't joke about that," she was eventually able to say. "If you knew how many times I have thought of such a thing—"

He hung his head. "I am truly sorry, Lise. You may have been thinking, but clearly I haven't been. Of course I shouldn't have suggested anything of the sort. You have—you have your duty to your family, to your aunt de Vimoutiers."

"And to myself," she said, so quietly she wasn't sure he'd heard her. "No more talk, now. We have to move quickly."

Four

"Have I just done something stupid?" Lise set down her wine goblet and looked at Rafael, perched on a chair on the opposite side of the parlor table like one of the gargoyles on the cathedral. "What if the cardinal's men are waiting for Juliette?"

"They will have no reason to detain her," Rafael said, taking a sip of his wine. "The message I gave her to deliver is not addressed to me but to Alain, and it concerns a matter of linens to be washed, and not an escape to be effected."

"And he will understand what it means?"

"He certainly will once he has laid hands on it. Alain wears a crucifix I have charmed for him. When the message is pressed to his breast it will reveal its truth to him—and to him alone."

"Thank you," she said. "I would not want anything to happen to Juliette."

"Nor I to Alain."

"Tell me," she asked picking up her goblet, "did de Ferreulle touch you at all?"

"I did not wish him to," Rafael said, "and therefore he did not."

Lise thought about the fight, and the shock of her épée hitting her opponent, and suddenly heat flared up in her. "I would like to touch you," she said, and now she was aware of a roaring in her ears. She was on her feet before she fully knew what she was doing. "But no prayers, please. Just you."

In his haste to reach her, Rafael knocked both their goblets to the floor.

"Just once," he muttered after kissing her for a delightfully long time, "I'd like to kiss you without having our moustaches in the way." Then he kissed her some more, and when he broke the kiss his hands were on her hips and she was in the air, dizzy for a brief moment before he let her down. She realized she was sitting; opening her eyes and looking down, she saw that he'd placed her on the table. *I don't care,* she thought. *Anywhere he wants.* Then he lifted her again, and when he set her back down she felt the smooth, time-polished oak against her bare skin. For a moment Rafael disappeared, crouching down to pull off her boots and tug the breeches and drawers from her legs.

Lise suddenly felt cold, wanted Rafael back up and holding her, so that she could lose herself in him and not have to think about what she was doing—not have to think about anything. She closed her eyes, knowing that there was a mirror on the wall across from her and not wanting to have to face herself just now.

She felt the brush of hair against her leg, and then Rafael was kissing the insides of her knees, her thighs—

She could not suppress her gasping intake of breath. How had he learned *that?*

A bright light flared behind her closed eyes and a powerful sensation blasted through her. In the time it took her to draw breath, the sensation resolved itself into a fierce, sickening pain. Someone was cursing, and she realized the voice was hers.

A Poisoned Prayer
February

"Are you unwell? Did I do something? I promise you, there was no magic this time!" Rafael stood before her. She opened her eyes to see him quickly wipe his mustache.

"I hit my damned *head* against the table!" she said, carefully touching the spot with a fingertip. There was going to be a bump there. "I lost my balance when you did—that thing you did." She felt the flickering of embarrassment, suddenly seeing how she must look, slumped back on the table. *No,* she thought. *I'm not going to think. This is not the time for thinking.* "And why did you stop?"

Rafael laughed. He also got back down into his crouch, and returned his wonderful, warm mouth to the junction between her thighs. His hands gripped her hips, as if to pull her further toward him. Lise let herself slide back into the warmth and the wonderful irritation that rose up and overwhelmed her.

She became aware that he had stopped again and opened her eyes to see why. He was standing again, looking down at her, and his eyes seemed to glow the silver-green of wild sage in late spring. "What?" she asked, suddenly unsure.

"Nothing," he said. "And everything." He slid his hands up her thighs to her hips; it tickled, and Lise was surprised to realize that this was because his hands were shaking. "This is a remarkable thing for me," he said. He wasn't smiling anymore. "I wanted you to know that."

I don't want talk. That was a surprise to her as well. "Is this all there is?" she heard herself ask.

Now he smiled. "Oh, no." Pulled her hips toward the edge of the table. "Not anywhere nearly all there is." Opened her with one hot, liquid thrust. She meant to say something in reply but found herself beyond words. Lise no longer cared about the pain in her head, or her aunt's opinions, or her reputation. Or anything. All that mattered was that these sensations continued. If the intensity increased, that would be good.

It increased. It was almost too much. Her body seemed to be singing, making a joyful noise. After the initial explosion of sensation had subsided, she realized that the noise was coming from her mouth. She didn't care.

When Rafael had sung his own song and they had eased apart, she felt the shock of air on her suddenly-cold skin. Now she was aware of how ludicrous she looked, laying on the table, legs limply dangling over one end. Her head rested right on the opposite edge, which was digging into the back of her skull. *That will probably bruise. I'm going to look as if I was in a tavern brawl.*

She was sure she should say something. But what? To thank him would be absurdly polite. To tell him that he had taken her heart would be ridiculous and theatrical. And she wasn't even sure if that was something he wanted to hear. As for herself, there was much that she wanted to hear—and words of love, she realized, were only a part of it.

"My lord," she began, feeling a bit of a flush as she did so, "you are indeed a splendid teacher." Before he could preen too much at the compliment, she added: "If you would be so good as help me down, I'd like to put something on. It's cold in here. And it seems a long way down, now." She pulled herself back into a sitting position and smiled at him.

He returned the smile, but with one eyebrow cocked a little. The green of his eyes had faded to a more brownish shade and for a moment she thought she saw confusion there. Then something appeared to close down, and his focus sharpened. "It's more safe than you think," Rafael said. Still, he grasped her by the hips—memory flared briefly in her, and her body warmed at the thought—and lifted her gently before setting her down on the floor. "You needn't be in such a hurry to resume your disguise," he said quietly.

"I was thinking more of putting on a robe," she told him. "After all, we don't know when Juliette will return. And don't you have to be on your way soon?"

"I am now thinking I should change my schedule." He leaned to kiss her, and she found herself pressing against him, and the heat beginning to flow through her again. After a moment she could feel heat—and more—from him as well.

Rafael stepped back, but kept his hands on her shoulders. "Well, well," he said, looking down. This is most interesting."

"Why?" she asked. The evidence of his interest seemed perfectly natural—and flattering, of course—to her.

He bent, put one hand behind her back and the other behind her knees, and swept her off the ground. "I'll explain later. Please allow me to stay?"

She laughed, wrapped her arms around his shoulders and kissed him. "I can't very well throw you out if my feet aren't even on the ground, can I?"

⚜

Rafael kissed her softly, then leaned back, propping himself on one elbow as he looked at her. "You are a very curious young woman," he said. "I am still not at all certain what possessed you to leap to my aid this afternoon."

"I am just a woman who recognizes a good teacher. I am hoping for another lesson," she added. "I am sure my technique needs work." She paused. "And my fencing skills as well." She felt a sudden, giddy rush as she spoke the words. Aunt would most definitely not approve. She couldn't suppress a tiny smile, though, as his smile broadened. *No matter what happens after this*, she thought, *nobody and nothing can take away today.*

"Might I ask a question, while I'm getting my breath back and, um, regaining my strength?" She nodded, enjoying the flush that continued to suffuse her face. "Why did you request no prayer? This was the second time you've said that to me. And what did I do that was so horribly wrong the last time I gave you—a lesson?"

"I wanted no prayer *because* of what you did last time."

"I don't understand. I'm not one to brag—well, not much, at any rate—but my love-prayers are rather well-regarded."

She looked at him closely, searching for some clue that this might be a test, or that he might have a hidden motive for asking. She found nothing. After a few breaths she said, "It wasn't you. It was—it *is*—me. I am Cursed, Rafael, or if not then my Blessing is its own curse. I suffer hideous headache whenever I'm exposed to God's Blessings in someone else. Anyone else." She turned away, but when she looked at him again his gaze appeared not to have shifted. Lise was suddenly somehow more aware of her nakedness.

"Have you confessed?"

"No! I cannot bear the thought of the Inquisition taking me! Oh, but I suppose I have, in a way. Lieutenant-General de La Reynie knows about it. He seems to think it's not a curse, for which I thank him."

"De La Reynie? What does this have to do with the police?"

"I can't tell you. He swore me to secrecy. I wasn't supposed to tell anyone about my Curse—or Blessing—either. But you—well, you're more than *anyone* to me, Rafael."

"You don't have to tell me that, my little fox," he said with a quick smile. "And I don't think you have to worry about the Inquisition, either. Whatever de La Reynie's interest in you, the mere fact of its existence is proof against anything those degenerate sons of Spaniards could get up to. Perhaps our exalted policeman is correct, and you ought to start treating this as an unusual sort of Blessing rather than a curse." He gazed at her a moment, then smiled, the smile broadening until it burst into a laugh. "Denise," he sputtered. "You spiked Denise because your headaches told you she was throwing a prayer at you!"

Lise felt her flush turning into a blush, and that didn't seem fair somehow. Why was it acceptable for Denise de L'Este to use prayer to attack a perceived rival, but unacceptable for Lise to use her sensitivity to prayer in her own defence?

Change the subject, she told herself. "It's my turn to ask a question, now. What were you doing when I found you in your hôtel, that last time?"

"That, like your arrangement with de La Reynie, ought to remain a secret. For your own safety," he added, seeing on her face a look she thought she had hidden better.

"Oh," he said abruptly. "That would be why de Ferreulle was my opponent today and not his master, d'Audemar. Get me out of the city and they can stop worrying about my vengeance; clearly I'm close to the truth now and they know it. And who would miss de Ferreulle? He's nothing." He had suddenly gone far away from her.

"Rafael?"

"Lise," he said. "The d'Audemars know—or have guessed—that you somehow stumbled on me as I was casting my—prayers. Why didn't I think of this before?"

"So it really was death-magic."

He stared into her eyes, and the intensity she saw there was, for a moment at least, not quite human. *He has spent too much time around that cat-devil, Shahrbàz*, she thought.

"Yes," he said. "But whatever you have been told about

what I'm doing, Lise, is probably wrong." He sat up in her bed, heedless of how he was exposed.

"Tell me what's right about it then," she said. "But before you do that, you have to tell me: who was the woman?"

Rafael's mouth dropped open. "Woman?"

"That day, when I came in to that room to find you and saw you praying surrounded by water—that's what it looked like to me, anyway. Then your creature, Shahrbàz, saw me, and the next thing I knew I was somewhere else, and I think I was in another woman's body." The horror of that fluid, ugly vision came flooding back into her, and the intensity of the memory had a physical presence. "They killed her, Rafael, they choked her and then they stabbed her with swords, and I could *feel* it!" She felt herself falling into crying, a wild and jagged crying that threatened to overwhelm her.

Then Rafael had pulled her up and into his arms, and she let herself cry out the pain and horror for a few minutes, until the worst of the memories was gone and she could once again feel the reassuring heat of his chest. Pulling her head back from the safety of his embrace, she said, "What did I see?"

"I have an idea," he said, "but I'd like you to tell me everything you can about what you—what happened."

In a way it was a relief to talk about what she'd—felt, she decided, was the best word for it. Words could put distance between her and the numbness, the fierce wild spiritual assault, the swords. When she'd finished, he sat back, his hands resting lightly on her shoulders. For long moments he just stared at her.

"Six months," he finally said. "For nearly half a year I have been trying to learn what happened to her. You spend a few minutes in the presence of my spells and you learn more than I could in six months—and you're spiritually deaf!"

The anger surprised her and she pulled back. "Why be angry with me? I've done nothing wrong."

Something she hoped was shame flashed across his face, and he dropped his hands to his side. "I'm sorry. I—I certainly don't blame you for anything. In fact, I'm in your debt, Lise." He shook his head slowly. "I realize I've done a terrible job of conveying that"—he looked up at her, venturing a tiny smile—"and I hope you'll forgive my thoughtlessness."

She released a breath she hadn't been aware of holding. She realized she had been almost as afraid of Rafael as she'd been of the vision she'd just relived. "I will accept your apology," she said, "if you will tell me who she—who that woman was, and why what I saw made you so upset."

"We should be comfortable," he said, getting to his feet and pulling the bedclothes back up so that she could cover herself. "This could take a while."

He climbed back into her bed; Lise felt a delightful spark go through her when his hip touched hers. "To answer your first question, the woman was my Aunt Génie. She was murdered last September near the Temple gate; there were no witnesses. None who survived, at any rate." Lise shifted to look directly at Rafael. He did not appear distressed; he looked nearly as angry as he had a few moments ago. "My aunt and I were very close," he said, "especially following my father's death eight years ago. Génie was more than a decade younger than my father, so she was more like a sister than an aunt. I valued her advice, and her husband, Bertrand de Montauban, became a close friend."

He turned away from her, to stare into the fire. "And

she was murdered by the Audemar family—by the Prince d'Aude, or on his orders."

"Why?"

He continued to stare at the fire. "I don't know. I can't even prove to my own satisfaction that a d'Audemar was responsible, much less convince the Parlement. I just *know* it. Perhaps God is speaking to me about this, and I have only understood a small part of what He is saying."

"And that is why you are using death-magic? To get the story from her?" Lise wasn't certain why, but she didn't find this knowledge as distressing as she suspected she ought to.

"I have to reach her," he said, and she suddenly thought she knew what he'd been like as a boy. "I have to know. I won't hesitate to kill the one responsible—I'll kill that entire damned family if I have to—but I have to know that I'm justified before I act. And I'll use any tool I can make work for me in order to know." Finally, he turned back to face Lise. "I'm sorry if I've upset you—and sometimes it seems as if all I've done is upset you"—here he smiled again, and this smile was more confident. "I suppose I am somewhat fixed in my ideas. And no doubt the cardinal would disagree with me, but as far as I'm concerned one prayer's as good as another, if it will give me the answers I need. If you decide you'd rather not associate with me, because some call me a heretic, I will understand."

"You should give me credit for more determination," she said.

He laughed. "You're right. I've seen you fight, after all. Twice, now." He looked into her eyes for a moment, then leaned in and kissed her. "Thank you," he said.

"Oh. You're welcome." *What an interesting sensation that was,* she thought. *And all he did was kiss me.* She was shifting back toward him when part of what he'd said earlier triggered a memory. "You said something a minute ago about the d'Audemar family knowing about me."

"Lise, I think the d'Audemar family have learned about what happened when you stumbled into my prayer. Or they've guessed it, for some reason—it doesn't matter how. I think you should be much more careful about where you go and who you see while I'm away. I'll assign one of my men to look after you, if you'd like. Or perhaps I should act as your bodyguard myself."

"Even if that was meant as a joke, don't you dare suggest it!" She thought about Guillaume d'Audemar's warning to her, and realized that if her aunt de Vimoutiers was in danger, Rafael was triply so.

"Lise, you could be in danger."

"And you *are* in danger!" It was wonderful, she realized, to think about Rafael acting as her paladin. All the more reason to reject it, and soundly. "If half of what you say is true, then you have the d'Audemar family looking for you as well as the cardinal."

"You need never worry about me where a fight is concerned," he said, smiling like a boy again. "There isn't a man in France who can best me with a sword—or a priest who can get at me if Shahrbàz objects."

"And yet you were wounded today."

"By treachery that may well help to bring down the d'Audemars," he said, shifting onto his side the better to be able to look at her. "The cardinal is not a stupid man, Lise, nor is de La Reynie. Between them they are going to get pretty much the full story of the duel, and it will not reflect well on the d'Audemars."

"Who weren't there."

"Nobody who matters will believe that de Ferreulle was

acting alone. He doesn't shit without permission from the chevalier d'Audemar. Under these circumstances I don't think they'll dare touch me."

"And yet I still believe you should go," she said. Her voice suddenly sounded flat in her ears.

"Just when I finally have a good reason to stay," he said, and abruptly kissed her. "But I promise I won't be gone long. The cardinal usually manages to get word to us when it's safe to return after a duel like this. In my case it'll likely be sooner than for de Ferreulle, because—beside that business with the crossbow—I just don't move in society that much. Few people notice when I'm away, so few will notice my eventual return."

"If you're trying to persuade me it wouldn't be difficult for you to stay, you can stop. I may be just your country cousin, but I'm not completely ignorant of how things work here, Rafael. The cardinal's guard isn't always as understanding as the cardinal himself. Is it?" Lise sat up, shivering.

"I should start the fire again." He picked up her nightdress from where it had fallen in her earlier haste to get at him, and wrapped her in it. "My poor fox, you must be freezing."

"I am," she said, "and you're evading the issue."

"I'm sorry, Lise. It's just that you've made me think. And it's not just me and it's not just you, either. If you assume that the d'Audemars are also behind the murder of that wine-provost's daughter—and I do assume that—then not only do they drive me out of the city, they force my Uncle Bertrand to marry the woman of their choosing, not his. I should be here to help him."

"What a shame this didn't occur to you before the fight," Lise said.

"Touché," he said. "There's no satisfying you, is there?"

"Yes there is. You should go. Before it's light."

A Poisoned Prayer
February

⚜

Lise was sitting up in bed, drinking more spiced wine and guessing that Rafael would be passing Chantilly on his way north, when it occurred to her how the d'Audemar family could have learned about her encounter with the spirit of Rafael's Aunt Génie. She hoped it hadn't occurred to him or that, if it had, with the sun was well up it was too late to return to Paris. She would explain her guess to him, she decided, when it was safe for him to come back to the city.

Sleep would not come for her.

⚜

It had been cold on the way to the dinner party, before the sun went down. Now that evening had settled in, some of that cold had muscled its way into Madame de Réalmont's house on the Place Imperial. Lise, shivering as she accepted a glass of warm, spiced wine from a lackey, wished the fashion wasn't for quite so much exposure. "It's hard to tell where goose flesh ends and these begin," she muttered, looking down at her modest décolletage.

Marguerite laughed. "No man would agree with you," she said. "And before you say it, I think that dress is perfect for you, and you for it."

"Thank you, Marguerite. I don't necessarily believe it, but it's good to hear it." Lise smiled at her friend. For the first time in days, Marguerite looked as happy as she claimed to be. It was possible that she had embraced the inevitability of her marriage. Of course, it was equally possible that she had realized that, in the aftermath of the horrific death of her bourgeois rival, there was no way that Bertrand was going to be able to insist on a marriage taking place before the Feast of St John the Baptist in mid-June. The talk now was that the wine-provost's daughter had been poisoned and then strangled to make it look like a robbery. It was quite the scandal and Bertrand du Montauban was said to be distraught; talk was he'd left Paris at the same time Raphael had vanished. Whatever the cause, though, Marguerite was smiling now, and the smile reached her eyes.

"It's nice to be together at a party again," Marguerite said. "I haven't seen you in days. It feels like weeks, you know."

Since I helped Rafael fight de Ferreulle, and since I made him leave the city, Lise realized. Aloud, she said, "I have missed you, Marguerite. Would it be rude of me to ask Madame de Réalmont if we could sit together at dinner?"

"I don't think so," Marguerite said, adding, "and you can ask her now if you'd like. She's on her way to us."

Lise turned, and sure enough their hostess was hurrying toward them, her skirts swishing and darting outward as though there were birds trapped in them and trying to escape. "Oh, Mademoiselle de Trouvaille," Madame de Réalmont said, her voice fluttering like her skirts, "you will never believe it. He is here! He has come here, to see you! Unannounced! It is quite the scandal."

Rafael? Lise thought, knowing better. "Did he say why he was here?" she asked. All but one of the men her aunt was pushing her toward were either at this dinner or away from Paris. It was not hard for her to guess who it was who had arrived uninvited to the party. "Does the captain wish to speak with me?"

"Good God, girl, of course he does! Why else would he come here and risk the tongues of the gossip-mongers in this neighbourhood?" Madame de Réalmont looked as excited as Lise supposed she herself ought to be. *Would that he were here to see you, madame, and not me,* she thought.

"Will you excuse me, Marguerite?" Lise was afraid of what she would see on Marguerite's face, but steeled herself to look anyway. Sure enough, the smile had gone, replaced by something superficially similar but brittle and false.

"Yes, of course." Marguerite turned away; when she spoke next it was to the window. "I will wait here for you, Lise."

Madame de Réalmont escorted Lise to a small room off the entry hall of the apartment. "I've put him in here," she whispered. "I will ensure that you aren't disturbed."

"Oh, please don't go to that effort," Lise said. "In fact, come in with me if you'd like. I assure you nothing interesting is going to happen." *That's one of the reasons,* she said silently to her hostess, *that I have no intention of marrying the good captain. The too-good captain.*

Whether out of a misguided sense of romance, or just perversity, Madame de Réalmont refused to go into the anteroom with her, so Lise was left to face Captain d'Oléron by herself. His great, bland, puppy face was beaming. Was it pride? Was he pleased with himself now, think himself the doer of something clever because he'd tracked her down to this party? Lise wished she could recover the days, now receding from memory, when d'Oléron had seemed a friend in the making—or even those long-ago days when he had appeared to disdain her. She might have been anguished at the thought of being ignored by the handsome musketeer, but that fancied anguish was easier to deal with than the reality of d'Oléron's attentions.

"Good evening, captain," she said, offering him a curtsy but not her hand. "I am surprised, I admit, to see you. Is this not highly irregular?"

"I am sorry mademoiselle." The idiot was positively preening with delight at the transgression. "I must leave Paris in the morning. And while I will only be gone a few days, I did not want to wait to give this to you. Such beauty as yours should never wait."

That was the worst sort of drivel—and at that d'Oléron had probably had to have someone teach it to him—but in spite of this Lise felt her breath flee out of her when the captain opened the plain wooden case he'd been holding.

Inside, resting amid folds of sky-blue silk, was a necklace unlike any she had seen. Tiny globes of what looked like frozen smoke were held in the embrace of red-orange metal claws; there appeared to be a dozen of the globes linked together, and what wasn't the colour of smoke—the metal claws and the links and clasp—was the colour of flame.

"I—It's beautiful," Lise said. "But this is—you should not have done this, captain."

"I had to do it," d'Oléron said, and now his face was stern and, yes, dutiful. "I saw it, and knew it was made for you."

"It is too much." *God in heaven,* she thought, *what am I to do with this?*

"It is not enough," he said, "but it is the best that I can do on a captain's pay."

You could never pay for this with a decade's worth of a captain's pay, Lise realized. With that, the spell of the necklace's exotic beauty broke; her only challenge now was to prevent him from seeing the truth of her understanding. Someone else had purchased this for him to give to her, and that someone was undoubtedly her aunt. The duchesse clearly still had not realized that the harder she pushed Captain d'Oléron on Lise, the further away from him Lise moved.

"I have no words," she said, adding silently, *That I am prepared to share with you.* "I do not know what you expect from me."

"Only that you should wear it," d'Oléron said. "I ask nothing more, expect nothing more. It is a gift, mademoiselle, and freely given."

"In that case I thank you." Lise nodded at him in lieu of another curtsy, and stepped back to the door of the small room. "And now I must ask you to excuse me, captain. I am being rude to my hostess."

"And I must go," he said. "Might I see you wear it before I leave?"

That was presumptuous if not rude, but Lise was desperate enough to be rid of him that she immediately opened the box again and pulled the necklace from it, fighting to keep her hands from shaking. Evidently she was unsuccessful in this, because d'Oléron said, "Don't worry, mademoiselle, I'm told the glass is quite stout." He smiled, and Lise felt a sourness in her mouth at the insincerity she saw there. "The necklace was made to be worn and appreciated by everyone, and not hidden away."

Lise turned, ostensibly to work at the clasp of the necklace but mostly so that he not see her face. Captain d'Oléron was disingenuous enough that his last comment could easily have been said in clumsy earnestness. It was also possible, though, that this was her aunt warning her, though the medium of the captain's clumsy suit, against continuing her association with Rafael. The implication was that Rafael, while keeping her from any of the suitors who wanted to marry her, would never himself offer her the respect of an honest marriage. *As if,* thought Lise, *marriage to a wine merchant or a lawyer would please me more than any time I could steal to be with Rafael.* And the point was moot anyway, so long as Rafael remained hidden in Picardy.

The necklace was, it turned out, easy enough to fasten and not at all fragile. It rested just above the swell of her breasts, near enough to the décolletage to draw attention without getting so close to her bosom as to be vulgar. It was an astonishing piece of work, mysteriously exotic and yet not audaciously demanding of attention. There was no chance, she decided, that the captain had commissioned or even chosen this himself.

Having composed her expression, she turned again so that he could see the necklace on her. His expressions of appreciation, she decided, were about as real as his claim to have paid for the necklace himself. As soon as she had opened the door for the captain to leave, she unclasped the necklace and put it back in its box. It was beautiful, and on that ground at least it would be a shame that it remain hidden. But she would never wear it. Somehow she had to find a way to persuade her aunt that she did not want to marry the captain.

Why, she wondered, was the captain suddenly so smitten with her? This interest couldn't be real; the two of them had settled into a sort of amicable accommodation that held out the promise of a long friendship, but this turn in behaviour, this sudden ardent solicitousness must be, she thought, pure theatre.

Then it struck her. *He wants to marry me because he can't marry Marguerite.*

It made sense. Marguerite came from a good family; it was most unlikely that her father would accept a musketeer captain, no matter how brave and how handsome, as a son. But if he couldn't have Marguerite in marriage, perhaps he could make her his mistress once they were both safely married.

Of course. And what had happened recently, coincident with Captain d'Oléron's sudden interest in her? Marguerite had announced that her father was negotiating a marraige, with Rafael's uncle, no less. It was comic, in a way: if she married d'Oléron and Marguerite married Rafael's uncle, they could all be free to carry on together, Lise with

A Poisoned Prayer
February

Marguerite's husband's nephew and Marguerite with Lise's husband. *I suppose,* she told herself, *that this is how it's done in Paris.*

It really was to laugh. What a pity she couldn't.

By the time she had returned to Madame de Réalmont's drawing room, she had come up with a plan for disposal of the necklace that was worth the potential long-term problems it might cause, because in the short term it could make two people happy.

⚜

"It's beautiful, Lise. I have never in my life seen something like this." Marguerite fingered one of the grey globes, lifting the necklace up from her more impressive bosom. Supper over, the party had adjourned to the long room that ran across the front of Madame de Réalmont's home. "But I should not be wearing this." She sighed. "He gave it to you."

"Only because my aunt told him to, Marguerite." Lise dropped her voice, though nobody was nearby, and steered her friend toward the window. "I could never wear it under those circumstances. I know that he does not love me, dear friend. And I have seen the way he looks at you." She was embellishing things rather extravagantly now. It was only her guess that the motivator of the gift was her aunt; for that matter, it was a guess that it was Marguerite who was the true object of d'Oléron's affections, though in this case she felt on firmer ground.

Even if it was a lie, it was evidently a welcome lie. Marguerite smiled a little for the first time since Lise had been summoned to speak to the importunate captain before dinner. "If only this could mean something real," Marguerite said, "instead of something I have to hide." She turned to stare out the window.

"I understand exactly how you feel," Lise said. Putting a hand on Marguerite's shoulder, she lowered her voice again. "I have had, ah, gifts from Rafael that I can never reveal to anyone save you." Those gifts involved deadly weapons and men's clothing rather than jewels, but the point, she thought, remained a valid one. "And like you, I will never truly have the man I love either."

"Oh, Lise; how did we ever get ourselves into this state? And is there anything we can do for ourselves?"

"Aside from taking many lovers, you mean? I think that perhaps more wine is likely the best thing we can do for ourselves." Lise frowned; outside, a pair of lackeys was arguing about something not quite audible, and that was annoying. Deliberately ignoring the noise, she took a healthy drink, admiring the way the candlelight made the wine glow through the glass. Madame de Réalmont was justifiably proud of the fact that all of her guests could drink from glasses rather than cups or goblets.

"My glass is empty."

"I can remedy that," Lise said, "even if there's nothing I can do about anything more significant than wine."

Michel, Marquis de Verteillac, was waiting at the sideboard when she arrived. "More wine, mademoiselle?" He seemed a bit nervous, which to Lise's surprise made him less pathetic. When he wasn't trying so hard to justify his recent, expensive, ennoblement, the lawyer showed hints of an appealing humanity that contrasted impressively with Captain d'Oléron's studied protestations. *I should have been nicer to him*, Lise thought. *And will be.*

"Thank you, sir," she said. "Not for me this time, I'm afraid. But my friend Marguerite de Courçon thanks you."

"Tell her she's very welcome," the marquis said with obvious pleasure. Lise looked back to the window, where

A Poisoned Prayer
February

Marguerite was now a study in concentration; perhaps the argument had turned into a fully-fledged sword fight. The marquis cleared his throat; turning around, Lise saw that he was holding out Marguerite's glass, almost but not quite brimming.

"Thank you, my lord marquis," Lise said, smiling.

"Can you make out what they're shouting?" Marguerite asked as Lise handed her the glass. "It doesn't sound like French at all."

Lise listened for a moment. "No, it doesn't, does it? It could almost be Latin—but who argues in Latin these days? Not even priests and students bother to curse in anything other than French." Stepping up to the window, she leaned so that her ear was against the glass. "Ai!" she said, recoiling back. "That's cold!" Staring into the darkness, she said, "I still can't make out what they're saying. They don't seem to be fighting, either—they're just standing there, shouting at each other. What in the world do you think they're doing, Marguerite?"

Something cold and wet splashed her foot at the same instant as she heard the sharp, abrupt song of breaking glass. Looking down, she saw candlelight reflected crazily from the broken wine glass and from pools of dark red. Looking up, she saw Marguerite had fallen, face-forward, against the windowpane. Unbelieving, she watched her friend collapse awkwardly to the floor.

Lise dropped to her knees, spilling her own wine in the process. Pushing her now-empty glass aside, she rolled Marguerite over onto her back. Then she sat back on her heels, stunned into breathlessness.

You didn't have to be a physician or a priest to know what the unfocused stare, angry gaping mouth and purple-grey lips meant.

✥

"What news do you bring?" The duchesse de Vimoutiers got up from the couch, where she had been sitting with Lise, and marched to the door of the salon where Cousin Robert stood, trying not to look anyone directly in the eye. "And let me warn you," she added in a voice that suggested the moment just before a summer storm, "that if this is purely a social call you can just crawl back into whatever wine pot you've been living in the past four days. We're none of us in the mood for frivolities, boy."

"I have news," he said in the quiet mumble that always appeared when he was unhappy or ashamed. "Not very good, though." For a moment Lise was occupied with feeling sorry for her cousin, who could never seem to be much in his mother's eyes. Then she remembered her situation, and sank back against the couch.

The duchesse pulled Robert into the room by one arm. "Well? Out with it! Honestly, you're worse than your father."

"Please, Marie-Françoise, control your temper. It isn't helping matters." The marquise d'Ombrevilles got up with difficulty from her chair on the opposite side of the salon and walked toward Lise. "If it's bad news I'm not in any hurry to hear it."

Aunt d'Ombrevilles had brought Lise here three days ago, following her second sleepless night in the aftermath of Marguerite's nightmarish death. A preliminary examination of the body had suggested, and a more thorough post-mortem by a physician and priest in the employ of the police had confirmed, that Marguerite had been killed by poison. Word had spread throughout Paris at the speed of a curse, and now it seemed as if even the emperor was on edge, waiting to see if Lise would be brought to the Bastille

A Poisoned Prayer
February

as a poisoner. Both of her aunts had decided, after a mutual consultation, that Lise needed to be with family at all times. The company served well enough as a distraction during the day; it had not, however, allowed her any sleep. Not even prayer had helped.

It was not the threat of trial that kept Lise awake at night, though. It was the knowledge, relearned every minute it seemed, that her friend was gone. She would never again share a clandestine cup of coffee with Marguerite, would never gossip about men or who had become whose mistress, would never again share fashion and dressing discoveries. Marguerite had, to a very great extent, *made* the person Lise had become in Paris.

And now Lise stared up at the ceiling every night, revisiting every instant of their last moments together, hoping that this time she would discover the one thing she could have done differently that would have saved her friend. What news could anyone bring that would possibly be worse than what she lived through when the sun went down?

"It's what we feared," Robert said after a long pause. "Monsieur de Courçon has sworn out a *lettre de cachet* against Lise. He accuses her of poisoning his daughter."

"My god," said Aunt d'Ombrevilles. "The fool."

Aunt de Vimoutiers didn't blink, didn't even acknowledge her kinswoman's outburst. "Has he signed it yet?"

"De Courçon?" Robert started to say more, but what emerged was a babble that quickly trailed away in an embarrassed clearing of the throat.

"The emperor," Lise said. Robert and Aunt d'Ombrevilles turned abruptly, as though startled to discover Lise in their midst. "He has to sign it before it can be enforced."

"At least in the case of capital crimes he does, yes." Aunt de Vimoutiers walked back to Lise and squeezed her shoulder. "Don't worry too much, dear. De Courçon is a minor entity, at least as far as the court is concerned. The emperor will think twice before he takes that man's word over my own."

"I don't know," Robert said. "He has more friends now than I would have thought, and some of them are pretty big, at court and outside of it. There are strange things being said at the parties I go to, Mother. Alliances of nobles and bourgeois, counts and lawyers and merchants all angry at the emperor for not doing more to enforce the laws. Old de Courçon might get his letter signed sooner than we think."

I should do something, Lise thought. But what? Almost as horrible as Marguerite's death was this smothering sense of lethargy that had wrapped itself around her in the past few days. She knew she ought to be doing things for herself, rather than having them done for her. But it was so much easier to be led.

"This is preposterous!" Aunt de Vimoutiers turned on her son as though everything that had happened was his fault. "Of course the emperor should be more forceful in keeping the rabble in line. That peasant uprising—what do they call it?"

"The *fronde?*" Aunt d'Ombrevilles suggested, the way a mouse might.

"Whatever it is—*that*, Charles should come down on top of like one of the old city walls falling down. But *we* aren't rabble! It's ridiculous that anyone thinks Lise would murder her closest friend in Paris—maybe her *only* friend in this cursed city. But even if anyone did suspect her, Lise deserves a proper hearing at court, not to be hauled off to the Bastille like some drunken younger son."

"I don't disagree with you, cousin," Aunt d'Ombrevilles began.

A Poisoned Prayer
February

The duchesse turned on her. "Of course you don't! Nobody in their right mind would!"

"But that's more or less the point, isn't it? Poor de Courçon has lost his daughter. He can't exactly be thinking clearly right now. He wants to strike out—I can see why he might."

"Well, he should strike out at someone at his own level! Surely the emperor realizes how ridiculous this all is."

"And right on the verge of marriage, too," Robert said.

"What?" His mother turned back to him. "De Courçon isn't getting married, you fool—" She stopped. "Ah. That. Yes; it was to de Montauban, wasn't it?"

"Rafael's uncle, yes." Robert scratched his chin absently. "Second fiancée he's lost in a matter of weeks, isn't it? I should be more careful with my women."

"Oh, don't be an idiot," Aunt de Vimoutiers said, but Lise couldn't suppress a smile. She had just about got Robert figured out, she decided. Idiots could get away with an awful lot, couldn't they?

Rafael's uncle. She thought about Rafael, wondered if he was bored nearly to death yet up in Picardy, wondered if he had come to the same conclusions she had, and realized that she was not likely to see him again, ever. *He could tell me what to do*, she thought.

And then she thought, *he just has, though he doesn't know it.* "I have to leave," she said.

The others continued to argue about which course of action they should pursue. "I have to leave," she said again, more loudly. She got to her feet.

Everyone stopped talking and stared at her. "What did you say?" the duchesse asked.

"I said that I have to leave. It's not safe if I stay here: not safe for me, not safe for you. If I'm arrested they may take you as well." Lise swallowed; it hurt. "I think I should leave France. Exiles usually go to England, don't they?"

"No!" Both her aunt and cousin de Vimoutiers rushed to her, each grabbing a shoulder.

"You cannot run," the duchesse said. "Go to England and you might as well paint your confession on bed sheets and hang it on the towers of the cathedral."

"And anyway," Robert said, "who will I go to for advice on *reversis* and women if you leave?"

"Think a moment, though," said Aunt d'Ombrevilles, soft-spoken and edging back to her corner of the room. "Lise has a point. As you yourself said, cousin, this situation makes little sense. And if it makes little sense now, with Lise safe in your home, how much less sense will it make if she's locked up? If de Courçon succeeds in getting his letter signed by the emperor, there's almost no way we can control what happens."

"Madame, you underestimate me," the duchesse snapped.

"I do no such thing," said the marquise, and Lise was startled to hear as much steel in this aunt's voice as in the more exalted one. "Quite the contrary. You have many friends at court, Marie-Françoise. But forgive me for pointing out that you also have more than your share of enemies. And those enemies might, for example, go to the cardinal—he dislikes you, does he not? Though he seems to have a warm corner in his heart for Lise." Aunt de Vimoutiers's face paled, save for spots of red on both cheeks that made her look as if she'd been slapped. *That hit home,* thought Lise. "Now think of how much more effectively we can lobby," Aunt d'Ombrevilles said, "if Lise is safely out of the hands of those who might use her fate to strike at you."

"I never thought for a second that this was all happening

because someone was trying to attack Mother." Robert stared at Lise; he looked to her as if he was trying to calculate the likelihood of her suddenly exploding.

"Of course not," Aunt de Vimoutiers said. "But I confess I hadn't thought this all the way through, either. You are probably right, cousin. And God knows it wouldn't be the first time a falsely accused member of our class had to defend his or her honour from Sussex or Kent."

"I will pack my bags," Robert said. His hand, Lise noted, had wrapped itself around the hilt of his ridiculous sword.

"Oh, I don't think that will be necessary," Aunt d'Ombrevilles said. "You wouldn't enjoy England very much, Robert. And—I mean no offense here—Lise needs someone a bit more, ah, experienced to take her there."

"I can take care of myself," Lise said. *Probably. Possibly.* "I don't want to cause any more trouble than I already have."

"Under no circumstances are you leaving my house by yourself." Aunt de Vimoutiers began shredding her handkerchief. "I don't even want you to go with an escort of less than a dozen men."

"I think," said Lise, "that I ought to be trying to *sneak* out of the city. You're describing an invasion of the *faubourgs.*"

"What about Rafael?" Robert had sidled over to her. He whispered, "He'd be happy to escort you, I'm sure. And I know you'd be safe with him."

"I can't ask him!" she whispered in response. "He's hiding from the cardinal himself. You know that, Robert."

"For you, he'd risk it. Why won't you let him?"

"What in the world are you two doing?" Aunt de Vimoutiers inserted herself between Lise and Robert. "Did I hear you mention that bastard Bellevasse?"

"I think he'd make an excellent escort, that's all," Robert muttered. "He likes Lise, his Blessing's so powerful even the cardinal would think twice before challenging him, and he's an excellent swordsman."

"He is a disaster waiting to happen to us," Aunt de Vimoutiers said. "Lise, I forbid you to even mention this to that man. The same goes for you, Robert. We will handle this in the family, Lise."

"The man has too many enemies, Lise," Aunt d'Ombrevilles said. "I have no doubt he's as strong and determined as you say, Robert. But this has to be done quickly and quietly. Do you not think that de La Reynie or the cardinal have men watching him, or looking for him? And if they do, his enemies won't be far behind. Get him involved and you might not save Lise—you could doom her."

Beaten down, Robert did not respond. Lise, though she said nothing either, was secretly grateful. It was bad enough that exile was the best outcome her circumstances promised her; not even for her own safety would she impose her own fate on Rafael.

"If not Robert, then who could be my escort?" she asked. "I don't know any other men in Paris well enough to trust them." There had been a few suitors, of course, but she hadn't really done anything to encourage them to get close to her. And the one man she had begun to feel more sympathy for—the Marquis de Verteillac—was the man who had poured the wine the doctors said had killed Marguerite. Lise knew that she hadn't poisoned the wine, so who had? De Verteillac, inexplicable as it sounded, was the best suspect. She knew he'd been questioned.

So it hardly made sense for her to put herself into his hands. "I still think the best solution would be for me and

A Poisoned Prayer
February

Juliette to sneak out of the city and make our way to the coast. I could travel up the Seine with one of the freight barges. Or go cross-country to Normandy. Nobody would expect me to go that way."

"That makes perfect sense," Aunt de Vimoutiers said. "Everything except the part about you and your maid sneaking out alone. That is impossible, Lise."

"But if you won't let me go alone and you won't let Robert escort me, then I'm trapped here." She didn't mention Rafael, couldn't because there was no way to do so without pain.

"Yes, you are, aren't you?" The duchesse kept her voice flat, so Lise couldn't tell if there was triumph or resignation behind the words.

"What about that young man you've been pushing at Lise?"

Everyone turned to look at Aunt d'Ombrevilles.

"Captain d'Oléron?" Lise stammered a moment. "He has duties," she said after collecting her thoughts. "He told me he had to leave Paris."

"He's back," Robert said. "Saw him last night."

"He would be violating his oath, then, if he left the princesse's side. Wouldn't he?" She thought of the eager musketeer sharing his clumsy devotions all the way to England and had to suppress her disgust. She didn't dare say anything aloud about this: d'Oléron was her aunt's favourite, or at least one of them, and she needed her aunt's support now more than she ever had. Still, the thought of weeks spent in the captain's company…

"You're a good friend of the princesse, aren't you, Marie-Françoise?" asked Aunt d'Ombrevilles. "Perhaps you could—"

"I will have a word with the princesse," Aunt de Vimoutiers said, as if it had been her own idea. "She doesn't have to know why I want the captain released from his duties, and she won't ask it of me." She nodded at her cousin. "Excellent idea, dear. Lise," she added, "I believe you should pack now. You'll want to leave this evening."

⚜

"Thank you for coming back to the city, monsieur." De La Reynie nodded, with more deference than was due, to the man hunched over the table opposite him and looking like an unhappy gargoyle. "It has been too long since we talked last."

"I could have stood it being a little bit longer," said Rafael. "I was enjoying my rustification very much, thank you, until your man here arrived at my mother's door with enough archers to invade the Low Countries. You gave her quite a start."

"Would that I could simply have asked you to come," de La Reynie said, smiling and knowing that he'd deflated de Bellevasse's indignation with the quiet comment.

"Touché," de Bellevasse replied. He leaned back in his chair and smiled. "I suppose I could take advantage of your invitation to see to some business that I've been neglecting during my—absence. I remind you of your promise, monsieur: not a word to the cardinal so long as I'm in the city."

"Not a word, monsieur, so long as you're in the city at my request. Once our interview is concluded, you have the rest of the day to get yourself beyond the gates under my protection. After that, I'm afraid I'll be obliged to treat you as I would treat any other noble suspected of duelling."

Rafael sighed. "It wasn't my intention to draw a crowd.

It was de Ferreulle who insisted we fight in the Place Imperial."

"I don't disbelieve you, monsieur. I'll be having rather stronger words with him, once we locate him." De La Reynie picked up a quill and sheet of paper. "Now, as to the reason for my invitation—"

"Wait. Did you say you can't find de Ferreulle?" Rafael leaned forward again. "You had no trouble finding me within a day or two of my leaving Paris, and I have many more options in terms of boltholes than does that fool. I've been under surveillance by your men the whole time I've been in Picardy. You are serious when you say you can't locate him?"

"It's not something I'm proud of," de La Reynie said. "Obviously the d'Audemars are hiding him somewhere. Equally obviously, I can't just go and ask old Simon what he's done with the man." He dipped the quill and wrote de Bellevasse's name at the top of the paper. "But I didn't bring you here to discuss de Ferreulle."

"You didn't?" De Bellevasse looked startled, and de La Reynie decided the surprise was genuine. So it was true: his men had intercepted the message before it reached the duc.

"As far as I'm concerned, your dramatic flouting of the cardinal's anti-duelling laws is—temporarily—a non-issue. It didn't happen.

"I want to talk to you about murder."

De Bellevasse smiled. "Whose?" *Presumably he thinks I'm joking*, de La Reynie thought. *He should know better.*

"Marguerite de Courçon's, monsieur. I believe you know her."

Again, surprise. Perhaps even shock. "Marguerite?" de Bellevasse asked. "Lise—Mademoiselle de Trouvaille's friend? When did this happen?"

"Four nights before last; I decided to send for you the next morning. And she was a friend of the young woman, yes. But I have been thinking of her as your uncle's fiancée."

"My uncle?" Rafael's brows lifted for the space of a breath, then dropped in understanding. "Why do you think Uncle Bertrand has anything to do with this? You can't think that he killed her. That wouldn't make any sense. And why didn't I know about this before now?"

"You have to admit, monsieur, that it is very hard to portray as coincidence the murder of not one but two young women in the past few weeks, both them affianced to your uncle." *Very likely not involved,* de La Reynie wrote on the paper. He decided that now wasn't the time to tell de Bellevasse why he hadn't heard of Mademoiselle de Courçon's murder.

"Of course it's no coincidence," de Bellevasse said, picking at a splinter on the table in an agitated fashion. "It's obviously a conspiracy." He lifted his head to stare at de La Reynie. "But my uncle is the one wronged: either of those women would have been a very advantageous match. Uncle Bertrand told me himself how badly he needed to make this sort of marriage. His finances are not good." De Bellevasse gestured with outspread hands. "If it had been one or the other, I'd understand your suspicion. Truth to tell, I wondered myself when that merchant's daughter came out of the river. But both of them dead? It's obvious that somebody has taken vile steps to prevent him from marrying again."

"And presumably you have some idea of who might have done so." Knowing what was coming, de La Reynie permitted himself a small smile.

"Obviously it's the d'Audemars."

"Obviously? Not to me."

A Poisoned Prayer
February

De Bellevasse gave him the sort of look one usually saved for the very young or imbeciles. "You know, monsieur, how that family is, the way they grasp and control. It's why they killed my aunt."

"Please, monsieur. We are not going to discuss that again. Unless you have something new to offer me." *And I know you don't,* de La Reynie thought.

"There's nothing new about the way old Simon gets his hooks into people and refuses to release them," de Bellevasse said, mouth forming a stubborn pout. "I know that my uncle had made these matches himself. It's clear to me that the d'Audemar family would never give up control of his next marriage. In fact, I have begun to suspect that my uncle may even be spying on me for the prince. No, I can't prove that either. But a certain incident seems to have been reported to them, and my uncle was one of the few who knew of it."

"How very interesting," de La Reynie said. "Blackmail, is it? Every day, old Simon becomes more and more like a common criminal." He wondered, not for the first time, what it would take to make this unhappy young man grow up. "My problem, my good duc, is that it is always clear to you that the d'Audemar family is responsible for—well, pretty much everything. You blame snow in the winter on the d'Audemar family. I need considerably more than you telling me it's 'clear' and 'obvious' if I'm going to be able to make any use of your evidence."

"I'm not at all sure why you think I can help, then." His eyes narrowed. "And perhaps you could tell me why I didn't hear about this until now."

"I had your man intercepted before he could reach you," de La Reynie said. "I wasn't sure how you'd respond when you got the news, and so I decided that you should be told under controlled conditions."

"How very kind of you."

De La Reynie felt the blood rise in his face. "Monsieur, that tone may be suitable for dealing with your lackeys and your friends, but I do not accept it." *Self-absorbed bastard,* he thought. "You no doubt feel that the entire world owes you a debt of restitution for the loss of your aunt, my lord duc, but I assure you that your own attitude is the single biggest obstacle standing in the way of any successful resolution of that case. Further, if in the next few hours or days I develop even the slightest suspicion that you are behaving with regard to this investigation the way you behave about your aunt's death, I will not hesitate to put you in a place where you will pose no threat to me—or to yourself."

De Bellevasse hunched forward again; a wooden squeal told de La Reynie he was pushing back his chair. "I do not like to be threatened, monsieur," the duc said, as slowly as he was moving his chair, "not even by you."

"You might learn to accept it, then, if you cannot like it." De La Reynie made sure that de Bellevasse could see both his hands. "I have always respected you, monsieur, for your intelligence as much as for your position and Blessing. I would regret having to move against you. But you must understand, de Bellevasse, that nobody in this empire is above the emperor's law. There are too many nobles in this city today who do not accept that truth, and they will soon enough realize the error of their ways. I beg you, monsieur, as one who respects you: do not place yourself in their company."

"I am not putting myself above the law," de Bellevasse said through clenched teeth. "I am trying to see that the law is enforced. But," he added, seeing the rejoinder about to reach de La Reynie's lips, "I do not wish to be ungrateful. I promise you I will not hinder your investigation, and I will pass on to you anything of relevance that I learn."

"I ask nothing more, monsieur," de La Reynie said, and bowed more formally to de Bellevasse as the duc left the chamber.

"So," he said after closing the door. "What did you think?"

Valentin emerged from behind the heavy carpet that had hidden him from view during the interview. "There's no doubt he firmly believes in his uncle's innocence," the investigator said. "I'm certain he knew I was here, because after a few minutes of your conversation he dropped all of his guards. I got a very clear reading."

"Imagine that." De La Reynie smiled. "So what else was he thinking?"

"Hard to be sure," Valentin said. "Aside from some confusion over his uncle's motives, he was quite—well, let's just say that even for one of our aristocrats he seems unusually self-absorbed. Mostly, though, I felt anger. Do you not think, monsieur, that de Bellevasse is actually a much better suspect than is his uncle? Everything he said about his uncle is essentially true. But every accusation he made against the prince d'Audemar could as easily be made against him."

"What a good thing," de La Reynie said, "that most of our cases don't revolve around *idées fixes* the way this one does. Our friend the duc's automatic response is to blame the d'Audemars for everything. And *your* automatic response, dear Valentin, is to blame him in turn. If de Bellevasse had been responsible for all the crimes you accuse him of, he'd have gone to the block long ago. Nobody is so clever as to hide their guilt for so many crimes for so long."

"But he does have motive, monsieur."

"True," de La Reynie said. "But allow me to say that while we have motive, *motif* is lacking. No," he said, waving off Valentin's objection, "I cannot agree with you. Both young women were poisoned, Valentin, and there's strange indirection in both cases. With the bourgeois girl it was the attempt to make it look as if she'd been strangled. With Mademoiselle de Courçon it's the way nobody can pinpoint how the poison got into her. But it's just as it was with that servant of d'Audemar's we pulled from the river a couple of months ago: the method is too crude for de Bellevasse. If he'd really wanted those women dead, we'd have had to employ one of the cardinal's stronger assistants to determine how it was done—if it were even possible to determine that."

"Perhaps he's simply using crude methods to persuade us that he couldn't be the guilty one." Valentin sat down. "It wouldn't be the first time someone had tried that."

"Remember Friar Punch and Occam's philosophy, Valentin. My explanation requires less convolution, so it makes more sense, unless you can present me with evidence of de Bellevasse ever using any weapons other than his rapiers and his magic in dealing with enemies."

"I am sorry, monsieur." Valentin shrugged, the expression on his face one of unhappy frustration. "I suppose I just want this to make sense. At the moment it's refusing to. It's like the reactivation of the city ward-stones, or the seditious talk our men keep overhearing in the bourgeois taverns and cafés. It's all pieces that refuse to come together in a way that makes sense."

"I've been wondering about that," de La Reynie said. "Perhaps it's refusing to come together for us because it simply isn't all together. Have we ever considered the possibility, Valentin, that there just is no connection between the conspiracy we know is out there and this low-key war between de Bellevasse and the d'Audemars?"

"But you said you were certain the prince is conspiring with the bourgeois to somehow attack the government."

"I am. I am also beginning to wonder if we've been trying to force de Bellevasse's vendetta into that conspiracy." He picked up the note-paper and pointed to the last remark he'd written. "As you yourself said a moment ago, Valentin, our friend is very self-absorbed. My man in his household tells me the same thing. This is all about *him*. Do you really think he'd settle for being just a cog in someone else's infernal machine? Or care what anyone else was doing, so long as it didn't affect his own dreams of vengeance?"

"If not de Bellevasse, then, who?"

"I am thinking, Valentin. Perhaps we should involve ourselves in the arrest of the young woman the duc mentioned—our informant Mademoiselle de Trouvaille. Perhaps she is more connected to these things than we have thought."

"You've been told that she is definitely being charged with the murder?"

"I don't know about any charge," de La Reynie said. "But there will definitely be an arrest. I understand the emperor will be signing the *lettre de cachet* tomorrow morning."

March

One

I AM NEVER going to ride a horse in the woman's style again, Lise told herself. *I would never have survived this day so well if I'd had to use a woman's seat.*

They had slipped out of Paris just before sundown yesterday, and this morning Lise had insisted on changing into her country-cousin costume, though this time without the moustache. She had sent Juliette home—two men would not have had a maid riding with them, and anyway she had decided it wasn't fair to reward Juliette's devotion by exposing her to this sort of risk. If they were caught, Lise and d'Oléron would be returned to Paris in chains and locked in the Bastille. Juliette would be tortured as part of her interrogation.

In breeches and boots it had been so much easier to ride, and she had enjoyed at least the horseback part of the day more than any similar excursion since her youth, when all children in the neighbourhood of the family château rode the same style. The weather was clear but cold; the chill that had come down on Paris the night Marguerite was murdered had not lifted, and Lise was sure it was only a matter of time before a blizzard hit. She prayed to all three of the Trinity that she reached England before the weather became worse, then wished her prayers had more effect.

Captain d'Oléron had been horrified at her dismissal of

her maid, and more horrified when he saw the ratty-looking young man she had become, but as they were now fugitives there wasn't all that much he could say, or expect her to do. He had scarcely spoken to her today, and if it was her costume that was responsible for his reticence, she was doubly convinced that she'd made the right choice.

On one score, at least, the musketeer's silence had frustrated her. Last night they had passed the blackened, gap-toothed visage of a burned-out building; at the time Captain d'Oléron had said something in passing about the poor, a riot and a grain merchant's warehouse, but today he'd dismissed her request for more information as being irrelevant to their current circumstances. This was true enough as things stood, but Lise still wanted to know what had happened. The city had seemed tense to her as she left it, and she wasn't convinced that this was entirely due to her own anxiety.

"Should we be stopping soon?" she asked. She knew she ought to demand that they ride as late into the night as they could. But d'Oléron's unexpected diffidence annoyed her, and now she wanted to do whatever it was he seemed unlikely to want. "It's going to be dark in another quarter-hour or so," she added. Unbidden, the memory of the loup-garou came snarling into her mind, and she thought she saw it shape in the swirling smoke of her expelled breath.

"I was about to suggest that," he said, bringing his horse alongside hers. *Damn,* she thought. "I know of a farm nearby where we can spend the night in safety. It's owned by the family of friends, and they'll ask no questions."

"How close are we to the coast?" she asked. "Is there a chance we'll be there tomorrow?"

He laughed; in the bitter cold it sounded unpleasant in her ears. "If we could fly, perhaps. Otherwise, we're several days away at best. And that assumes that we're able to get a boat down the Seine without interference from soldiers or police." He turned to her, and there was something different about him. "I didn't say anything last night because it wouldn't have done any good. But after your aunt charged me with seeing you safely out of France, I heard at the palace that de La Reynie himself is interested in you. We may not be able to take the river at all."

"Monsieur de La Reynie?" Mention of the lieutenant-general of police saddened her. Yes, he'd frightened her at their first meeting, but subsequently she'd come to think of him as a man of pleasant temper, had allowed herself to think that he liked her a little. At the very least he was interested in her; he'd even described her magical handicap as an ability. And now he was coming after her himself? "I think that I would rather keep to the roads, if Monsieur de La Reynie is watching the river."

"Very wise," d'Oléron said.

"I wish I could fly," she said, thinking of Rafael's horrible companion, Shahrbàz. It wasn't fair that creatures of that sort could fly, and men and women could not.

She sat up in the saddle. "Do you hear that?"

"What? Ah—horses."

They stopped their horses, and now there were definitely hoofbeats, sounding crisply in the late afternoon cold.

He twisted around in his saddle. "Nobody is back there— yet. But you are right, mademoiselle: there are horsemen behind us, at least four."

"And they're not walking." On the frozen mud of the road the hoofbeats sounded like military drummers playing the charge. That speed meant there was a good chance they were after her. "Would de La Reynie—?"

"Yes, he would. He plots and calculates the way a spider

spins a web. And he respects nothing but the law, and nobody but the emperor." Captain d'Oléron nudged his horse to a faster walk. "My advice, mademoiselle, is that we move more quickly. And be prepared to gallop."

What would de La Reynie do if he caught her trying to get out of the country? Had she effectively announced her guilt by leaving for England? Aunt de Vimoutiers may have been right in her first instinct; perhaps Lise should have agreed to stay and fight.

Horsemen emerged from around a bend in the road. Captain d'Oléron had guessed well: there seemed to be four of them. Their affiliation wasn't advertised by the nondescript hats and cloaks they wore. But they were moving at a trot when they came into view, and as Lise watched them they picked up the pace.

She heard a click and turned in time to see d'Oléron, holding the reins and a cocked pistol in one hand, draw the second pistol from its saddle holster. "Go, mademoiselle," he said, and now she realized what it was that had seemed different about him this morning. The urgent suitor had completely disappeared, and she was looking now at the cool, dispassionate musketeer he had been when she first met him.

"What are you going to do?" she asked him.

"Whatever is needed to hold them off, mademoiselle," he said. "But you have to go, now. Fast."

"Thank you," she said. It wasn't much, especially in light of the way she had treated him since deciding she didn't love him after all. But it was the best she could do under these circumstances. She spurred her horse into a gallop, hoping its shoes would provide adequate purchase on the frost-slick ground.

I should have asked for directions to his friend's farm,

she thought. But when she turned her head, she saw him galloping in the opposite direction toward her pursuers. There was nothing to do now but fly and hope she could improvise passage to England by herself. Assuming she made it as far as the coast.

She made it as far as the next bend in the road.

As she galloped, a horseman emerged from the woods alongside the road and began to chase her. A companion to the rider launched into the road as she passed him, and a third and fourth, who had been waiting further up, came into the road and blocked her path. Cursing, Lise tugged her rapier from its scabbard, wrestling with it because her arms weren't quite long enough to draw it on horseback.

"Easy, boy," one of the galloping riders gasped. "No point in getting yourself poked for nothing." What the horsemen said next surprised her: "Where is the woman de Trouvaille? Where is d'Oléron?"

It took a moment for the meaning to reach her. "You're his friends? From the farm?" The man nodded. "I am Lise de Trouvaille," she said. The other man, who had now come up alongside her, cursed with a laugh, then reached for her bridle. She didn't resist when the riders slowed her horse, and the other two riders joined them. "There were men following us," she said. "Captain d'Oléron went back to stop them."

The rider nearest her smiled. "Good for him," he said. "Come with us, mademoiselle." The man's laconic comment seemed odd to her, given d'Oléron's likely fate. That wasn't all, either. As the party cantered down a rugged dirt track off the main road, Lise realized that the man didn't look like any farmer she'd ever seen. Perhaps peasants looked differently in the north.

That they likely weren't peasants at all became clear to

her when her party rode into the courtyard of a well-made farmhouse.

The first person she saw was Guillaume, comte d'Audemar.

Before she could say or do anything, Lise felt a hammer blow inside her skull, a blast of magic unlike anything she had ever experienced. As from a distance she heard a howl of pain and anguish, and then the world went away.

⚜

The headache would not stop. Neither did the screaming, and Lise had been conscious for some moments before she fully realized that the screams were coming from someone other than her. "What happened?" she asked.

"You fainted." She turned to see the comte de Ferreulle, seated with his épée across his lap, regarding her as if she were some sort of specimen. "I wanted to wake you in my own inimitable fashion—I don't think I've ever had a woman dressed as a man before—but Guillaume and Étienne saw fit to deny me my fun." He made an extremely rude gesture in the direction of her crotch, and Lise flushed with furious helplessness.

"You'll pay for that insult," she said. "Eventually." Another blast of magic and another hideous scream hit her simultaneously. "Sweet Jesus," she gasped, fighting the urge to vomit. "What is that?"

"One of Étienne's father's more amusing little experiments." De Ferreulle gripped the hilt of his sword and got to his feet. "Up you get, girl. I'm supposed to take you to them as soon as you're awake."

He didn't take her far: the d'Audemars were gathered in the farmhouse's main room. In front of the fire at the far end of the room, on an old-fashioned bed, a woman thrashed and howled, surrounded by people only some of whom Lise recognized. De Ferreulle pushed her forward, but Lise was already walking in horrified fascination.

The woman was young, possibly even younger than Lise—though the pain was making her look much older. By the roughness of her dress and hands she was clearly a peasant, the one person in this room who seemed truly to belong in it. The source of the pain was obvious as soon as Lise reached the bed: the woman was hugely pregnant, and obviously in the throes of birthing. That would make the unhappy-looking woman holding the pregnant woman's hand a midwife. An even less-happy woman, clearly noble, sat in a corner staring at nothing; occasionally she would look at the woman on the bed with a sort of horrified fascination that immediately turned into repugnance.

The presence of women here, even a noblewoman, made a certain amount of sense. The presence of the prince d'Aude and his sons made no sense whatever. Men *never* attended a birthing.

Hadn't de Ferreulle, though, referred to an experiment? Could the farm girl thrashing on the bed be the experiment? The woman, thin blond hair sweat-stuck to her forehead and face, twisted and opened her mouth to scream again; Lise felt the coming blast of magic and fought against it with all the skill she'd been able to learn in the past few weeks.

Then she realized the nature of the experiment.

"Good Lord," she said. Another blast, almost too strong for her to resist. "Sweet Mother of God. She's a witch, and one of you has made her pregnant."

"I told you she was too clever for her own good."

Lise spun around. Captain d'Oléron had entered the room, accompanied by the four men she had thought him to be attacking. At first she could find no words, could only stare at him. His insolent smile, though, warned her that she had to say something biting, if she wanted to retain a shred of self-respect concerning this bastard. "Looks as if I was right about you," she said. "What a pity my aunt wouldn't believe me."

"You don't know how right you are, girl," he said, and his thin, cold smile made Lise terrified for her aunt. For both aunts; they had both been involved in handing her over to d'Oléron, so whatever he had in mind for the duchesse would no doubt befall her cousin as well.

"I don't care about any of that," the chevalier said. "You told me, d'Oléron, that she had unusual gifts. So make her use them to help Anaïs through this!"

Shrugging, d'Oléron lifted one of his pistols. "You heard the man," he said. "Do something to ease the girl."

"What?" Had they confused her with someone Blessed? "I don't have any God-given gifts; everybody knows that. And I've never been at a lying-in, so I can't even do anything as a midwife's assistant."

The musketeer walked toward her and leveled the pistol at her breast. "This is not the time," he said in a cold, quiet voice, "to play imbecile. All the talk at court is of your mysterious gift; de Bellevasse as much as confirmed it, and even de La Reynie seems to think you're some new and marvellous prodigy. Don't pretend ignorance: it wouldn't disturb me in the slightest to shut up that insolent mouth of yours."

"I have no idea what the duc de Bellevasse or the lieutenant-general of police think of my so-called gift," she said, "but the only court talk I'm aware of was because I knew when a scheming bitch was trying to use a prayer to humiliate me. And if that's what you're talking about, my little soldier, then it's a gift you're welcome to. Yes, apparently I can feel prayers being cast. It's brought me nothing but pain and embarrassment." She was surprised at how calm she sounded; she felt terrified almost to the point of being unable to stand up.

The woman Anaïs went through another series of paroxysms that lasted, at Lise's guess, nearly five minutes. She noticed now that the prince d'Aude did not appear the slightest bit upset by the screaming and thrashing. Instead, he observed with attention that seemed almost obscene. His younger son, though, was clearly going through agonies almost as wrenching as those the young woman was suffering. *I think,* Lise thought, *that I know who the father is.*

And then she had to ask herself, *What noble worthy of his name would make his son service a peasant broodmare—and a witch, at that?* Any child born from this blasphemous union would be cursed. The moment word of this reached Paris the cardinal would have the woman put to the torture, broken on the wheel, and burned. And not even the prince's exalted status could save him from a blasphemy conviction. The prince d'Aude was in the process of destroying his family. And for what purpose?

"This is a waste of time," the chevalier said when quiet eventually returned to the room. "Get her out of here, somebody. At best she's in the way; at worst she might affect the baby somehow. Take her to the cellar, de Ferreulle. You know what to do."

"It will be my pleasure, my lord chevalier." De Ferreulle winked at Lise and grabbed her shoulder.

"I did warn you, mademoiselle," the comte d'Audemar said, smiling nastily. "What a pity you're not that bright."

"Hold on a moment." The prince broke his gaze from the panting, sweating girl on the bed and fixed his eye on Lise.

"I think I may have another use for this one. Get her to the cellar, de Ferreulle, but make sure no harm comes to her."

"Define 'harm,' my lord prince."

"Don't be an ass, de Ferreulle," the prince said. "I scarcely tolerate you as it is. Annoy me any further and you'll find yourself beginning a stay in the cardinal's prison. A short stay."

"I wonder if that old man realizes how much harm I could do him?" de Ferreulle said as he pushed Lise out of the farmhouse's back door. "He might treat me differently if he did."

"He almost certainly would," Lise said. "So you'd best pray that he never does realize the threat you could represent." She smiled at him until his face showed that he'd finally understood what she'd said.

He slapped her. Hard. Stunned, she couldn't even curse as she fell to the frozen ground of the yard.

"Shut up, mademoiselle," he said. "You're the one who should be praying now."

Scrambling to get to her feet, Lise risked a surreptitious check of her boot for the knife she'd placed there this morning. It was gone; someone must have searched her while she was dead to the world. Her cheek stung where he'd hit her, the cold and the frustration of being weaponless making it feel worse. *I never want to be without a weapon again*, she decided. *I am sick of feeling helpless.*

"I've no time for prayer," she said. "I'm adding up your account."

"You seem to think I should spend all of my time being afraid of people," he told her. "From where I stand, it seems as if I'm the person to be feared, and you're the one who should be afraid." Standing behind her, he grabbed her hair with one hand, bunching it in his fist until her scalp burned.

She cursed and kicked back at him, but he dodged, gave her hair a sharp pull that forced a yelp from her, and then pushed her forward. His treatment had pulled tears from her eyes, so she couldn't see where he was pushing her. After a few paces, though, he stopped. Reaching past her with his free hand, he pulled something; she heard a brief scraping sound. Blinking back the tears, she saw a worn, scarred wooden door. He tugged it open. "Get in."

A set of steep, narrow stairs led down into a small, low-ceilinged room. As she reached the bottom of the steps, de Ferreulle conjured up God-light, and she could see her prison. The floor was hard-packed earth, the walls and ceiling old rose-coloured brick. The ceiling was vaulted; all in all, the place had an ancient look to it that suggesting something from the decadence of Rome.

"Up against that wall," de Ferreulle said, giving her another shove. At least he'd had to let go her hair when they made their way down the steps. "Hands behind you."

"I warn you, bastard, that if you try to do anything to me you'll have to kill me to keep me from tearing out your throat." *He has a sword*, she thought. *So there's a good chance that I'm going to die now.* It didn't matter, she realized. She was going to die here, later if not now. If she was able to kill de Ferreulle she might at least have a chance of escaping.

"Don't flatter yourself," he said. He tugged at her cloak, and she heard and felt it tear. "I'm going to tie you up and leave you here. Perhaps d'Audemar will give you to his lackeys. Or to the pigs." He tied her hands behind her, and he wasn't gentle about it. The scratchiness against her wrist told her he'd bound her with a strip he'd cut from her cloak; he was putting away his knife when she turned around again.

As he opened the door at the top of the stairs, de Ferreulle turned to look down on her. "Enjoy yourself, mademoiselle," he said. "I'm off to find someone more cultured and beddable. A maid, perhaps." The God-light faded, the door closed with a thump, locking with another thump, and then Lise was alone in the darkness.

From the farmhouse came another blast of unfocused spiritual energy, muted enough by distance that Lise wasn't immediately shocked into insensibility. She leaned back against the rough brick of the cellar wall, flexed her wrists and found the knotted cloth too firmly tied to work loose. *Look on the bright side,* she told herself. *You haven't had to give up your life in defence of your honour. The d'Audemars and their lackeys are all preoccupied with their mad broodmare. You're alone in the dark, but that just means you've got a bit of time to work with. You're not dead yet, and if you can start thinking calmly, rationally, you might just survive this.*

The energy level coming from the witch increased, and Lise found herself gritting her teeth in a futile attempt to resist the pain. *I don't think I've ever felt anything this powerful,* she thought. *If that woman doesn't give birth soon, the d'Audemars may not have to worry about killing me: I'll have gone mad from that woman's pain.*

That thought made her stop. *How do I know it's the most powerful force I've ever felt?* Rather than try to resist the power, she forced herself to relax, to open up to it. Something poured into her, a sort of sensation that was not actually of the senses. And she had encountered this before. If it had been taste, it would have been something bitter, like stale coffee or the herbs monks used in medicines. *It's not at all like Rafael,* she thought—and then realized what that meant. *She is using the same sort of power we do.*

That couldn't be. The Church was adamant about it, and so were the Empire and the King of England and the rulers of every country in Christendom. Nobles were Blessed and the Church spoke with and for God; anyone else who could manipulate the physical world in the way Rabbi Weiss had described to her was in the grip of the Devil. The woman upstairs was clearly possessed, and would be burnt the instant the Cardinal or the Inquisition learned of her existence.

And yet, just as Lise had been training herself to identify the different sensations she received from different Blessings, she had been able to match a particular sensation to this witch's madness. Individual Blessings or curses might have their own flavour to her—but that seemed to mean that in essence they were the same thing.

If this truly was the case, then the witch-woman Anaïs was a creature of the cardinal's nightmares. The d'Audemars may not have understood magic in the way that it had been revealed to Lise, but they did understand breeding: the prince was famous for the horses produced on his estates. This woman was having a child by the chevalier d'Audemar, undoubtedly in the hope that the child would inherit that power that raged, only fitfully controlled, in its mother. Lise was sure the child would be brought up in the prince's household, and now she knew who the noblewoman was who sat, so miserable, in the corner while the chevalier's mistress birthed his child. No doubt the offspring would be passed off as the child of the chevalier's poor, miserable wife. At least that woman would have a child to raise; Anaïs, the true mother, would no doubt end up in the river.

He could get away with this, she realized. The prince could, if the child inherited its mother's power and that power was properly controlled—and served the interests of the child's adoptive family—then the next generation of d'Audemars would wield a power that could challenge the emperor himself.

I have to get out of here, she realized. *D'Audemar knows that his life depends on the silence of everyone at this place. He might not feel obligated to kill everyone who has witnessed this, but he will certainly kill me.*

And then she knew where she had encountered this specific flavour of madness before. It hadn't been in her own experience; she had encountered it in a dream. Or, rather, in Rafael's dream.

This was the power that had blasted her when she was inside the spirit of Rafael's murdered Aunt Génie. Rafael might have been annoyingly obsessed, to borrow a sentiment from de La Reynie, but he was also right: the d'Audemars had in fact murdered his aunt, and they had used this witch as the weapon, as surely as if she had been the blade that pierced Génie's heart.

Two

"WHY DON'T YOU leave now, monsieur, and let me join you at the inn on the road to Chantilly once all the preparations are complete?" The servant Alain handed the half-packed satchel to de Bellevasse. "The lieutenant-general of police is sure to be watching you, and once he finds you're still in the city it'll only be minutes before the cardinal's guard is here." *The man speaks the truth*, de La Reynie thought, watching from a safe distance and listening to their voices amplified by a prayer Valentin had taught him. *I am appalled that you're still here, you immature idiot.* He had wanted to disbelieve his agent when the man—a footman who had helped unpack de Bellevasse's travelling bags—had sent word that the duc hadn't left the city as instructed at the conclusion of his interview with de La Reynie.

"A good idea, Alain," Rafael said. "But not one I'm inclined to follow." *You never were one to follow good advice*, de La Reynie thought. Turning from his observations for a moment, he scratched a note to his secretary, instructing him to send a squad of archers to this run-down inn near the Temple Gate. No point in bothering Valentin about it; with any luck de Bellevasse would recognize the danger he was in—or start listening to his servant—and leave before the archers arrived. Calling the owner of the tavern in which he had set up his observation post, he gave instructions for delivery of the note.

He heard de Bellevasse's servant sigh and returned to his observations. "I felt it my duty to try, monsieur. May I ask why you are so determined to talk to these people yourself?" The sound of creaking leather filled de La Reynie's ear; by squinting a bit he could see what might be a leather satchel.

"You may," de Bellevasse said. "And I will tell you: it is because at this point I can only trust the evidence of my own eyes and ears, Alain. Nobody can help me now but me." He seemed to be wrestling with the satchel.

After a moment de Bellevasse dropped the satchel and turned to his servant. "I am stuck, Alain. I admit it. I have exhausted all of the exotic prayers my Hebrew friend has been able to acquire for me; the one time I successfully recalled my aunt's spirit she simply made me—and Mademoiselle de Trouvaille—relive her murder without telling me anything new." De La Reynie whistled, quietly. *What a good thing for you I'm not prone to taking the cardinal into my confidences. You must be an unhappy young man to be so dangerously forthright in public.*

"I have to do something or give up, and I'm not willing yet to give up. And since I cannot seem to do anything to strike at the d'Audemars, I am going to do the one thing in which I do have some freedom to act—I am going to find de Ferreulle."

"Are you doing this for yourself or as a sop to the cardinal and de La Reynie?" Alain's voice was dry and sardonic and de La Reynie chuckled softly to himself, imagining the look that must have accompanied those words.

"A good question, and one I can't honestly answer just now. I admit that at the moment I am rather cherishing the thought of putting both rapiers right through that posturing little prick. But it's also possible that I could benefit from delivering de Ferreulle to the cardinal, and let the cardinal exact my revenge." A crackling sound drowned out Alain's reply; probably the rustling of paper. "Either way, I have to start by tracking down de Ferreulle's servants. So let's go through this again, Alain. The two of us working together will finish the job faster, and then I promise I will follow your advice."

"Bellevasse!" The voice shouting the duc's name was so unexpected de La Reynie's chin slipped from the palm on which it had been resting, and he nearly did himself an injury. *Vimoutiers?*

"By the good God," de Bellevasse said. "If you can find me, de Vimoutiers, then anyone can." *You had best hope not,* thought de La Reynie.

Even at this distance Robert de Vimoutiers looked unhappy; it was not a style de La Reynie had ever seen the boy adopt, and it did not much suit him. "What has happened?" de Bellevasse asked. "Wine!" he called over his shoulder, the volume of the shout making de La Reynie's head rattle.

"According to Mother and her cousin," de Vimoutiers said, "nothing has. But I am worried, de Bellevasse. No— I'm frightened. They've sent Lise off with nobody but her maid and that arse-licking musketeer—and a few hours ago the maid showed up at our place, saying that Lise had dismissed her and was riding in her mannish disguise. And I don't see what's so funny about that."

"Sorry, de Vimoutiers. I was just remembering the last time I saw her dressed that way. Your cousin is quite remarkable, you know."

"Of course I know. And it's because I knew you felt that way that I'm here. I tried to talk her into getting you to take her to England, but she wouldn't have it. I asked her again yesterday before she left, and she told me she wasn't going to put you at risk of falling into the cardinal's hands." He glared. "And now I find you in the city, running the risk yourself."

The duc's angry embarrassment was audible. "I don't appreciate your tone." *But he's absolutely right*, thought de La Reynie at de Bellevasse, *and you know he is.* It was also a bit of a relief, he realized, to know that mademoiselle de Trouvaille was safely out of Paris. *I still have to talk with her, but I would be just as happy to correspond.*

"And I don't appreciate having to threaten your servants with the cardinal's guard to get you to do something to help her." De Vimoutiers challenged de Bellevasse with a glare; de La Reynie could only stare with silent admiration. He'd never seen de Vimoutiers this exercised. It had made the boy quite forceful, and in a way that was rather more charming than that of his overbearing mother.

"That's how you found me?" De Bellevasse seemed to be recovering his *sangfroid*.

"Yes. I told your man François that if he didn't tell me where you were holed up I would enlist the cardinal's guard to help me find you."

"I'm sorry I inconvenienced you," de Bellevasse said. "I only came into Paris because I'd been summoned—in secrecy, no less—by de La Reynie. Everyone else may think that your cousin killed her friend, but our clever policeman thinks it was my uncle Bertrand. And his investigators all think it was me, though why I should have wanted to murder a charming young lady is beyond me." *That has the ring of truth to it,* de La Reynie thought. *Thank you, boy.*

"I'm sure that having to be in Paris instead of Picardy is indeed a grave inconvenience," de Vimoutiers said. "But why don't we try something different this evening? Why don't we pretend that, just this once, what is going on isn't all about you?"

Hand twitching to where his swords would normally be, de Bellevasse stepped back. "I appreciate that you're upset, de Vimoutiers," he said, "but I'd advise you to take more care with your words and tone. I fight under less provocation than this."

"That's exactly what I'm talking about!" The younger man was practically shouting now. "Lise is going off to exile—if she's lucky—and you're worried that I might be insulting you? God! If we're all like this, no wonder women murder their husbands."

De La Reynie couldn't suppress his smile. *It's not often one is privileged to see somebody growing up in a matter of moments. Is it too much to hope that both of them—?* He left the thought unfinished. "So what should I do?" de Bellevasse demanded. "She already told you—twice, if I hear you correctly—that she doesn't want me with her."

"Oh, for God's sake." The boy rolled his eyes, then turned on Alain as the latter rejoined them. "Give me that," he said, and de La Reynie heard the sing-song gurgle of wine pouring. "I obviously need to be very drunk if I'm going to make any sense of your master."

Taking a large gulp of wine—the distant-hearing prayer made the swallowing sound quite diabolical—de Vimoutiers turned back to de Bellevasse. "I wonder that I ever doubted you two belonged together—you're easily the two stubbornest people I've ever met. She won't admit that she needs you, so she pretends that she's concerned for your safety. You won't admit that you're worried for her, so you pretend that—well, what is it that you're telling yourself?"

Again de La Reynie was stunned. Normally at this point arrangements would be made, and the whole idiotic process of the duel would repeat itself. Then de Bellevasse sucked in a slow, miserable breath, letting it go out of him in a rush. "I've been telling myself that I have to find de Ferreulle," he said, "because I can't find the proof that the d'Audemars murdered my aunt." He paused. "And save for a few moments with your cousin, this is all I've done with my life for nearly seven months. God help me, de Vimoutiers, but I really have behaved like a turd, haven't I?"

"There's nothing I can say about that," said de Vimoutiers, "that won't bring me trouble at some point. So let's both stop beating on you and decide what's to be done."

"I continue to follow the plans my man Alain has carefully laid out for me," de Bellevasse said. "But instead of chasing after de Ferreulle's servants, we go chasing after your cousin."

"She's a good eighteen hours ahead of us," de Vimoutiers said. "And we don't even know what route she's following."

"Not an issue," de Bellevasse said, draining his cup and gesturing for de Vimoutiers to follow him. "As long as Alain ensures that I'm upright on my horse, I can look ahead while we ride, and check out the roads leading to the ports. And if I can't find Lise, I have someone who can—and who can travel faster than we can."

Well, thought de La Reynie after the young men had disappeared from view, *that was most interesting. Thank you, Lord, for letting me live to see this.* With de Bellevasse safely out of Paris—and perhaps a bit more grown-up than he had been an hour ago—de La Reynie could return to his primary concern, the identities of those who had been trying to restore Paris's magical defences as a weapon against the emperor.

A Poisoned Prayer
March

Still he found himself thinking more about Lise de Trouvaille as he made his way back to the centre of the city. It really was a relief to know that she was safely out of Paris; however much her cousin feared for her, she was unlikely to find more danger outside the capital than she would have had she stayed.

⚜

Let's see, thought Lise, *what I have to work with here.* It was cold in the cellar, but not as cold as it was outside. *I will tell myself that this temperature is bracing,* she decided, *and that it will help me think.* Just about anyone else—even Cousin Robert—would have been able to pray for sufficient warmth to make the cellar comfortable. She would have to make do with the gifts she had, not the gifts she wanted.

She slumped back against the wall, then eased herself down to the floor. Closing her eyes, she began to recite the prayer for light. Remembering how it had felt when she let in the witch's power, she tried to open her soul and mind to whatever power she might be Blessed with.

It made no difference, she decided. Eventually, though, she was able to coax a weak, jaundiced light into being. There wasn't enough to provide decent illumination even in this small space, but Lise was still able to explore the cellar, because as she moved the light moved with her.

It was not a successful exploration. The cellar might well have been cleared just to accommodate her, because it was utterly bare: no barrels, no coal or oil, no old tools or farm implements. The light wavered, and for a moment Lise felt light-headed and sick. *I can't keep this up for much longer,* she thought.

Her salvation was hiding just beyond the stairs up to the door, in a small alcove—apparently a cold store that had been dug out after the main cellar had been finished. In the last of her flickering God-light Lise found, half-buried in a corner, a single, small chamber-stick, its candle dusty and short but still intact and its cheap iron base free of rust. She had just enough strength left in body and spirit to move the candle to the centre of the floor and will it to light—against the dampening power of the iron base—before she sagged against the wall and fell to the floor.

For a few minutes she just lay there, the only sounds her ragged breathing and the quiet crackle of the burning candle. Eventually the discomfort forced her to act: the angle at which she'd collapsed was threatening to wrench one of her shoulders apart.

Slowly she got to her knees, then up onto her feet. She'd have to free her hands before she could do anything else; even running would be awkward with her arms pinioned and hands behind her back. It would be easier to deal with the bonds if she could get her hands in front of, rather than behind, her.

Try though she might, Lise could not bend herself to the extent needed to let her step through the circle made by her arms. The circle was too tight, presumably because de Ferreulle had bound her at the wrists.

Muttering a series of curses, she stepped up to where the candle sat, turned carefully so that her back was to it, and then crouched down onto her haunches. Moving slowly so that she could retain her balance, she shifted her hands and wrists away from the small of her back, letting the heat from the flame guide her.

She wobbled, suddenly lurched backward, and knocked over the candle.

I am not going to cry, she thought. *I am going to get out of here.* Rolling over, she got to her knees again. This time, she edged herself to where the candle had fallen, turned around and sat down. Feeling her way back to the candle, she found and righted it. Then, holding her wrists just above the wick, she prayed the candle into flame. When she was sure she wasn't going to hit the candle again, she whispered the igniting prayer.

After a few moments of only gentle warmth, the prayer burst into reality, in exactly the way it had when she last had tried it in her Aunt de Vimoutiers's salon in her first week in Paris. The candle flared up, crackling and spitting. Pain burned its way up both wrists and forearms. She gasped at its intensity, then bit down on her lower lip, trying to ignore the need to scream. The smell of burning wool she took as evidence that her plan, such as it was, was working.

Eventually she stopped noticing the pain.

When she was finally able to pull apart the scorched threads that had bound her, she had to look away from the mess she had made of her forearms. She could not block out, however, an image of red, weeping skin and bits of blackened fabric. She decided it was just as well when the candle suddenly went out and she no longer had to worry about accidentally catching another glimpse of her ruined arms.

There was still the door to open, and her arms hurt so badly now that she had little confidence in her ability to do anything that required strength. It took almost no strength, though, to discover that the door was locked from the outside. The lock wasn't magical, so possibly this cellar had been intended to imprison others besides herself, others more Blessed.

A thin line of moonlight came through the gap between the door and the jamb, and that gave Lise an idea. Recovering the chamber stick, she pulled the stub of the candle from it.

Yes: the flat base of the stick was thin enough to fit between door and jamb, at least as far as the small spike in the centre on which the candle had been impaled. The stick was cheap and old, though, and even with her near-useless arms it was easy for Lise to push the base against the door until the spike snapped off.

Now she could push the base through the door for nearly its full diameter. And when she lifted the base—crying and gasping with the pain—the bar lifted with it, and then the door was open and she was out in the icy night.

There were horses here somewhere, but she could not afford to risk the possibility that they were being guarded. So she made her way to the back side of the barn and, using it as protection from any eyes that might be watching the courtyard, stole her way to the edge of the farmyard. At the base of a tree she found a deep snowdrift from which she grabbed handfuls of snow to press against her burns. It wasn't much, but it reduced the pain a little, and that was enough.

As she made her way back to the road, Lise realized that the blasts of power had stopped coming. Instead of the screams of the witch, she was hearing a tinier cry, interspersed with the excited babble of male voices.

⚜

There was enough light coming from the moon that she was able to recognize the stretch of road on which she'd been riding a few hours earlier, and thus take the right direction to return to Paris. Now that she was away from the d'Audemars, she realized she had to come up with some sort of plan of action. Getting away was no longer enough.

What do I say, she wondered, *assuming I actually make it back to Paris? The police want to arrest me; are they going to be prepared to listen to my accusations against one of the great families of France? And won't the d'Audemars try to stop me from reaching Paris once they realize I've gone?*

The idea, when it occurred to her, was embarrassing—and not just because it should have been obvious. Rafael's family estate was in Picardy, somewhere to the north of where she stood. Possibly it was as near as a few leagues. She had been prepared to accept exile—just about anything—in order to spare Rafael the need to be involved in her problems. But he was the obvious person to look to, she told herself. He would be able to help her, regardless of what the cardinal and his men thought. Besides, Rafael would be very interested in what she had learned about the d'Audemars and their witch-concubine. And it was far less likely that anyone would expect her to be moving away from Paris with the knowledge she now possessed.

She turned and began to walk north.

Ten minutes later she was shivering, and it was increasingly hard to keep moving in a straight line. Night sounds were alternately frighteningly clear and loud, or muffled and distant; her head was beginning to feel as if it had been wrapped in unspun wool. What she wanted more than anything else was sleep. If she could find a safe place off the road, she could rest until the sun rose.

A shadow flew across the moon.

Lise didn't know that Shahrbàz had found her until the djinn dropped to the road right in front of her and she came to an abrupt halt in front of that nightmarish face. The creature eyed her with disdain for a moment, then opened its jaws in an elaborate display of fangs disguised as a yawn. *Come,* Lise heard in her head. *Rafael looks for you. Shahrbàz finds you. Hah.*

"Rafael? He's here?" Lise looked around, wondering if Rafael might be hiding behind one of the trees.

Stupid human. Shahrbàz said come. Take you to him. The creature looked at her for a heartbeat, before apparently deciding that it was pointless to wait longer for an answer and rising into the night with a quick beat of massive wings.

A second later Lise felt dagger-length talons hook into her cloak and jacket, and she was flying south.

⁂

"You sweet fool," she said as Rafael sat back on his haunches, wiping his forehead. He was exhausted, she knew, and hoping it didn't show. "Why did you do that, when I told you what was waiting for us up there? You're going to need your strength in a few hours."

"I need you now," he said, and she was thrilled to know how good it felt to hear something like that, and to know it had been said without reservation. "If I hadn't healed those burns, you likely would been so ill by the time we could get you to a physician that you'd have lost your arms—if you were lucky. There was never any question in my mind about helping you."

They were around a small fire that burned on the edge of the road. Shahrbàz had found her, Rafael had told Lise, after flying for perhaps two hours—it would have taken days to cover that ground. While the creature had searched for her, Rafael and her cousin had taken the faithful Alain and a quartet of Rafael's most bloody-minded lackeys and had ridden hard, exhausting two horses apiece, trying to cover in ten hours ground that Lise had taken eighteen hours to travel.

"Don't think I don't appreciate your helping me this way," she said, walking over to where he was squatting and sitting beside him. "I was beginning to wonder if I'd ever lift a sword again." She smiled at him, and squeezed his hand. It felt pleasingly *right* to do so.

"That's the other reason I healed you first," he said.

"What?" She looked up from the fire. His eyes glittered in the light, and she felt her heart begin to sink. "What's the other reason?"

"I need your sword. I've got a half-dozen men and Shahrbàz—assuming I can persuade her to fight—but I'm pretty sure we're outnumbered by the d'Audemars. I need every blade I can get if I'm going to deal with them tonight. And you use a sword better than many men I know."

"I believe he's referring to me," Cousin Robert said from the dark beyond the fire's light.

Now she felt sick again, but a heart-sickness rather than the shock the burns had caused. "I can't help you," she said softly. "It's not that I wouldn't want to. You're not the only one, now, with a reason to settle with de Ferreulle. But I have to get to Paris immediately, Rafael. Captain d'Oléron threatened my aunts, and I have to warn them."

"We can get a warning to them," he said. "In fact, if you'll help me you'll probably be able to warn them sooner than if you were to set out by horse this minute." He shifted position, putting his hand on Lise's shoulder to steady himself. When she put her hand on top of his, she again felt a surge of something good, and vital, go through her. He seemed to feel it as well, if his sudden surprised smile was any indication.

"And anyway," he said, "this isn't about vengeance anymore, Lise. But there's one other thing I haven't mentioned. This farm that you've told us about—if it's the one I think it is—is just under two hours from my estate. My mother lives there, pretty much by herself. If the d'Audemars wanted to attack my mother the way you say they killed my aunt, they'd be able to do so after a short ride. I love you, Lise—I realized, this afternoon when your cousin came to me, that I wanted you more than I wanted vengeance—but we both have family members at risk here. If we work together we can save them both."

He would have said more, but she touched a finger to his lips. "You've convinced me," she said. Shuddering, she added, "though if your promise to get me to Paris faster than I could ride involves flying to the city while held in Shahrbàz's talons, I'm not sure I like the idea. The journey to here was terrifying enough. I will never again wish that I could fly."

"There have been many times since I met you," he said, "that I have rather envied your freedom from the weight of a Blessing. You just continue to be what you are, Lise, and don't wish for things that don't matter."

He got to his feet. "And now, if you're feeling up to it, my love, we have a fight to go to." He reached out to her, and she took his hands and let him pull her to her feet. She still felt a trace of uncertainty—but Rafael was right, and before d'Oléron could do anything to her aunts he had to get back to Paris, so it was in her best interest to stop him here before he could escape. She felt her jaw set, and when she took the sword he offered her it was the most natural thing that she shift into a fighting stance as she strapped the scabbard belt around her waist.

When she looked up, Rafael was smiling. "I think," he said, "that I *really* like women who carry swords."

⚜

"There should be more men here." Lise kept her voice low, though Rafael had assured her that his prayers would prevent anyone in or near the farmhouse from hearing them. The situation just demanded low voices and hiding behind hedges or trees. "I saw dozens of people when I was brought here." And now only four men, looking like the worst sort of street thugs from the city, were visible. Two leaned against the farmhouse on either side of the front door; two were sitting in the remains of two haystacks that, judging from their diameters, had once dominated the U-shaped courtyard formed by the farmhouse and two small barns.

"Some will be sleeping," said Robert, in a voice that implied he envied them.

"And some may well be looking for you," Rafael said to her, giving her shoulder a squeeze that turned into a caress. "I can't believe they haven't found out that you escaped. Though they could be forgiven for not believing it." She heard pride in his voice and wrestled with a glorious disbelief, afraid to accept that it might be inspired by her. "Shahrbàz will take care of any who are outside this farm; we don't have to worry."

Lise looked again through the gap in the hedge. Her shoulder brushed a branch; a small snow-shower tickled her scalp and forehead. One of the men in the farmyard was wrestling with a tinderbox, trying to restart a small fire whose remains huddled in apparent misery just beyond the doorstep. She understood the man's desperation: the cold was so bitter she was having trouble thinking of anything beyond how numb she was becoming. *I have to start moving again soon*, she thought, or *I'm going to take root here.*

"Wherever they may be, though," Rafael said, "this is good news and we should take advantage of it."

"I was going to ask about that," Robert said. "What exactly is your plan, de Bellevasse?"

"To kill those people and prevent that unnatural child from being used to put a d'Audemar on the throne." The moon had set long ago, but even in the darkness Lise could see Rafael's mouth twist into something she hoped was exceptional. *Prevent:* there was the possibility of something very ugly hidden within that word.

"Well, yes, that's all very good," Robert said. "But that's a goal, de Bellevasse. I meant, how are we going to do this?"

"And how are we going to get the child away from the prince and chevalier?" Lise pulled her scorched cloak more tightly around herself. "The poor baby isn't responsible for what the prince is trying to do."

"How we are going to do this," Rafael said, "is simple. We walk up to those men and kill them. Then we go inside the farmhouse and kill anyone who resists us. This is not theatrics, de Vimoutiers, or the sort of duel one fights in order to impress a woman. This is treason, and the d'Audemars can't be in any doubt of that. They are without honour, but we can still fight honourably ourselves."

He turned to her. "As for the child, I confess I don't much care how we get it away from the d'Audemars. If you think you can get it out alive, my love, then you should go in the back way while I and my men are dealing with the rabble in the yard. The distraction should be sufficient." He put his hands on her shoulders and gently pulled her back from the hedge. "But you are not to take risks, Lise. Please. You have to know that the cardinal is not likely to suffer this baby to live, if it could grow to be as powerful as you suggest. A Curse that powerful might not be subject to overturning, even by batteries of priests."

"But it isn't cursed," Lise said. "There's no such thing as the Devil's Curse. That's why we have to save the child."

"No such thing?" Robert crossed himself. "I think the cold has reached your mind, Lise. Of course there's such a thing as the Devil's Curse. Everybody knows that. You're talking nonsense."

"I am not. It's God's truth—I've seen it. That baby has the

same kind of Blessing you were born with. I'm sure of it: I've seen it in its mother."

"You've... *seen* it?"

Hurriedly, Lise told them of the conclusions she had reached in the cellar. She had worried, in the aftermath of Rafael's healing prayer, how she would explain this to him, but the words poured out of her like the benediction at the end of Mass. And she realized, as she told them, that in truth the only difference between Blessing and Curse was training. The Blessed were brought up in the knowledge of their Blessing, and taught to use it correctly—safely. In the Cursed—when magical power appeared in a peasant or bourgeois family—there was no training, no safety. Just power, wild and dangerous—a deformation of the spirit. That explained the miserable, hollow-eyed men and women she'd seen in Paris, with their iron collars and cuffs, holy symbols scarred or tattooed into their flesh.

"Lise." Rafael's hands were on her shoulders now, and the expression he wore made her immediately conclude that he was about to disown her. Instead, he said, "If you say this to the cardinal he is going to want to know why you believe it. In fact, I'm rather sure he will insist on it. I believe you—I have learned in the last few months the cost of doubting you—but not everyone will feel about you as I do."

"Even those who merely like you, cousin," Robert said, "are going to have a lot of trouble accepting the idea that we're all born equal. By God, I'm not at all sure I accept it, and I'm family." He paused a moment, then winced. "And what in the world will Mother have to say about this?"

"I don't know," Lise said. "But I do know what I can sense. And where spirituality is concerned I sense no difference in kind between that Anaïs woman and you, Robert. Only a difference in strength and control."

"Oh please," Robert said. "Sense? Nobody can sense spirituality, Lise. The effects of prayer, certainly. But prayer itself? You might as well claim to be able to read my mind."

"It doesn't take a Blessing to know what you're thinking, most of the time," Lise said. "As for what I sense, I would love for you to be right, Robert. But I seem to be able to know when prayers are being cast—and who is casting them. Every encounter I've had in Paris—and now this—convinces me of it."

"Can you prove it, Lise?" Rafael's face had become progressively grimmer.

"I'm sorry, Rafael," she said. "I didn't want to be this way. I would much rather not have told you about it. And if you feel you must—"

He kissed her, and the fierceness of the kiss set chills spiraling through her until she thought she'd faint. When he released her he was smiling. "Beautiful idiot," he said. "Did you think I would suddenly decide you were unworthy because you have finally revealed your Blessing? I'm only asking because I want to keep you out of the hands of the Inquisition, and I'd rather do it by your proving your Blessing than by fighting the entire Church."

"Oh," she said.

Then she thought about it. "I think Monsieur de La Reynie has actually been performing his own experiments on me—trying, as you say, to prove it. We can ask him when we get back to Paris." After a pause she added, "With the baby."

"With the baby, then," Rafael said. "If it's possible."

"We will make it work," she said, turning to her cousin.

"We?" Robert said. "I know nothing about babies. Well, aside from some suspicions of how they're made."

"You won't have to do a thing with the infant," she

said, getting to her feet. She felt stiff, her calves sore. *We shouldn't have stayed here so long*, she thought. "Just help me to get to it, that's all."

"That's all?" Robert got to his feet. "Oh, good. For a moment I thought I was going to be put at risk or something."

"If you're determined to just march up to them and issue your challenge," Lise said to Rafael, "please give me and Robert a chance to get around the back of that barn on the left before you start." After a moment's hesitation, she leaned in and kissed him. It was supposed to be something quick, a good-luck gesture, but then his hands were on her face and the heat from his mouth and hands were driving the cold into some faraway place. She was grateful when Robert eventually coughed, in gentlemanly fashion, because without his interruption she was sure she'd never have been able to pull herself away. "Please take care of yourself," she said as Rafael pulled back and got to his feet.

"I always do," he said. "Permit me to worry more about you."

"You've nothing to worry about. Remember: you taught me."

He laughed, low and slowly. "Make me proud," he said, and then went to collect his men.

"Come on, Robert," she said, pulling on his sleeve. "Let's go collect a baby."

Three

"Speaking of babies," Robert said as they skirted the edge of the woods behind the barn, "How long before you two are making one of your own?" he asked.

Lise paused, replaying the question in search of anything malicious. But this was Robert; of course there was nothing like that. "Never," she said, feeling something leaving her as she spoke the word. "We might be lovers, Robert, but we'll never have children outside of marriage. And we'll never marry. So let's just make this thing happen, and not talk about things that can't happen."

"Sorry, cousin," Robert muttered, following her from behind the hedge and across the narrow road that led into the farmyard. "Didn't mean anything by it, you know."

"I know."

"It's just that you look, you know, *right* together." He was silent a second, as they passed behind a barn that smelled, slightly sweetly, of manure and cattle and reminded Lise for a moment of home. "I like to think," Robert continued, "that Mama and Papa looked the way you two look together." Another pause. "You know. Once upon a time. A long time." He was silent for another moment. "Sorry. I'm babbling."

"It's all right," she said, wanting to hug him for his guileless honesty. "I'm nervous as well. Don't worry—we won't do anything until we hear Rafael fighting. With any luck at all, the d'Audemars will all run out the front door and we'll be able to jump in and out without having to draw our swords."

"You believe the d'Audemars will run outside to be slaughtered?"

"I've fought two of them, Robert. Yes. They're idiots." It occurred to her that the man she loved was equally eager to rush into harm's way, and she was essentially doing the same thing; but she put that thought out of her head, carefully drawing her borrowed sword from its scabbard. She moved forward a few more paces, then stopped. Any further and they would lose the protection of the barn and be visible to anyone outside the house who happened to look this way. Lise stopped, sword raised, and listened for sounds of movement. Where was Rafael? All she heard were night sounds, unnaturally loud in the cold night air, and a murmur of what could have been conversation from the opposite side of the barn.

Looking back at Robert, she raised a finger to her lips. Then, heart pounding, she walked slowly, deliberately past the opening between barn and house. When she reached the safety of the back of the house she realized she'd been holding her breath; it took an effort of will not to gasp her relief at the absence of a challenge. They were safe, she thought, for at least a few minutes longer.

Then the shouting she'd been dreading began—but it began behind her, back at the entrance to the farmyard. *Rafael.* She'd been steeling herself against it, but she couldn't stop the fear that slashed her when she thought of him confronting the d'Audemars. *I should be with him*, she realized. *Damn the baby, damn the emperor.*

"Robert," she whispered, "we have to go—" The creak of a door opening stopped her.

She turned back, away from Robert, just in time to see a man emerging from the open cellar door. He was in the midst of drawing his sword when he saw her. No, not *his* sword.

"Monsieur," she said, "you have my sword." Stepping forward, she slashed at his sword arm, and felt the tug as her blade connected with something.

The lackey yelled and leapt back, clutching his arm for a moment before trying to draw the stolen rapier. Lise didn't give him the chance to finish or think or even find his footing; she darted forward and flicked the épée at his exposed arm. She felt the shock of contact, knew she'd caught him with the edge and not the point, and slashed downward.

The lackey was on his back and on the ground before he realized what she'd done to him. When Lise saw the blood pooling, blackly, up through his shirt and coat, she braced herself for a scream. What emerged from his mouth, though, was a sort of strangled whimper. The man rolled over and furled himself up, as if tightening himself into a ball could protect him from a killing blow.

Lise realized she had no desire to deliver it. "You have some of my things," she said, poking his left shoulder with the tip of her blade. "Give them back to me and you can live. Provided you start running now and don't stop for the next hour or so."

"Take it," the man gasped. "It's done me no good." He fumbled for a moment, and then awkwardly tossed her scabbard to the snow at her feet. A moment later her pistol and powder case were there as well, and the man was trying to get to his feet using only his good arm. Lise had a momentary absurd desire to help him.

When he was standing before her, Lise was surprised at what she saw. His face was pale and drawn, and he suddenly looked no older than thirteen. For a moment he just stared at her, as though daring her to prove that she'd been lying a moment ago.

"What's the matter with you?" she asked. Her voice sounded tight in her ears, betraying the strain she felt. "Don't you want to live? Get going!" The boy—she could no longer think of him as a man—looked away, no longer able to hold her gaze. After a moment he turned, jerkily, and headed away from her, slipping and sliding as he went.

"I hope you don't regret doing that," Robert said as the boy staggered into the woods and disappeared.

"If I've made a mistake," she said to him, "I won't regret it for long. Let's get that baby and get out of here."

A curse and the sound of something scraping against the walls of the farmhouse stayed her. Her throat tightening, Lise drew the rapier she had so carefully arranged. *Now what?*

The "what" turned out to be de Ferreulle, who rounded the corner to the back of the house, saw her and skidded to a halt, cursing in a most un-aristocratic fashion. His sword, she saw, was already out of its scabbard, but the blade was clean. Impossible for him to have fought with any degree of success without blooding his blade; that he himself did not appear to be wounded confirmed everything she had suspected about his character.

"You go on," she said to Robert, drawing her dagger. "Get the child if you can, and if there are too many men still in there, go around to the front and get Rafael to help you. I will deal with this"—she spat on the ground for emphasis—"excrescence."

"Fine words, slut," de Ferreulle said, hissing the sibilant. "I will enjoy cutting out your tongue for that effrontery."

"What?" Lise asked, "the way you so bravely fought in the yard a moment ago?" From the way his eyes widened she knew that her guess had been accurate, and she laughed, not so much in amusement as in the sheer pleasure of knowing herself to having been *right*. "It's fine, Robert," she said, adopting a casual guard that owed more to her grandfather than to Rafael. "You get going. I'll be fine here."

"I believe you," Robert said, and she heard something of a deeper respect in his voice. She did not turn to watch as he opened the back door of the house.

"Now," she said, taking a step toward de Ferreulle. "I believe you owe me satisfaction for the way you treated me earlier today, when I was unable to defend myself. I only regret that Captain d'Oléron isn't here to share your punishment. His turn will come, though."

"You grasping little *whore*," de Ferreulle said, false surprise and outrage dripping from his words. "You pretend to suggest that this is about *honour?* You need to be put in your place, trollop, and I am just the one to do it." He darted toward her, his blade wavering slightly. At the same time Lise felt a shimmer move through her head of something that wanted to be pain but wasn't quite.

"I have had quite enough of your vulgarities," she said, parrying his attack with her rapier, keeping the dagger in reserve. "And your pathetic attempts at magic. You'll not defeat me through prayer, you worm—there's too much metal here, and your Blessing is about as effective as your wit." She made a tentative cut at him, but without putting too much strength into it. *I'm going to insult him some more,* she decided, *before I stick this blade into his throat.* "You're right about this not being about honour, though. It's easy for me to see that you have none."

De Ferreulle didn't reply, other than to curse as he lunged at her. On level ground it would have been an unadvisable move; here it was insanely stupid. Over-extended, he had to throw his dagger-hand outward in order to keep his balance. Lise had a free cut at him—or would have, had he not suddenly slid sideways and shot down the shallow slope leading to a small wooden structure behind the house. Lise lost her own balance when her sword-thrust ended in empty space rather than de Ferreulle's breast, and she landed hard on her bottom.

He was running away when she recovered her wits and got to her feet. "Coward!" she said, but it wasn't likely he heard: short of wind after her fall, she couldn't raise more than an outraged croak of a voice. Waving her arms to keep her balance, she slid down the icy slope until her boots encountered snow again, and then she ran toward the small wooden box behind which de Ferreulle was now hiding. "So much for honour," she hissed. Feinting to her left, she waited until he began to move, then darted right and around the structure, hoping to catch him before he could reverse direction.

Something soft but heavy crashed into her cheek, then bounced off her right shoulder with an outraged squawk and a small explosion of...feathers. De Ferreulle was hiding behind the henhouse: he had thrown a chicken at her. The poor thing had no doubt been happily dozing, dreaming of whatever it was chickens dreamed of, and this vile coward had grabbed it and turned it into an avian grenade.

Lise stopped for a second—but only a second. What in world could you say to a man who assaulted you with poultry? He was evidently preparing to do it again, though the bird now in his hand was already awake and had thus become her ally, pecking angrily at the hand holding its feet. With a shout she charged, dagger turned so that she could deflect any flying fowl with the flat of the blade, rapier held overhead and the blade angled down. Too late, de Ferreulle tried to transfer his épée back from left hand to right. The hen fluttered for a brief moment, flying clumsily to freedom as he released his grip on its legs.

The shock of the rapier's impact travelled up through Lise's arm to her shoulder, spreading to her breast and ribs. Then the hilt was ripped from her hand and again she struggled to keep her balance. Only through a sort of controlled crash into the side of the henhouse was she able to keep her feet.

Once she'd regained her balance, Lise saw why the rapier had been pulled from her hand. It was embedded in de Ferreulle's chest, nearly a third of the blade invisible now. Grandfather had told her stories of battles in which blades got themselves trapped between the ribs of the men they'd impaled, and presumably this had just happened to her.

He was not dead—not yet, anyway. A horrible, wet sound was coming from his mouth as he breathed, and in the faint light of the moon the spreading stain on his pale coat looked shiny and thickly wet, like spilled ink. His eyes were closed tight, and from time to time as Lise watched his fists clenched equally tightly, then relaxed. Whether from force of will or simple inability to speak, de Ferreulle said nothing.

It was awful, in every sense of the word. Lise could think of nothing to say—all of the anger she'd felt just moments ago had itself turned coward and hidden from her, leaving just the shock of realizing what she had done. And her sword: to get it back she would have to—

The sound of a gunshot rocketed around the woods.

Lise turned. The sound was too sharp to have come from where Rafael was fighting, in the courtyard. Robert had gone into the house. Robert did not carry a firearm.

Without thinking, Lise grabbed the hilt of her sword and, in a single quick motion, hauled the blade from de Ferreulle's chest. "Robert!" she screamed, and ran toward the rear door of the house.

Before she reached the door, though, it opened, and the comte d'Audemar stepped through it. "My cousin," she said. "What did you do to him?" She put her weight on her back foot and brought her rapier to *quarte* and her dagger to *tierce.*

"You can ask him yourself," d'Audemar said, "when you join him in hell." He drew the pistol he'd hidden in the folds of his cloak.

The right sort of prayer might have worked, but there wasn't time to find it even if she had been capable of using it. With de Ferreulle dead or dying there was nobody near to hand for Lise to use as a shield. She had no choice.

She attacked.

If Rafael had seen this lunge in practice he'd have beaten her for her stupidity. This was more a matter of desperation, with d'Audemar too many paces away for a normal attack to reach him in time. It took the space of a breath for d'Audemar to cock the pistol and pull the trigger, and that was enough time for Lise's idiot lunge; as the lock swung the hammer down onto the flint and ignited the powder, she threw herself forward, all her weight on her right leg and with the left stretched out behind her, thrusting her rapier forward with only the tip making the smallest of slashes, and cut, not for d'Audemar's hand but for the barrel of the pistol.

The outward movement of the tip of the blade wasn't much, but it caused d'Audemar's hand to clench as the pistol fired. The tension pulled the barrel to Lise's left just far enough that the ball passed her without hitting.

Lise lost her balance and fell over, dropping her dagger in a vain attempt to steady herself. All she accomplished was to scrape her left hand on the rock-hard frozen mud of the courtyard. "God damn you for a coward, d'Audemar," she gasped as she reached for the fallen dagger. "Pistols? That's pathetic."

"Pathetic?" D'Audemar threw back his cloak and drew his sword. "You're one to talk, you abominable bitch!" he shouted, then made a cut at her. "Get up and help me!" he added to de Ferreulle's corpse.

Lise shifted to avoid the slashing blade; then, pulling back out of reach, she straightened up and settled into a proper fighting stance. "He's not playing the coward anymore," she said, "He won't be getting up for you or for anyone."

"My brother," d'Audemar said after a moment, "has no taste whatever. In friends or in mistresses."

"I can't argue with you about that," Lise said, going back *en garde*. "Unfortunately, we still have far too many other points of contention for this to end other than with your death, d'Audemar. Either I kill you or the emperor's headsman does."

"I disagree with your conclusion, blasphemer." D'Audemar drew a long dagger with his left hand, and stepped off the threshold and toward her. "Though not with the fact that someone has to die."

Lise feinted around d'Audemar's dagger hand, but didn't press. She suddenly felt tired, and while the weight of the rapier wasn't yet dragging her arm down, she could feel that it would only be a matter of time before her parries were a fatal second too slow. *I feel old,* she thought as he stepped back away from d'Audemar's riposte.

"You seem to be incapable of understanding your best interests," d'Audemar said. "Warning you against getting involved was clearly a waste of my time." He raised both dagger and sword and stepped to the attack.

"Criticize me," Lise said as she parried, "when you've won." *I don't feel old,* she realized. *I don't feel tired. I feel angry.* She feinted a further step back, then darted forward, her rapier thrusting up from the level of her hip. It was only at the last second that d'Audemar got his dagger in the way of the thrust and parried the rapier down and to her right. *I've just killed a man, and now I'm joking with another man who seems to think that this is all just a game. And it isn't.*

From the front of the house the sound of combat continued, and Lise prayed that Rafael was still alive. A scuff of boot on stone betrayed d'Audemar's next attack in just enough time to allow Lise to parry and step aside. She was cold, and sweating, and her muscles sang a song of pain. Suddenly Lise found herself furious at the absurdity of it all. *I only hope I can make Rafael see how ridiculous this is,* she thought. *Fighting as if it's fun—because they're all of them boys.* She stopped circling and glared at d'Audemar. *Some of us can't afford to be children. Not any longer.*

"I'm finished with this," she said to him. Her voice seemed soft in her own ears, and she wondered for a moment if d'Audemar had heard her. Then she decided that it didn't matter. "We are finished," she said, more loudly this time, and then shifted onto the balls of her feet. She didn't leave d'Audemar the chance to ask the question forming behind his eyes; raising her rapier she darted forward. There was no art in this attack, and very little science. Mostly there was anger, a cold, clear anger at these people—and at herself, for what she had nearly let them make of her.

A strong, inward slash with her attacking blade forced d'Audemar to parry with his épée and then to bring his dagger across his body to fend off the force of the blow. At that point it was easy for Lise to drive her parrying blade into the thigh d'Audemar had left unguarded.

"What?" D'Audemar stood for a moment, as if unable to accept what had happened. His gaze alternated between Lise and the dark stain spreading rapidly along the front of one leg of his breeches.

"You shouldn't have threatened my family," she said. Lise narrowed her eyes at d'Audemar. Then, without any flourish, she stepped forward and thrust her rapier into d'Audemar's chest. Then she pulled back with the rapier and drove the guard blade into the man's belly. D'Audemar's eyes opened wide, and he made an inarticulate sound that might have been a plea, or a prayer. Lise didn't wait to see him fall.

⚜

She tore open the door with enough force, it seemed to her, that it ought to have left its hinges. Crumpled just inside the door, like a flame on the point of being extinguished, was the orange-clad body of her cousin. For a moment all she could do was stare at him; he seemed so small, suddenly. Then a scream filled her ears, the sort of sound Shahrbàz would make, and she knew somehow that the scream had come from her throat.

Directly opposite her, his back braced against the front door, was Rafael. Like hers, the rapier he held was black with blood, to nearly half the length of the blade. For a moment he seemed not to see her; then his eyes met hers, and he smiled thinly, a grim and savage sort of acknowledgment.

As she became numb to the thought of her cousin's fate Lise understood what had held Rafael's interest. The inside of the house suggested the inner workings of a whirlpool or hurricane. A motley collection of non-metal items—wooden shoes, bowls, spoons, even what looked like a collar for oxen—circled in a mad race. As Lise watched, a bowl and a sabot collided, the shoe spinning out of the circle and toward the large double-sided fireplace that divided what was essentially one big room.

At the far side of the fireplace, the Prince d'Aude raised a pistol from whose barrel smoke still issued, and casually batted the shoe away from his head. In his other hand was another pistol, this one cocked. To Lise's right there was a large bed, in front of which stood her nemesis, the young Chevalier d'Audemar. In the bed, twisting against the efforts of a peasant woman to hold her down, was the witch.

The prince, now aware of the threats on either side of him, seemed possessed by uncertainty. It was only after several moments of alternating between Rafael and Lise that he finally settled on Rafael as the greater threat, and aimed the pistol at him.

"It doesn't matter," Rafael said to him. "Whatever you do, it doesn't matter. The thing is over, d'Audemar. You are finished."

"Not yet," growled the prince. His youngest son said nothing, but Lise could tell by the way he looked at his father that the chevalier knew the game was done.

"Your men are dead, dying, or running," Rafael said. "Your eldest son is dead. You may have stopped de Vimoutiers there, but you've only one ball left. You can't stop all of us—and that's assuming you can hit me, which I don't believe."

"Believe," the prince said. "And then I'll face: what? A boy? And not a very big one, at that. You've become broader-minded, de Bellevasse." Lise sucked in a hissing breath and stepped forward. The prince ignored her. *You are an idiot*, she thought to the old man. *Now I know where your son obtained his stupidity.*

"I suggest," Rafael said, "that you look carefully at that blade. I suspect you're not the first to assume that because of her size she—he—doesn't know how to fight." As he finished, Lise stepped around the fireplace. The prince was now sandwiched between herself and Rafael; an attack on him would end with the prince on the point of her rapier.

"So you may be right," the prince said. "There is a first time for everything, after all. It's over, then."

He did not lower the pistol, though. Instead, he walked toward the bed.

"No!" The chevalier raised his sword against his father. "I told you—you cannot do this! She is my love!"

"You imbecile." The Prince d'Aude did not admonish his youngest son, nor was there any affection in his voice. The words were weirdly flat, uninflected.

Raising his arm, the prince shot his son in the breast.

The chevalier staggered under the impact of the ball, his sword arm instinctively swinging around to clutch at the wound. "You—" he began. Whatever he had intended to call his father, however, died when he did.

Now the prince drew his dagger. Lise, horrified, shouted "No!" and, grabbing for the first blunt object she could reach, darted toward the bed. Whatever madness was possessing the witch granted her enough clarity that she, too, understood the prince's intent. For, as he slashed at her infant, Anaïs twisted to place the baby on the side of the bed furthest from his grandfather. The dagger struck her instead. And struck her again, and again, baby, mother and midwife screaming, as the old man cursed in that chillingly uninflected voice.

He stopped only when Lise smashed him on the back of the skull with the wooden shoe she had picked up from the floor. The prince dropped to the floor, almost on top of his son's body.

A second later, the wood and leather objects spinning around the farmhouse dropped as one. A brief, clattering crescendo of sound was followed by a near-silence that startled Lise, who had, she realized become accustomed to the raucous music of combat and the swirling hell of this possessed farmhouse. Without having to think she knew what the sudden silence meant.

"She's dead," she said when Rafael reached her. "The mother of his grandson, and he just killed her. And his own son. Why?"

Rafael did not answer. Instead he grabbed her shoulders, turning her to him, and then wrapped his arms around her. He only let her go when the baby began to cry.

The infant's face and swaddling clothes were spattered with its mother's blood. "Why?" Lise asked again.

"Because he was possessed? Because he realized that he and his children would likely go under the headsman's sword anyway? Perhaps because he hated when he had done, and this child is the personification of that. Who knows, Lise? I'd like to think it was because he was just an evil old man. But that's no longer enough to believe in. Perhaps he'll tell us, before we hand him over to de La Reynie and the emperor's justice." He took a deep breath. "But really, love—does it matter?"

Lise took a corner of a sweat-soaked bed-sheet and began to dab the blood from the baby's face. "No," she said. "I suppose it doesn't. I'd like to understand, that's all. Not that understanding would make any difference. The baby is still an orphan, isn't it?" Her voice shook, and sounded thin, like a little girl's.

She was, she realized, on the verge of going into shock after all she'd done and seen. Rafael realized it as well. He looked around, then grabbed a bottle and forced a draught into her mouth. "Swallow," he said. "And then go check on your cousin. He may not be—it may be you can still help him."

Lise coughed when the brandy hit the back of her throat, but she swallowed, and then tilted the bottle to take another sip. "Thank you," she said as she handed the bottle back to him. A furtive glance around the room, and then she kissed him, lightly, on the mouth. "You should be looking for some iron."

"Iron?"

"You'll want to chain him," she said, pointing to the prince, who lay where he'd fallen when Lise had smashed him with the sabot. "I don't know how powerful he is."

"Good point." Rafael smiled, and she wondered what he could find to amuse himself here. "Go, now: tend to your cousin, and then we'll decide what's to be done next."

⁂

"It's the best I can do, I'm afraid." Rafael wiped his brow with the back of his gloved hand. The glove came away wet. "I can't heal it, but at least it's clean now."

"It's more than you should have done," Lise said, surreptitiously placing a hand in the small of Rafael's back to steady him. "You were weak to begin with."

"Hey!" In the back of the wagon on which he'd been placed, cousin Robert raised himself on the mattress they'd laid for him. "I'm bleeding here, and you're telling him he's done too much?"

"Too much," Lise said, nodding her head. "He should have left you unconscious."

"You're just jealous," Robert said with a grin. "I've got this amazingly picturesque hole in me that is going to leave the sort of scar that makes the right sort of woman swoon with lust. And you're such a good swordsman—woman—fighter—that you haven't got a mark on you to show for your efforts."

"And to think I was worried that he was dead," she said to Rafael. He grinned back at her and she felt a small jolt go through her, and decided she would never tire of seeing him smile at her.

"The wound itself isn't a bad one," Rafael said, "and no bones are broken as far as I can tell. My mother and her servants will be able to deal with it once we can get to her." He smiled again. "As for his missing the last of the fight, we will be charitable and assume he was knocked unconscious when he fell, after the ball hit him."

Robert snorted. "See if I ever let myself be shot for you again," he said. He looked, Lise decided, immensely pleased with himself. No doubt entire theaters-full of actresses were going to find themselves listening to the story of this night's fight.

"Don't be too smug, my friend," Rafael said to him. "The ball is still in you, and someone is going to have to dig or draw it out. Unless my mother is in a generous mood, you're not done with pain just yet." Some of the self-satisfaction drained from Robert's face, and he slowly lowered himself to a prone position. Lise couldn't resist a small giggle of amusement.

Rafael's man, Alain, emerged from the house carrying a small, heavily bundled body. "Are you sure about this, Lise?" Rafael asked as Alain handed the baby into the wagon, where it was collected by the nervous-looking midwife, conscripted into nursemaid duty with the promise that her part in the night's events might not lead to torture and execution if she cooperated now. "You know what this baby represents, and you've never met my mother." His eyes looked, in the flickering torchlight, as if they'd been hollowed out, and Lise wondered how much longer he'd be able to stay on his feet.

"I have never met her, it's true," she said. *Though I hope to—want to.* "But I trust you, Rafael. His chances of getting through the night are better if he goes north than if we try to take him to Paris on horseback." *Or worse*, she thought, thinking of Shahrbàz's talons and fangs, and the cat-like, capricious viciousness of the creature's behaviour.

Rafael nodded, and reached over to squeeze her shoulder. "Thank you," he said; she could hear the weariness in his voice. "That makes our job a bit easier." He went to the front of the wagon, and Lise heard mutterings of what she presumed to be instructions to the lackey who was on the driver's bench.

To the east, a small shift in the degree of blackness announced the approach of dawn. Lise realized with a start of surprise that she had been awake, save for those minutes under Rafael's curing prayers, for a full twenty-four hours. How long had Rafael been awake? And how hard had he ridden, in order to get to her as quickly as he had? *We have to sleep, and soon*, she thought. *But how do we do that and still save my aunts from d'Oléron and his friends—whoever they turn out to be?* An inventory of the bodies had not discovered the musketeer captain; either he had escaped, or he had already left the farm when Rafael's little army had invaded it.

The ad hoc teamster cracked his whip and the wagon jerked into forward motion. "That's one task dealt with," Rafael said, coming up beside her and sliding an arm around her waist in a fashion that suggested it had always belonged there. For a lovely moment they stood together, leaning in to one another, watching as the wagon rumbled away from the small circle of torchlight.

"Now for the less-pleasant of our responsibilities." He stepped away from her—his hand sliding around her waist as if reluctant to go—and walked to where the Prince d'Aude sat, pike-straight, on the mule to which he'd been chained. He wore an iron collar improvised from the blades of two hoes; his wrists were confined in the iron-studded straps from a set of oxen harness, and he was fixed to the mule by chains from some sort of agricultural implement. Those of his lackeys who had survived Rafael's assault were tightly bound and then roped together; they would walk to Paris.

"I have one question for you, monsieur," Rafael said to the old man.

"I have no answers," the prince replied. "Not for you, not for anyone save God."

"You will answer soon enough, I think," Rafael said. To Lise he sounded alert again, and she wondered what was animating him. Then he spoke again, and she knew: "But you can tell me now: why did you have to murder my Aunt Génie? What possible threat did she pose to you?"

"Perhaps your hearing is failing you," d'Aude said. "I have nothing to say to you."

"Not even if it means your freedom?"

Lise froze in place.

"My freedom?" The prince turned, slowly, to face Rafael, and Lise could see in his eyes a greed in the process of relighting itself. "Define that, monsieur."

"It means exactly what it seems to. You tell me why it was so important that my aunt be murdered, and I will remove your fetters and let you ride away. I'll tell de La Reynie that you escaped during the fighting. If you'd like I'll even tell him that it was I who shot your son, and not you." He nearly spat out that last sentence, and Lise found herself holding her breath. After all they'd done tonight, surely he wasn't going to let this most treacherous of enemies escape, and just for the sake of information that could mean nothing to him now?

"You promise this on your honour?" The prince's voice was hoarse with what Lise concluded was a sort of selfish excitement, and if he leaned any closer to Rafael he would likely fall off the mule. Perhaps he'd choke to death on his chains.

"You and your sons have commented more than once that I have no honour worthy of that name," Rafael said. "Why now are you so suddenly willing to invest me with it again?"

"Don't be a cretin," the prince said. "Swear, or you'll get nothing from me, and when they put me to the torture I'll implicate you in this as well." He sneered, and Lise thought she'd seldom seen anything so ugly. She was reminded of the look on the loup-garou's face as it looked at her through the shattered front of the hired coach, all those months ago.

"I am happy to swear," Rafael said. "On my honour, if you tell me why you killed my aunt, I will let you go. For now." He patted the hilt of one of his rapiers. "Surely you will accept that this is a one-time offer, and that the next time I see you I will kill you."

"You won't see me," the prince said, showing his teeth. "If you do, it will be the last thing you see."

"Enough threats," Rafael said. "I am out of patience with you."

"Very well." The prince leaned forward. "Your aunt was in possession of information that made her a danger to us. She had been given this information because her participation in our plan had been promised. When she refused to help us, we could not risk letting her take the information to the emperor or the cardinal. So we had to—remove her. Of course, she tried to send that information anyway. We learned that she detailed a monk to take some letters to the emperor, at Fontainebleau. He seems to have gone into hiding at his patron's death, and not tried to reach the emperor until several months later. But we found him and we dealt with him in a way much like we'd dealt with her."

He straightened himself up. "It was my son's idea to use his mistress to beat down her defences. I was happy enough to let the witch attack her, since none of my sons was up to it."

"Which is why you put your son to stud with the witch in the first place," Rafael said. "It's a revolting thing, d'Aude, that you would resort to something so blasphemous; but you can't persuade me that this was a dark enough secret to justify murdering a woman who was kin to you, if only by marriage."

The prince laughed, a shrill sound that echoed through the night. "You think I would care that she knew about the witch? Are you so stupid, de Bellevasse, that you can't see what's going on right in front of you?"

"Insulting me is not helping you," Rafael said, but Lise

heard the uncertainty in his growl even if the prince didn't. She shook her head, fighting off the sleep that beckoned her. There was something to what the prince was saying, and it was true—Rafael had been so fixated on his aunt's murder that he had failed—or just refused—to see even the things that she had noticed in her few months in Paris.

"You don't think the emperor is doing enough to end the peasant insurrections, do you?" she said to the prince.

He laughed again. "You should be paying more attention to your catamite, de Bellevasse," he said. "He has, I'll wager, figured it out already while you still grasp at trivialities."

"I am nobody's—what did you call me?" Lise said, tugging the hilt of her sword to free it from the scabbard's grip.

"He doesn't seem to have realized that you are a woman, love," Rafael said, gesturing at her to return the rapier to its resting position. "Speaking of people being obtuse." He turned to the Prince. "And my aunt's murder is not a triviality, d'Audemar."

"I'm afraid it is, in the greater picture." The prince looked from Rafael to Lise, and back. "But it doesn't matter anymore; it's too late for you to do anything to stop it. Your mistress is correct, de Bellevasse: a group of us has concluded that these insurrections are going to bring disaster to France unless they're stopped—quickly, brutally if need be. And our Charles XIII is clearly not the man to do this. He has let himself be turned by the cardinal into a woman in emperor's robes. So he must be replaced with someone who will act where action is necessary."

"With someone who will act as you tell him," Lise said. Then the realization hit her: *that* was why Captain d'Oléron had brought her here. He was part of the conspiracy. "Or should I say, 'as you tell *her*,'" she said. "You're going to try to place the princesse on the throne. Is all of her bodyguard part of your conspiracy, or is it just Captain d'Oléron?"

"There is no 'try,' young woman. The princesse takes the throne"—he shifted on the mule to look to the east—"today. In just a few hours, I expect. And the captain will have friends to assist him, you can be sure of that." The prince turned again, this time to Rafael. "Now, monsieur le duc, if you will have your man remove these impediments, I believe I will undertake a journey to the coast."

"We're not finished, monsieur le prince. You said earlier that my aunt's participation in your conspiracy had been promised. Why would she promise to assist you in something like this? What could she possibly have had to gain by joining you?"

"Did I say that *she* had promised anything?" The prince grinned at Rafael, and Lise stepped back involuntarily from that grin. *There is*, she thought, *madness there, and it might be contagious.* "I said her participation had been promised," the prince said. "Génie might have had nothing to gain by her joining us. But her husband certainly did."

Rafael said nothing. She could not see his face, but from the look of petulant disappointment on the prince's face she concluded that he had showed nothing outwardly either. *Perhaps he has already guessed, as I did, that his uncle betrayed us to the prince. And if he was capable of this betrayal, why not much more?* But the confirmation still had to hurt.

The silence was excruciating, so she broke it. "We can still get to Paris in time," she said to the back of Rafael's head. "Do what you must with this sorry excuse for a prince, and then summon Shahrbàz. She'll be willing to carry us, yes?"

Rafael turned slowly. When he was facing her, he smiled—something of a death's-head smile, but at least a smile—and said, "It's never easy to predict how Shahrbàz will respond to a request. But you're right, my love: it's our best chance."

He turned around again. "Alain!" When Alain appeared by his side, Rafael said, "We are finished here. There's been a small change of plan, though. You will have to make your way to Paris without me, Alain. Lise and I have to make our own way to the Tuileries; with luck we'll be there in an hour or so. I'll look for you tomorrow, at the St-Martin gate."

The prince coughed. "You've forgotten something, de Bellevasse."

Rafael sighed. "You're right, of course." He turned back to Alain. "If this filth tries to escape, you are to do anything you feel necessary to prevent this—short of killing him. Take any or all of his limbs, take his eyes or his tongue. But I want him alive when we deliver him to the emperor."

The prince howled, and the animal fury of the sound startled the mule into motion. "Your honour!" the prince shouted. "You promised me!"

"My honour would have been far more tarnished had I let you go than it will for breaking my word," Rafael said, and in his voice Lise heard a cold fury that he had evidently been fighting to suppress as he drew from the prince the details of his aunt's betrayal. "As for my promise, if you had ever bothered to consult my Aunt Génie—instead of my Uncle Bertrand—you would have learned that I am a notorious liar whose word can never be trusted."

He walked away, in the direction of the house. Lise left him alone until Alain had chivvied his convoy of lackeys and prisoners out of the yard and onto the road to Paris.

Four

"She's not at home either?" Rafael looked haggard, the late-morning light and flecks of dark whiskers emphasizing the death-like pallor of his face. Lise wrestled with guilt at having insisted they try to find her aunts before warning the emperor. Finally, she decided that if Rafael could ignore, for months, a conspiracy that was right under his nose to pursue family matters, she could indulge herself for an hour.

"No." She stepped down from the door to the building she shared with her aunt d'Ombrevilles and remounted the horse Rafael had given her. "Nobody knows where she is, either."

"Well, there's little we can do about it, then," Rafael said. "At least we know where the Duchesse de Vimoutiers is. Off to the palace, then?"

"Yes. I don't know how much trouble we'll have getting into the palace"—she smiled at him—"since we're not exactly dressed for an audience. But let's assume we do get in. I am going to find my aunt, and you will speak to whichever of the emperor or cardinal you find first." She looked across at him as they rode to the bridge, and smiled in what she hoped was a reassuring fashion. "Oh, and if you happen to find Captain d'Oléron, would you please kill him for me?"

Rafael laughed, though it sounded a little forced. "It will be my pleasure, mademoiselle."

They crossed the bridge to the right bank of the Seine, and had nearly passed the building when it occurred to Lise exactly where they were. She stopped the horse. "Wait a moment," she said as Rafael passed her. "I know how we can get into the palace."

He looked back at her, and then his gaze shifted up and over her shoulder. He smiled, and this time there was nothing forced about it. "Excellent woman," he said. "If I could, I would bow before your brilliance. Let's hope he's in his office."

"He thinks you're out of Paris," Lise said, smiling back at him, "so by logical deduction there is no aristocratic wrong-doing worthy of his investigations."

He laughed. "You'll pay for that impertinence, mademoiselle. One day."

"I'll hold you to that threat," she said, unable to contain her smile. Dismounting, she walked up the door to the Châtelet.

⚜

De La Reynie looked up from the overnight arrest report to find a haggard yet effeminate young man standing in his office doorway. Behind the young man was Rafael, Duc de Bellevasse. It took a long moment for de La Reynie to put it all together.

"Good God," he said eventually. "Mademoiselle de Trouvaille? Did he make you dress like that? Bellevasse, you really are the most—"

"This was my idea," Lise de Trouvaille said. "You might be surprised, Monsieur le Lieutenant, how much more easily a woman can move about if she's dressed this way."

De La Reynie slowly raised an eyebrow, and was quietly pleased at how quickly the recognition appeared on the young woman's face. "Apparently not surprised," she said, in a breathy voice.

"Perhaps we could discuss your investigative methods some other time, monsieur," said de Bellevasse. "There's going to be an attempt to overthrow the emperor, possibly as early as today. We thought you should be warned as soon as possible."

De La Reynie's nerves sang with that delicious mix of tension and anticipation that was one of the things he loved about his job. One hand grabbed the small bell from the bookshelf behind his desk while the other hand liberated a quill from the stand; as he rang the bell he recited a short prayer under his breath: within the limits of his Blessing it seemed to him that de Bellevasse was speaking the truth, or at least what he believed to be the truth.

Valentin appeared in the doorway as de La Reynie had begun writing date and time on his report. "That plot we've been discussing is coming to a head, Valentin. And it may be worse than we thought. Assemble a squad of Archers. Direct them to the Tuileries; they're to wait at the major-domo's office for my instructions. Send a messenger to the Musketeers as well; have the commander of the day watch ready to receive me." He turned to de Bellevasse. "You'll come with me and explain yourselves as we walk to the palace." Seeing the look of concern on Valentin's face, he added, "Walking will be faster than trying to assemble a chair or saddle a horse, Valentin. Feel free to test them yourself if you wish, but I'm in no doubt this is a real threat. Once you've got things moving, catch up with me as fast as you can."

"If I might make a suggestion," de Bellevasse said, "could

you send a second squad of Archers out onto the Paris-Amiens road? About ten hours' ride north of the city gates they'll encounter some of my men escorting the Prince d'Aude back to Paris."

"They'll be closer now," Mademoiselle de Trouvaille said. "It's been at least three hours since we left them."

"Good point," de Bellevasse said. "If they leave now they could meet up with my man just north of Chantilly. Oh, and there's a farmhouse a couple of hours south of Amiens at which you'll find the bodies of the Marquis and the Chevalier d'Audemar, along with some lackeys and peasants. The elder d'Audemar Lise killed in as fair a fight as he was ever going to offer. The chevalier was killed by his own father."

"Sweet Jesus," Valentin said. "What is going on?"

"A conspiracy," said de Bellevasse, "that I'll wager even your mind might not have suspected." He turned to de La Reynie. "One more thing. You'll want to arrest Bertrand de Montauban, Marquis de Valérien. The charge is murder, more specifically the murder of his wife, Génie de Montauban. I will swear out a *lettre de cachet* if you'd like, though I'd rather take care of paperwork after we've ensured the emperor's safety."

De La Reynie couldn't suppress his smile. "Good heavens," he said, getting to his feet. "The duc de Bellevasse displaying a sense of civic duty. I can retire now, Valentin. I truly have seen everything." He scratched out the orders on two sheets of paper, then got to his feet. "Let's go."

⚜

"It's ridiculous," de La Reynie said to Lise as they walked. "The emperor is showing a superb instinct for reacting to a crisis in the way he's handling this so-called *fronde*. How in the world could d'Aude and his friends think that the princesse imperiale would do any better?"

"Perhaps it's the very fact that he's proving clever that bothers them," she said. This was unfamiliar terrain for her, but over the past several months she had concluded that many of the lessons she had learned growing up in the backwaters of Trouvaille were surprisingly applicable to life in Paris. "Perhaps they've convinced themselves that any strength the emperor gains will be at the expense of their own privileges. A stronger emperor is not in their best interests; a more easily biddable empress probably would be."

"Are you sure you're not a courtier in disguise?" de La Reynie asked.

"Impressive, isn't she?" Rafael said. Embarrassed as she was by the attention, Lise was absurdly pleased that he was proud of her.

"I don't suppose you know the identities of any of the other conspirators," de La Reynie said to the two of them. "We have our suspicions, of course, but I've been forbidden to act without conclusive evidence—I haven't even been allowed to do more than routine surveillance."

"Sorry," de Bellevasse said. "I thought it more important to get to Paris quickly than to continue interrogating the prince. Besides, once he'd realized I was going to hand him over to the emperor's justice he refused to talk at all. He seems to have been upset with me for some reason." Lise remembered the lies Rafael had told to pry out what little information he'd been able to get from the prince, and wondered what it had cost him. The thought of lying to someone like the Prince d'Aude didn't bother her at all, but she suspected that Rafael put rather more store in things like honour.

"Incidentally," de La Reynie added, "the d'Audemars have always been on my list, de Bellevasse, and I probably would have paid them closer attention if you hadn't been so ridiculously determined to make this a personal matter."

"I'm sorry," Rafael said, and to Lise it seemed he was apologizing to her as well. "It *was* a personal matter. My fault was in being happy that it be nothing more than that. Not a mistake I'll make again, I assure you."

"You're a young man yet," de La Reynie said. "Indeed, young enough to even recognize the lesson, much less to learn it. Ah, Valentin. Good to see you." De La Reynie slowed to allow his deputy to catch up.

"Sorry to run you around like this, Valentin, but I have another task for you." De La Reynie spread his hands in a sort of half-apology. "Fortunately, I think we have a few hours left to us. According to his schedule the emperor is meeting with his ministers this morning. There's a recital for the princesse, in one of the salons, but he's not expected there. My best guess is that the conspirators will strike during his audience early this afternoon. So you have time to run around the city for me."

"Around the city?" Valentin gasped, bending at the waist and resting his hands on the fronts of his thighs. "It's all right, monsieur. Clearly I need the exercise."

"Better you than me," de La Reynie said with a sardonic laugh. "It turns out, from what the young people have been telling me, that this really is the culmination of that obscure threat we've been investigating the past several months. So you're going to have to organize groups of the gendarmerie to go out and check again to ensure that nobody has tried to replace the city ward-stones you removed earlier. Be quick but be thorough; the defences of Paris must either be in the emperor's hands or no one's."

"It really sounds as if the garrison should be notified," Valentin said.

"Not yet," de La Reynie replied. "De Bellevasse says that the Musketeers have been compromised, at least the princesse's company. So it might be wiser to keep this in police hands. For a while longer, at least."

Valentin acknowledged, then turned and began trotting back in the direction of the Châtelet. A moment later they were at the gates of the palace, where de La Reynie's mere appearance was sufficient to open the gates and see them through to the entrance of the long, narrow building. As de La Reynie and Rafael turned to go to the major-domo's quarters, Lise slowed and said, "If it's all right with you gentlemen, I'd like to try to find my Aunt de Vimoutiers. Captain d'Oléron threatened her, in my presence, when he was leaving yesterday to ride back to the city. I want to be sure that she's not in any danger."

"Please do so," de La Reynie said. "You have already provided sufficient help that the emperor is going to be very much in your debt." He smiled. "I think his majesty might enjoy being in your debt, mademoiselle. As I understand it, you've been in search of a husband. You can probably stop worrying about that now: the emperor will make a most satisfactory match-maker."

It was meant to be both reassurance and compliment, Lise knew, but the lieutenant-general's words stung. The match she wanted was the one she could never attain to, no matter what favour the emperor chose to hold her in. She could, she supposed, be satisfied with having Rafael as a lover. *But I'm selfish,* she thought as she acknowledged de La Reynie with a blush and a curtsey. *And I'm greedy. I don't want to share him with anyone. And I don't want him to have to share me, either.*

The first servant she encountered refused to tell where the recital was taking place, and threatened to call the guards. Lise decided she didn't have time to argue, so she simply left the man gawking after her and, guessing based on her previous visits to the palace, went up the stairs and in the direction of the princesse's apartments. The second servant was less upset by her costume—perhaps the servants in the princesse's employ were accustomed to wild-looking young men appearing at all hours—and the servants outside the door of the salon to which Lise was directed were more concerned that she might interrupt the music than they were at her mud-spattered jacket and breeches. She finally obtained entrance by swearing to the servants that she would give up her rapier and dagger and be silent as a mouse once the doors were opened to her. This mostly matched her own desires anyway: in the event that her aunt was inside, Lise wanted to be able to watch her without drawing attention to herself. *It would have been better to have been armed*, she said to herself, *but really: you're so tired now you couldn't do much more than draw a blade, and fighting a Musketeer would be out of the question.*

As soon as she stepped through the door she knew that something was wrong. She sensed the soft, soothing hush of the imperial ward-spells enveloping the salon—though it was overlaid with something harsh, like the screech of a carrion-bird. Her aunt, the duchesse, sat in a chair midway between the door and the opposite end of the salon—and Captain d'Oléron was sitting right beside her. Lise didn't have time to determine what the Musketeer was doing there, because her gaze was drawn toward the far end of the salon.

And there, on a dais, sat the emperor and empresse— and next to them sat the emperor's sister, the princesse imperiale.

A Poisoned Prayer
March

Lise was still absorbing this fact when she realized what she was listening to. A few paces from the imperial dais, a quartet of singers was intoning a bastard mix of French and Latin. The words themselves made no sense to Lise, but the flow and pattern of them were familiar. She had heard them, without music, in the street below Madame de Réalmont's house the night Marguerite died. And there were, she realized, more voices than just the four singers she could see. A small wave of nausea passed through her, and she closed her eyes.

When she opened them again she saw what the emperor was wearing.

Her first instinct was to shout out. But if Captain d'Oléron wasn't the only conspirator in the room, she'd be silenced before she could do anything to save the emperor's life. *Well,* she thought, *Mother always told me my voice was my own special gift.*

Lise began to sing.

The first song that came to her was "The Maiden and the Captain"—of course it would be one of Grandfather's nasty campaign songs—but after a stanza she realized that the actual song didn't matter nearly so much as the volume and atonality of its delivery. So she stepped back to the doors, her hands behind her gripping both doorknobs, abandoned all modesty and all pride and delivered the tune with the same uninhibited gusto with which she'd sung to Grandfather as a child.

Faces were turned to look at her now, and from outside servants rattled at the doors trying to open them. Lise ignored everything and continued to sing: inside her head the screeching assault on the wards had decreased in volume as, in the salon, the singers fumbled, distracted by her aural assault.

Movement caught her eye, and just in time she was able to dodge away as Captain d'Oléron lunged for her. "Shut up, bitch!" he snarled. Then, stepping back, he drew his sword. *Oh, of course,* she thought as the blade sparkled in the candlelight. *He's a member of her bodyguard—of course he's allowed to be armed.*

"Keep singing!" someone shouted as d'Oléron stepped into an attack. A woman's voice, Lise thought as she dodged away from the doors. Someone screamed and leapt off the stool on which she'd been sitting. *Thank you,* thought Lise, grabbing the stool as it began to tip over. It wasn't the perfect weapon, but it might make a useful shield. She managed to raise it in time to deflect the blow of d'Oléron's épée. She didn't realize that he was also holding a dagger until the blade had stabbed through the heavy wool of her jacket and cut into the flesh of her upper right arm. Lise howled, not so much because the cut hurt—though it did—as because any noise might serve to prevent the singers from reaching the fatal climax of their song.

"First one cut loses the fight, you trollop," d'Oléron said. The smug bastard didn't even have the decency to sound winded. So Lise threw the stool at him. Then, as he dodged, still smirking, she kicked him, as hard as she could, in the groin.

As he collapsed to the floor, retching, Lise said, "Last one standing *wins* the fight, you little prick." Then she picked up another piece of abandoned furniture—a more substantial chair, this time—and smashed it across the back of his head.

"Your majesty," she said, once she was sure d'Oléron wouldn't be moving anytime soon, "please take off your *torque*—very carefully." There was no response. Looking up, Lise saw that the emperor and empress had gone.

"They're safe now, mademoiselle." Lise turned around, to see the welcome hook-nosed face of Nicolas de La Reynie standing in the doorway. "I'm still not entirely sure what you did here, but I thank you anyway."

If de La Reynie said anything more, Lise didn't hear it. A powerful wave of nausea overwhelmed her, and the same screeching she'd felt earlier—now magnified a thousand times—filled her ears, and suddenly she couldn't breathe. Bright colours appeared behind her eyes; she felt a sharp pain in her shoulder and then her head. Now the pain was in her chest, and through the violent torment in her mind Lise realized that she was dying. *They say it doesn't actually hurt once you cross over the threshold,* she thought.

But it does *hurt,* she realized. *Which means I'm no longer dying.* "Oh," she said. "That *really* hurts."

"What does?" The voice was Rafael's. Where had he come from? Through the pain she realized that her head was actually in his lap, and that he was stroking her cheek with a fingertip. *Mmmm, that feels nice,* she thought.

Aloud she said, "Just about everything. I'm cut on my right arm, my left shoulder feels as if it's broken—and I hope I never find the words to describe how the inside of my head feels. Who attacked me like that?"

"If you'll get up I'll show you," Rafael said. "Can you stand?"

"My legs appear to be the one part of me that works." She struggled for a moment, then lay back, waiting until the nausea passed. "You'll have to help me up, though."

"It will be my pleasure," Rafael said.

"And mine," added de La Reynie.

Each of them took an arm—Rafael taking the wounded one, which Lise saw had been bandaged with lace from a lady's bodice—and they gently got her to her feet.

In front of her, eyes wide in shock, holding a second strip of cloth she had torn from her bodice, was Aunt de Vimoutiers. "Child," she said. "Are you hurt badly? I cannot believe that anyone would do this to you."

Lise looked at Rafael. " It wasn't her," he said, leading her past the duchesse. "Though you could be forgiven for suspecting her. I certainly did."

"As did I," de La Reynie said. "And it may yet turn out that she had something to do with this." He looked at the duchesse, whose face, already grey, paled another shade closer to white. "Certainly it seems that the archbishop, her lover, was involved." He gestured to a body that lay in front of a large tapestry. The archbishop's head was pillowed in a growing pool of red. "He always wanted to wear red," de La Reynie said. "This is as close to a cardinal's robes as he'll get, now."

"I didn't want to kill him," Rafael said. "But he wouldn't shut up. I don't know what that song was about, but all I needed to know was that you wanted it disrupted." He smiled at Lise. "That was enough for me."

Rafael let go of her arm and reached out to the tapestry. When he pulled it away from the wall, Lise saw another body on the floor.

"Aunt d'Ombrevilles?"

"A surprisingly strong woman, notwithstanding her dowdy appearance." Rafael flushed. "I had to hit her; I still haven't regained enough strength to engage someone of her Blessing in a battle of prayers."

"You hit a woman?" De La Reynie chuckled.

"I've long since ceased to have honour, monsieur. And nothing I see or encounter can surprise me any longer, I suspect. I fell in love with this one"—he nodded at Lise—

"when she was disguised as her cousin. Once I'd accepted that, I was, I think, prepared for just about anything."

"This doesn't seem to be the time for joking," Lise said, though she felt her mouth curving upward. "Why was my aunt involved with this? She had no great name, no great privilege to protect or extend."

"We will find out the why," de La Reynie said in a quiet voice. "I am still unsure of the what, though. What was that song? And what was it you were shouting after you kicked d'Oléron in the privates?"

"I was telling the emperor to remove his *torque*," Lise said. "The flame-coloured piece with the pale grey glass balls. There's poison inside at least one of those globes."

De La Reynie gave out with a strangled yelp and darted—with surprising speed and grace for one of his age and bulk—back to the doorway of the salon. "Poison?" Rafael asked her. "How could you know that?"

"Because that's how they killed my friend Marguerite," Lise said. A lot had happened since that night, she realized—and she'd killed at least two men—but the pain of that evening still hurt far more even than the dagger wound she'd taken from d'Oléron.

Rafael reached out as if to hug, or at least touch, her; at the last minute he held back. *He knows I'm too sore*, she thought, and again she thought of de La Reynie's cheerful offer of the emperor's help in finding her a husband. *I'm tired*, she thought, *and I want to go to bed. For about a week.*

"What was that I heard?" De La Reynie was back with them, presumably having sent someone to very carefully remove the emperor's *torque*. "You were talking about the Courçon murder?"

"I think it must have been a trial run for this assassination attempt," Lise said. Her voice sounded odd in her ears. "I know everyone thinks I put poison into her wine, but I loved her—I would never do that. Whereas Captain d'Oléron" — she found herself shaking—"he gave me the necklace. Oh! It wasn't supposed to be Marguerite who died at all! Oh, God!"

Rafael put his arms around her now, and heedless of the pain she clung to him, sobbing into his chest. "I want to go home," she said into the fabric.

"Of course," Rafael said. "That would make perfect sense."

"A weapon that was neither fully magic nor completely man-made," de La Reynie said. "The poison could easily be given to the emperor because it was hidden and thus benign—"

"And the combined strength of six nobles could overcome the wards just enough to shatter a glass ball," Rafael said. "But how is it that Marguerite died, if Lise was supposed to be the victim?"

"Because I despised Captain d'Oléron for the insincerity of his attentions," Lise said, pulling herself back from Rafael's chest so that she could be heard. "And Marguerite loved him anyway. So I thought that I would give it to her, and for a while at least she could pretend he'd given it to her instead of me. Stupid!"

"That's enough," Rafael said. "I think that it has been long enough that we've been without sleep that no self-criticism should be paid any notice at all. Instead, we should just go to bed. Monsieur de La Reynie, do you have any further need of us?"

"Not today, I think." De La Reynie bowed to Lise. "Mademoiselle, one of my men will escort you to your home and see that you are put safely to bed. Monsieur, I trust you can get yourself to your hôtel without difficulty?"

"So long as any *lettres de cachet* against me are nullified," Rafael said, "I will happily make my own way home without an escort."

"You are free to go," de La Reynie said. "But please be prepared to present yourselves at the Châtelet when I send for you. You will both have to be interviewed—extensively, I fear—as part of my investigation into this."

"I understand," Lise said, a heartbeat before Rafael said exactly the same thing.

Five

"**How long was** I asleep?" Lise asked. She wished Juliette wouldn't fuss quite so much: the maid had been a human whirlwind since Lise had first opened her eyes.

"All of yesterday afternoon, and last night, and this morning, mademoiselle." For at least the fourth time in the past five minutes Juliette rearranged the pillows under Lise's head. "I was so worried this morning when you didn't wake, I thought you were dead. But the nice archer from downstairs came up when I asked him and he said you were fine."

"The what?" Lise struggled to sit up, and a sequence of pains and aches reminded her that she really needed to see a priest or physician. She had, she realized, got used to Rafael casually erasing any injuries she'd suffered. "There's an archer downstairs?"

"Oh, yes, mademoiselle. Not always the same one, but always one there. There was a lot of talk, too, when I went down this morning to get the water. A lot of fine people in the Bastille or the Temple today, mademoiselle, and they say you had a big part in that. Is that why you left—why you had to leave me like that?"

Lise closed her eyes. "It was for your own safety, Juliette. Yes." Well, that was mostly true. "As for my putting people into prison, I just wanted to rescue my aunts." *At least one of* whom turned out to be one of the leaders of the d'Audemar conspiracy.

"Do you have time now to look at this, mademoiselle?" Juliette reached behind a trunk and tugged at something. Eventually she hauled up a battered leather satchel. It looked familiar.

"Isn't that the satchel I sent back to my family at the new year?" she asked. "Why do you have it?"

"I don't have it, mademoiselle—you do. It came a couple of days ago—while you were away on your mission for the emperor and the cardinal." *Oh, dear,* thought Lise. *I am never going to live this down.*

"My father and mother sent it back?"

"Don't know for certain, mademoiselle. Could be that, I suppose. There's a letter for you." Juliette passed the folded paper to Lise, who broke the wax seal with an urgency that surprised her. Of all the things she had expected to feel after what she'd been through, homesickness was nowhere near the top of the list.

Daughter, read the letter. The handwriting was her mother's, which was to be expected. *We are shocked and saddened to hear of the attack you suffered, and the death of poor Julien. This satchel is, however, not his. Julien did not read, and the contents of this are mostly papers. They are sealed and so we cannot tell you more about their contents. We can only trust that you will be able to find their rightful owner and return them.* The rest of the letter consisted of descriptions of the progress of the winter crop and preparations for the spring planting. Apparently Andrée had come more fully into her Blessing after Lise's departure for Paris, and Mother and Father were confident that this year's crops would be good, and that the taxes would be paid and the peasants still have plenty to eat.

Lise carefully refolded the letter. *I will read it again soon*, she said to herself. Then she gestured to Juliette, who placed the satchel on her bed. "I will bring you your chocolate now, mademoiselle," Juliette said, "unless you think you would like to go back to sleep."

"No, that's fine. I'm awake. And chocolate sounds good."

She'd hardly eaten anything in three days, she realized. So not all of her headaches yesterday morning were likely prayer-related. The wave of dizziness that hit her when she tried to sit upright and open the satchel convinced her that, whatever was in the satchel, it had waited long enough for her to look at it, and could perfectly well wait a bit longer, until she had eaten something and drunk several cups of chocolate. And coffee. And brandy, if she could persuade Juliette to go get some.

When she opened the satchel and looked at its contents, she was at first shocked. Then she laughed. There was nothing else to do. Other than pay a visit to Nicolas de La Reynie, anyway.

⚜

"If I had held onto this, instead of being a dutiful *seigneur's* daughter and sending it straight back to Trouvaille, none of this need have happened." Lise opened the first letter and spread it before de La Reynie. "To the emperor, and dated last fourteenth of September," she said. "From Génie de Montauban. This satchel is the dossier that the prince d'Audemar told us about. It all seems to be here, monsieur: names of the conspirators, plans—from what I saw before I got dressed to bring this to you, the people you've arrested were not only going to use the *fronde* as an excuse to replace—and then to assassinate—the emperor, they were surreptitiously *assisting* the fronde. There are several impoverished nobles in the north who were apparently going to employ weather magic to damage or destroy crops; if anyone suspected, they were going to pretend to be agents of the Hapsburgs in the Low Countries."

"And you sent this to your parents in the south?"

"I thought I was sending it back to my parents. Monsieur, what I believed was that a loup-garou attacked a man we met on the road, and then attacked me and my servants. I thought the satchel belonged to one of those servants."

"Whereas what seems to have happened is that the man you met actually was the loup-garou." De La Reynie scratched his head and picked up a pipe. Sucking on it—though it had clearly been cold for some time—he said, "If d'Aude or your aunt d'Ombrevilles couldn't reach Brother Marçal directly, perhaps they were able to place a curse on him from a distance. Infection with lycanthropy is a death sentence in the Ile de France, mademoiselle. Loup-garou are despised by farmers for the way they prey on livestock, and it doesn't matter whether one is a noble three weeks out of the month—in that fourth week one is vermin. The wonder is that the poor man survived for more than three months before you shot him."

Lise shook her head. "Poor man. Not that I could have done any differently."

"I would be grateful if you would remember that, mademoiselle, should you be stricken with any feelings of guilt or regret in the days to come." De La Reynie took the pipe from his mouth, stared at it a moment as if surprised at its dormant state, then tapped the ashes onto the floor and reached across his desk and into a ceramic jar; when his hand emerged a clump of tobacco rested between thumb and forefinger. As he stuffed the pipe he said, "You should know that it is not going to go well for the marquise d'Ombrevilles, and even your aunt the duchesse is likely to be tainted by this scandal."

"But she wasn't involved!" That was what Rafael had told her, at any rate.

"She was used. Her antipathy to the cardinal, and her disdain for the emperor's policies, made her an easy dupe of the conspirators." Holding a taper to his lamp until it flamed, de La Reynie lit his pipe, sucking furiously at it until it was drawing well. The smoke smelled rather pleasant, Lise thought.

"She will not be executed or even jailed, I think. It does seem likely that she will be banished to her estates, at least for a year or two." A thoughtful expression crossed the policeman's face as he sucked on the pipe-stem. "You might help her," he said, "by mentioning—however formally you think appropriate—that the emperor himself wishes to be lenient toward her. It is the sincere wish of his advisors"—de La Reynie bowed his head and smiled tightly—"that only some mild form of punishment be invoked—to encourage others, as it were."

Lise smiled back. "Either the emperor or... his advisor is a very clever man." She felt her smile fading. "And the marquise?"

De La Reynie sighed. "There is only one outcome for her, I'm afraid. She is being interrogated now, in the Bastille. The cardinal's priests have a variety of methods available to them, and I fear that they are not being gentle. I would prefer it that physical torture not be used—that was the emperor's express wish—but the interrogators will do what they feel they must in order to obtain the answers they need.

"After that, she will face the sword. Only her age and sex save her from being broken first."

Lise hung her head. "I should be sorry. I should pity her.

But she killed my friend. She tried to kill me." Tears were rising, Lise felt. *Mustn't cry. Not for her.* "What I don't understand, monsieur, is why she did it. Was it greed? I don't see how she could have gained anything, herself. Was she being used by the Prince d'Aude?"

"Hard to be certain," de La Reynie said through a cloud of smoke. "My guess is that it was more fear than greed. The emperor considers himself the father of all his people, not just the nobles and clergy. Some members of the first and second estates are convinced that any gain to the third estate—whether townsfolk or peasants in the provinces— can only come at the expense of themselves. So they consider any action, no matter how treasonous, justifiable if it means the saving of their privilege and what they consider to be their God-bestowed superiority over the other estate."

Lise straightened up in her chair. *If I'm ever going to tell anyone else of my conclusions about magic and Blessings,* she thought, *this is the time to do it.*

Then she felt her shoulders slump and knew that she would say nothing. Cousin Robert had spoken more truth than he'd known when he'd joked about her overturning the entire basis of society. *I can't be the first person to think about this,* she thought. *Even if I might be the first person to be in a position to prove it. So there is probably a reason nobody has said or done anything about this before me.*

The baby, though. The baby might be a way to prove something. To herself as well as to the world. *If anyone asks me, I'll just say the baby died. It will make everyone happier anyway.*

"Well, whatever twisted thinking prompted her," Lise told de La Reynie, "I am now certain that it was mostly my aunt whose magic was being used to recharge the ward-stones. I wasn't certain—until the other day."

"And now you are. Certain enough to testify to that effect?"

She shook her head. "Who would believe me? I am certain, but only have my peculiar Blessing to support me."

"Ah. The last time we spoke you said you thought you could tell one Blessing from another."

"Yes, and now I am even more convinced of it. It seems to me," she said, "that everyone's Blessing has its own distinct—I use the word 'flavour,' but I suppose you could say it's like one's handwriting, or voice. No two people write or speak in exactly the same way, do they?"

"We have solved some crimes by assuming that," de La Reynie said. "Continue, please."

"Well, I have been paying more attention, and, well, looking within myself, and I am convinced I am able to taste the differences between Blessings. Please don't play the naïf with me, monsieur. You have already admitted you knew I was exploring the ward-stones the way I did."

He smiled, and leaned back in his chair. " You're not the only one who has befriended actresses, young woman."

Lise laughed, feeling a bit of the weight she'd been carrying lifted from her soul. "I will never underestimate you again, monsieur." There was still one issue to be dealt with, though, so she narrowed her eyes and fixed her gaze on the lieutenant-general. "Rafael warned me to keep this Blessing to myself, monsieur, because he was afraid I might be turned over to the Inquisition as a blasphemer."

"A wise man, despite his occasionally idiotic behaviour," de La Reynie said. "You would indeed be better off if you did not feel compelled to discuss some aspects of your conclusions with the cardinal, over a glass of wine. Please let me assure you, however, that you can discuss most aspects of this with me in perfect confidence." He re-lit his pipe, and after another minute of gurgling, sucking noises, said, "Mademoiselle? What have you learned?"

"I learned nothing, monsieur, of any use—until the other day, when it all came together." She paused, wishing that thoughts of Aunt d'Ombrevilles didn't sicken her so much. "There was the recognizable flavour to the two Blessings that were reactivating the ward-stones. But neither was one I had any knowledge or experience of. The fact that the same prayers, uttered by the same persons, were activating all the ward-stones was of no use to you if I couldn't say who was speaking those prayers."

"And you say it all came together the other day. What happened the other day?"

"My aunt d'Ombrevilles tried to kill me." Lise shook, remembering the suffocating feeling as the prayer was drowning her. "I didn't think about it at the time, but this morning, as I was looking through the satchel, I suddenly realized that the marquise had never performed any sort of prayer-magic around me. Until she tried to kill me, that is."

"If she'd never prayed near you, how can you be sure that the flavour of her attack is the same as that you detected around the ward-stones?" He returned her stare. "This is important, mademoiselle."

"Trust me, monsieur. The conditions under which I identified the flavour of my aunt's Blessing were such that I doubt I will ever forget how that felt." She sniffed and carefully wiped the corner of an eye. "I don't quite know what to think now. She provided me a place to live, and helped me when the duchesse my aunt was too demanding of me. And all the time she was conspiring to kill the emperor—and she was prepared to do away with me when she thought it necessary."

"There is no prescribed way you should think of her," de La Reynie said. "If it helps, though, you could remind yourself that, the priests notwithstanding, there is no such thing as absolute evil, at least not on this plane of existence. The worst regicide can still feel warmth toward his family."

"I will try to remember that."

"In the meantime, mademoiselle, might I request one small favor from you?"

"Why do I suddenly feel cautious?"

De La Reynie laughed, a sputtering burst that, curiously, made Lise feel far better than his words had. "Because you are an intelligent woman," he said, "and I am never to be trusted, not fully at any rate."

"Very well; what would you like of me?"

"I would like you to simply try to—ah, taste, is it?—what I am about to do." He closed his eyes and began muttering, so softly she could not make out the words. The sudden sharp headache, though, made it obvious what was happening. When she opened her eyes, Lise saw the papers on de La Reynie's desk shuffling themselves into neat piles.

"Does everyone suffer massive headache," she asked, "when they invoke their Blessing?" She rubbed her temples but it didn't help; only when the last of the papers had settled down did the pain ease.

"It sometimes afflicts me, yes," he said. "As well, I gather, as it does others. But I consider it a small price to pay, and so should you."

"I will try to remember that," she said, "the next time it feels as if God is hammering nails into my head."

"Let me get you some wine," he said, and got up from his chair. "I will be right back."

A moment later the headache returned, but at much less intensity—and with a flavour she remembered from her last visit to this office. Lise was not in the least surprised when, after a minute, de La Reynie returned to the office carrying a carafe and three pewter goblets and accompanied by his subordinate—what was his name? Valentin, she remembered.

"It wasn't you, monsieur," she said to de La Reynie. "And you tested me in a similar fashion the last time I was here. I remembered the feeling of prayer as invoked by Monsieur Valentin here."

De La Reynie laughed, set down the bottle and goblets and, with great ceremony, accepted the coin Valentin proffered. "Mademoiselle, you have exceeded my expectation," he said. "You see, Valentin? There is a—what would we call it?—predictability to her Blessing. Perhaps 'control' is a better word. It is just as we hoped. This could prove very useful indeed." He turned to look at Lise. "And now, mademoiselle, I would like to offer you a—well, think of it as a combination request and proposal."

I am not much interested in proposals now, she thought. But she said, "I am listening, monsieur."

"I gather that your presence in Paris is owed as much to your family's circumstances as it is to your actual desire to be married. Is that a reasonably accurate interpretation?" She nodded. "Well, then: allow me to offer a possible solution to the financial aspect of your position. I would like you to consider the possibility of—ah, consulting for me. There are, from time to time, crimes the unmasking of which your special Blessing would make much easier than any method of detection or enforcement I currently have at my disposal. It would of course be my pleasure to reimburse you for your consultations."

"I thought that nobles were prohibited from engaging in any sort of business," she said.

"This is the business of the state," de La Reynie said, "and as such is not subject to those restrictions. Otherwise, why would so many bourgeois be so eager to purchase offices with the primary goal of ennobling themselves? Besides," he added, "you might be surprised at the extent to which the empire's great families are engaged in business under the cloak of anonymity."

Lise looked down at the desk. Her headache had gone, so there was no excuse for fuzzy thinking now. It would be nice, she thought, to have an income that didn't depend on the turn of a card or the willingness of a fleeced aristocrat to accept defeat. At the same time, what would Grandfather think of a granddaughter who became essentially a town watchman?

"A noblewoman working," she said slowly. "Not the sort of thing that's likely to lead to invitations to the better sorts of hôtel."

"No less so than a noblewoman skulking about the city in breeches and attacking men with an ancient sword," de La Reynie said with an edged smile.

"Touché," she said. Put that way, there was a certain attraction to the offer. Freedom, she realized—that's what he was offering.

"I am inclined to accept, monsieur," she said. "But please, if I may think on it for a while? I'd like to be absolutely certain."

"And so you should be." De La Reynie poured the wine. "Let us drink to your good health, mademoiselle." He handed her a goblet. As she drank, he added, "If you were looking for sound counsel concerning my proposition, you might do far worse than to discuss this with the duc de Bellevasse."

Lise nearly choked on her wine.

⚜

Bertrand de Montauban's cell was not one of the luxurious suites normally made available to imprisoned nobles, but neither was it the fetid pit into which Lise thought the man ought to have been thrown. It had a window, for one thing, and it had been whitewashed at some point in the not-too-distant past. And the mattress had been stuffed entirely too recently: the straw was still crisp and hardly stank at all.

"How did you pay for this treatment?" Rafael asked after the jailer had closed and locked the door behind them. He wore a heavy iron collar that must have been painfully uncomfortable; in mocking recognition of the poverty of her own Blessing Lise had been let off with a chain of metal links that was cold but not especially heavy.

Though she thought herself better able now to recognize Rafael's moods, Lise had no idea at all of what his current expression implied. *I am beginning to regret insisting on being here for this interview,* she thought at Rafael. *And here I was worried you might kill him.*

"A loan, of course, nephew. Against the significant improvement in my finances that will happen when I inherit from my dead d'Audemar relatives. I would have thought, incidentally, that you would have come to see me before now. I've been three days in here. And why have you brought—her?" Lise, as much shocked as disgusted at this self-centredness, decided that Bertrand hadn't suffered nearly enough.

"I've been recovering," Rafael said. *From the mess you made,* Lise added silently. "As for Lise's presence, she insisted on coming. She has suffered far too much for your greed and selfishness, and I would not deny her this. But please tell me, uncle: what makes you think you'll live to inherit anything?"

"Why wouldn't I? Not everyone de La Reynie has arrested is guilty of anything beyond poor judgment at worst. In my case I merely happen to be unfortunate in my choice of relatives."

"You promised my aunt's support to your relatives," Rafael said, and now Lise could hear the trembling anger working its way into his voice. "And then you gave her up to be murdered when she refused to help you. And you have the nerve to call this 'unfortunate'?"

"There is no proof of any of that," Bertrand said. "Everyone who was on the bridge that night is now dead, save for my uncle the prince. And he soon will be, and his confession won't convict me, because he won't speak unless compelled by the priests. And if his testimony is compelled it will of necessity include my many refusals to countenance the death of the emperor or even to participate in this conspiracy. At worst I am guilty of taking my wife to a meeting with the prince."

"You knew they would have their witch with them. You knew what they intended to do. You delivered my aunt to her death, you pig!"

Bertrand cocked an eye at him. "Prove it," he said.

Prompted by a growing rage, Lise moved toward him; Rafael's hand on her shoulder stopped her. After steadying her with his gaze Rafael said, "Lise knows. She has already met with de La Reynie. If I ask her to, she will testify."

"This freak will testify?" Now it was Rafael who moved toward Bertrand and Lise whose touch stayed him, even as Bertrand stepped back so abruptly he nearly fell backward onto the bed. For a moment the two men just stared at each other; when Rafael made no further move Bertrand's nerve seemed to return. "That was an interesting reaction, nephew. I'll make certain my lawyers know of it. They will of course want to investigate this woman quite a bit, to learn all they can about this blasphemous curse she supposedly possesses—or possesses her." He leaned back against the wall. "No, nephew, I don't think that she will testify. The Parlement of Paris won't accept her as a credible witness— though I'm sure the Inquisition will want to... hear from her."

Rafael dropped his hand to his belt—but of course the rapiers weren't there, having been confiscated when he was fitted with his collar. Nobody entered the cells armed or magically enabled. His hand twitched, helpless, for a moment. Then he straightened up and, with a half-turn of his head toward Lise, smiled. He shifted the hand inside his jacket, and when he withdrew it again he was holding what looked like a set of long, narrow keys.

"So the worst that can happen to me," Bertrand said, "is that I may—*may*—be tried as an accomplice to this shameful conspiracy." He glared at Rafael. "And let me remind you, nephew, that the prince ordered the murder of not one but *two* young women to whom I'd become betrothed, in order to enforce my silence about his conspiracy. Not only will I not be convicted, I may even be awarded a pension to compensate for my suffering."

"Shut up." Rafael stopped the work he'd been doing with the mysterious keys and turned to face his uncle. "You're wrong, uncle. For one thing, only the wine-merchant's daughter was murdered on the prince's order. The poison that killed Marguerite de Courçon was actually intended to silence Lise. For another, you never cared for either of those girls—they were walking dowries and nothing more. Tell me, *uncle*: have you ever had an honest conviction in your life, beyond that of self-aggrandizement?"

"Fine words, coming from you. You possess one of the great fortunes of the empire, and you've spent it in a self-destructive pursuit of the most selfish of desires known to God."

"The difference between us, pig, is that I now know what a fool I was. Whereas you are determined to believe yourself the victim. No doubt you believe that your wife betrayed you as well, when she refused to let you prostitute her to your uncle's regicidal schemes."

"Poor boy. Will you ever be able to let her go?"

"Go ahead and laugh," Rafael said. "You think I was wasting my time, do you?"

"It didn't profit you any, and it cost you plenty." Bertrand turned his back on his nephew and, standing on tip-toe, glanced out his window. Lise stared as Rafael's hands flew to the heavy steel collar around his throat; a momentary scratching was the only evidence that he was working the lock with those mysterious tiny keys. "Whereas I," Bertrand told the world outside his window, "will soon be out of this cell and into something more appropriate to my station. Of all the people involved in this, everyone but me had some *lofty* goal to attain to. And look at how you've all wound up. You've spent a fortune on nothing but some old paper, and now you're become a bitter old man long before your time. The d'Audemars and the d'Ombrevilles woman are dead or soon will be. Even the emperor has lost: because he refuses to show a strong hand to the peasants, they will be further emboldened, and in the end they'll have his head—or his son's."

"How very eloquently argued. And how self-centred—as

always. But I must disagree with you, monsieur. I got a lot for the money I spent. For one thing, I learned that there will be times when it's appropriate to know the less-exalted skills of the bourgeoisie." A twist of the wrist, and the lock that held the iron collar together snapped open. The sound of the metal striking the floor of the cell caused Bertrand to fall away from the window and spin around.

His eyes wide, his face pale, Bertrand said, "You wouldn't. Rafael—nephew—whatever you think, I'm kin. You can't just kill me." Unwilling, or unable, to avoid the unjust word, though, he added, "If you kill me it will mean the block for you."

"Oh, I have no intention of killing you, monsieur." Rafael kicked the iron into the furthest corner of the cell, then murmured what Lise recognized as a simple memory-prayer; he was trying to recall some other, more difficult prayer. After a moment he smiled. "No, I've learned a lot, in the course of my travels and through my purchases. At one time I despaired that I would never find the exact prayer I wanted, to get the revenge I desired. But now I know that one's happiness depends not on getting what one wants, but rather what one needs. I'm not entirely sure of getting what I need, monsieur. But I know, now, what that is. So when I leave you today, I will put you and everything associated with you behind me. I have a life I'm looking forward to living."

He recited the prayer, in full voice so that his uncle heard every word. Lise, who had been training her mind to suffer less in the presence of Rafael's Blessing, still recoiled at the power of those words. "This is another thing I learned in the course of my travels, monsieur: the ancients, the Romans and before them the Greeks, were every bit our equals when it came to violence and depravity. This is one of the first prayers I collected; at the time I had no idea why anyone would want it."

Bertrand de Montauban, horribly mistaken, laughed. "I feel nothing. You have failed—again, I might add." *Rafael,* Lise thought, *what have you done to him?*

"Have I?" Rafael smiled. "Let me explain something."

He walked to where the collar had fetched up; Bertrand skipped out of his way as he approached. "What I did is a small enough thing, in itself. As for whether it worked or not, there is only one way for you to find out. You will continue to live, uncle, and so long as you take good care of yourself you may even outlive me. However, that prayer has just bound your heart—indissolubly, I'm afraid—to this cell. To this very space, in perpetuity." He paused a moment, letting the words penetrate his uncle's selfishness. "So long as you stay in this cell, you will live. Happily or not is up to you, but you will live. The moment you leave this place, however, your heart leaves you. And should this place be demolished or broken in any way, your heart will break too." Rafael fastened the collar around his neck again, and locked it.

"The only way you'll ever know if the spell worked or not is to walk out of this cell." Rafael took Lise's hand in his and walked her to the door. Pounding on it, he said, "Since I'm not at all sure myself whether or not I did it properly, I will be most interested to see what happens should you decide to attend your trial." A clumping of hobnailed boots announced the arrival of the turnkey. As he and Lise stepped into the open doorway, Rafael turned. Bertrand was cowering in the corner.

"I wish you long life, uncle," Rafael said.

Six

ROBERT WAS—RATHER indelicately, Lise thought—showing off the scar just below his left shoulder when a servant announced the arrival of the duc de Bellevasse.

"Oh, not him again," Robert said. "That man is nothing but trouble."

"I'm glad to see you recovered, Vimoutiers," Rafael said from the salon's doorway. Lise felt her heart jump a bit at the sound of his voice. "When did you arrive?"

"This morning. Already been interviewed by de La Reynie and the cardinal and Lord knows who else. Not fair—I wasn't even in town for the big finish." Robert grinned as he buttoned up his shirt, but to Lise the grin seemed a bit forced. There was nothing forced, though, about his bow to Rafael, who returned the bow. "Your good mother sends her regards and her love," Robert said to Rafael, "and reminds you that you left her house looking as if the Turks had been rampaging through it. I am instructed to tell you to return at once and clean up after yourself."

"My love to her, too," Rafael said. "I trust your wound is suitably healed?"

"What a woman," Robert said. "I had to argue with her for a good three hours to prevent her from wiping away the scar. Does she not understand women at all?"

"How could she?" Lise asked, laughing. "She only is one, after all."

"Whereas you have so much more knowledge," Rafael added. His eyes were very bright, Lise realized. *He's not thinking about his aunt,* she thought. *Please let it be that. Jesus and the saints, please give him peace.*

"Did you come here just to abuse me?" Robert asked.

"Not at all," Rafael said. "That is merely an unexpected side-benefit. Is your mother here?"

Lise felt herself stiffen, and Robert's smile faded a bit. "She has gone to the country," he said. "The emperor has personally promised that she will neither be tried nor asked to witness concerning the conspiracy scandal. But he has also asked her to spend some time at our estates. So for the time being I am master of this hôtel. Though I've been told in no uncertain terms that I will be paying for any damages caused by partying, so it's something of a mixed blessing." He laughed, but to Lise it was clear that Robert found the change in his family's circumstances disturbing at the least.

"Well, monsieur, I may have a request to make of you, then, in your mother's absence. But in the meantime, would you accede to my request for a moment alone with your cousin?"

"Of course," Robert said. "I will arrange for wine." As he passed Rafael, Robert leaned over and spoke, briefly, in Rafael's ear.

"What was that about?" Lise asked when Rafael joined her by the fireplace.

"In time," he said. After a moment's pause, he turned away and looked out one of the windows. "I sense spring coming, at last," he said. "It was an unusually bitter winter; I have hopes for a warm spring."

"I am pleased at the way I survived the cold," she said.

"It's not something I'm used to." *What is wrong with him?* she wondered. *Who talks about the weather after what we've been through?*

Evidently something similar had occurred to him, because Rafael abruptly turned and took her hand. "Lise," he began. A pause, and then, "Mademoiselle de Trouvaille, would you"—

"Lise," she corrected. "My name is Lise."

He laughed, and squeezed her hand. "And a good name it is, too." He took a deep breath. "I would like to join it to mine."

She stepped back. Yes, it had entered her mind that he might say something like this. But to actually hear it—she felt her heart sink.

"No." How could such a simple word be so hard to say?

Now it was his turn to step back. "What? You can't be serious."

"I have to be." She swallowed, and forced the words out of herself in a rush. "I love you, don't doubt that. I will gladly be your mistress, your lover—whatever, wherever I end up, know that I am yours forever. But you cannot marry me, Rafael. I have nothing to give you."

"After what we've just been through, how can you possibly believe that, much less say it?" She found herself staring at him, despite her desire to look away. He didn't look all that unhappy, and this should have been a source of satisfaction. Somehow it wasn't.

"You owe your family more than me," she said. "Surely you know that, Rafael. Powerful families marry into other powerful families. My family can scarcely survive on the income from its estate, and then only by being as tied to its land as peasants are."

"I believe," said Robert from the doorway, "that this is the point in the conversation at which I intrude."

"Get out!" Lise was startled at the anger she felt. "I—" She hung her head. "I'm sorry, cousin. That was unforgivable, but I ask your forgiveness anyway. It's just that this is the wrong time for jokes."

"I'm not joking," said Robert. "I have a summons, here, from the emperor.

"For both of you," he added.

⚜

I could spend all of my time here, Lise thought. *I have never felt so at peace as I do inside His Majesty's wards.* "Lise de Trouvaille is at her emperor's service," she said, curtsying until her back leg was parallel to the parquet floor.

"Please rise," Charles said. "You as well, our lord duc. Rafael. It has been too long since we have enjoyed your company."

"My fault entirely, Majesty," Rafael said. "An oversight I hope I'll be allowed to correct."

"We hope so as well," Charles said, a slight smile playing across his face. "And that, in part at least, explains my summoning you here."

I don't understand, Lise wanted to say. She knew better, though, so she simply remained standing where she was.

"Before we go further, though," Charles said, "please allow me to provide seats for you." He nodded, and a pair of footmen brought heavily upholstered, three-legged stools, placing them to Rafael's left and Lise's right. "Sit," the emperor said, "and let's talk a while."

"But Your Majesty—" Lise couldn't contain her shock. Rafael, in the act of sitting on his stool, stopped and stared at her, eyebrows raised. "Only ducs and duchesses have the right to sit in front of the emperor," she said to him. Rafael smiled at her, and she felt the flush rising.

"I think His Majesty can be trusted to be aware of the protocol in this instance," Rafael said.

"I'll just shut up, then, shall I?"

"Your confusion is understandable," Charles told her, settling back onto his throne. "I gather, from your cousin, that you believe yourself to be unworthy of the proposal of marriage you received a few hours ago."

Rafael had to lean over and thump her on the back to stop her sudden explosion of coughing.

Amused, the emperor added, "And we are told that our lieutenant-general of police has promised you our services as matchmaker. So allow us, lady, to assist you in resolving the issue that brought you to our city in the first place."

Leaning forward, the emperor lifted a hand. "You think you have nothing to bring to a marriage," he said. He raised a finger. "You have brains, as you proved in detecting certain aspects of the conspiracy against us."

A second finger. "You have courage, in amazing quantity, as shown by the way you escaped your captors and then defeated them before they could assault us in our city."

A third finger. "You have, in your own way, a more powerful Blessing than most have." He frowned. "We are not entirely certain how this Blessing works, and the cardinal has yet to discuss it with us. Or even show that he is aware of it." The emperor smiled, a little. "But de La Reynie is very enthusiastic, as we believe you have learned." Lise, too amazed to speak, simply nodded. *The emperor is playing matchmaker for me,* she thought. *But why does he have to sell me to Rafael?*

"Do you dispute these things?" the emperor asked, and

Lise suddenly realized, *He's selling me to—me.* She shook her head, dazed.

"So that leaves us with the one thing that apparently concerns you the most," Charles said. "Social standing. A lady such as yourself, possessed of neither title nor estate, is not a fit match for one of the most exalted families in the empire. Do we understand your position properly?"

Lise nodded.

"Well," the emperor said, "there are two possible responses to this. The first is to point out what we would have thought should have been obvious to your aunt the duchesse: Rafael, duc de Bellevasse, can either be the most exalted bachelor in our empire or he can be a social outcast who consorts with the Devil, but he can't be both at the same time. We have until recently been operating on the latter assumption, which would suggest that your social status, mademoiselle, might have been higher than that of de Bellevasse." Rafael's shoulders tensed, but only briefly. Then he smiled at Lise, as if to reassure her that he wasn't that sort of person anymore.

"If you remain to be convinced, lady," the emperor said, "we have but one course of action left to us." He stood, and motioned Lise to come to him. Suddenly shy, she stumbled in rising from her stool. She managed to reach him without further incident, though, and at his gesture she knelt before him.

"The throne has recently come into a rather substantial amount of property," the emperor said, "as the result of the confiscation of the estates of the d'Audemar family. As Lise de Trouvaille performed such laudatory service on our behalf in destroying an attempt on our person, and as it pleases us to reward such devotion, we hereby bestow on Lise de Trouvaille that portion of the d'Audemar estates centred on the village of Combray, and declare her Lise, comtesse de Combray." He placed his hands on her shoulders, then bent to kiss the top of her head. "Please rise, comtesse."

Lise felt her cheeks burning as she turned to face the others—and Cousin Robert had somehow snuck into the audience chamber along with de La Reynie. *This must be a dream*, she thought. *If so, it's a lovely dream.* The rest of the world may have been tossed and turned on waves of prayer, of Blessing and Curse, but in the emperor's presence, with Rafael smiling at her, she felt as if she could float.

"*Now* will you marry me?" Rafael asked, getting up from his stool.

"If it is my emperor's wish," she began.

"Of *course* it's his wish, you ninny!" shouted Robert. "Say yes already!"

"That's a horrible violation of protocol," Lise said to Robert. To Rafael she said, "Yes."

⚜

"I have one request to make, love."

"The answer's yes," she said, rolling over and stretching. The afternoon sun was wonderfully warm on her skin. "What's the request?"

"When you come north with me to meet Mother—"

"Yes?"

"You have to wear your sword."

Lise laughed. Then, looking up, she said, "My sword is at your service, my lord duc. But I have one request to make of you, as well."

"The answer's yes. What's the request?"

Lise pointed to the window. Outside, Shahrbàz hovered, tail lashing furiously. "You have to explain this—us—to her."

About the Author

Michael Skeet is an award-winning Canadian writer and broadcaster. Born in Calgary, Alberta, he began writing for radio before finishing college. He has sold short stories in the science fiction, dark fantasy and horror fields in addition to extensive publishing credits as a film and music critic. A two-time winner of Canada's Aurora Award for excellence in Science Fiction and Fantasy, Skeet lives in Toronto with his wife, Lorna Toolis.

Books by Five Rivers

NON-FICTION

Big Buttes Book: Annotated Dyets Dry Dinner, (1599), by Henry Buttes, with Elizabethan Recipes, by Michelle Enzinas
Al Capone: Chicago's King of Crime, by Nate Hendley
Crystal Death: North America's Most Dangerous Drug, by Nate Hendley
Dutch Schultz: Brazen Beer Baron of New York, by Nate Hendley
John Lennon: Music, Myth and Madness, by Nate Hendley
Motivate to Create: a guide for writers, by Nate Hendley
Steven Truscott, Decades of Injustice by Nate Hendley
King Kwong: Larry Kwong, the China Clipper Who Broke the NHL Colour Barrier, by Paula Johanson
Shakespeare for Slackers: by Aaron Kite, et al
  Romeo and Juliet
  Hamlet
  Macbeth
The Organic Home Gardener, by Patrick Lima and John Scanlan
Shakespeare for Readers' Theatre: Hamlet, Romeo & Juliet, Midsummer Night's Dream, by John Poulson
Shakespeare for Reader's Theatre, Book 2: Shakespeare's Greatest Villains, The Merry Wives of Windsor; Othello, the Moor of Venice; Richard III; King Lear, by John Poulsen
Beyond Media Literacy: New Paradigms in Media Education, by Colin Scheyen
Stonehouse Cooks, by Lorina Stephens

FICTION

Black Wine, by Candas Jane Dorsey
Eocene Station, by Dave Duncan
Immunity to Strange Tales, by Susan J. Forest
The Legend of Sarah, by Leslie Gadallah
The Empire of Kaz, by Leslie Gadallah
  Cat's Pawn
  Cat's Gambit

Growing Up Bronx, by H.A. Hargreaves
North by 2000+, a collection of short, speculative fiction, by H.A. Hargreaves
A Subtle Thing, by Alicia Hendley
The Tattooed Witch Trilogy, by Susan MacGregor
  The Tattooed Witch
  The Tattooed Seer
  The Tattooed Queen
A Time and a Place, by Joe Mahoney
The Rune Blades of Celi, by Ann Marston
  Kingmaker's Sword, Book 1
  Western King, Book 2
  Broken Blade, Book 3
  Cloudbearer's Shadow, Book 4
  King of Shadows, Book 5
  Sword and Shadow, Book 6
A Still and Bitter Grave, by Ann Marston
Indigo Time, by Sally McBride
Wasps at the Speed of Sound, by Derryl Murphy
A Quiet Place, by J.W. Schnarr
Things Falling Apart, by J.W. Schnarr
A Poisoned Prayer, by Michael Skeet
And the Angels Sang: a collection of short speculative fiction, by Lorina Stephens
Caliban, by Lorina Stephens
From Mountains of Ice, by Lorina Stephens
Memories, Mother and a Christmas Addiction, by Lorina Stephens
Shadow Song, by Lorina Stephens
The Mermaid's Tale, by D. G. Valdron

YA FICTION

My Life as a Troll, by Susan Bohnet
Eye of Strife, by Dave Duncan
Ivor of Glenbroch, by Dave Duncan
  The Runner and the Wizard
  The Runner and the Saint
  The Runner and the Kelpie
Avians, by Timothy Gwyn
Type, by Alicia Hendley
Type 2, by Alicia Hendley

Tower in the Crooked Wood, by Paula Johanson
A Touch of Poison, by Aaron Kite
The Great Sky, by D.G. Laderoute
Out of Time, by D.G. Laderoute
Diamonds in Black Sand, by Ann Marston
Hawk, by Marie Powell

YA NON-FICTION

The Prime Ministers of Canada Series:
  Sir John A. Macdonald
  Alexander Mackenzie
  Sir John Abbott
  Sir John Thompson
  Sir Mackenzie Bowell
  Sir Charles Tupper
  Sir Wilfred Laurier
  Sir Robert Borden
  Arthur Meighen
  William Lyon Mackenzie King
  R. B. Bennett
  Louis St. Laurent
  John Diefenbaker
  Lester B. Pearson
  Pierre Trudeau
  Joe Clark
  John Turner
  Brian Mulroney
  Kim Campbell
  Jean Chretien
  Paul Martin
  Stephen Harper

WWW.FIVERIVERSPUBLISHING.COM

The Tattooed Queen
ISBN 9781988274171
eISBN 9781988274188
by Susan MacGregor
Trade Paperback 6 x 9
December 1, 2016

In this last book of The Tattooed Witch trilogy, Miriam, Joachín, and Alonso finally reach the New World. Here, their destinies are larger than any of them could have dreamed. They also learn a hard truth–the fulfilment of love is not without its sacrifice.

Sick at heart because her husband, Joachín, is captive on a slave ship bound for the New World, Miriam finds her own crossing of the Great Ocean Sea, with its lack of privacy and vermin infested quarters, the least of her troubles. The crew suspect witchcraft of her and her ragtag tribe of Diaphani. Alonso, her ghostly love, does what he can to help, but at a growing, personal cost. As for Joachín, his situation improves little when his slave ship is taken by pirates off the coast of Afrik. Still in hot pursuit, Tomás, the Grand Inquisitor, hunts them both, sailing for Xaymaca with his pet sorceress Rana, and a bokor, (a voodoo sorcerer) who takes their blood magic to a new, diabolical level.

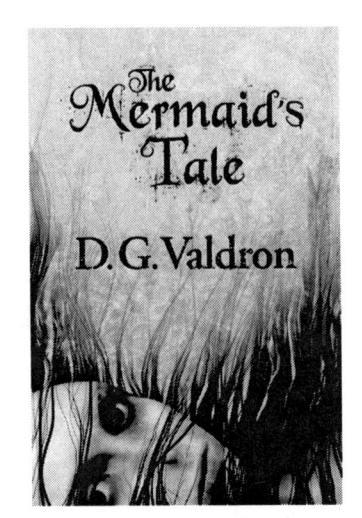

The Mermaid's Tale
ISBN 9781927400975
eISBN 9781927400982
by D.G. Valdron
Trade Paperback 6 x 9
August 1, 2016

In a city of majesty and brutality, of warring races and fragile alliances, a sacred mermaid has been brutally murdered. An abomination, a soulless Arukh is summoned to hunt the killer. As the world around the Arukh drifts into war and madness, her search for justice leads her on a journey to discover redemption and even beauty in the midst of chaos.

The Mermaid's Tale is violent and brutal and haunting and beautiful. Highly recommended.
            Michael R. Fletcher, Beyond Redemption, and 88

Fantasy fans, read this book for a different perspective, I can guarantee you will be thinking about it for a long wile after you have read the last word.
            LibraryThing

I'll admit that this book is quite far out of my comfort zone. It is a genre that I rarely read and within the first few pages, assumed that I would not be able to enjoy. But I was so wrong. This story is raw and painful and in many places quite ugly. There is war and murder and rage. But the story starts to weave so intricately that it draws you in and makes you feel invested in it.
            booksable

Diamonds in Black Sand
ISBN 9781988274195
eISBN 9781988274201
by Ann Marston
Trade Paperback 6 x 9
April 1, 2017

Master story-teller, Ann Marston, weaves a bright new tale about the lure of the sea.

Iain dreams of sailing beyond the treacherous Barrier Reefs to the tumultuous Wildesea, to become an Outsider like his father before him. But he is bound in service to his uncle Durstan for raising him after the death of his parents, and may not go until he has paid back the time he owes.

The new King of Celyddon bans the magic that keeps the Out-ships safe on the demanding Wildesea where Iain longs to be, and makes outlaws of those who work that magic. Neither the ships nor the men and women who sail them are allowed in the Realm. Iain has no means of escaping his bondage.

He is almost resigned to his fate and trying to make the best of it when he himself develops some of that banned magic, and becomes an Outlaw on the run from the authorities.

Immunity to Strange Tales
ISBN 9781927400142
eISBN 9781927400159
by Susan Forest
Trade Paperback 6 x 9
August 1, 2012

A collection of 12 short stories by one of Canada's rising stars of speculative fiction.

Forest takes you from death-bed wishes to the eerie regions of madness employing subtle skill and fresh prose. Nine of the stories have appeared in publications such as Asimov's, On Spec, Analog, Tesseracts Ten, Tesseracts Eleven, Tesseracts 14, and AE Science Fiction Review. Three of the stories make their debut in this collection, with an introduction by one of Canada's respected editors and experts, Mark Leslie Lefebvre.

Enjoyable, and an author worth keeping an eye on.

LibraryThing

Immunity to Strange Tales *is a superb premier collection of short science fiction and fantasy by Canadian author Susan Forest. These intriguing stories are varied in voice and style, spanning years of literary experimentation by the author, and most are told with delightful sophistication.*

Steve Stanton

author of *Freenet*

I can wholeheartedly recommend this collection to anyone who enjoys Sci-Fi and short stories.

Amazon

Wasps at the Speed of Sound
ISBN 9781927400432
eISBN 97819274004499
by Derryl Murphy
Trade Paperback 6 x 9
November 1, 2013

Derryl Murphy's first collection is back.
There are eleven stories in this collection, ten of them gathered together for the first time and one making its debut in these pages. All of them examine our experience with the worlds around us, anticipating dread and disaster with every turn, even while hope is sometimes allowed to win out. Come witness: the destruction of the Earth; an alien tourist and the death of a species; Earth at the end of time, coming back from a very long trip; a man and his father, lost in time; sailing on seas of garbage; an insect rebellion; a virtual future that creates an unrealistic past; water, politics, and a big machine; monkey-wrenching taken to a new level; lessons in photography; and rebellion on a distant world. Eleven stories that take you into the future even as you wrestle with the present.

A great book of short stories, chosen as for the UNBC Reads campaign at the University of Northern British Columbia in 2007.
Goodreads

Murphy constructs the world of each story so well, with little extraneous language as possible so the reader can create a vivid image of their own. Truly a pleasure to read for any science fiction fan and possibly for any environmentalist too.
LibraryThing

Very thought-provoking and entertaining stories.
Amazon